THE DEALER

Ajit Menon and **Anil Verma** are authors, screenwriters, music and film producers. Ajit is also a philanthropist and a unique nation-builder in his own right, and was featured among the change-makers of 2025. Anil Verma, apart from being an ad man, is also a well-known lyricist whose songs are blockbuster hits. Their previous books in the Panther's Ghosts series, *The Beginning* and *The Puppeteer*, featured in the top 15 must-read books of 2023 and in the top 100 books on Amazon. Both Ajit and Anil live with their respective families in Mumbai.

Praise for *The Panther's Ghosts*

'A compelling espionage thriller that does not border on didacticism or sensationalism ...'

The Telegraph Online

'... full of mysteries, plots and twists. ... the fictionalised version of what transpires in the real world.'

ABP News

'Ajit's thrillers take you on an absolute rollercoaster ride through different countries, situations, and scenes even as they unveil one mystery after another ...'

Lokmat Times

'Thriller duo Ajit Menon and Anil Verma are back with *The Dealer*, the third instalment in their blockbuster series The Panther's Ghosts, and this one isn't just heading to the bookshelves—it's heading to the big screen.'

Mid-Day

'In the world of high-stakes thrillers and pulse-pounding espionage, India has long been waiting for its own answer to *Mission Impossible*—and it may have finally arrived.'

Republic World

'Celebrated for their ability to weave real-world events into visually rich narratives, the duo [Ajit Menon and Anil Verma] has gained recognition as India's leading cinematic writers, crafting stories with dynamic and visually engaging narratives.'

Outlook

THE PANTHER'S GHOSTS SERIES

THE DEALER

AJIT & ANIL

Published by Westland Books, a division of Nasadiya Technologies Private Limited, in 2026

No. 269/2B, First Floor, 'Irai Arul', Vimalraj Street, Nethaji Nagar, Alapakkam Main Road, Maduravoyal, Chennai 600095

Westland and the Westland logo are the trademarks of Nasadiya Technologies Private Limited, or its affiliates.

ISBN: 9789371973052

10 9 8 7 6 5 4 3 2 1

This is a work of fiction. Names, characters, organisations, places, events and incidents are either products of the author's imagination or used fictitiously.

Typeset by Mukul

Printed at Thomson Press India Private Limited

Dedicated to our families
and
our parents,
who have nothing but love and blessings for us

PROLOGUE

22 January 2024, 6.30 a.m.
Ayodhya, Uttar Pradesh, India

AYODHYA WAS DARK AND COLD. Although the city was generally not too chilly at this time of year, unforeseen showers and heavy snowfall in the northern states had caused the temperature to drop to 6°C.

While the commandos stationed outside struggled to keep their blood circulation going, thirty-six-year-old Inspector General Arul Marwar was warm inside his specially designed black Mitsubishi surveillance van. Half Tamilian and half Marwari, Arul was born and raised in Rajasthan. He now headed the Special Police Operations Team, a unit created to handle high-risk operations such as anti-terrorist activities and organised crime, and execute critical interventions in sensitive cases. His vehicle was parked on the western boundary, 500 metres from the Ram Mandir. He was wearing a white pyjama–kurta, a woollen waistcoat and a black woollen jacket—just like a politician.

Twenty-seven-year-old data specialist Jeremy 'Jerry' Coutinho, a Christian from Goa, sat confidently inside the sleek, black surveillance van, surrounded by an arsenal of cutting-edge technology. The dimly lit interior hummed with activity as multiple high-resolution screens mounted on the walls displayed live feeds from surveillance cameras, their lenses discreetly positioned across the city. A cluster of powerful computers, their fans whirring softly, processed streams of data in real-time, while a rack of servers blinked with green and blue LEDs, handling encrypted communications and running advanced AI algorithms. The AI system, seamlessly integrated into the set-up, analysed patterns in the camera feeds, flagged anomalies, and cross-referenced faces and voices against global databases. Jerry's fingers danced across a touchscreen interface, pulling up thermal imaging and audio interceptions, his eyes scanning the flood of intelligence pouring in from the van's sophisticated array of tools.

'With this unexpected fog, can you still relay the live footage to the SPOT team outside?' Arul asked the young man.

'No issues, sir. This Korean equipment is incredible. I am dispatching the footage to our team: Mr Dhariwal in Delhi and Mr Hublikar right away,' Jerry answered.

Ajit Dhariwal was the national security advisor and Mandar Hublikar was the police commissioner of Uttar Pradesh.

'Your father-in-law, you mean,' said Arul, smiling at Jerry.

Jerry was engaged to Ritu, Mandar Hublikar's daughter. Jerry and Ritu had been friends since their days in engineering college, and Ayodhya was his last assignment before he got married next week.

Jerry gave an embarrassed smile and changed the topic. 'So, how is Mr Dhariwal? I don't know much about him. Is he very strict?' he asked.

Arul opened his phone and showed him a picture of Dhariwal and him at a programme. 'You tell me, Jerry. Does he look strict?'

Jerry looked at the NSA with his thick moustache, meticulously styled hair and intense black eyes, and nodded. 'He does, sir.'

Arul laughed loudly at Jerry's innocence. 'He looks strict, but he has a great heart.'

'What is his background?' asked Jeremy curiously.

'He was the director of the Research & Analysis Wing and has made extensive efforts to combat insurgency operations nationwide. He spent many years in the Indian High Commission in Islamabad.'

'Was he also on the field?'

'Yes, he was. In fact, in 1990, he targeted hard-line terrorists funded by Pakistan and persuaded militants in Kashmir to become counter-insurgents. After DD took over in 2014, he appointed Dhariwal as India's seventh national security advisor,' said Arul.

'No other prime minister in the world is addressed with an initialism. How did "DD" come about?' Jerry was curious.

'Indeed,' Arul nodded. 'DD is truly unique. But it is just the short form of his name, Damodar Das. His mother called him that when he was a kid. It stuck with friends and colleagues, and now, that's what everyone calls our prime minister.'

'Do you also call him DD?'

'Yes, I do.' Arul smiled and looked at the array of devices around Jerry. 'You love these gadgets, don't you?'

'I do. Anything you want to know about anyone in the world, I have it right in here. This,' Jerry said, tapping the computer, its sleek interface pulsing with life, 'is an AI-powered comp. The machine's neural core churns through terabytes of data, instantly decoding encrypted signals and pinpointing targets on the screens above.' He pressed a tab, and the screens above flickered to life. 'With just a tap, it unleashes algorithms that sift live feeds, spotting threats faster than any human can.' He smiled at Arul and, patting the computer, added, 'As as long it's humming, it will unveil secrets. If you want to learn anything about dreaded terrorists and criminals, dead or alive, I'll tell you in a flash.'

'Who do you love more? Ritu or your gadgets?' Arul asked teasingly. Seeing Jerry hesitate, he added, 'Thought as much.'

'What about you, sir? Was yours a love marriage, or did your parents choose Sulekha ma'am for you?'

'You can say both,' Arul admitted with a chuckle. 'We met in college, fell in love and told our parents. Before we knew it, our families pushed us together. So, we tied the knot within three months of falling in love. We were in our early twenties at that time.'

'So, you met a random girl in college, fell in love and your parents got you guys married in three months?'

'Not a random girl. Sulekha is the daughter of my father's business partner. We went to school together and then to the same college in Jaipur. Unknown to us, our parents had promised each other that when Sulekha and I grew up, they would get us married. They were business partners but also friends. And now, family!'

'But you hardly got time to really romance and love Sulekha ma'am before getting married ...'

'That's true, but we learnt to love each other after we got married. We have been happily married for eleven years now. But I spent only half this time with her.'

'How come?'

'The other half was spent in police training, special forces training and my stint with the Marine Commandos. MARCOS. In fact, I could spend time with Sulekha only after I was transferred to SPOT and shifted to UP.'

'And how did you end up in SPOT?'

'I worked with Dhariwal on a special assignment. After I completed that assignment, he asked me to head the SPOT team. That photo I showed you was from my farewell in MARCOS.'

'And you won the President's Police Medal and a gallantry award for that assignment,' said Jerry.

'How did you know?'

Jerry tapped his computer. 'I told you I know everything.'

'Then how come you did not know about Sulekha and my early marriage?' asked Arul sarcastically.

Jerry looked at Arul, and both burst out laughing.

'Do you still report to Mr Dhariwal, sir?'

'Yes. But I also report to your father-in-law,' Arul winked.

Jerry was about to ask another question when Mandar Hublikar's voice crackled over the speaker connected to Arul's and Jerry's phones. Jerry hit the answer button.

'Good morning, sir,' said Arul.

'May not be a good morning, Arul. We have worrying news,' said Mandar.

'What is it?' asked Arul.

'The intel from the RAW to the Anti-Terrorism Squad is correct. Three Lashkar-e-Taiba terrorists are here in Ayodhya. They plan to blast improvised explosive devices in the Ram Mandir during the consecration.'

The Ram Mandir was a brand-new temple constructed in Ayodhya, the birthplace of Lord Ram. After winning a 470-year-old fight for the temple, the government had built the grand temple and installed the deity in the sanctum sanctorum. Today was the consecration, and Prime Minister DD would be present.

'The surveillance footage captured four men in saffron clothes and one of my ATS officers, Sukhi—I mean Sukhwinder Singh Barnala—entering a lodge a kilometre from the temple at 6 a.m. today. A few minutes later, they re-emerged, wearing press IDs and carrying two video cameras and a microphone. Three of those men, along with Sukhi, proceeded towards the temple. The other guy took an autorickshaw and left the city,' said Mandar. After a pause, he added, 'I trained that man myself. He was a patriotic Sikh with a spine of steel! And now this betrayal.' His jaw tightened, fury flashing in his eyes.

'Can you send us the footage?' asked Arul.

'I have already shared it with you,' said Mandar. 'Jerry, can you run it through your database and tell me who they are, son?'

Arul and Jerry exchanged glances at the word 'son'.

'Sure, sir,' said Jerry as he ran the footage through a special software.

After a five-minute-long search, he grinned. 'Got them,' he declared.

'Great. Tell me their names,' asked Mandar.

'The tall one with a black golf cap is thirty-two-year-old Shahnawaz Alam.'

Jerry hit a few more buttons. Two other faces appeared on the large screen. 'The one with the straw hat is Arshad Warsi. The one wearing spectacles is Mohammad Rizwan. Warsi is twenty-two, and Rizwan is twenty-one. They are cousins. Both are dressed in blue jeans and red T-shirts.'

'Are you sure?' asked Arul.

'My son is never wrong,' said Mandar proudly.

'Anything else you have for us?' asked Arul, grinning at Jerry.

'Alam, Warsi and Rizwan were in the LeT but now have joined ISIS. They are Sri Lankans,' Jerry reported.

Then he keyed in more information, and a second image which Mandar did not have emerged. In the image a fourth man was getting into the auto. Jerry enlarged the footage, scanned it, fed it into the software and waited. After two minutes, he said, 'This is Shahid Faisal.'

'Of course. I know him,' said Arul, recognising the face.

'Shahid Faisal is the son-in-law of Farhatullah Gauri, the primary accused in the attack on the Akshardham temple that happened on 24 September 2002. Twenty-seven innocent civilians, two state police officers and one commando lost their lives. One more commando, Surjan Singh Bhandari, was hit in the head with a bullet and died after nearly two years in a coma. Shahid Faisal is LeT's sniper. He can shoot. And hit his target positioned even 2,000 yards away,' Jerry read the information.

'You're damn good,' Arul praised Jerry.

Jerry blushed and continued. 'Both were under ISI protection for a long time, but recently, Shahid has been absorbed into the ISI and is now a major in the Pakistani spy agency. Gauri and Shahid operate from Quetta.'

'Jerry is right. Shahid is now an ISI officer,' said Mandar.

'Zoom in on the cameras, please,' requested Arul.

In a second, Jerry had zoomed in on the cameras and said, 'They are too big for press video cameras.'

'Precisely. So, what do you infer, genius?' asked Arul.

'The video cameras they are carrying are the IEDs,' said Jerry.

'Which means?' asked Arul again.

'These are suicide bombers,' whispered Jerry. His face was etched with fear; he had never been this close to a terrorist attack. 'If they detonate the explosives when DD is there ...'

'It's not an "if", Jerry,' said Arul. 'They will detonate the IEDs *when* DD is here. That is the plan. Destroy the temple and assassinate the prime minister of the world's largest democracy.'

'There are over 3,000 VVIPs and foreign dignitaries sitting inside the temple premises. If they succeed, this will be the worst terror attack of the decade, not to mention the communal riots that would follow later. The nation will burn,' added Mandar.

'Should we postpone the function?' asked Jerry.

'It would be an embarrassment and a clear acceptance of our defeat,' argued Arul.

'But this is too big a risk. We have to inform DD,' said Jerry.

'Yes, we will,' Mandar agreed.

While Arul and Jerry waited, Mandar called Dhariwal.

In New Delhi, a world away from Ayodhya's tension-soaked streets, the air was thick with power and protocol. Dhariwal was in a meeting with DD at his library in 7, Lok Kalyan Marg, the prime minister's official residence in New Delhi, when he received Mandar's call. He excused himself and stepped out of the room. 'Yes, Mandar. What happened?'

Mandar explained everything in detail to Dhariwal. 'How should we proceed, sir?'

Dhariwal exhaled slowly. 'Wait. I am returning to the library and will get DD on the line.'

Damodar Das, aka DD, was busy discussing the plans for the consecration with the ministers for defence and home affairs. Dhariwal stepped inside and cleared his throat. DD's white hair and well-trimmed white beard gave the prime minister the appearance of a saint. His deep brown eyes were razor-sharp. He wore a white pyjama, a white kurta and a brown waistcoat. He looked up at Dhariwal and immediately understood something wasn't quite right. Excusing himself from the meeting, he stepped into an adjoining study, gesturing to Dhariwal to follow.

'What happened?' he asked softly.

Dhariwal briefed him on the situation unfolding in Ayodhya. For a brief second, he noticed DD's eyes burn with rage. But the prime minister swiftly regained his calm and said,

'There is no question of postponing the event. The consecration will go on as per plan, and I will be there at noon.'

Then he looked towards the library and said, 'Ajit, reschedule the meeting and patch me into the team at Ayodhya.'

Seven minutes later, DD joined the video call. There was silence in the group as everyone waited for him to speak. After a pause, DD asked Mandar, 'Commissioner, do we know where the terrorists are as of this moment?'

'According to the CCTV footage, they are inside the temple premises, sir. That traitor, Sukhi, escorted them,' Mandar was quick to reply.

'Where specifically?' DD asked.

While everyone was quiet, an amusing *whoop* broke the silence.

'I am sorry, Prime Minister,' came an immediate apology from Jerry.

'What is your name, young man?' asked DD.

'Jeremy Coutinho, sir,' Jerry replied.

'What do you have for us, Jeremy?' DD asked with a smile.

Within seconds, Jerry displayed a section where a crowd had assembled. Then, he circled his cursor around three people in the second row. 'These are the bombers, sir.'

'That's the section reserved for the media,' said Arul.

'Excellent work, Jeremy. How did you trace the bombers so quickly?' asked DD.

It was the first time he was getting a chance to showcase his talent to the PM—and probably his last—so he did not want to waste the opportunity. 'First, I performed data aggregation, then followed it up with geospatial clustering. I then applied heat mapping and pin clustering to converge on the bombers' locations accurately,' Jerry answered proudly.

'Fantastic. Meet me after the consecration. I'd like to know more about these techniques,' DD said encouragingly.

'Not to be left behind,' Mandar quipped, 'he is going to be my son-in-law next week, sir.'

'Congratulations, Commissioner Hublikar. Your daughter has chosen wisely,' said DD. Then he looked at Dhariwal and said, 'We have identified the threat, and you have the best man to deal with terrorists. Get the job done. Arul, I am confident your team will neutralise this threat. I will be there on time, as always. Thank you for your service, gentlemen.'

With those words, DD left the call. Once he did, Dhariwal looked at the screen and said, 'Guys, you will be given anything you need. Apart from the ATS, I will have the National Security Guard arriving in Ayodhya in an hour. Mandar, throw a second layer of security inside the premises without creating a scene.' Then, after a pause, he added, 'Arul, it's your show now.'

Arul looked at the watch his wife had gifted him on his fortieth birthday. It was 7.30 a.m. He braced himself, ready to command his team.

He looked at his young assistant. 'Jerry, I want every CCTV camera and drone following the three bombers.'

Then, he addressed Mandar. 'Sir, I want a chopper posing as a media helicopter hovering above and covering the bombers.'

Finally, he addressed the three members of his team positioned close to the media section. They were walking around the arena in the guise of devotees dressed in saffron robes. All three carried silencer-topped GLOCK 19s inside their robes and were wearing AI-enabled Ray-Ban Meta Glasses with a 12 megapixel camera and a high-powered Bluetooth mic. Whatever they were looking at or discussing was promptly recorded and sent to Jerry, who ran it through facial and voice recognition software inside the van in real time.

'Officers, I hope you can see the targets clearly?' asked Arul.

'We do,' came their replies.

Arul looked at the large screens in front of him. Each one covered the bombers from every possible angle, including an aerial view. He checked his GLOCK 19, tucked it into his waistband and turned towards Jerry.

'I am disappointed that you have still not invited me to your wedding.'

'You haven't seen the invite?' Jerry asked, a worried look on his face. 'I handed it to Sulekha ma'am last night.'

Arul patted him on his back and smiled. 'Just joking, buddy.' Then he pointed at the screens which displayed HD resolution live feed of everything and said, 'I am a fan of yours from today.'

Arul addressed Mandar. 'This operation is code-named *Mirage*. I am going after the bombers, sir. Can you take care of Sukhi for me?'

'Absolutely, Arul,' said Mandar.

Arul stepped out of the surveillance van and stretched. 'Team, I am on my way. Stay sharp.'

On the other side of the temple, Mandar stepped out of his police SUV and walked towards the temple. As he walked, he asked Jerry, 'Can you see Sukhi, son?'

Jerry opened another screen and keyed in information. In a few minutes, Sukhi popped up on the screen. 'He is heading for ... wait, he is now at the main gate and is talking to another man in civilian dress. Let me check who he is.' Jerry zoomed the frame, captured the face and fed it into one of his apps. 'Sir, he is talking to Paramjit Punia.'

'Who is he?' asked Mandar as he walked towards the main gate.

'He is the anchor of KHALI TV.'

'When you say KHALI, do you mean the banned terrorist organisation ...' Mandar began.

'No, sir. What you are referring to is the Khalistani Liberation Group. KHALI is an offshoot of the KLG but is more dangerous. They're based in Birmingham,' Jerry explained. 'Gurwinder Singh Pannu started the organisation a year ago.'

Pannu is a Khalistani terrorist mastermind operating from the shadows of the United States of America. A charismatic yet ruthless leader, he was the head of the KLG, but he had a difference of opinion with the other members a year ago. So he left and started KHALI, a venomous organisation; a cocktail of radical and rogue elements from the KLG, LeT and ISIS dedicated to executing terror activities in India. Their singular obsession is to carve out an independent Sikh state called Khalistan by severing Punjab from India by 2030.

Pannu started KHALI TV to spew propaganda against India and the Indian government by orchestrating sophisticated anti-India campaigns. He leveraged KHALI's global network to incite unrest and division amongst radical Sikhs. His cunning and unyielding ambition made him a formidable threat, always staying one step ahead of international authorities.

'Paramjit Punia is the prime-time anchor of KHALI TV. He is always spewing anti-India and pro-Khalistan propaganda on the channel, but he has a huge fan base, sir.'

'Thank you, son. And stop calling me sir when we are alone. You can call me dad,' said Mandar.

Jerry hesitated momentarily before saying, 'Thank you, Dad.'

It was 8 a.m. Inside the temple premises, around 15,000 devotees and more than 3,000 VVIPs were seated in two groups on either side of the ornate stairs at the entrance. Giant screens were live broadcasting the rituals happening in the sanctum sanctorum. Everyone was patiently waiting for DD to arrive at noon.

Arul could see his three commandos hovering near the media section. He spotted Warsi holding the mic, while Alam and Rizwan were carrying the cameras.

He fixed his gaze on them and spoke into his lapel mic, 'Officers, listen up: those video cameras are rigged with IEDs, and the microphone's the detonator. These bombers think they're headed for their seventy-two hoors today, but we're rewriting their script. We must move them fast, away from the crowd, and guide them to the bomb squad stationed at the southeast corner, behind the temple and near the goods receiving door. SPOT Team Leader, Operation Mirage is green—go now!'

'Yes, sir,' said Inspector Meera Sharma, known for her sharp instincts and tactical brilliance in high-stakes operations.

'Junior, please activate the jammers and override the central PA system,' said Meera. The team affectionately called Jerry 'Junior' since he was the youngest of the lot.

'Done, ma'am. And?' asked Jerry, adrenaline coursing through his veins. This was his first on-field assignment where he was part of the action.

'Wear your seatbelt and enjoy the ride,' said Meera. He looked at his mobile phone and saw a missed call from Ritu. He made a video call to her and propped the phone on a stand below one of the screens in front of him so he could see her and work.

'Still in your favourite van?' Ritu asked.

'I am in the thick of Operation Mirage,' he said proudly.

'What is that?' asked Ritu.

'Confidential.'

'What time will you come home? We have to get your suit from the tailors, and I need to collect the lehenga.'

Jerry looked at the screen and his watch. 'If I know Arul sir, he will close shop before noon.'

'So, will you be home for lunch?'

'Yes, my darling.'

'Should I wait then?' asked Ritu.

Jerry's eyes darted to one of the surveillance cameras. Sukhi and Punia were walking towards the police surveillance van.

'Dad, they are coming here ...'

A piercing shot rang through the van. Jerry's eyes went blank. He slumped forward and fell onto the keyboard. Ritu screamed, watching in horror as blood flowed down a gaping wound in his head.

Suddenly, the internal speaker came alive. It was Mandar. 'Jerry, I heard a noise. Are you okay? Jerry ... son ...'

Sukhi turned off the speaker, walked up to the table and looked at Ritu's terrified face.

'Sorry, dear,' he said in a sinister voice. 'Wrong place, wrong time. Next, I will have to come for you.'

Ritu disconnected the call with trembling hands.

Sukhi turned to Punia and said, 'You know what Pannu said. There should be no witnesses. So, I am going for the girl. You make sure the explosion and the assassination are telecast live. Let the world see what KHALI can do.'

Punia pushed Jerry's body off the chair and sat down. Then, he took a buffing cloth from his bag, wiped the table clean and pulled out a flexi keyboard, which he placed on the table.

'Khalistan zindabad.'

Mandar, who had run to the van after hearing the shot, was almost near it when the door opened, and Sukhi stepped out. They saw each other at the same time. Sukhi raised his gun, but Mandar was faster. He dived sideways and drew his GLOCK 19. A neat double tap to Sukhi's forehead. Sukhi's body flew three feet back, crashed onto the van and slid down to the floor.

Mandar ran up to him, confirmed he was dead and slowly turned the door handle. He had just about opened it when he saw Punia standing with his gun pointed at him. Before Mandar could lift his weapon, Punia fired. The bullet hit Mandar in his left lung. But before Punia could take another shot, Mandar fired his GLOCK again. The bullet hit Punia's right eye, and as he fell to the ground, the right side of his head exploded like a melon.

Mandar was bleeding from his chest and mouth, but he still managed to climb into the van. He looked at his son-in-law's lifeless body on the floor and fell to his knees.

'My son,' he said, then fell forward beside him.

It was 8.30 a.m. Inspector Meera walked towards the media arena carrying a tray of flowers, blending seamlessly with the throng of devotees. Her teammates, Arjun Rathore and Vikram Tyagi, approached the crowd from different angles, ensuring a quiet boundary around the terrorists.

Meera stopped a few feet from the media and announced, 'The Ram Mandir's trust is happy to accommodate a media crew from two channels inside the sanctum sanctorum during the consecration. A maximum of three people per team, please.'

Immediately, every channel started pleading their case with her. She scanned the crowd and stopped at the bombers. 'You. Which channel are you from?' she asked, pointing her finger at Warsi.

'Me? Eh … we …' Warsi stammered, taken aback by being suddenly singled out.

Alam stepped forward and said, 'Channel 24, ma'am. Please give us a chance.'

Personnel from other media houses were shouting for Meera's attention, but she only wanted Rizwan, Alam and Warsi. With a warm smile, she said, 'Brothers, today is your lucky day. Lord Ram has blessed you.' Then, identifying another channel, she said, 'All of you, follow me.'

While the ATS members cordoned off the rest of the media, the three bombers and the other journalists eagerly followed Meera inside the temple. The promise of exclusivity had lowered their guard.

As the group moved towards a corridor running along the side of the temple, Rathore and Tyagi flanked them. They smiled and engaged the group in small talk. The passage led to a storeroom where the groceries were stored, near the temple's southeast corner. As they approached the storeroom, Arul joined the commandos and covered them from the back.

As soon as they entered the storeroom, Arul took over. 'Good morning. I am from the temple's trust. Before you enter the sanctuary, please leave your bags here. Those aren't allowed during the ritual,' he said.

While the other journalists put down their bags, the bombers hesitated. 'We don't have any bags. We only have our equipment to cover the rituals,' Alam argued.

Arul sensed the resistance and did not want to raise any doubts. 'Of course, I understand,' he smiled. 'You can carry your mics and cameras. It's no issue, but before entering, you must wash your hands, face and feet with Gangajal.'

Arul pointed to a storage drum in the corner of the storeroom. 'Please put your gear here and take water from the drum.'

While two ATS officers took the other journalists to a separate room for frisking, the bombers were allowed to stay back. Following Arul's instructions, they carefully lowered their gear and approached the drum.

As soon as the gear was placed on the floor, the ATS team grabbed it and sprinted out of the room. Rizwan and Warsi realised they had been exposed and turned on Arul. Instantaneously, Rathore and Tyagi pounced on the cousins, pinning them against the wall and disarming them with precision. Alam heard the commotion and turned, but Meera was already on him. The bombers struggled to free themselves, but Arul pulled out his GLOCK, aimed it at them and said, 'You move, you die.'

By now, the other journalists had already been taken to the sanctum sanctorum for a short video shoot and then escorted back outside.

'Parcel acquired,' said Arul, speaking into his lapel mic. But he got no response. 'ATS to move in and take possession of the parcel.'

Within minutes, the ATS swept in with surgical precision, their movements cloaked in secrecy. As they entered the dimly lit storeroom, the air crackled with urgency. The bombers, their plans unravelled, sat in a corner, their hands tied with zip cords from the storeroom. Moving swiftly, the ATS officers snapped handcuffs on the bombers with a metallic clink, each click a countdown to safety. The leader of the ATS looked at the storeroom's heavy entrance door and then at a back door hidden behind stacks of crates. 'Where does that lead to?' he asked one of his officers who had already conducted a reconnaissance of the storeroom before Operation Mirage started.

'That one leads to the corridor to the goods receiving gate behind the temple.' The ATS leader looked at another officer and said, 'Clear the crates and break open the door. We must avoid the thronging devotees outside.'

Within minutes, two officers moved the crates, broke the door locks, and opened the doors to the corridor. With calculated steps, the officers guided the bombers through the narrow, shadowed corridor leading to the goods receiving gate—a discreet exit veiled by high walls and overgrown vines. The team synchronised their movements to the rhythm of the temple's loud chants, drowning out any stray sounds. Within minutes, they reached the goods receiving gate, opened it, and slipped out into the bright winter sun. Outside, the bombers were loaded into an unmarked van stationed just behind the gate. Not a single devotee caught a glimpse of anything.

Operation Mirage had been sealed in silence.

After the ATS team departed with the bombers, Arul congratulated Meera and her team, exited the premises and started walking towards the surveillance van. On his way, he spoke into his lapel mic, 'Jerry, release the jammers. The threat has been neutralised.' When he didn't receive a response, he repeated his message. No response again. Worried, he called Mandar. 'Mandar sir, parcel is on its way to the safe house.'

When he did not receive an answer from Mandar, Arul knew something was amiss. He called the SPOT team and the second ATS team. 'Come to the van now. I think something is wrong.'

When Arul and his team arrived at the site, they found that ATS members were already present. Mandar's body was on a stretcher, being carried to another vehicle. Arul looked at one of the ATS men. He shook his head sadly, a sign which confirmed Arul's doubts. Commissioner Mandar Hublikar was dead. He saw Sukhi's dead body outside and Punia's lying half in and half out of the van.

His stomach in a knot, Arul stepped over Punia's body and entered the van. A loud gasp escaped his mouth. A dull ache seared through his heart, and tears gushed out of his eyes. He knelt beside Jerry's body and sobbed like a child.

1

23 January 2024, 9 a.m.
Cointrin Business Tower, Geneva, Switzerland

'YOU FAILED, AND YOU FAILED miserably,' Robert Azman, the Council's consigliere, said to the man on the large video conferencing screen before the Council members. His voice was strained and gave away his anger.

Bob, as he was called, was a coiled serpent of ambition, his every move laced with cunning and restless discontent. Though his role commanded respect, he loathed its confines, his sharp mind perpetually scheming for greater power, his loyalty to the Council a mere facade for his own ascent. His personality was a volatile blend of charm and menace—disarming in conversation, but his piercing hazel eyes betrayed a relentless hunger, always calculating, always plotting the next manoeuvre.

He wielded his influence like a blade, his silver tongue earning him the Council's ear while his heart brewed plans to eclipse them all one day. His appearance was meticulously curated to project control: a lean frame draped in bespoke navy suits, the fabric hugging his form with predatory elegance. A blood-red silk tie, knotted with precision, hinted at his ruthless streak, while a platinum cufflink engraved with a subtle crest glinted with his concealed pride. His jet-black hair, streaked with deliberate grey, was swept back, framing a gaunt face whose every smile was a trap and every frown a warning of the storm within.

The conference hall on the twenty-fifth floor of the Geneva Business Centre was a cathedral of intrigue, its floor-to-ceiling windows offering a relentless view of the snow-capped Alps slicing through a restless, silver sky.

The room thrummed with an unspoken tension, its air laced with the sharp scent of polished teak and the distant hum of the city below. A commanding circular conference table, crafted from dark granite, anchored the space, its glossy surface reflecting the cold, diffused light from sleek overhead panels, casting the five figures seated around it in a chiaroscuro of shadow and resolve.

The walls, adorned with muted steel panels, seemed to lean inward, muffling sound and amplifying the weight of every glance exchanged. A lone chandelier, all jagged edges and frosted crystal, hung like a suspended threat, its fractured light dancing across the room's severe elegance, illuminating secrets yet to be spoken.

Beyond the glass, the Jet d'Eau pierced Lake Geneva's surface in the distance, a fleeting reminder of the world outside this high-altitude crucible.

Apart from Bob, there were four others in the room.

Eighty-year-old Leon Fink, the Council's chairman, was a man whose presence commanded attention despite his unassuming frame. His sharp, angular face, etched with lines of calculated experience, bore the weight of countless clandestine decisions. Steel-grey eyes, cold and unyielding, flickered with a barely restrained intensity, betraying the storm of anger beneath his composed exterior. His silver hair, impeccably slicked back, framed a high forehead that seemed to carry the burden of secrets. Dressed in a tailored charcoal suit, he exuded an air of ruthless authority, his lean fingers drumming softly on the table—a subtle tic that hinted at the volatility simmering within. He had founded Blue Rock, a mighty American multinational investment management corporation with the world's largest asset managers supervising over $10.5 trillion in assets. To Leon's right was Stephen Favier, CEO and owner of the Redstone Group, who carried the weight of his $5 trillion real estate empire with a polished, predatory grace. A member of the Council and a shade younger than Leon Fink, his mid-seventies were cloaked in an aura of timeless ambition. Tall and broad-shouldered, his commanding presence filled any room, his piercing blue eyes scanning for opportunity with the precision of a hawk. His chiselled features, framed by a mane of faded brown hair, bore a faint smirk that hinted at his unshakable confidence. Stephen's personality was a blend of charisma and calculation; he was charming enough to win allies, yet ruthless enough to crush rivals, his every word measured to maintain his grip on power. His wardrobe was a testament to his status: a dark blue custom-made suit tailored to perfection, paired with a crisp white shirt and understated gold cufflinks engraved with the Redstone crest. A Patek Philippe watch gleamed on his wrist, a subtle flex of his wealth. Beneath the veneer of sophistication, a restless drive simmered—he was a man who owned cities but always hungered for more.

Next to Favier sat Jim Brodsky, founder and CEO of the World News Network. A colossus of influence, Brodsky's media empire stretched across news and entertainment channels in over 150 nations. With a net worth approaching $4 trillion, he held the power to mould global narratives, his vast cross-media holdings amplifying his voice to a near-ubiquitous presence. In his late sixties, Jim's stocky frame and weathered face exuded the authority of a man who had outmanoeuvred countless adversaries. His deep-set brown eyes, shadowed by heavy brows, sparkled with a blend of cunning and scepticism, perpetually scanning for advantage. His personality was both captivating and formidable—a gifted storyteller capable of swaying millions, yet his charisma concealed an unyielding drive for control.

Jim, dressed to command attention, sat a few feet away from Brodsky, wearing a flawlessly tailored navy pinstripe suit accented by a signature burgundy pocket square that lent a touch of panache. On his feet were polished oxfords that had clicked with purpose when he had entered the conference hall, each step a testament to his dominance. Though in his late sixties, his thinning red hair revealed the onset of baldness, barely concealed by careful combing. On his finger gleamed a chunky gold signet ring engraved with the WNN crest, a constant symbol of his reign over the world's discourse.

To the left of Leon was Tim Butler, the visionary architect of Bioguard Group. He was a biotechnology prodigy whose company had, in just a decade, become the largest owner of pharmaceutical firms through bold investments and intricate cross-holdings. In his early sixties, Tim had a lean and wiry frame, and his intense green eyes and sharp features gave him an almost ascetic air, as if he thrived on ideas rather than sustenance. His personality was a paradox—publicly a champion of 'safety and innovation', privately a calculating strategist who saw humanity as a chessboard for his biotech gambits. Charismatic in boardrooms, he could inspire trust, but his restless mind was always three moves ahead, plotting expansions and acquisitions. Tim's style was understated yet deliberate: a slim-fit beige suit paired with an open-collared shirt and a heavy gold chain hanging around his neck. His wavy blond hair and rimless glasses lent him the look of a rock star, while a sleek smartwatch on his wrist ticked like a metronome to his relentless ambition.

The Council was born in the shadows of the 1929 global financial crash, a cataclysm that exposed the fragility of unchecked markets and the desperation of nations. On a stormy November night in 1929, four visionaries—each a titan in their own right—met in a secluded chateau outside Zurich. They were Alexander Favier, a real estate magnate with empires spanning continents; Tony Brodsky, a media baron whose newspapers shaped public thought; Josh Butler, a pharmaceutical pioneer with patents that controlled life and death; and Garry Fink, a cunning financier whose connections ran deeper than any vault. Disgusted by the chaos of democracy and the unpredictability of sovereign states, they forged a pact to impose order—a totalitarian world order under their iron grip. And thus was formed the Council, a secret society modelled on the whispered legends of the Illuminati but far more ruthless. Its mission was to bend the world's nations to their will through a clandestine entity: Apuni Malo.

Apuni Malo, meaning 'Silent Hand' in a forgotten dialect, was the Council's invisible fist—a shadow government operating beyond borders, accountability or morality. It comprised 312 agents, a carefully curated legion of operatives drawn from the world's elite: forty-seven CEOs of central banks, twenty-nine retired intelligence chiefs from agencies like the CIA and MI6, sixty-three ex-politicians whose names still echoed in corridors of power, and 173 strategists from privately funded think tanks that crafted policies for unsuspecting governments. Each agent was vetted through a gruelling five-year process, their loyalty ensured by a mix of blackmail, obscene wealth and a shared ideology of absolute control. Apuni Malo's headquarters, codenamed Obsidian Vault, was rumoured to be hidden beneath a private island in the North Atlantic, its location known only to the Council's inner circle. From this nerve centre, they orchestrate global machinations with surgical precision, their encrypted networks untouchable by even the most advanced cyber defences.

The Council's singular goal was global business dominance, a vision where every market, resource and transaction bends to their design. Apuni Malo was the instrument that made this possible, infiltrating and subverting democratically elected governments to serve as puppets for the Council's agenda. They cared not for nations' development or their people—citizens were mere cogs in their machine, their struggles irrelevant unless they disrupted profit or power. To achieve this, Apuni Malo toppled governments with chilling efficiency, using tailored strategies: engineered coups backed by private mercenaries, civil unrest fuelled by propaganda campaigns, or economic strangulation through manipulated markets. Once a puppet regime was installed, Apuni Malo's agents moved in, embedding advisors in key ministries, rigging legislation and redirecting national wealth to Council-controlled enterprises. Over decades, they'd perfected this playbook, ensuring that entire economies—oil in the Middle East, tech in East Asia, minerals in Africa—flowed into their coffers.

The Council was no mere cabal; it was a machine of unrelenting ambition, its every move calculated decades in advance. They'd survived world wars, economic collapses, and revolutions, adapting with a chameleon's ease. Their agents were trained in psychological warfare, cyber espionage and assassination, capable of dismantling a government or silencing a whistleblower without leaving a trace. Their history was a tapestry of domination: the 1930s saw them profit from rearmament, funding both sides of conflicts to corner arms markets; the Cold War was their chessboard, with proxy regimes feeding their coffers; the 2008 financial crisis was their masterpiece, as they bought collapsing banks for pennies, cementing their grip on global finance.

Since its inception, the Council had left an indelibled mark on history, its influence woven into events most attributed to chance or ideology. In the 1950s, they orchestrated the fall of a Latin American democracy, replacing it with a junta that opened vast oil fields to their conglomerates. The 1970s saw them destabilise a European nation's coalition government, installing a prime minister who gave his industries into their hands. By the 1990s, Apuni Malo had infiltrated seventy-three governments, with operatives whispering in the ears of presidents, premiers and kings. Their agents had sparked riots in capitals, crashed currencies overnight and redrawn borders through proxy wars, all to secure monopolies over steel, pharmaceuticals and data. The Council's wealth was incalculable, with slush funds estimated at $9 trillion, hidden in layered shell companies across tax havens. Their think tanks published white papers that shaped UN policies, while their media arms—controlled by Brodsky's empire—spun narratives that kept the world distracted.

By 2022, Apuni Malo reached suffocating heights. One hundred twenty-eight nations had leaders or advisors on their payroll, and their surveillance grid, built by Butler's biotech innovations, monitored billions through back doors in global telecoms. The Council's strength lay in its unity and their commitment to the goal over several generations.

The Council's most recent triumph was the 2023 Bangladesh Gambit, in which they engineered a silent coup in Bangladesh, leveraging a manufactured corruption scandal to oust Jamila Begum, a reformist prime minister. Within weeks, they installed Syyed Jafri, a pliant banker handpicked from their ranks, who signed over a complete island to them with exclusive mining rights for rare earth metals to a Council-linked consortium.

The operation was flawless: they created student protests to overthrow Jamila, and when Syyed took over, the students were quashed by hired militias. With the global media focused completely on the Russia–Ukraine war, the world barely noticed, and apart from having control over another

Asian country, $700 billion in assets flowed into their network. The Bangladesh Gambit solidified their stranglehold on the global supply chain, proving their ability to continue bending even developing nations to their will.

Apart from the business angle, the island was also going to be developed as a military base for the Americans, from where they could easily launch missiles into Iran and Russia.

Now, in 2024, the second generation of the Council was at play. Favier's real estate empire provided safehouses and logistics, Brodsky's media buried their tracks, Butler's biotech ensured compliance through chemical persuasion, and Fink's financial web laundered their gains. They'd crushed upstarts who dared challenge them, from rogue tycoons to idealistic hackers, leaving no rival standing.

However, their present goal to destabilise India, as they had Bangladesh, had hit a roadblock. With 1.47 billion people, for the Council, India was the world's largest consumer market. Moreover, an American military base on India's eastern border would be a direct threat to their arch-rival, China. It was to this effect that the Ayodhya operation was planned, but it failed. It was their first failure in nine decades.

The Ayodhya failure stung, and it stung badly. Today's Council meeting was to understand the reasons for the failure and recalibrate their next move.

The four Council members looked at the man on the large screen in front of them, waiting for him to respond to Bob's statement.

When the man did not respond, Bob leaned closer to his table mic and repeated. 'Mr Sorosi, do you have anything to say about your spectacular failure in India?'

Joseph Sorosi, sitting in his steel-clad office on the seventh floor of the Empress Towers, a Manhattan high-rise, loomed large on the big video conferencing screen.

Even though he was in his early sixties, his broad shoulders and 6'4" frame radiated a menace that silenced rooms before he spoke. He was dressed in a tailored black suit that hugged his muscular build, a crisp white shirt open at the collar to reveal a glimpse of a scarred neck, and a single silver ring on his right hand with a small silver skull on it.

His army-style crew cut highlighted his high cheekbones and square jaw. The short silver hair crowned a face carved by decades of ruthless decisions, and his piercing grey eyes glinted like cold steel. As the man entrusted with the Ayodhya operation, the response to Bob's question reflected on his face as a storm cloud of controlled fury.

A tough-looking man, Sorosi had not liked Bob from day one. There was something about Bob that had pissed him off the moment he had set his eyes on him. Sorosi clenched his jaws and stared at Bob for a good fifteen seconds, then turned his attention to Leon Fink.

'Chairman Fink, you had asked me to neutralise DD and wreak havoc in India. I presented a simple and effective plan to the Council three weeks ago.' Eyeing Bob with disgust, he added, 'But Bob here convinced you to opt for another route, which is to blow up the temple. I raised my objections to you and told you it has only a 50 per cent chance of success as there were too many variables and probabilities, but Bob here convinced you all, and you insisted that I do the Ayodhya job. Though I knew the plan was ridiculous, I did not argue. I executed it, but unfortunately, as I had predicted, we failed. And now, to cover up his tracks, Bob is going on the offensive. I find no reason to answer Bob's inane question.'

Bob was ready to retort and defend himself, but Fink raised his hand. He looked around the table and asked, 'What about the rest of you? What are your views on this?'

Butler switched on his microphone. 'Sorosi, before we share our opinions, can you educate us on what happened in India?'

'I don't have too much information, but all I know is the mission failed.'

'Yes, we are aware of that fact. What happened to your team? Are they dead?' asked Favier.

'I have no idea. Even Shahid Faisal, their handler, has no clue what happened to his team. There is no mention of the incident in any newspaper or media. It is as if nothing happened.'

'I think the Government of India is deliberately keeping quiet, as they do not want anyone to know that such an attempt was even made. Because if they do, it will be fodder for the Opposition. Brodsky here cannot discuss an incident that never occurred in the first place. They are smart,' said Fink.

'I think they got wind of the operation and nipped it in the bud. Which is exactly what I had feared,' Sorosi replied.

'And now they are aware of the plans, they will be more alert,' added Butler.

'Are you saying the mission was sabotaged?' asked Brodsky.

'Either that, or the bombers goofed up somewhere and the RAW caught on to it. Either the team is in custody, or they have been neutralised efficiently. If they had been neutralised, we would have received some news from our moles in the hospitals. Which means they are alive and in RAW's custody. And I also fear that the Indians have covered up the entire incident to avoid any external scrutiny. I am betting on the latter—that the RAW got wind of the operation,' Sorosi admitted.

'You mean there is a leak in the Council's system?' asked Fink.

'Yes.'

'So, who is the mole?' asked Favier.

'I don't know. It could be Pannu, Shahid or Bob,' Sorosi said, looking at Bob with a slight smirk. His insinuation was a deliberate attempt to create suspicion in the minds of the Council members.

Bob knew what Sorosi was doing. 'As they say, a bad workman always blames his tools,' he countered.

Realising that the two most important people in the meeting were caught in a blame game, Fink decided to step in and abate the rising tensions, but not without subtly letting Sorosi know that he had failed before, too. 'Sorosi, isn't it true that every mission *you* attempted in India in the last decade, based on *your* plans, has failed? The farmers' agitation in Punjab, the innumerable riots in the south and north, and the recent violence in Manipur. These were all *your* ideas, and we invested a lot of money in all the projects. *You* asked, and we gave you everything.'

'Precisely. We gave you $1 billion to get DD out democratically. You even went public, stating that you have the money to oust DD, yet he remains in place. In fact, he won the subsequent elections with a higher mandate,' Butler reminded them.

'When we met four weeks ago, you said the Opposition in India is very weak, and there is no way that the People's Congress Party can defeat DD in the next elections. So, we decided on this mission. The mission was a disaster and we can learn to live with that. But what is worrying is that you lost your entire crew, and you have no idea what happened yesterday in Ayodhya,' Fink explained, carefully measuring his words not to antagonise Sorosi.

'Yes, it is worrying. Do you think I am not aware of it?' Sorosi snapped at Fink. 'A similar thing happened on 6 January 2022, when, with the Punjab CM's help, we boxed DD near Piareana on the Firozpur–Moga highway, approximately 30 km from the National Martyrs Memorial at Hussainiwala. We influenced the farmers to create a roadblock and agitate around him, preventing his cavalcade from moving forward. The only thing left was for the shooters to fire their goddamn guns, but they mysteriously did not turn up. After an embarrassing twenty-minute wait on the flyover, DD was escorted safely to the airport by the Special Protection Group and flown back to New Delhi. The only thing that came out of it was that the People's Congress Party lost the state of Punjab in the next election.

'Do you think the failure of the Hussainiwala incident and yesterday's mission in Ayodhya are mere coincidences? No. We have a mole in the system who is leaking information to the Indians. But I will find out who the rat on board my ship is,' Sorosi said, glaring at Bob.

Fink sensed the deep animosity between Bob and Sorosi. He needed to intervene. 'Sorosi, in our long-standing relationship, you have delivered 100 per cent on all global projects. We admire your strategic manoeuvring of the Arab Spring and the Iraq, Yemeni and Sudan wars. With the booming sale of the COVID-19 vaccines, we made a lot of financial gains, and thanks to your move, Bangladesh will soon be in our control. But somehow, the operations in India seem to be failing. For decades, we have orchestrated chaos and control. But now, our carefully woven tapestry of global control appears to be unravelling thread by thread. The name on every president and prime minister's lips is a single, unshakable syllable: *India*.'

Fink leaned forward, his hands trembling as he clutched the edge of the table. His voice, usually a calm blade slicing through uncertainty, now quivered urgently. 'We are losing,' he hissed, his eyes darting to the flickering screen on his computer displaying live economic projections, trade routes and geopolitical maps. 'India is rising—faster, stronger and more defiant than we ever anticipated.'

With its 1.45 billion souls, India is no longer just a market but a colossus awakening. Under the leadership of DD, a man who has become a living legend, India is transforming into the world's manufacturing juggernaut. Their factories are churning out everything from microchips to fighter jets, smartphones to solar panels. The 'Made in India' stamp is now a global hallmark, rivalling and surpassing the fading echo of 'Made in China'.

'We worked tirelessly to dismantle China's manufacturing dominance, but in its place, India has risen like a phoenix, its economic might now threatening to eclipse even the US. Once a modest currency, the rupee is gaining strength, whispered in global trade talks as a viable alternative to the dollar. India's ports are buzzing with activity, exporting goods to every corner of the globe. The Asian subcontinent views India as a benevolent elder, while the African Union, long a battleground for Western influence, has now aligned itself with New Delhi's vision of mutual prosperity. India is not just a nation—it is becoming the heartbeat of a new world order.'

'DD must go, and the People's Congress Party must come. Apuni Malo should take control of India!' barked Fink, slamming his fist on the table, his voice echoing through the chamber, a desperate plea wrapped in rage. 'He's turned India into a fortress of loyalty. The people worship him! Every village and city chants his name as if he were a god. If we don't act now, India will not just rival America—it will bury us.'

Then, after a long pause where he calmed himself, he said, 'We will go by your suggestions. But give us results.'

'Give me a one-line brief, and let me execute it independently without discussing it with anybody else, including the Council.'

Fink looked at Butler, Brodsky and Favier, who nodded their acceptance. 'Your one-line brief is: DD must die,' Fink said.

Sorosi took a deep breath, his chest rising as if to brace against the storm brewing within the room. He turned to Bob, his voice laced with venomous sarcasm, each word a dagger aimed at the man's pride. 'Do I have your permission, Your Highness?' The title dripped with mockery, a challenge to Bob's faltering authority within the Council's fracturing ranks.

Bob's face contorted, his eyes flashing like twin infernos. He leaned forward, his voice a low, guttural hiss that carried the weight of a curse. 'Go to hell,' he mouthed, the words silent but searing, a declaration of war in the suffocating silence.

The room held its breath, the tension a living thing, coiling tighter with every heartbeat. Sorosi's lips curled into a smirk, a predator's grin that masked the terror gnawing at his core. He turned slowly to Fink, the Council's quiet enforcer, whose cold, calculating eyes betrayed no emotion. Sorosi's voice dropped to a chilling whisper, each syllable a promise carved in ice. 'Thank you, Council. By the end of this year, only *one man* will stand between DD and me.'

The words hung in the air like a guillotine's blade, sharp and final.

2

23 January 2024, 9.30 a.m.
Seventh floor, Empress Towers, Fifth Avenue, Manhattan, New York City

SOROSI SAT BEHIND A LARGE mahogany table in his office, drumming his fingers and eyeing a small tape recorder connected to his phone. He removed the tape from it, walked over to a metal safe and placed it inside along with a thousand others.

These tapes—recordings of all his conversations with the Council—were his insurance in case he ever faced any trouble from them in the future. He put his official phone away, picked up his other phone and dialled a Canadian number.

After two rings, Gurwinder Singh Pannu answered the call. 'Good morning, Mr Sorosi,' he said respectfully.

Sorosi came straight to the point. 'Any information on your team in India yet?'

'No, sir. No news from anywhere. It is as though the earth swallowed them.'

'And Shahid?'

'I told him to activate the B team at Gandhinagar. DD's arriving there to address a rally. We will get him there,' reported Pannu.

'When is DD coming?'

'Next Monday. He will be giving a speech at a rally. This time, we will not fail, sir.'

'Who else knows of this plan, Pannu?' asked Sorosi.

'Apart from us, only Shahid and the handler on the ground know about this plan.'

'Good. I doubt that the bastard Bob is the mole in the system. Anyway, keep me posted.'

'Understood, sir,' came Pannu's clipped reply before the line went dead, the faint hum of disconnection echoing in the room like a fading heartbeat.

Pannu leaned back in his chair, his fingers drumming against the armrest, his frame betraying the weight of years spent weaving conspiracies against India. At fifty-eight, his once-lean physique had softened, a slight paunch now straining against the tailored fabric of his suit—a subtle reminder of time's relentless march. He rose and crossed to the full-length mirror in the corner, his reflection staring back with weary eyes. The lines etched into his face reflected the repeated failures he had suffered since DD had taken over. He looked at his midsection, which mocked his former vigour. 'Need to sharpen up, if I have to get the old bastard,' he muttered, the words meant for the man he hated the most—DD.

After his call with Pannu, Sorosi dialled a second number—that of the only person he trusted his life with. 'I am exhausted,' he said as soon as his call connected.

'Come home and talk to me,' Susan answered.

'On my way, darling. Make sure you have a bottle of Chianti ready.'

Susan Nikolov was John Sorosi's most valuable mistress. He confided everything in her, even matters he did not discuss with his wife, Rebecca Goldstein, and their sons, the twins Gabriel and John.

For fifty years, Sorosi and Rebecca had been bound by marriage, but their union had long since withered into a hollow formality. The day Rebecca gave birth to their twins, Sorosi's affection for her had evaporated, his disdain for children casting a shadow over their shared life. Now, at fifty-seven, Rebecca moved through her days like a ghost in Sorosi's world, their lives running parallel like twin rails of a railway track—stretching endlessly side by side, yet fated never to meet. The twins, now nearing thirties, had grown into adults who carried no warmth for their father, their hearts as distant from Sorosi as his own had been from them since their birth.

Susan, now fifty-two, had once been a high-profile escort dispatched to Sorosi nine years ago by Eros, a discreet Hungarian agency catering to the elite. Born into a poor Hungarian farming family, Susan vowed at fifteen to escape the shackles of poverty. Her striking beauty and physique were her only assets, and she wielded them with ruthless determination. By seventeen, she had won the trust of a local pimp, swiftly rising from his most prized prostitute to his assistant, managing his illicit business with cunning precision. But ambition bred greed, and when Susan schemed to seize control, the pimp uncovered her betrayal. Marked for death, she fled, drifting through cities and working for various pimps until she found refuge at Eros, a high-end escort agency serving a select clientele of billionaires—politicians, judges, actors, even notorious criminals.

Eros operated with impeccable secrecy, providing mistresses to its exclusive patrons while covertly recording their exploits as leverage against future liabilities. Within this shadowy world, Susan's charm and guile propelled her to a coveted role: Sorosi's personal escort. Unlike her previous assignments, her time with Sorosi took an unexpected turn. After two years, Susan severed ties with Eros, stepping away from the agency's web of intrigue, to chart her own path alongside the world's most ruthless strategist.

Although the agency attempted to initiate action against her, Sorosi intervened and protected her. From the moment Susan entered Sorosi's shadowed world, she carved a permanent place in his guarded heart, becoming not just his lover but his truest companion. In a life defined by calculated moves and ruthless ambition, Susan was the one constant that anchored Sorosi, the flame that warmed the cold machinery of his existence. Though he indulged in fleeting liaisons with new escorts from Eros during his travels beyond New York, none could rival the profound connection he shared with Susan. She was his soulmate, the one who saw through the façade of the Council's master strategist to the man beneath—a man who, despite his disdain for vulnerability, found solace in her presence.

Their bond was forged in a rare alchemy of mutual devotion. Susan showered Sorosi with unconditional respect and love, her unwavering loyalty a balm to his battle-worn spirit. She listened to his darkest fears, counselled him through the labyrinth of global conspiracies, and celebrated his triumphs, no matter how morally ambiguous. In return, Sorosi poured his resources into fulfilling her every desire, ensuring her life was one of opulence and security. He gifted her a high-rise luxury penthouse in Manhattan's glittering skyline, a sanctuary where she lived alone yet never felt isolated, surrounded by the echoes of his devotion. Her bank account swelled with wealth that surpassed even the fortunes of A-list Hollywood stars, a testament to Sorosi's commitment to her comfort.

But their connection transcended material gifts. Susan was more than a lover—she was Sorosi's confidante, his partner in navigating the treacherous currents of power. In quiet moments, when the weight of the Council's faltering empire pressed down on him, it was Susan's voice that steadied his resolve, her insight that sharpened his strategies. They were inseparable, their lives intertwined like vines, each drawing strength from the other. Whether dining in the glow of candlelit restaurants or plotting in the secrecy of his office, they moved as one, their thoughts and dreams synchronised in a dance of mutual trust. Soon, Sorosi's devotion culminated in a quiet, irrevocable act. His new will named Susan as the legal heir to eighty per cent of his vast fortune. It was a declaration that she was not just his heart's keeper but the guardian of his legacy.

In stark contrast to Susan's gritty ascent from poverty, Rebecca hailed from the rarefied world of aristocracy. Her father, Joseph Goldstein, was a renowned jeweller whose craftsmanship adorned the elite, his name synonymous with wealth and prestige. Rebecca's mother descended from the venerable House of Varnholt, a dynasty whose storied lineage stretched back centuries to the courts of medieval Europe, where their ancestors were whispered to have been advisors to emperors and architects of trade empires. This noble heritage imbued Rebecca with an air of untouchable elegance, setting her apart from Susan's hard-won nouveau richness and anchoring her in a legacy of power and refinement.

Tall, beautiful and fierce, she was known for her righteousness and strong moral compass, and commanded the world's respect. Everyone looked up to her, in awe of her charismatic personality.

Sorosi married Rebecca only to benefit from her social standing. But, deep in his heart, Sorosi despised her for all her qualities. Despite all his money, he felt inferior in front of her. To Sorosi, Rebecca was an unavoidable liability, and their social circles viewed him with quiet suspicion.

Sorosi's name alone was not enough to open the vaults of the world's financial titans. The banks and institutions that funded his labyrinthine projects did so not out of faith in his cunning, but because he was tethered to Rebecca Goldstein, the aristocratic daughter of Joseph Goldstein, the famed jeweller, and scion of the illustrious House of Varnholt.

Rebecca did not run any of her father's businesses, as they were managed by a trust that swore utmost loyalty to the Goldstein family and its business empire. But she was the owner and CEO of Goldstein Charities, a global foundation that her father had handed over to her before dying. The foundation looked after and rehabilitated homeless children across the globe and had earned the respect of being one of the world's top five most honest and charitable foundations. It received billions in charitable donations from almost all the world's top companies and banking institutions and was managed efficiently by her sons.

Rebecca and her sons were well aware of Sorosi's shady business ventures, though they did not know the extent of his ruthless life. They all stayed in the same house, but the father and sons didn't interact with each other. The sons deliberately avoided their father; they wanted no part in his life or to have him in theirs.

While Rebecca and her sons did not need Sorosi, he needed them. Without her name shielding him, Sorosi was a pariah to the financial elite, his reputation stained by whispers of deceit and ruthless ambition.

The distrust ran deep, etched into moments that fuelled Sorosi's smouldering hatred for the system that dared to question his worth. At a private meeting with the board of Zurich's prestigious Falken Bank, Sorosi had presented a meticulously crafted business proposal to start a futuristic tech company; in reality, it was to fund an investment in Dubai. The bankers, their faces cold as the marble walls surrounding them, barely glanced at his documents. One leaned forward, his voice dripping with condescension, and remarked, 'We don't lend money so that you can loan it further to make money. And we know you do this. To be honest, we don't believe a single thing you say as you lie through your teeth. But we'll consider this only because Mrs Goldstein's family has been one of our largest clients for thirty years. We will do this because their lawyer vouched for you.' The words stung like the whip of a lash, reducing Sorosi's decades of manoeuvring to a mere footnote in Rebecca's legacy.

In another instance, Sorosi sought a billion-dollar loan from the London-based Crest Moor Financial Group to restart his failed solar farm project in Angola. The meeting had been tense, with the group's chairman openly questioning Sorosi's integrity, citing rumours of his involvement in a failed currency manipulation scheme in Eastern Europe. 'We trust the Goldstein name,' the chairman had said, his eyes narrowing, 'but you, Mr Sorosi, are a risk we'd rather not take.' The loan was granted only after Rebecca's attorney provided assurances, a humiliation that left Sorosi seething again, his fists clenched under the table as he swallowed his pride.

The final slight came at a New York gala hosted by the elite Meridian Trust. Sorosi, standing beside Rebecca, overheard a group of bankers chuckling about his latest project. 'He's a loose cannon,' one muttered, 'but with Goldstein's daughter as his wife, we can't afford to say no.'

'I recently spotted him in a hotel in Monaco with a blonde who had "tart" written all over her. I don't know why Rebecca tolerates this ass,' asked a CEO.

'I don't think poor Rebecca knows about his nefarious activities. She would have thrown him out if she did,' replied the banker.

Unknown to Sorosi and the rest of the world, Imane Keram, their family lawyer, close confidante and childhood friend of Rebecca, suspected Sorosi of geopolitical conspiracies. So, he hired a well-known private investigation firm to keep an eye on Sorosi. Over a period of four years, the firm collected enough data to prove that Sorosi had some hand in various geopolitical disturbances.

The PI firm soon started collecting evidence to prosecute him. During the process, they discovered via wiretap that Sorosi had willed over 80 per cent of his wealth to Susan in case anything untoward happened to him. Imane directed the PI firm to find and destroy the will, but it was easier said than done; the will document, prepared by another lawyer, was kept safely in a locker in Empress Towers.

This was a big problem for Rebecca and her sons. If Sorosi were prosecuted, the will would become active, and Susan would inherit most of the wealth.

'I am telling the financial institutions and banks to stop any more loans. Let him sweat a little. He will make some mistakes, and we will capitalise on them. If he confronts you, say that the trust made the decision without informing you and that they are no longer listening to you. He cannot question the trust,' Imane told Rebecca.

Soon, Sorosi's hatred for Rebecca grew into a consuming fire as the banks rejected all his loans. His hatred stemmed from his loathing not just of the banks' distrust but also of the fact that he knew she was behind it all. The rejections stoked an inferno inside him, and he vowed to ruin Rebecca completely. He called for the mysterious lawyer as he decided to leave 100 per cent of his wealth to Susan. Unfortunately for him, the lawyer was undergoing a major surgery and said he would need four months before he returned to work. Sorosi had no choice but to painfully await his return, as he did not want to introduce a new lawyer again.

In the quiet elegance of Rebecca's bungalow, the two friends sat across from each other, New York's skyline a glittering backdrop to their hushed conversation. Rebecca's fingers traced the rim of her coffee cup; her aristocratic poise tinged with unease. Imane leaned forward, his eyes sharp with purpose.

'Rebecca,' Imane began, his voice low but urgent, 'the PI firm called. They picked up a wiretap on Sorosi talking to his lawyer. He's planning on rewriting his will, giving *everything* to Susan—one hundred per cent. We've got four months to act, or we lose it all. We need to get our hands on that will and make sure it's destroyed.'

Rebecca's grip tightened on her cup, her knuckles paling. 'How do we even begin to do that?' she asked, her voice betraying a flicker of desperation.

Imane's lips curved into a knowing smile. 'We don't do it alone. We bring in someone who's got just as much to lose as we do—someone who'd jump at the chance to stop Sorosi.'

Rebecca's brow furrowed. 'Who?'

'Dhariwal,' Imane replied, his tone deliberate. 'Ajit Dhariwal, India's national security advisor. The PI firm also overheard Sorosi telling Susan he's planning something big in India to destabilise it before he skips the country with her. If we tip Dhariwal off, he'll act. And whatever happens next, it'll work in our favour. Sorosi won't even suspect we're behind it.'

Rebecca shook her head, her voice wavering. 'You can't just call him up and say, "Hey, Dhariwal, Sorosi's plotting something against India." He may not even answer your call, for all I know.'

Imane's eyes softened, a shared memory surfacing. 'Don't you remember, Rebecca? When Gabriel was in the hospital, fighting for his life during Covid?'

Rebecca's gaze drifted, her eyes misting over. 'How could I forget? His immune system was failing, his oxygen levels dropping so fast that the doctors gave up. They told me he had 72 hours left and sent us home to say goodbye,' her voice cracked, the pain still raw. 'I was lost, Imane. I turned to you, and you saved him.'

Imane shook his head, his expression solemn. 'No, I did not. I reached out to Ajit Dhariwal that night. I knew he had connections, that India's doctors were pulling off miracles. He didn't hesitate. He sent two AIIMS specialists in New Delhi to oversee Gabriel's treatment. Four months later, your son was walking again, Rebecca. Dhariwal made that happen, not me.'

Rebecca's lips trembled as she recalled those months.

'Though Ajit and I had common friends, I got to know Ajit a lot better during that time. He'd call me every alternate day and talk about Gabriel, you, life and also about Sorosi,' Imane said.

'What about Sorosi?' asked Rebecca.

'I told Dhariwal then that I suspected Sorosi of meddling in India's elections, trying to undermine DD and destabilise the country, and he listened. From his reactions, I realised he greatly cared for his country. Six months later, when Gabriel had fully recovered, I made you speak to him. Do you remember what you told him that night?'

'I told him that I was forever in his debt. That he and his nation had saved my son, and I'll never forget that,' replied Rebecca.

Imane's eyes gleamed with intent. 'That debt, Rebecca—it's time to call it in. We will tell Dhariwal that Sorosi is scheming something big against India. DD's India isn't the same as it used to be—they're fierce and relentless, and more ruthless than Mossad when it comes to protecting their own. Dhariwal will crush Sorosi like a bug, and we'll be free of him. Two birds, one stone: we protect our future, and India gets its revenge.'

Rebecca's jaw tightened, a spark of resolve igniting in her eyes. 'Anything to be rid of that monster,' she whispered. 'Let's do it.'

Imane nodded, a conspiratorial glint in his gaze. The game was set, and with Dhariwal as their unwitting ally, Sorosi's empire—and his betrayal—would crumble under the weight of India's rising power.

~

As Imane got into his car, he heard two beeps. He took out a small gadget from his coat pocket and pressed the play button. A new conversation between Sorosi and Susan played out. He smiled and muttered, 'Once you are in chains, Sorosi, I will have Rebecca. Then my life would be complete.'

~

As he was being driven through the bustling streets of Manhattan, Sorosi had his mind already in Susan's penthouse, where solace and strategy awaited.

His phone buzzed, shattering his thoughts. The screen flashed the name of Henry Hunt, the steely CEO of Sorosi's Open Forum Foundation (OFF), his trusted lieutenant who orchestrated the intricate web of payments, political machinations and covert operations that kept the Council's influence alive.

OFF was more than an NGO—it was Sorosi's meticulously crafted front, a façade of philanthropy that funnelled the Council's 'charitable donations' into funding coups, civil unrest, and the toppling of governments that dared defy their agenda. Henry Hunt was the maestro of these dark symphonies, executing Sorosi's orders with ruthless precision.

'Yes, Henry, what is it?' Sorosi answered, his voice clipped, betraying the urgency of his mission.

'The payments to Yunus Khan have been made, sir,' Hunt replied, his tone as cold and efficient as ever.

Sorosi's lips curled into a faint, predatory smile. Yunus Khan was no mere humanitarian. Despite the world's adoring gaze, the Bangladeshi social entrepreneur and economist—celebrated for his microfinance innovations and crowned with the 2006 Nobel Peace Prize—was a carefully cultivated asset of the Council. His philanthropy and saintly image were a masquerade, a meticulously woven tapestry of deception designed to cloak his true purpose. Over the decades, the Council had moulded Yunus into their perfect instrument, his global acclaim a shield that allowed him to move unchecked across borders, his every gesture cloaked in the guise of altruism.

The Council's latest gambit was their boldest yet—to seize control of Bangladesh by ousting its sitting prime minister, Sheikh Nasreen. Through Sorosi, they had dangled the ultimate prize before Yunus—the premiership of Bangladesh, a role that would cement him as a puppet of the Apuni Malo, the Council's shadowy proxy for manipulating governments. Yunus, seduced by power and oblivious to the strings attached, had become the lynchpin in their plan to destabilise the nation. The strategy was ruthless—ignite civil unrest by mobilising students, flooding the streets with whispers that Nasreen was a corrupt megalomaniac, a tyrant strangling democracy. These lies, spread through OFF's covert channels, would fan the flames of rebellion, paving the way for Yunus to rise as the Council's chosen saviour.

But the Council's ambitions stretched beyond mere regime change. Bangladesh was a prize—its thriving textile industry a golden goose they sought to control, funnelling billions into their coffers. More critically, they coveted Jupiter Island, a strategic speck in the Bay of Bengal, perfectly positioned to host an American military base. With missiles trained on China, it would be a brazen checkmate in the geopolitical chess game, a signal to Beijing that the Council—and America—has them in its sights. Yunus, with his halo of nobility, was the ideal figurehead to mask this imperialist grab, his every move choreographed by Sorosi's unseen hand.

As Sorosi quickened his pace towards Susan's penthouse, a flicker of satisfaction warmed his chest. Yunus was in place, the payments secured, and the stage set for chaos in Bangladesh. The Council's grip would tighten, and with Susan by his side, Sorosi would wield their power to reshape the world, starting with the fall of Sheikh Nasreen and the rise of their carefully crafted puppet.

'Has he started his work?' asked Sorosi.

'Yes. Yunus is speaking to all the student unions across Bangladesh. He expects a massive student revolt by mid-August. If all goes well, Sheikh Nasreen will be out of power by the end of August, and we can install him as the head of the caretaker government. Once he is on board, we can quickly get approvals sanctioned for the military base.'

'Good work. How are the election preparations coming along in India?' asked Sorosi.

'We have sufficiently funded the PCP this time, and the PCP leader, Rahul Singh Yadav, has galvanised support from more Opposition parties. He has formed a new coalition to jointly fight elections against DD's Bharatiya Lok Party (BLP) and its allies. As you said, if we can't neutralise him, we should at least get him out of power,' said Hunt.

'And what do you think are the chances he will not form the government this time?'

'If Rahul follows our instructions, we will be able to defeat DD this time.'

'Once he is out of power, I will make sure he does not live to see another day,' growled Sorosi as his car entered Susan's compound.

'But what if Rahul loses again?' asked Hunt.

Sorosi leaned back in his seat, his voice sharp and deliberate as he outlined the intricate plan to Henry. 'Why do you think I'm orchestrating this chaos in Bangladesh?' he asked, his eyes glinting with purpose. 'This is no random act of disruption. It's a carefully crafted strategy to bring India to its knees, to rewind its progress by decades, and to make it a subservient, debt-ridden nation once again, beholden to the Western powers and the Apuni Malo Council. The success of the first phase of the plan hinges on undermining the grip of DD's party on India,' Sorosi explained. 'Rahul and the PCP have been working tirelessly to erode DD's support base. They've spread a narrative among India's Muslim community that a third term for DD would lead to a constitutional overhaul, transforming India into a Hindu nation.'

'This fear has taken root, amplified through social media campaigns funded by our networks. Posts, videos and influencers have flooded platforms with this message, creating distrust and division. But what if, despite all this, DD wins?' asked Henry.

Sorosi smirked. 'Even if DD wins the elections, it will be with a wafer-thin margin. Their coalition will be fragile, and governing will be a nightmare. Every policy, every decision will face resistance from a polarised populace and an emboldened Opposition. The PCP will capitalise on this, positioning itself as the only viable alternative.'

'What is step two?' asked Henry.

'The next piece of the puzzle lies across the border in Bangladesh. I plan to exploit the country's volatile political landscape. The current Bangladeshi government is teetering,' Sorosi said. 'It will collapse under internal dissent and economic strain in a few months. Once it does, we will ensure that Yunus steps in as the interim government advisor. His appointment will delay elections indefinitely, citing the need for "stability". This will frustrate the student movements and the general populace, who are already restless.

'The delay in elections will create a power vacuum, giving us fertile ground for chaos,' Sorosi continued. 'We've been quietly funding Islamic fundamentalist groups in Bangladesh. These groups will seize the moment, inciting civilians with promises of Sharia law as a solution to the country's woes. The rhetoric will be simple but powerful: a return to "purity" and "order". Meanwhile, rogue elements—our proxies—will target Hindu minorities with calculated atrocities. Homes will be burned, temples desecrated and families displaced. The violence will be relentless, designed to provoke a desperate response from India.'

'The escalating violence against Hindus in Bangladesh will leave DD with no choice. The Hindu minority will beg for India's intervention,' added Henry.

'Precisely. DD, already weakened and facing domestic pressure, will be forced to act. He'll see it as a moral and political necessity to protect his kin across the border. Just like Indira Gandhi intervened in East Pakistan in 1971, DD will mobilise troops, perhaps even launch a limited military operation.'

Sorosi leaned forward, his voice dropping to a whisper. 'That's when we spring the trap. One shot, Henry—one shot fired by India into Bangladesh will be enough. I've already secured assurances from the Bangladeshi general, loyal to our cause, to retaliate with missile strikes into West Bengal. This will escalate the conflict into a full-scale war.'

'But the war will not be a simple bilateral affair. Pakistan and China will back Bangladesh,' Henry said.

'Pakistan, eager to weaken its rival, will provide military and logistical support to Bangladesh; and China, with its own geopolitical ambitions, will supply advanced weaponry and economic aid too. Both will frame it as a defence against Indian aggression,' Sorosi said.

'What about Russia? It is a strong ally of India,' asked Henry.

Sorosi smiled, 'Russia, caught between its alliances with India and China, will opt for neutrality, leaving India isolated. To ensure India's defeat, I will force the Council to make sure that our army and the armies of our allies clandestinely funnel weapons and ammunition to Bangladesh via Pakistan.'

'And, just like you've prolonged the Ukraine conflict, you'll keep Bangladesh armed and fighting, right?' asked Henry.

Sorosi nodded. 'Drones, missiles and small arms will flow through covert channels, ensuring a prolonged and bloody stalemate.'

'How will you ensure India's international isolation and economic strangulation?' asked Henry.

Sorosi's eyes sparkled. 'Ah! That will be the final nail in India's coffin. The Apuni Malo and the Council will ensure that global opinion turns against India. Within three days of the war's outbreak, the Council will lobby the American Senate to declare India the aggressor,' he explained. 'We'll draw parallels to Russia's invasion of Ukraine, painting India as a reckless imperialist power. The US will impose crippling economic sanctions, cutting India off from global trade networks, foreign investment and critical resources.

Other nations, aligned with or dependent on the US, will follow suit.'

'India will be starved of money, oil and technology,' Henry said.

'Yes. Its economy will grind to a halt. Supply chains will collapse, inflation will soar, and the Indian rupee will plummet. The Indian public, already frustrated with DD's leadership, will turn against him, blaming him for the war and the ensuing hardship. With India in chaos, the PCP will seize the moment. They'll position themselves as the saviours of a broken nation,' Sorosi said.

'Backed by our funding and propaganda, they'll promise stability, secularism and economic recovery. The public, desperate for change, will rally behind them. Before long, the PCP will control India's government and, through them, the Apuni Malo will pull the strings,' Henry added.

Sorosi's voice grew cold. 'India will be reduced to what it was seventy years ago—an underdeveloped, debt-ridden nation, dependent on Western aid and dictated by our interests. Its dreams of being a global power will be shattered, its military weakened, and its people subdued.'

Henry, listening intently, raised a concern. 'What if India wins the war? What if they overwhelm Bangladesh before our plan unfolds?'

Sorosi laughed, dismissing the possibility. 'They won't. Our intelligence networks have mapped India's military capabilities. Thanks to the sustained terror attacks from Pakistan, their forces are spread thin, and their economy can't sustain a prolonged conflict. Even if they gain early victories, the sanctions and international pressure will cripple them. And if that's not enough, we have sleeper cells within India—politicians, bureaucrats and media figures—who will amplify dissent and sabotage DD's efforts from within.'

Henry shook his head, marvelling at the plan's ruthlessness. 'You really have a criminal mind,' he said.

Sorosi's laughter echoed through the room. 'I'm no criminal, Henry. I'm merely the executor. The council sets the agenda; I make it happen. The fall of the largest democracy in the world will be a masterpiece of strategy, a testament to the power of those who control the world's shadows. And I will be known as the architect who reduced a rising power to a shadow of its former self, turning it into a nation enslaved by debt and beholden to its will.'

'If you pull this off, it will be etched in history and the Council will be very pleased with you,' said Henry.

'That is what the Council pays me for, Henry,' replied Sorosi.

'What about Bob?' asked Henry, as he knew of the enmity between them.

'He is a thorn in my flesh, but I will deal with him later. Now, I need to brief Susan about all this,' Sorosi disconnected as the car entered Susan's apartment building.

3

25 January 2024, 8.30 p.m.
7, Lok Kalyan Marg, New Delhi

'IS THE PANTHER IN?' ASKED Shiva Kumar Raju, an SPG officer and DD's personal bodyguard, to his colleague from the PM's security detail, who was lounging outside DD's library. DD's nickname, Panther, wasn't given lightly by the SPG. It wasn't just how DD walked—precise and fierce—but the calculated accuracy with which he destroyed every thorn in his path.

'Yes. He is expecting you,' the officer answered. Shiva knocked and entered the library.

DD was leafing through the incident report on what had transpired in Ayodhya while Dhariwal sat beside him, watching him intently. The prime minister motioned Shiva to sit as he reviewed the report. Shiva walked across the room and sat on one of the living room chairs to DD's left.

After a few minutes, DD placed the file on the table in front of him. 'This is a thorough report, Ajit. The bombers have revealed vital information. ATS has done a good job.'

'DD, the report says that if the Ayodhya mission failed, Shahid would use his second team to assassinate you in Gandhinagar,' said Dhariwal.

'Yes, I read that,' said DD.

'Despite every precaution, the ISI and LeT have infiltrated the BLP. The bombers revealed that Rafique Abubakar is a part of the conspiracy.'

'Faith and belief can make you do anything, especially if you are uneducated. Abubakar was a loyal grassroots-level worker for decades. He grew from the ranks, eventually becoming the president of BLP's Gujarat wing. But it looks like the ISIS and the LeT have finally caught up with him. Anyway, what is the plan now that we know their intentions?'

'We must strike the Gandhinagar team before you land there on 31 January,' said Dhariwal.

'Do we have enough intel to execute it?'

'Yes. The bombers were very cooperative,' Ajit replied sarcastically.

'Then I will attend the rally and give my speech. Like Ayodhya, we will keep this under wraps. I don't want the news of the assassination attempts to take centre stage and dilute the narrative around the polls,' DD said. Then, as an afterthought, he asked, 'Since you used the word strike, I am presuming you will use the "Ghosts" for this mission?'

Dhariwal nodded, 'Yes, we plan to use the Panther's Ghosts for this. That is why I called Shiva in for the meeting, sir.'

For a while, DD and Dhariwal had wanted to change India's defence strategy as it was highly defensive and portrayed India as a meek country. Post 2014, DD and

Dhariwal had initiated a new defence doctrine for India, called 'Defensive Offence', where India, like the CIA and the MOSSAD, worked towards proactively neutralising terrorists, both within India and in enemy states. To this effect, they wanted to create a new unit under the Special Forces wing. However, the PCP and the Opposition in the parliament boycotted it, saying it was too draconian.

Determined to proceed with their plans, DD and Dhariwal chose an unconventional approach. They decided to create a clandestine group that would operate outside the boundaries of the government. Unknown to anyone, this team would fulfil the expectations of the new doctrine. Since no one was aware of the existence of such a team, this covert group was called the Ghosts. And as they belonged to DD aka the Panther, they came to be called 'The Panther's Ghosts'.

The Ghosts were a group of six elite anti-terrorist commandos drawn from the Special Forces. The team was created to orchestrate covert, false-flag operations on terrorist organisations even before they could launch an attack. And Shiva was part of the group.

'Where are the Ghosts?' DD asked Shiva.

'AV and Geeta will arrive tonight from Mumbai. Raj and Lala are on a "strike" in Tibet,' Shiva answered. Every mission of the Ghosts was termed as a 'strike'.

'What is the news from them?' asked DD.

'Thanks to all the help from Madam Paitoon Luan, they safely reached Tibet a month ago.'

'When is the strike expected?'

'Raj will inform me when they are ready, sir,' answered Dhariwal.

'So, who will handle the Gandhinagar strike?' DD asked Shiva.

'Geeta, AV and I, sir. AV will be leading it,' Shiva informed them.

'Where is Abubakar right now?' asked DD.

'He flew to the UK yesterday under the pretext of medical treatment for his liver. But our sources confirmed he is now with Abdul Rashid Abdullah in Kandahar.'

'The same Rashid who has been radicalising innocent Indians and Sri Lankans to join ISIS for a while now?' asked DD.

'Yes, sir.'

'Where is Shahid Faisal? Is he in Gandhinagar?' asked DD.

'We don't know. My team is still trying to locate him.'

'Let me help you with Kandahar. The Ghosts are spread thin already,' said DD. Then he picked up his Thuraya SAT phone and dialled S. Jaikrishna, the minister for external affairs.

'Good evening, Jai. How did the discussions with the Iranians on the Chabahar Port go?'

'Went off very well, sir. We have signed a ninety-nine-year lease with them,' said Jaikrishna. 'Tonight, I have dinner with the Khamenei. So, I am flying back tomorrow.'

'Jai, I want you to stop by Kandahar and meet the prime minister of Afghanistan.'

'Maulvi Abdul Kadir?' Jaikrishna asked.

'Yes.'

'Okay, and ...?'

'We have two gentlemen in Kandahar creating problems for us. I want them extradited. Dhariwal will explain everything to you separately. Just make sure they are sent back, please.'

'Sure, sir. I'll wait for Ajit's brief,' Jaikrishna said as he looked at the clock. It read 7.00 p.m. local time.

After disconnecting the call, DD turned to Dhariwal. 'Give Jai the basics only. Do not mention the assassination attempts.'

'Sure, sir,' Dhariwal replied. 'And since we recently reopened our embassy in Kabul, we have a technical team headed by R. Singh there. I will arrange for him to set up a meeting between Maulvi and Jai, making it an official visit to avoid raising any suspicions. We will throw in a few goodies that we were planning to announce by the end of the year in Kabul. That will help cement the relationship between Jai and Maulvi.'

DD turned to Shiva and said, 'Get the Ghost ready for a meeting with Ajit.' Then he shook hands with Shiva and said softly, 'All the best, son.'

Shiva stood up, saluted and left the room quietly. After Shiva left, DD leaned back into his chair and asked Dhariwal, 'How is your father now? Is he still in the ICU?'

'Yes, sir. But you know TB of the stomach has no cure, so his doctors have requested me to take him home.'

'Who will look after him if he is brought home?' asked DD.

'I need to figure it out. I plan to leave after the Gandhinagar strike and sort this out. I may even bring him back to Delhi because it is easier for me here.'

'Let me know if you need any help,' said DD.

Thirteen hours later, at 9.00 a.m. local time, Kandahar, the doors of Ariana Afghan Airlines Flight FG401 slid open, releasing a rush of warm, dusty air. S. Jaikrishna stepped out first, a sleek iPad in his left hand. He was immaculately dressed in a tailored black suit, a crisp white shirt, and a blazing red tie that stood out like a streak of fire against the muted tones of the tarmac. His salt-and-pepper hair was neatly parted, his eyes sharp behind thin-rimmed glasses. Flanking him were his loyal secretary and two SPG officers, their presence understated but unmistakably alert.

After collecting their luggage, the group exited the terminal into the blinding Afghan sunlight. At the curb stood Ravinder Singh, waiting anxiously, dabbing his forehead with a monogrammed handkerchief.

Singh, a compact man barely 5'2" tall, was entirely bald, with a cherubic face that belied the sharp bureaucratic instincts beneath. He wore beige slacks, a matching hat and a loosely tucked white shirt that billowed in the dry wind.

'Welcome to Kandahar, sir,' Singh beamed, extending his hand as Jaikrishna approached.

'Thank you, Ravinder,' Jaikrishna replied, his tone warm but clipped with purpose.

After a brief round of introductions and polite smiles, the group split. Jaikrishna and Singh climbed into a black, dust-coated Land Rover with tinted windows and a hardened frame—clearly retrofitted for secure VIP movement. The rest of the entourage, including the secretary and the SPG officers, were ushered into a white Toyota Fortuner. On

Singh's instructions, the Fortuner peeled off towards the Indian Embassy, while the Land Rover turned left, taking a less-frequented road that snaked through the rocky outskirts of Kandahar.

The drive offered a grim beauty. The arid terrain stretched endlessly, broken only by occasional mounds of rubble, abandoned Soviet-era watchtowers, and pockets of tan-brick dwellings huddled together like survivors of a long-forgotten siege. Dust storms whispered across the roads, and wild shrubs clung stubbornly to the earth. In the distance, rugged hills rose like silent sentinels guarding the region's bloodstained history.

'I hope the flight was comfortable,' Singh said politely, his voice barely audible over the grumble of the Land Rover's engine and the occasional bump in the rugged path.

'Nothing to complain about, except the layover in Dubai,' Jaikrishna replied, adjusting his collar. 'I was stuck inside the aircraft for half an hour without air conditioning. Felt like a damn oven. Anyway, how are things here?'

'The Taliban has been cooperative, sir,' Singh reported, glancing at his tablet. 'They're appreciative of India's assistance—food, clothing, medicines, infrastructure. As requested, the office of Maulvi Abdul Kadir released an official press note about your visit late last night. Everything is above board.'

He reached into his bag and handed Jaikrishna a sealed envelope.

'I've also received a few instructions from the PMO,' Singh continued. 'Once your meeting with Kadir ends, a short press conference has been organised. You'll be announcing some new development projects. The Maulvi has been informed.'

Jaikrishna nodded, eyes narrowing slightly as he broke the seal on the envelope, his mind already preparing for the political tightrope ahead.

An hour later, on the dusty fringes of Kandahar, the black Land Rover pulled up to a high-walled compound, flanked by mud-brick barriers and guarded by two heavily armed men in loose salwar–kameez and dusty combat boots. Beyond the crude security post stood the private residence of Maulvi Abdul Kadir, a man whose quiet presence now commanded the highest authority in Taliban-controlled Afghanistan.

Since the Taliban's return to power, Maulvi Kadir had chosen to govern not from the opulence of the presidential palace in Kabul, but from this modest, fortified bungalow nestled on the outskirts of Kandahar. The road leading here was unpaved and uneven, flanked by thorny acacia trees, discarded tyres and scattered ruins from past wars. Yet, it radiated a strange calm, almost like the eye of a storm.

The gates creaked open slowly, revealing a surprisingly well-maintained courtyard shaded by grapevines and scattered with rose shrubs. The house itself was low-slung and rectangular, built in traditional Afghan style—flat-roofed with arched windows and sun-faded sandstone walls. A Taliban flag fluttered gently atop a narrow mast, catching the desert wind.

Inside, there was a large foyer with no furniture. The floors were lined with Persian carpets dulled by age and sand. Whitewashed walls bore Islamic calligraphy in black ink and green paint, invoking verses of strength, mercy and divine justice. The reception area, where guests were received, was simple—large cushions and bolsters lined the perimeter, with no furniture save a single carved wooden table bearing a copper tray of dates, almonds and spiced tea.

There was no air of grandeur here, only a fierce assertion of humility blended with power. It was a space built not to impress but to remind: the new leadership had returned to its roots—austere, inward and deeply grounded in ideology.

As the Land Rover rolled to a stop, Jaikrishna adjusted his blazer, picked up his iPad and stepped out. The thick silence of the compound was broken only by the distant bleat of goats and the whirr of an old ceiling fan heard through an open window.

This was where the real talk would begin—in a room stripped of diplomacy's glitter, but heavy with consequence.

As soon as Jaikrishna and Singh stepped out of the Land Rover, a flurry of motion surrounded them. Six Taliban fighters, faces half-covered with black scarves and eyes sharp with suspicion, quickly encircled them. The men were armed to the teeth—each carrying an AK-47, and some with sidearms strapped to their thighs and traditional curved daggers tucked into their belts.

The leader among them, Ayub Khan, was hard to miss—a towering figure with broad shoulders, sun-baked skin and a neatly trimmed beard streaked with grey. An AK-47 hung casually from his shoulder like an accessory, but his stance said otherwise—alert, commanding, ready. He stepped forward with a half-smile, the kind that didn't quite reach the eyes.

'Mr Minister,' he said, nodding respectfully at Jaikrishna and giving a subtle tilt of the head to Singh, 'this way.'

They were led past the reception into the primary residence through a heavy teakwood door studded with iron bolts. Before entering, Ayub gestured politely but firmly towards a carpeted vestibule. As per custom, the two Indian dignitaries removed their shoes and placed them on a worn wooden rack by the entrance. The air inside was cool and mildly fragrant—a faint blend of attar, gun oil and dried herbs.

The living room was surprisingly spacious yet sparse. The walls were whitewashed but bore the signs of ageing—faint watermarks near the ceiling, and cracks where plaster had peeled under the desert heat. Arabic calligraphy adorned one side, framed under glass, while the other held a faded tapestry in deep maroon and gold.

Thick Afghan carpets in shades of rust, olive and indigo covered the entire floor. Cushions lined the walls, and in the centre, a low table held a brass samovar, a bowl of sugared almonds and a plate of dry dates. Natural light filtered in through slatted wooden shutters, casting warm streaks across the room.

Ayub motioned for them to sit, then disappeared behind a curtain, into an inner chamber. They could hear the murmur of his voice through the wall—speaking in Pashto, sharp but calm. A minute later, he returned and positioned himself silently near the main entrance, now guarding it like a sentry.

Then came the soft creak of a door, and Maulvi Abdul Kadir entered.

He was smaller than expected—no more than 5'4", with a wiry build and intense eyes that missed nothing. His face was lean, framed by a thick black beard, and his gait carried the confidence of someone used to commanding authority. Despite his size, there was an unmistakable toughness about him. A matte black GLOCK pistol was tucked without ceremony into the waistband of his salwar trousers.

He wore black from head to toe—a stark kurta, a matching vest and a black turban wrapped tightly around his head. And yet, his face beamed with warmth as he approached, a smile stretching from ear to ear as he extended his hand.

'Mr Minister,' he said, gripping Jaikrishna's hand firmly. His palm was rough and calloused—not the hand of a ceremonial leader, but of a man who had weathered both mountains and war zones. 'How are you today?'

'I'm well, thank you,' Jaikrishna replied, smiling back. 'And please, call me Jaikrishna. If that's too long, Jai will do.'

Kadir chuckled softly. 'This is what I like about you, Indians—no ego. Not pompous like the Americans or the Russians ... or even the Pakistanis.' He winked, a flash of mischief in his eyes. 'Please, be seated.'

He gestured towards a long white sofa positioned beside the window. Behind it, a battered air cooler wheezed gently, offering some reprieve from the outside heat. The atmosphere, while polite, was charged—a meeting of two worlds, wrapped in pleasantries, yet brimming with unspoken intent.

Jaishankar sat to the right and Maulvi to the left. Once they were comfortably seated, a lady in a burqa walked out of one of the rooms, presumably the kitchen, and served them fresh kahwa, dates and a cake. Jaikrishna's surprise was evident on his face when he saw a woman serving them.

Maulvi Kadir smiled, 'I know you are wondering about the Taliban's restrictions on women; you are our special guest, thereby an exception. This is Roya, my wife.'

'Roya means vision,' said Jaikrishna, politely accepting the tea and cake.

'Yes. I value her advice. She has better vision than me,' Maulvi Kadir said. His expression suddenly turned serious, and he leaned forward, 'I heard about the announcements you wish to make. The people of Afghanistan will join me in thanking you, Jai. Your help is always greatly appreciated.'

Jaikrishna took a few seconds to respond. He enjoyed the cake while Maulvi Kadir watched. Once he had finished it, Jaikrishna washed it down with a sip of kahwa and handed Maulvi Kadir an envelope. 'This is the service contract for the Afghan–India Friendship Dam that we built eight years ago on the Harirud River. This was a long-pending request from your end.'

Maulvi Kadir's eyes scanned the letter carefully and put it on the coffee table. 'Thank you, Jai. This will solve much of our water crisis. We also received your tractors last week.'

Unaware of any such deal, Jaikrishna quickly looked at Singh, who immediately jumped to his rescue. 'Sir, about the farming and agriculture aid you approved last month, industrialist Pavak Dahia was contracted to deliver hundred tractors to Kandahar's agricultural department. Mr Dahia's consignment arrived last week.'

'Oh, yes. It slipped my mind,' said Jaikrishna.

Kadir smiled from ear to ear. 'Let's not forget the seed money you approved for our farmers. It has been of great help to our cultivators. Most Afghan farmers have transitioned from poppy farming to wheat and rice production. Now we can feed our people without begging for food from anyone.'

Jaikrishna nodded and handed him another letter. 'Mr Prime Minister, as you requested, AIIMS will be opening three medical colleges in Kabul, Kandahar and Herat. Within the next three years, Afghanistan will have three state-of-the-art medical facilities, enabling locals to receive treatment locally instead of travelling to India. The work will start early next month.'

Maulvi Kadir could not contain his happiness when he was handed the second letter. He embraced Jaikrishna tightly and said, 'Jai, your people and you are truly farishtas.'

'You are very kind, Mr Prime Minister,' Jaikrishna said.

'But this is too much for one day, Jai,' Maulvi Kadir said with a small laugh. 'Now tell me, how can I help you?'

Jaikrishna paused for a second and then handed Maulvi Kadir two pictures. He tapped on them and said, 'They are here in Afghanistan, and we need them.'

Maulvi Kadir recognised Abdul Rashid Abdullah at once but could not place the second face. 'Who is this man?' asked Maulvi Kadir.

'He is Abubakar. He is Rashid's man in Gujarat. On Rashid's instructions, he has planned a big terror attack in India.'

'You want to take both of them back to India?'

'We only need Rashid to be extradited. You can decide what to do with Abubakar,' said Jaishankar. For a moment their eyes locked and then Kadir nodded, understanding the meaning of the second statement.

'Do you know where they are?' Maulvi Kadir asked Ayub Khan, handing over the photographs.

Ayub looked at the pictures and nodded. 'They are in Kandahar.'

'Rashid has been recruiting Indians from Kerala and sending them to Syria to fight the ISIS war for a long time. Now he is recruiting Sri Lankan ISIS terrorists and sending them to India. At the same time, we have been proactively neutralising them. If we get Rashid, we can shut off the recruitment tap and also find out who is behind this operation. We need your help in getting Rashid,' Jaikrishna said.

'ISIS is our enemy, too,' Maulvi Kadir said, his voice steely. 'They have already expanded their presence in our eastern provinces and targeted civilians in suicide attacks. We will cooperate, Jai. Ayub, find Rashid and hand him over to Mr Singh for extradition.'

'And Abubakar?' asked Ayub.

'He will be collateral damage,' replied Maulvi Kadir, his face expressionless.

Forty-eight hours after their successful meeting with Maulvi Abdul Kadir, Singh called Jaikrishna. 'Ayub has Abdul Rashid Abdullah in our safe house in Kabul for extradition.'

'And Abubakar?'

'Buried six feet under.'

4

27 January 2024, 9 p.m.
Biju Patnaik International Airport, Bhubaneshwar, India

DHARIWAL STEPPED OUT OF A private aircraft and got into a waiting car that would take him to the hospital where his father was admitted. He was about to call the doctor when he received a call from one of his agents in Canada.

'Yes, Angel?' asked Dhariwal.

'Shahid Faisal is in Bhubaneshwar, but I do not know where in the city. You need to be careful because you are the target.'

'Thank you, Angel. I will handle this from here. You take care,' said Dhariwal.

After disconnecting Angel's call, Dhariwal called the state's home minister, who answered after two rings.

'Good evening, Mr Dhariwal. How may I help you?' he asked.

'Mr Minister, we have reasons to believe that the wanted terrorist Shahid Faisal is in Bhubaneshwar. Inform the police commissioner, the local police and state ATS to take action. Every check post, bus terminal, train station and airport should be on high alert. Throw a massive security ring around the city.'

'I am on it and will keep you posted,' the home minister assured Dhariwal.

As he neared the hospital, Dhariwal received a call from an unknown number. Assuming it was from someone in the NSA office as not many people had his direct number, Dhariwal answered the call. 'Yes?' he asked.

'Good evening, sir. This is Major Indrajit Rathode from Mumbai.'

Major Rathode, nearing sixty, was an ex-military intelligence officer. He had worked closely with Dhariwal on several missions before his voluntary retirement. Later, he joined an IT company called Info Dynamics as its security head.

'Hey, Indrajit. I did not recognise the number. Is it a new one?' Dhariwal asked.

'No, sir. My phone has a double SIM facility. This is the number I use at ID. I am sorry I called you from this number.'

'That's okay. Long time no see. How come you called? All okay?'

'All okay, sir. Are you in Delhi? I wanted to meet with you.'

'I am in Odisha to meet my father. He has been hospitalised and it doesn't look too good. I plan to return to Delhi tomorrow with him so he can spend his final days with me. But I need to assess his condition before I take that decision. I will call you once I am back. I hope it is nothing urgent.'

'Nothing urgent. Where are you staying in Odisha?'

'I will be in Pipili at my dad's place till I return to Delhi.'

'I will pray for your father, sir,' said Indrajit.

'Thank you, Inder. I will see you in Delhi.'

Minutes later, Dhariwal's car screeched to a halt outside AIIMS. Without waiting for the driver to open the door, he stepped out, his heart pounding heavily in his chest. The morning air was cool, but he felt none of it. His feet carried him almost mechanically towards the ICU building, the world around him blurring into a distant hum.

He was halfway to the private suite when he saw the doctor approaching—a familiar figure in a white coat, his expression grave.

Dhariwal forced a smile, clinging to hope. 'Is everything okay?' he asked, his voice unnaturally calm.

The doctor hesitated for a heartbeat—just a heartbeat—but it was enough. Dhariwal saw the truth even before the words came.

The doctor lowered his gaze and said quietly, almost apologetically, 'He is no more, Mr Dhariwal. I was coming to find you.'

For a moment, Dhariwal just stood there, as if the earth had slipped out from under his feet. A searing pain gripped his chest, burning a hollow into his very soul. He dropped his eyes to his polished black shoes, blinking hard, willing himself not to break down.

The doctor stepped closer, placing a steadying hand on Dhariwal's shoulder. His voice was gentle, full of reverence. 'Your father asked me ... to tell you how proud he was of you.'

That was it. The dam broke.

Dhariwal stumbled to the nearest bench, dropped onto it heavily, and buried his face in his hands. The quiet corridor echoed with the raw sounds of his grief—deep, guttural sobs he could no longer contain. In that moment, the man who had shaped the country's security doctrine—the sharp strategist, the unbreakable NSA—was simply a son, broken by the loss of the man who had given him everything. By dawn, the news had spread across India—the NSA had lost his beloved father. And when the ambulance carrying Dhariwal and his father's body reached his hometown of Pipili later that afternoon, almost every senior minister of the government, along with countless villagers, stood waiting silently, heads bowed in mourning, to pay their respects to the man who had raised a son that now carried the hopes of a nation.

The cremation was over by noon, and by 4 p.m., almost everyone had left. DD stayed a while longer, and Dhariwal briefed him about Shahid Faisal's presence in Odisha and how the ATS and the local police had been activated. After an hour's discussion, DD left to attend a meeting with the president later that evening.

By 5.30 p.m., Pipili had already surrendered to darkness. Winter had crept in early, swallowing the horizon in shadows. Inside the ancestral farmhouse, a quiet, mournful stillness filled the air.

The old cook, who had served the family for decades, prepared a simple meal—a bowl of warm soup and a modest dinner before leaving for the day. Dhariwal, hollowed out by grief and exhaustion, forced himself to eat by 6.30 p.m. The food was tasteless on his tongue, but tradition demanded respect for life, even amidst mourning.

After the meal, he made his way upstairs, into the bedroom where he had spent most of his time as a child—his father's bedroom.

The air inside was heavy, scented faintly with sandalwood and old cotton—his father's scent, lingering like a ghost. A lump rose in Dhariwal's throat as he stepped towards the bed, trembling slightly. Without thinking, he sank, hugging his father's pillow to his chest. It still bore the imprint of the man who had once seemed invincible to him. The last time he had slept in this bed was with his father when he had come home to announce that he had cleared the UPSC exams.

For the first time in months, he surrendered to sleep—deep, unguarded, childlike. And in that broken sleep, he dreamed. He dreamed he was once again a boy, wrapped safely in his father's arms. He dreamed of laughter among the fields. And of lessons whispered under the old banyan tree.

Outside, the SPG quietly fanned out around the property, forming a silent ring of steel. Hours slipped by unnoticed. Then, at precisely 2.30 a.m., his eyes snapped open.

A chill gripped him; not from the winter air but deep within his soul. For a fleeting moment, he could *feel* his father's presence—not in memory, but real, almost tangible, as if a voice was calling him through the veil of the night.

Dressed in a simple white kurta and dark pyjamas, Dhariwal slipped out of the farmhouse silently and walked onto the large courtyard overlooking the fields. Outside, the world was painted in shadows and silver. The stars glittered fiercely against a pitch-black sky, and the crisp winter breeze carried the sweet, earthy scent of tilled fields. The night sang a lonely symphony—the faint hum of crickets, the rustle of paddy leaves, the distant bark of a dog across the village. Beyond the house, the fields stretched endlessly, a living memory of a boyhood long past.

The SPG commandos maintained a ghost-like perimeter around the property, their figures melting into the darkness. Only Akash, the lead security officer, approached quietly and stood beside him, not as a bodyguard, but as a silent witness to the moment.

Dhariwal leaned heavily against the old wooden fence that separated the courtyard from the fields, staring into the misty expanse beyond.

'This is where I grew up, Akash,' he said, his voice raw with nostalgia.

His eyes glistened as he watched the pastures sway gently in the cold breeze. 'As a kid, I would run through those vegetable and paddy fields ... and my father would chase after me, shouting, "Ajit, you'll fall!"'

A tender, broken smile crossed his face. The fields before him, lit faintly by the scattered stars, seemed to breathe, as if the earth itself was waiting, listening. Dhariwal took a deep breath, the night air sharp and real in his lungs.

'Tomorrow,' he said softly, almost to himself, 'we will sprinkle his ashes in these fields.'

Above them, a shooting star traced a bright arc across the dark heavens, as if sealing the moment with the silent blessing of the universe.

Two thousand yards away, hidden in a dense grove of trees atop a distant hill, Shahid Faisal adjusted the tripod of his .50 calibre ceramic sniper rifle. A high-strength, low-weight weapon resistant to wear and heat, Faisal's gun was made from an advanced-grade ceramic known as silicon carbide. It was non-magnetic, easily dismantlable and capable of passing undetected through metal detectors and scanners. A few years ago, Shahid had it custom-made by a rifle maker in Hungary.

Shahid peered through the scope and saw Dhariwal's face. He checked the wind speed and aligned the cross hairs over Dhariwal's chest, accounting for the breeze, the curvature of the earth and even the slight sway of the man's movement. Then he locked the cross hairs and took a deep breath.

'*Bismillah al Rahman e Rahim*,' he whispered, squeezing the trigger.

The polymer-coated bullet shot out of the barrel and silently sliced through the night.

Back at the farmhouse, Dhariwal's conversation was interrupted by the faintest sound—like a sharp whip cracking in the distance. He looked confused, but before he could react, the polymer bullet slammed into his chest with brutal force. It pierced him cleanly, and for a moment, he staggered, disbelief etched on his face.

The SPG guards whirled around with their weapons drawn, but it was too late. Dhariwal's knees buckled, and he collapsed on his back, sinking into the soft earth of the paddy field, his arms stretched out as though reaching for something unseen. His blood started pooling around his body, staining the vibrant green of the crops and dark soil.

The SPG team scrambled into action, their shouts echoing through the fields. 'Contact! Sniper fire! Secure the perimeter!' But the origin of the shot was too distant, too concealed.

Dhariwal lay motionless, his body becoming one with the land his father had cultivated and cherished. A faint breeze carried the scent of blood and damp earth, a surreal symphony of life and death.

The guards, pale with shock, gathered around their fallen hero. One of the guards knelt beside Dhariwal, placing trembling fingers on his neck, but the outcome was clear.

'He's gone,' the guard muttered, his voice heavy with disbelief.

Moments ago, the serene farmland, a picture of peace, was now a silent witness to a violent end. Far away, Shahid efficiently packed his weapon, ran down the mountain to a hired car and disappeared into the night.

When the call came, the cabinet secretary was still fast asleep. His phone buzzed angrily on the nightstand. Groggy, he groped for it, blinking against the darkness. 'What is it?' he muttered, his voice thick with sleep.

'Sir,' came the urgent voice of the SPG director, 'we have bad news. The NSA has been shot.'

The words sliced through his drowsiness like a blade.

'What ... what happened?' he asked, sitting upright, fully awake, heart hammering against his ribs.

The SPG director wasted no time. In clipped, grim sentences, he briefed the cabinet secretary on what had transpired—the location, the emergency airlift, the critical condition—every word heavier than the last.

The cabinet secretary listened in silence, a growing sense of dread wrapping around him like a noose. When the call ended, he took a deep, shaky breath and muttered, 'I need to inform the prime minister.'

Within fifteen minutes of receiving the director's call, a sombre gathering assembled in the private conference room of the prime minister's residence. The head of RAW, the home minister, the defence minister and the leader of the Opposition sat around the heavy teak table, the weight of the moment pressing down on them. DD sat at the head of the table, his hands folded tightly before him, his face carved in stone. The air was thick with tension. No one spoke, and even the clock ticking on the wall seemed too loud.

Finally, DD's voice broke the silence. Low, steady, but brimming with controlled rage.

'Where is Dhariwal now?'

'He is being airlifted to Delhi as we speak, sir,' replied the defence minister Rajnath Thakur, his voice tight. 'Doctors are standing by, but ...' he hesitated, glancing at the others.

DD's jaw clenched. He turned sharply to Rajnath, making a decision without hesitation. 'Dhariwal's sudden demise was unexpected. We all knew he was close to his father, but that he would be so aggrieved that he would have a seizure and leave us is something I did not anticipate.' The coverup was by design. Before the leader of the Opposition could say anything, DD moved on to Rajnath. 'With immediate effect, you will assume Dhariwal's responsibilities.'

Rajnath stiffened and nodded curtly.

DD's gaze shifted next to the home minister. His voice remained steady, but the weight behind his words made everyone sit straighter. 'After the postmortem, we will do the cremation. Make all arrangements to cremate him with full state honours.'

The home minister scribbled a note feverishly. Without pausing, DD picked up the secure phone on the table and dialled. Within moments, he spoke to the director of the National Investigation Agency. 'I want the best forensic experts on this case,' he ordered. 'I want every shred of evidence analysed and a preliminary list of suspects on my table within twenty-four hours.'

He hung up and turned to Rahul, the head of PCP and the leader of the Opposition, his gaze razor-sharp. 'This is a moment of national crisis.' His voice grew sharper with each word. 'I don't want the PCP or anyone from the Opposition exploiting this sad moment for political mileage. We must project unity before the nation and the world.'

Rahul swallowed hard, but he understood the stakes. Public sentiment could swing violently against them if they appeared petty and political at such a solemn time.

'We will stand with you, Prime Minister,' he said earnestly. 'You have my assurance.'

DD gave a brief nod of acknowledgment. His face softened just slightly, and he rose from his chair. 'Thank you, gentlemen. Let us bring our hero home,' he said, his voice heavy with emotion.

One by one, the ministers filed out of the room, their faces grim. But DD caught Rajnath's arm before he could leave. 'We need to discuss something ... confidential,' he said.

The atmosphere shifted again, growing heavier. DD led Rajnath to a large oak desk in his library. Behind it, mounted on the wall, was a map of India—marked with invisible wars fought secretly. He gently pressed the right-hand corner of the map, and the frame split into two; each half moving to either side, revealing a hidden steel safe behind it. He opened the safe and pulled out six thick files, their covers stamped TOP SECRET. He laid them out carefully on the oak desk before Rajnath.

'This,' DD said, his voice low, 'is something only Dhariwal and I knew about.' He slid a small slip of paper across the desk. On it was a single phone number. 'On my instructions, Dhariwal had created a covert strike team—the Ghosts—to execute the "Defensive Offence" strategy clandestinely. These are their files.'

Rajnath nodded. 'I am aware of the Panther's Ghosts.'

DD looked surprised for a moment, and then he smiled wryly. 'So, Dhariwal already created his successor. It was as though he knew his future.'

'He has been grooming me for the last six months without anyone's knowledge. I am aware of every mission that has happened till now. The only thing missing in the succession plan was a personal interaction with the Ghosts,' said Rajnath softly.

DD pointed at the paper. 'The number belongs to Ashok Vashisht. We call him AV. He is the senior-most Ghost.' DD's gaze bore into Rajnath's. 'Call him. Use my codename—Panther. Tell him I sent you. Meet him as soon as possible. He will brief you on everyone and everything. Once briefed, take over the Panther's Ghosts because we have an ongoing mission at play.'

Rajnath stared at the files, feeling the crushing weight of the responsibility now resting squarely on his shoulders. 'What mission?' he asked.

'Neutralising Lashkar-e-Taiba's suicide bombers in Gandhinagar. As of tonight, the Ghosts have tracked down the terrorists' hideout. So, they will be moving in soon.'

5

29 January 2024, 6.00 p.m.
7/17, Akbar Road, New Delhi

THE CREMATION FLAMES HAD BARELY died down when Rajnath Thakur convened a discreet meeting at his official residence. The man seated before him was no ordinary operative—he was a legend, according to Dhariwal.

Ashok Vashisht, known simply as AV, sat across from Rajnath—a quiet, unassuming figure who exuded an air of calm authority. He was sixty-one, of medium build, his salt-and-pepper hair neatly combed back, and a pair of simple, rectangular spectacles resting lightly on his nose. He wore a plain navy-blue sweater over crisp white pants, his look almost scholarly—more that of a retired professor than the invisible force Dhariwal had trusted with missions that would have been deemed impossible even by the special operations group in India.

But Rajnath knew better. Behind that mild demeanour was a man who had outwitted terrorist cells, eliminated a Pakistani general and the head of ISI, facilitated the dismantling of an entire government in Albania, and walked out of all this with little more than a scratch—a man honed by a lifetime of fighting battles that could never be traced back to the Ghosts.

Rajnath observed him closely, and his politician's instincts sharpened. Over the past six months, Dhariwal had personally groomed Rajnath, preparing him for this hidden world. He had briefed him on the Ghosts, their missions, their unorthodox methods, and their unparalleled loyalty to the nation, to Dhariwal and to DD—the Panther.

After Dhariwal's death, Rajnath poured over every classified file DD had handed him, meticulously studying every page until he knew each Ghost's history, strengths and even weaknesses. Yet, as DD had advised him, neither Dhariwal's detailing nor the papers in the file ever told the whole story. Rajnath needed to look each Ghost in the eye—to judge them for himself. That's why he called AV after the cremation and told him to meet him privately.

Sitting back slightly in his chair, AV spoke first. His voice was measured and low, yet it carried a steely resonance that immediately commanded respect.

'Dhariwal's death is a big blow to us,' AV said, folding his hands neatly on his lap. 'No one can truly fill his shoes.' Then, after a moment, he added, 'All the media channels reported that Dhariwal, who was extremely close to his father, could not bear the grief of his death and passed away from cardiac arrest. Good move denying the assassins the pleasure of taking credit for the death.' Pausing for a moment, he said, 'Also, the LoP the opportunity to take advantage and paint India's national security as weak.'

Rajnath nodded gravely. 'DD felt that we should let the perpetrator and the handler stew in frustration that their attempt to create chaos in the country had failed. More of a psychological victory.'

Then, with the weight of responsibility settling heavier on his shoulders, he studied the man before him; calm, deliberate, unshaken even in the face of tragedy. Everything that Dhariwal had told him about AV was true. But that and the files hadn't captured the quiet fire in AV's eyes or how he held himself—relaxed yet ready to move at a second's notice. *A wolf in sheep's clothing, trained to strike only when necessary.*

'I know,' Rajnath replied thoughtfully, his voice firm. 'Dhariwal prepared me well. He briefed me personally over the past six months. I have also read all your files, and I know the missions, the risks and the sacrifices all of you have made.' He paused, letting the silence stretch between them, then added, 'But I wanted to hear it all once again from you. Not from a file. Not from a report. From the man who has kept the Ghosts breathing in the shadows, despite the tragedy of losing two senior Ghosts—Veer in Mumbai during Strike 1 and Arvind in Albania during Strike 4, the Albanian mission.' Rajnath deliberately mentioned names, places, etc., to let AV know he was aware of every detail.

AV gave a slight, approving nod, with the barest flicker of a smile appearing on his lips. 'Very well,' he said, adjusting his spectacles. 'I'll tell you everything you need to know … as Dhariwal would have wanted.'

'And DD as well,' added Rajnath.

Outside the room, Delhi's winter wind brushed against the windows, rattling them slightly, as if the world was holding its breath for what was to come.

Inside, two men—one seasoned in the art of shadows, the other stepping into the storm—prepared to weave together the future of the Ghosts.

'As you know, I retired as the deputy commissioner of Pune a long time ago and am now a business consultant. I live with my wife, Ameeta, in Pune.

'I am. The cover under which you operate is all in there,' Rajnath tapped on his file.

'There were six Ghosts when we started: Veer Pratap Rana, Indrajit Rathode, Arvind Singh, Ram Madhav Lala, Shiv Kumar Raju and I. As you mentioned earlier, we lost Veer halfway through Strike 1. Indrajit couldn't take his death, so he took voluntary retirement. Then we were four. But we became six again when Indrajit's daughter, Geeta Rathode, and Veer's son, Raj Pratap Rana, joined us. Unfortunately, my legacy will end with me, as both my sons have opted to join the corporate world.' He paused a bit and then, with a wry smile, continued, 'We had another fatality in Strike 4 when Arvind Singh, the Sniper as we called him, was killed.'

'I know. Now you are down to five,' said Rajnath. Then he looked at AV and said, 'You lost men, but you never lost a mission.'

'That's right. We, Panther's Ghosts, may be martyred during an operation, but we never lose a mission. We have a 100 per cent strike rate,' said AV proudly.

'That's what I said. Please carry on,' said Rajnath politely.

AV leaned back in his chair. 'We all are ex-Special Forces, before we ended up in the police or the military intelligence unit.'

'All?' asked Rajnath.

'All, except Veer's son, Raj Pratap Rana. He was the CEO of Info Dynamics. When we lost Veer, we were still in the police force and operating as Ghosts clandestinely. With his death, we had been exposed and could not continue with Strike 1. We needed someone with the same passion as Veer, but someone unknown to our enemy. That's when Dhariwal discovered that Raj was working solo to avenge his father's death. Dhariwal felt that he had all the makings of a Ghost, so he invited him to join us—and to our surprise, he did.'

'How is he?'

'Raj? He is talented and blessed with HSAM.'

'I know. Dhariwal told me he has a highly superior memory that allows him to recall past events in great detail, including the exact time and date. In fact, Dhariwal said that the man memorises almost anything he sees or reads even once. But my question was different. Is he soft-hearted, or is he rough and tough? You know him better than anyone else. How is his personality according to you?'

'He is hard. Please don't go by his boyish looks. The man is lethal and has proven his capabilities right from Strike 1. He knows six languages, is a martial arts expert and a reservoir of violence.'

'Those are his strengths. What is his weakness?' asked Rajnath.

'Indrajit's daughter, Geeta Rathode. She is his weakness.'

'Really? Dhariwal did not tell me that. Neither is it there in the files.' Rajnath was convinced that this conversation with AV would throw up a lot of details that he did not know about the Ghosts.

'Yes. Raj loves her deeply, but after his father's and Sniper's death, he distanced himself from her.'

'Why?'

'Raj thinks those close to him left us much before their time.'

'Oh! So he blames himself for their deaths. Interesting,' said Rajnath. Then, after a pause, he asked, 'Didn't Don Mohammad Adnan kill Veer Pratap Rana? Adnan once ran a massive crime syndicate across Mumbai. And Raj was in Paris at that time, wasn't he?'

'Yes, he was. The then CM Sushil Kumar Katyal, Police Commissioner Rajiv Prasad and Adnan were a team. They fed off each other, but Adnan did not trust Katyal and RP, and recorded all their dealings in a black book. We designed Strike 1 to get the black book and nail all three. We were almost successful and Veer was close to getting his hands on the black book, but ...'

'People in his own team betrayed him and Adnan's bodyguard, Kalia Rafa, assassinated Veer in his own bungalow in Bandra,' Rajnath finished it.

'When Raj got to know, he packed his bags and returned to Mumbai with the sole ambition of avenging Veer's death. As I mentioned earlier, Dhariwal asked me to convince him to join us, and I was able to do so successfully. Once he joined us, he took off from where Veer had left. He led Strike 1, killed Kalia Rafa, to whom Adnan had entrusted the black book, and gave us the breakthrough that we wanted. Once we had it, we nailed Katyal and Adnan. One is rotting in jail and the other is in a safe house in Maharashtra. Rajiv

Prasad and Inspector Dharma, who had helped Kalia in the assassination of Veer, were eliminated by Geeta and Lala.'

'You said that after Veer's death, Indrajit retired and joined Info Dynamics. Isn't that Raj's company?'

'Yes. Indrajit told Raj about his relationship with Veer and joined his company as the head of security for ID. He is still there.'

'What is Inder's backstory? I did not find much information about him in any of the files. Neither did Dhariwal discuss much about him.'

'Indrajit worked with MI and was married to Sharada Iyer, whom Dhariwal had recruited as a RAW agent. He lost Sharada very early in life. She died in a car accident while on duty. The unfortunate part was that they could not recover her body as the car had fallen into a river. Geeta was a toddler at that time. The loss shattered Indrajit, but he continued. He was very close to Veer, and after he, too, died, Indrajit was devastated. When Dhariwal recruited Geeta, he quit. He said he had lost his edge. He built a house in Nainital and lived there for a while. Then, when Raj set up ID in Mumbai, Indrajit approached him and joined his company.'

'Does he keep in touch with the team?' asked Rajnath.

'Not really,' replied AV.

'I think he did with Dhariwal. His was the last call Dhariwal answered before he was shot the next day.'

'What are you trying to say?' AV snapped, sitting up straight. 'Indrajit killed Dhariwal?'

Rajnath's response was calm. 'No. I checked him out. Indrajit was in Mumbai when Dhariwal was killed.'

AV looked deeply upset. That Rajnath suspected a Ghost of killing Dhariwal had clearly shaken AV. He sat quietly in front of Rajnath.

Rajnath caught the subtle flicker in AV's eyes—a shadow of hurt that flashed and disappeared in a heartbeat. He immediately realised he had trodden too close to personal scars, and instinctively shifted gears, steering the conversation away from Indrajit. He leaned forward slightly and asked, his tone gentler, 'Tell me about Geeta Rathode.'

A faint smile touched AV's lips—not of amusement, but of quiet pride. 'She's one of our finest,' he said, reaching for the glass of lemonade on the table. He took a deliberate sip, as if gathering his thoughts before speaking.

'Geeta is ex-Special Forces. Dhariwal recruited her straight out of her advanced training course. She was too good to pass up—raw, sharp, fearless.' AV's voice grew warmer as he continued, 'Officially, she works under the cover of a freelance crime reporter for *India Times*, one of the largest English dailies in the country. She's based out of Mumbai, which gives her perfect access to the underworld, corrupt politicians and foreign agents who think the city is theirs to exploit.'

Rajnath listened intently, picturing her in his mind.

'She's tall, around 5'7', with an athletic frame honed by years of brutal training,' AV said, his voice lowering slightly with admiration. 'She has light-coloured eyes that miss nothing, a complexion tanned by sun and fieldwork, and a quiet, no-nonsense demeanour. You could mistake her for a typical ambitious journalist—until you watch her move. Then you realise that she's a weapon.' He paused, the memory vivid. 'After Sniper's death—you might've read about him—his M24 sniper rifle, his most trusted weapon, was passed on to her. Not just as a tool, but as a legacy.'

AV leaned back, his eyes briefly distant as if seeing old battlegrounds.

'She trained under him personally. And today, Geeta can drop a target clean at 2,000 yards without blinking. Wind, distance, pressure—nothing rattles her. She's cold, calculating, patient—everything a Ghost sniper needs to be.' He looked back at Rajnath, his voice steady now. 'She's not just a shooter, sir. She's a Ghost in the purest sense—unseen, unpredictable, unstoppable.'

Rajnath leaned back. Exhaling slowly, he said, 'Like the assassin who killed Dhariwal,' said Rajnath.

The room fell into a silence again for a moment, filled only by the soft clinking of ice melting in AV's lemonade glass.

'What do you mean?' asked AV, sitting up straight.

'I received a copy of the forensic report. The shot originated from the top of a hill in a forest about 2,000 yards away. The NIA found footprints of a male shoe, size ten, and a .50 calibre bullet casing.'

'The killer left the casing behind?' asked AV.

'It was a polymer-jacketed bullet. The light casing flew into the bushes. The killer did not have time, and he fled without it.'

'How do we know he did not have time?' asked AV.

'The footsteps going down the hill were longer. The assassin was running. He may have slid as he reached the bottom; there were skid marks, which also tell us that he came at high speed. There were also skid marks on the ground of the tyres. All of this suggests that he was in a hurry.'

'A polymer-coated bullet?' reconfirmed AV.

'Yes. It is used in long-range ceramic rifles made of silicon carbide. Hardly a handful are in circulation, and all are in museums.'

'Then how did the killer get it and why?'

'The *why* is easy. You can carry a ceramic rifle in parts, hidden in a suitcase and travel undetected under any scanner. *How* he got it was difficult to ascertain, but I used my sources and solved that part of the puzzle.'

'So, how did he get it?'

'The gun was custom-made by a rifle maker in Hungary. My source met with him and used our strong methods to convince him to share the details of the killer.' Rajnath pulled a photo from his pocket and placed it on the table. 'Shahid Faisal is your man. He came to Odisha to assassinate Dhariwal. Someone who knew Dhariwal was going to Odisha tipped Faisal, who then waited for Dhariwal to arrive.'

'Is that why you suspected Indrajit?' asked AV.

'Yes. But I was proved wrong. Nonetheless, I am convinced we have a mole in the system, and I am convinced it has to be one of the Ghosts, as no one other than the Ghosts, the PM and I knew that Dhariwal had plans of going to Odisha to visit his father.'

'In that case, am I also a suspect?' AV asked, raising the glass to his lips.

'Not anymore. You were in Pune with Ameeta that night,' said Rajnath.

'You tracked me?' asked AV, his eyebrows raised.

'Nothing personal. I am doing my job,' said Rajnath, his face expressionless.

AV felt a newfound respect for Rajnath.

'Let's move on to the next Ghost. Tell me about Shiva,' said Rajnath, tactfully shifting the conversation forward.

AV gave a knowing nod and leaned back slightly, gathering his thoughts. 'The next Ghost is Shivkumar Raju—known to most of us simply as Shiva,' he began. 'You may have already crossed paths with him at 7, Lok Kalyan Marg. He's almost always by the Panther's side.'

Rajnath nodded immediately. 'I have. Tall, dark, heavily built man, thinning grey hair, always a step behind DD. Silent, but you can feel the force around him. What's his story?'

AV's eyes softened with a tinge of respect. 'Shiva, Veer and I were batchmates during our SPG training days. All three of us started together, side by side. Shiva was Special Para before he moved to the elite Ghost unit. During Strike 1, Shiva was working closely with Veer on external surveillance. But then, tragedy struck.' AV's voice grew heavier. 'It was during the time Veer was after Adnan and his black book. One day, Adnan's men were targeting Veer's wife, Shanti. But by a cruel twist of fate, Shiva's wife, Leela, happened to borrow Shanti's car that day. They mistook her identity.' He paused for a beat. 'They shot Leela dead ... in front of Shiva's eyes. Wrong place, wrong time. But to Shiva, it was everything. She was his world.'

Rajnath's jaw tightened instinctively.

'Seeing him broken, Dhariwal moved him close to the Panther—not just as a protection detail, but to help him find a new purpose. Since that day, Shiva has remained the Panther's most trusted shadow.' AV's voice shifted slightly, carrying pride. 'He was the spotter for our best sniper—Arvind Menon—during Strike 2 in Quetta, when we eliminated global terrorist Hafiz Salahuddin.'

Rajnath leaned forward. 'Tell me about Sniper. I know a lot about him, but what's his full story?'

AV's expression turned grim, his voice dropping to almost a whisper. 'Sniper is his call sign. His real name was Arvind Menon. He was one of the finest products of the Special Forces—our official Ghost sharpshooter. Ruthlessly precise, fiercely disciplined, a master in ballistics and long-range kill shots. He trained most of us in marksmanship, including Geeta.'

'But,' AV continued, his voice hardening, 'Arvind's life was shattered during a mission in Quetta, much before he became a Ghost. ISI operatives captured him during a covert operation. They threw him into a prison controlled by the global terrorist and the head of LeT, Hafiz Salahuddin—a brutal hellhole on the outskirts of Quetta.'

Rajnath stiffened, sensing the gravity.

'For weeks, they tortured him. Tried to break him. When that failed, Hafiz escalated the cruelty. He orchestrated the abduction of Arvind's three children back in India using their proxies, the Indian Mujahideen.'

AV's voice caught slightly before he continued. 'They executed the children … one by one … sent Arvind the proof while he was shackled in that prison.'

A thick silence hung between them.

'But Arvind Menon wasn't a man you could break.' AV's eyes gleamed coldly now, as if reliving the fury that had followed.

'Fuelled by unimaginable rage, Arvind slaughtered the ISI guards, broke out of that Quetta jail and turned into a phantom of death. In the span of forty-eight hours, he hunted down seventeen of Hafiz's top men—one by one. Even hardened Lashkar men whisper Arvind's name in terror.'

Rajnath's heart pounded as AV continued. This is what he wanted. To hear the story in its raw form; a narrative that flowed like a slow-burning inferno.

'Yet, he wasn't done. Arvind waited, biding his time, perfecting his vengeance.' AV leaned closer, his voice dropping, 'And then, during Strike 2, one silent night under the Quetta moon, Arvind and Shiva set up camp on a dune 2 km away from Hafiz Salahuddin's heavily guarded mansion. They waited over twelve hours on the dunes and finally, the next evening, with the M24 rifle he'd sworn to his children's memory, he pulled the trigger.'

The silence stretched as AV's voice turned almost reverent, 'One shot. Two thousand yards. Straight through Salahuddin's head as he sat in his own living room.' He sat back slowly. 'After killing Hafiz, he went on to mutilate Hafiz's most trusted general, Jangrid. He left him half-dead, and battered so that he could narrate the terrifying ordeal.'

Rajnath exhaled slowly, feeling the enormity of the Ghosts' battles—battles fought not just with bullets, but with broken hearts, pain and unyielding loyalty.

'And after Arvind's death during Strike 4 in Albania,' AV added quietly, 'his M24 rifle was passed on to Geeta—a symbol of everything we fight for, and everything we have lost.'

For a moment, neither man spoke. Outside, Delhi's winter night deepened, wrapping their conversation in a heavy, ghostly hush.

'We are still missing one more ghost, right?' asked Rajnath.

'Yes. Ram Madhav Lala. He is a 5'11" tall, stocky and barrel-chested Punjabi Sikh with the strength of a gorilla. He is the youngest of three brothers. His two brothers were martyred in the Kargil War. Within a year of their death, Lala lost his parents, leaving him all alone. That is when Dhariwal recruited him. He was actively involved in all four strikes. He stays with Raj in our safe house in Pune. It is called Veer's Bungalow, in memory of Veer, who spent most of his time there.'

'I am given to understand that Raj and Lala are currently in Tibet executing Strike 5,' said AV.

'Yes,' replied AV.

Rajnath opened a side drawer, pulled out two slim, untouched files, and slid them across the table towards AV. His voice was casual but probing. 'Tell me about these two,' he said, tapping the covers. 'Dhariwal mentioned they handle the funding and logistics for the Ghosts. But there's barely anything on them in the files. I want to know more.'

AV's eyes dropped to the names stamped on the folders—Pavak Dahiya and Safi Doha. He closed the files quietly, almost protectively, and placed them back on the growing pile before him.

He exhaled slowly and began, 'All our strikes—every bullet fired, every mission executed—have been funded and facilitated by these two patriot brothers,' he said. 'Pavak Dahiya and Safi Doha are first cousins. Two sides of the same bloodline.'

AV's voice grew warmer as he spoke, tinged with a mixture of admiration and gratitude. 'Pavak lives here in Delhi. Safi operates out of Karachi.'

Rajnath raised an eyebrow. 'I heard. How did that happen?'

AV smiled faintly, as if he had anticipated the question. 'Their families lived together in Karachi before Partition. They owned vast cement and sugar businesses spread across India and Pakistan. But when Partition ripped the land apart, Pavak's great-grandfather moved his branch of the family to Delhi, to protect the Indian assets. Safi's side stayed back in Karachi, to guard the business there.'

AV's voice darkened slightly. 'In the early years, things were manageable. Business thrived. But over time, the Pakistani establishment turned hostile. Hindu businessmen were targeted systematically—their factories attacked, their trade licences revoked, their safety threatened.'

Rajnath leaned forward, listening intently.

'Safi's grandfather fought hard. But when legal battles failed and friends turned to foes, he was given a brutal ultimatum: convert to Islam or watch your family, your wealth, your life be destroyed.' AV's voice hardened, 'Cornered and betrayed, he chose to convert—but only outwardly. Behind closed doors, they remained Hindus in spirit, secretly worshipping, teaching their children who they truly were.'

He paused for a beat, letting the gravity sink in. 'Safi was raised a Hindu at heart—fiercely loyal to the motherland he had never set foot in.'

Rajnath absorbed it all, then asked, 'How do the brothers coordinate across borders?'

'They meet in Bangkok often,' AV replied smoothly. 'Away from prying eyes. It's neutral ground for business and blood,' he continued, his voice brimming with pride. 'Dhariwal first brought Pavak into the fold. Through him, Safi followed. They fund every strike. They arrange fake passports, visas, smuggle us Ghosts into hostile countries, forge documents, create identities—every logistical thread that keeps us invisible, they weave.'

'And it doesn't stop there,' AV added, his eyes flashing. 'They have powerful friends in the media network spanning India and abroad. They manipulate the narrative whenever necessary, ensuring our strikes appear as false flag operations or internal insurgencies.'

Rajnath sat back, impressed by the scale and sophistication of what he was hearing.

He asked the obvious question. 'What's in it for them? Surely it's not just patriotism.'

AV's expression turned sombre. 'Safi dreams bigger than his ancestors. He's buying up vast tracts of land in Pakistan-occupied Kashmir—betting everything on one future.' AV's eyes burned with a fierce certainty. 'Though the entire family stays in Karachi, he has sold off most of his sugar factories in Karachi. He is planning to move his empire to PoK because he and Pavak believe India will take it back. They are driven by a patriotism so deep and personal, they are willing to risk their lives, fortunes and everything their families have built—for the day India raises its flag over PoK once again.'

Rajnath allowed himself a thin smile. 'Do you think India will really reclaim PoK?' he asked.

AV looked at him steadily. 'You should know better, sir. Two weeks ago, you stood in Kashmir and declared that PoK and Gilgit-Baltistan belong to India ... and that we *will* take them back. When the defence minister of India says it, men like Pavak and Safi believe it, and so do we.'

Rajnath chuckled softly, his voice carrying a note of promise. 'Yes. PoK becoming part of India will soon be a reality. Safi has made the right investment.'

The mood in the room shifted. It became a little lighter, but only slightly, the shadows still lingering. Then AV grew serious again, his voice quieter, his words deliberate. 'So, now you have it, Mr Thakur. You now know everything—the Ghosts, their stories, their scars. Do you still think one of us is the mole?'

Rajnath stood up slowly, walking towards the bar in the corner of the room. He picked up a bottle and turned, smiling. 'Maybe, maybe not,' he said. Then he added, 'This was everything I needed to hear. Thank you, AV, for your time ... and for your trust.' He reached for two glasses. 'Care for something stronger than lemonade?' Rajnath asked, a spark in his eye.

AV allowed himself a rare, genuine smile; the kind forged only between soldiers who know they fight for something greater than themselves. 'A dark rum,' he said, 'with Thums Up.'

Rajnath poured the drinks as Delhi's winter wind whispered outside, carrying the scent of rain and revolution—a storm coming not just for PoK, but for history itself.

The dark liquor glinted under the muted yellow lights as Rajnath and AV raised their glasses in a quiet, wordless toast. As the warmth of the drink settled into their veins, a more dangerous conversation unfolded between them. AV leaned back, swirling his glass slowly, the ice clinking against its sides. His voice was casual, but his eyes stayed sharp.

'Now that you're certain Shahid Faisal was the assassin ...' he said, pausing for effect, 'do you know where he is?'

Rajnath set his glass down carefully, his expression grave. 'My source tells me Faisal crossed into Nepal by road last evening. He caught a flight to the US early this morning.'

AV's brows furrowed. 'That fast?'

Rajnath's eyes hardened. 'Dhariwal was shot around 3.00 a.m. The drive from Bhubaneswar to Kathmandu is roughly 1,074 km—about sixteen hours if the roads are clear and the border crossing is smooth. My source confirms Faisal crossed over at 8.00 p.m.—almost like clockwork. No mistakes. No delays.' He leaned forward slightly, his voice dropping into a razor's whisper, 'Someone close to Dhariwal knew about his travel plans ... someone who tipped Faisal off *beforehand*. Someone who knew Dhariwal would be in Odisha, knew about the farmhouse in Pipili, and made sure Faisal's exit was clean.'

The air in the room grew heavier. AV frowned, processing the implications. 'Who is this source of yours?'

'Confidential.'

AV nodded. 'I understand.' Then he asked quietly, 'But why kill Dhariwal?'

Rajnath took a slow sip of whisky, the burn down his throat fitting the burn in his gut. 'In my village,' he said, 'we have a saying: If you can't kill the man, chop off his right hand first. Then, when he's weak ... go for the kill.' He looked AV straight in the eye. 'Dhariwal was DD's right hand. They couldn't get to DD in Ayodhya, so they cut Dhariwal down. Now, they'll come for the Panther again, this time more confidently.'

The words hung between them like a funeral bell tolling in the distance. AV was silent for a beat, then asked, 'But if they have another team waiting in Gandhinagar, why risk drawing attention by killing Dhariwal now?'

Rajnath smiled grimly. 'Because they knew we'd scramble. That we'd focus all our resources on chasing Faisal, and while we chase a ghost across oceans ... their Gandhinagar team will have a clean shot at DD during his rally there.'

AV nodded, a soldier understanding the enemy's cleverness—and cruelty. 'So what's your call, sir? We go ahead with the strike on 30 January, I presume?'

Rajnath tapped the files in front of him thoughtfully before asking, 'For the Ghosts ... what number is this strike?'

'Strike 6,' AV answered crisply. 'Raj and Lala are still executing Strike 5 in Tibet.'

Rajnath nodded firmly. 'Then the answer is yes. Strike 6 goes ahead, as planned. Like Ayodhya, no leaks, no chatter. The fewer the people who know, the fewer who can betray us.'

AV caught the nuance instantly. Though Rajnath spoke with confidence, there was a razor-thin undercurrent of suspicion; a lingering doubt gnawing at him. Somewhere deep inside, Rajnath still believed there was a mole, hiding in plain sight. He didn't voice it. He didn't need to. AV could see it in his eyes.

'Sure,' AV said, standing taller now, shoulders squared.

Rajnath's gaze sharpened. 'AV,' he said slowly, 'how prepared are you really? Do you have a rock-solid plan, the right people, the weapons, for a strike this sudden?'

AV downed the last of his drink, wiped his mouth with the back of his hand and smiled; a cold, confident smile. 'The Ghosts,' he said, 'are trained for exactly this. Guerilla warfare. High-end stealth tech. Dark web infiltration. We have informants embedded in terror cells and political parties, both in India and abroad. We live civilian lives until the signal comes. And then, we become what we were trained to be.' His voice dropped lower, more lethal, 'When Dhariwal uncovered the Gandhinagar plot, he gave us the green light. Plans were already in motion. So yes, we are ready.'

Rajnath felt a surge of pride. Yet, deep within, a faint whisper of mistrust flickered; a reminder that not everything hidden in the dark is an ally. He stood up and raised his glass again. 'Then, all the best for Strike 6. Keep me patched throughout the operation.'

'I will,' AV promised, his voice solid. He turned to leave, his figure blending into the shadows of the room. But just as he reached the door, he paused, turned and said with a rare, genuine smile, 'Welcome to the Panther's Ghosts, Mr Thakur.'

Rajnath raised his glass one last time. 'The honour is mine.'

The door clicked shut, and Rajnath was left alone, staring at the empty glass in his hand, the firelight flickering across the files scattered on his desk. He picked up his phone and called his source. 'Somewhere among us, a traitor still breathes. So please be careful. This hunt for Faisal is only the beginning for a larger purpose.'

6

30 January 2024, 1.51 a.m.
Gandhinagar, Gujarat, India

THE FULL MOON HUNG LOW over Gandhinagar, draping the world in a ghostly silver glow. It bathed the deserted streets and tall fruit trees in cold light, sharpening every shadow, deepening every silence. The Ghosts moved like wraiths through that spectral night; silent, lethal, unseen. Their target was clear: three Sri Lankan ISIS assassins holed up inside Abubakar's isolated bungalow on the outskirts of town.

The house stood alone, wrapped in the embrace of a crumbling compound wall and towering fruit trees that rustled ominously in the winter breeze. Tonight was not a *capture* mission. It was a *cleansing* mission, as they knew there was nothing much they would get from team B that they hadn't already got from team A in Ayodhya. Also, since it was a silent mission, they could not inform the local police or get help arresting the assassins.

Each Ghost was clad in full black combat gear, night-vision optics clipped to their helmets, field glasses tucked into their vests. Their weapons—silencer-topped GLOCK 19s, stun grenades, razor-sharp bowie knives and AK-47s—were strapped tight against their bodies. Except for Geeta, who carried something deadlier: the legendary M24 sniper rifle once wielded by Sniper himself, now slung across her shoulder like a sacred relic.

Hugging the shadows of the abandoned road, the team crept forward in synchronised silence, every step melting them deeper into the darkness. A few hundred yards from the bungalow, AV, leading the front, suddenly raised his fist. The team froze instantly, vanishing into the black like living shadows. AV lifted his field glass, its matte surface barely catching the moonlight. Slowly, he scanned the distant rooftop where he had seen a faint flicker of movement.

Through the lens, he spotted the first target: a man in a woollen cap and heavy sweater, standing casually on the terrace, exhaling long trails of smoke into the cold night air, utterly oblivious to the death circling him.

AV's tight and commanding voice crackled quietly through the comms. 'Target 1, terrace. Cap and sweater. Geeta, all yours.'

There was the briefest beat of silence, then Geeta's calm voice responded, ice-sharp and professional, 'Roger that, AV.' Without hesitation, she slipped into position, the M24 cradled lovingly in her gloved hands. She lowered herself to one knee, scanning through her high-powered scope. Her breath slowed as she whispered, 'Angle shot, sir. Need a spotter.'

Before she had finished speaking, Shiva cat-footed three steps back, raising his spotting scope with swift, deliberate precision. He adjusted it against the gravelly road, his movements economical, his mind already calculating even as the world shrank to heartbeats and numbers. For a split second, he was transported to Strike 2, where he was the spotter for Sniper on the dunes. Then he snapped back to the reality in front of him and whispered, 'Wind: three knots westward.' After a few seconds, he whispered again, his voice blending with the gentle rustle of the fields around them. 'Elevation correction 2.3. Target drop: 1.5 over distance.'

Geeta's fingers turned the dials with practised grace, calibrating until the cross hairs aligned perfectly over the unsuspecting target. In her mind, she said, 'No bipod. No margin for error.'

Shiva crouched beside her, looked at the target through his scope, sensing the raw, terrifying stillness between life and death.

Geeta had anchored her rifle to the curve of an old streetlamp using a leather strap—a field improvisation born of instinct and training—and her body had become a sculpture of lethal focus. She took a deep breath and slowly exhaled. And then she pulled the trigger. There was no deafening blast. Only a soft, dry *pop* from the silencer—like a whisper of vengeance. The supersonic bullet tore through the freezing air with a deadly hiss. For a split second, the night stood frozen. Then, far ahead, on the terrace, Shiva saw the man's head jerk violently backwards, his cigarette spinning out of his fingers as the bullet shredded through his heart with brutal precision.

For one agonising heartbeat, his body hung in mid-air, arms outstretched in a grotesque dance, before crumpling forward, lifeless like a marionette whose strings had been severed. Then, the terrace swallowed him in silence. Through her scope, Geeta calmly watched him fall, unblinking.

'Target 1 down,' she whispered into her comms, her voice devoid of emotion, already scanning for the next threat.

'Just like Sniper,' whispered Shiva.

'Good job,' said AV as he signalled to move. The Ghosts melted forward once again, shadows within shadows, as the moon stared down from above; a pale, silent witness to a perfect kill.

As the team moved forward, they exhaled collectively; their expressions were grim, but they were satisfied at their first win.

A few minutes later, AV's voice came quietly through the comms, a ghostly whisper that sliced through the darkness. 'Reset. Eyes on Targets 2 and 3. First-floor, right window.'

Instantly, the Ghosts shifted position, rifles steady, eyes narrowing towards the first-floor window. But just as they adjusted their sights, the bedroom light flickered off, plunging the room into pitch-black darkness. A beat later, another light snapped on the ground floor.

Hidden in the shadows, AV's eyes scanned the bungalow with razor focus, his field glasses flicking from window to window, analysing every detail, every shadow. After a few tense moments, he was satisfied. No alarms. No movement near the periphery. He gave a series of swift hand signals—sharp, clean.

Shiva peeled off to the right, circling towards the back of the house and then coming up front. Geeta took the left flank, moving with the silent grace of a predator, the M24 still cradled across her back. They melted into position, silently encircling the target.

Inside Abubakar's bungalow, tension of a very different kind gripped the Sri Lankan ISIS team.

In the dimly lit drawing room, Nusrat Janum and Nassar Farid sat huddled around a crude, lethal creation—a garland bomb made of rusted nails, explosives and shrapnel tubes, carefully wired and primed for destruction. The clock ticked loudly on the wall, each second a hammer blow against the growing dread in their hearts. They had arrived with the Ayodhya team months ago, hidden in Delhi like sleeping vipers. When Team A departed for Ayodhya, Team B—*them*—had been whisked away by Abubakar to the relative obscurity of Gandhinagar and housed secretly in the basement of this quiet bungalow. The material for the bomb and the weapons had arrived from Meerut through one of Abubakar's friends. For weeks, they had lain low, unseen and unnoticed, hoping they would not have to sacrifice themselves.

But after the Ayodhya team's failure, everything changed. Fear had replaced faith. Worse, Abubakar, their guardian, had left them a few days ago, forcing them to fend for themselves, and there was no news from Shahid Faisal either. Though the fridge was stocked, and riders were delivering food, the feeling of being abandoned by their masters and mentors killed them.

The eldest of the three, Farid, clenched his fists. His sunken eyes, ringed with exhaustion, darted towards Nusrat, who sat staring at the garland bomb, her face pale and tight with suppressed fear. Deep inside, she was beginning to have second thoughts about blowing herself up.

'Where's that idiot Razdan?' Farid hissed.

Nusrat didn't look up. Her voice was flat, mechanical. 'Gone to the terrace for a smoke.'

Farid's jaw clenched. 'I told him to stay indoors! The fool will get us caught.' He glanced at his battered watch, then at Nusrat, and grimly smiled. 'Just nine more hours …' he whispered, leaning close to Nusrat. 'Nine hours … and we'll be martyrs. We'll find our place in Jannat.'

Nusrat said nothing, but her trembling hands betrayed the storm brewing inside her.

Outside, the real storm was about to break. The clock struck 2 a.m. After circling the bungalow and confirming that there was no way out from the back, Geeta and Shiva had positioned themselves on both sides of the entrance door. There was a black SUV with tinted glasses parked in the garage. AV peeped into it but did not see anyone. He raised his hand from his position by the garage and gave the signal even as he moved forward. Geeta and Shiva also moved in, boots barely kissing the earth. The trio approached the main door, a dark, hulking outline against the moon-washed wall. AV counted silently two feet from the main door—one, two, three—then pointed.

In an instant of synchronised fury, the Ghosts exploded into action. Shiva man-rammed the door open with a battering device. As the door burst open, Geeta tossed two flashbang grenades through the entryway—tiny steel bombs that clattered against the marble floor inside. BOOM! BOOM!

The night was ripped apart with twin thunderclaps of deafening sound and blinding white light.

Inside, the world became chaotic. Farid and Nusrat were hurled backwards by the blast, disoriented, clutching their ears as the grenades shattered their senses. The garland bomb slipped off the table, rolling away harmlessly. Before the ISIS team knew what was happening, the Ghosts poured in—shadows inside the chaos, guns raised, sights locked.

Farid reached for his weapon, but he was far too slow. AV's GLOCK barked once, the silenced bullet slamming into Farid's shoulder and pinning him against the wall. Nusrat screamed and lunged for her AK-47, but Geeta dived and blocked her. As she slid towards the opposite wall, she tried to pull the pin from a grenade tucked in her belt. Shiva, who was three feet away from her, swung his left leg and kicked the grenade out of her hand. Before Nusrat could react, he came up on one knee and fired. The first bullet hit her in her throat, smashing the voice box. The second went between her eyes. She was dead even before she fell against the suitcases kept on the side. A wounded Farid tried to grab the garland bomb, but AV shot him in the head, killing him instantly.

Shiva and Geeta looked at the assassins lying sprawled and dead, their dreams of martyrdom crushed beneath the black boots of India's most secret warriors. 'Sanitise the area,' said AV as he began dismantling the garland bomb.

As the Ghosts turned to search the room, a shot rang out from the kitchen. A bullet hit Shiva on his thigh. All eyes turned towards the shot. It was the driver of the SUV, standing at the kitchen door with a revolver in his hand. He pulled the trigger again, but it was a wild shot. That was enough time for Geeta to slide a bowie knife out of the sheath and throw it at the cook. The heavy knife sliced through the air and plunged into the middle of his face. The driver screamed as he went down and hit the floor. Geeta quickly surveyed the bungalow and said, 'All targets down.'

'Great,' said AV, not looking happy. He had missed the driver who was hiding in the SUV, and Shiva had paid for his mistake. He looked at the wound and said, 'I am sorry, Shiva.'

'Come on, AV. It happens. It's just a flesh wound,' replied Shiva with a weak smile.

'You are lucky it missed the thigh bone, and the bullet went through and through,' said Geeta as she pulled out a first aid pouch from her backpack and dressed Shiva's wound.

'Let's go,' said AV as he helped Shiva to his feet. Geeta searched the driver's pocket and found the keys to the SUV. Between her and AV, they helped Shiva into the SUV. AV took the wheel while Geeta sat with Shiva in the back seat. The operation lasted only seven minutes, a new record even for the Ghosts.

As they drove off into the night, the air inside the SUV was tense. After a prolonged silence, Shiva asked softly, 'Do we have beers back home?' And that broke the ice. Geeta laughed even as AV shook his head and muttered, 'Bloody alcoholic.'

In the rear seat, Shiva looked at Geeta, smiled, and said, 'Good job, Sniper.' Geeta looked at him and winked. AV looked at both in his rearview and nodded his appreciation. Then he called Rajnath. 'Strike 6 complete.'

'Great. Any casualties?' asked Rajnath.

AV looked at Shiva in the rearview, who was shaking his head vigorously. AV smiled and replied to Rajnath, 'All four terrorists have been eliminated. Please send in the cleaners and the bomb squad.'

'Roger that,' said Rajnath.

7

1 March 2024 , 7.30 p.m.
Empress Towers, Fifth Avenue, Manhattan, New York City

SPRING HAD CREPT INTO THE air, washing away the harshness of winter. The temperature outside hovered at a cool 11°C, but inside Sorosi's penthouse office, the air-conditioning kept the space at a comfortable 25°C—crisp, controlled, clinical. Sorosi sat alone at his expansive glass desk, the lights dimmed to a moody amber. In one hand, he swirled a half-empty glass of Jack Daniel's, the other resting lightly on the remote control. His lean frame—still sculpted, still powerful—rippled beneath a pristine white satin shirt as he leaned forward and raised the volume of the giant television mounted on the wall. On the screen, an Indian news anchor droned on about the elections, oblivious to the storm brewing elsewhere: 'The 2024 Indian general elections for constituting the eighteenth Lok Sabha will be conducted in seven phases, from 19 April to 1 June. The results will be declared on 4 June ...'

Sorosi wasn't truly listening. His sharp grey eyes stared through the television, his mind lost in turmoil. He took another long sip of his whisky, the liquid burning down his throat, failing to douse the fire in his chest. Everything he had meticulously planned for India—Ayodhya, Gandhinagar, the political destabilisation—had collapsed spectacularly. Ayodhya: Failed. Gandhinagar: Failed. Dhariwal's assassination—the trump card—had been masterfully covered up by DD's government as a cardiac arrest induced by grief. And the world bought the lie.

Even Gurwinder Singh Pannu's attempt to claim responsibility for the assassination had backfired. The Indian public ridiculed him as a delusional fool, flooding social media with mocking memes. No outrage. No international headlines. No uprising. Nothing. To make it worse, there had been no trace of the Sri Lankan suicide bombers. No trace of Rashid. No mention of Abubakar. DD's machinery had carefully and ruthlessly severed every thread he had left dangling.

Sorosi clenched the glass so hard that his knuckles whitened. What boiled inside him wasn't just frustration; it was fear—a fear he wasn't used to feeling. For the first time, a chilling thought gnawed at him: *Maybe I'm not in control anymore.*

He muttered to himself, the words bitter on his tongue. 'Two failures ... in such a short time. Someone's playing me ... and I don't even know who.' He gulped down the rest of his whisky in one savage motion, slammed the glass onto the side table, and switched off the television with a jab of the remote.

The room fell into a cold, suffocating silence. Desperate for an anchor, he picked up his phone and called Susan. 'I need some advice,' he said, his voice hoarse.

'Come home,' she replied softly, the love in her voice a brief balm to his shredded nerves.

Sorosi buzzed his driver through the intercom. 'Bring the car around to the porch.' Then, without a glance back at the darkened room, he pocketed his phone, straightened his sleeves and stepped into the private elevator. Behind him, the city lights twinkled indifferently—a city that no longer belonged to him.

Around 6,230 km away, in Geneva, Switzerland, the air inside the Council's secretive meeting room was thick with tension. The oak-panelled walls seemed to close in as the world's most powerful men sat around a long, oval table; faces grim, eyes cold and fists clenched on polished wood. The stakes could not have been higher. The clock was ticking, and Damodar Das was still alive. And Sorosi, their 'brilliant agent', had failed them. Twice.

Bob stood at the head of the table, his jaw tight, his voice sharp with restrained fury. 'I hope now,' he said, scanning the hardened faces around him, 'you will all agree, dealing with Sorosi was a catastrophic mistake. He failed our India plan again. And we are already down $1 billion.'

The words hung in the air like a death sentence. Brodsky, the old warhorse, was sitting with his eyes closed in tight concentration. Finally, he opened them slowly and growled, 'Sorosi's arrogance is his downfall. He still believes he's indispensable—even after delivering us nothing but losses. I don't trust the guy anymore. And I think if he feels cornered, he'll expose us too.'

The murmurs around the table were bitter, dark. Fink turned towards Favier and Butler, his voice low and cutting. 'Your views?'

Favier didn't hesitate. 'We can't let him dangle. Release his pending payments. Sever all ties. Bob can begin the search for a new operator.'

Butler nodded grimly. 'Agreed. End it now before he pulls us into his disaster.'

There was no argument. The Council had seen enough. Fink looked at Bob and delivered the final blow. 'It's done. Pay Sorosi off. End all dealings. Start the search for his replacement immediately.'

Fink was about to conclude the meeting when Bob's voice cut through the room. He looked calm, calculated and deadly serious. 'If the Council permits, I want to put myself forward as Sorosi's replacement.'

For a moment, there was stunned silence. Fink leaned back, studying him intently.

Bob's expression was a mask of calm, but inside, adrenaline raced through his veins. This was his moment. His coronation. Before Fink could reply, Brodsky grunted, 'Let him try.'

Fink looked at Butler, who shrugged indifferently, and then at Favier, who nodded in agreement. The room moved with the silent, ruthless efficiency of men used to pulling the strings of empires.

'It's yours, Bob,' Fink said finally. 'End Sorosi first and then take over.'

A thrill shot through Bob's body. He felt the invisible crown settle on his head: the power to shape nations, destroy leaders, topple regimes. All his years of quiet ambition, of patience, were finally rewarded. 'Thank you,' he said, his voice steady but burning inside, 'Thank you all.'

Later that night, after the Council had adjourned, Bob picked up his encrypted phone and dialled Sorosi. The call rang twice, and then the automated voice answered coldly, 'The number you have dialled is switched off.' Bob frowned, his jaw tightening. Without hesitation, he left a voice message—one Sorosi would understand all too well: 'Call me back. We need to talk.'

He ended the call and put the phone down with a soft click; a click that sounded, somehow, like the slamming of a coffin lid.

It was late evening, and the view from Susan's penthouse was breathtaking. The city sprawled endlessly outside the massive glass windows of her living room, its lights twinkling like a thousand restless souls under a dark, velvet sky. It was late—past 10 p.m.—the kind of hour when the world slows down, and hidden fears creep out from their corners. Inside the luxurious penthouse, the mood was sombre, heavy with unspoken dread.

Sorosi sat on a plush, cream-coloured diwan beside the glass wall, his jacket discarded, sleeves rolled up, a glass of untouched Jack Daniel's sweating on the low marble table beside him. He had been sitting there for over an hour now, motionless, brooding, his hand absent-mindedly holding Susan's slender fingers.

His eyes weren't really seeing the glittering cityscape before him. They were searching for something beyond the lights; perhaps redemption, perhaps revenge. At last, he sighed; a long, tired breath that seemed to come from the depths of a soul worn down by invisible battles. 'Sometimes,' he muttered softly, his voice barely above a whisper, 'I think we should just leave all this behind and disappear ... go to some quiet place where we can live the rest of our lives in peace and tranquillity.'

Susan, dressed in a soft ivory satin robe, leaned against the side of the diwan, her head resting lightly against his shoulder. She ran her fingers tenderly across his knuckles; a touch meant to ground him, to tether him back from the abyss. 'When the going gets tough,' she said gently, 'the tough get going.'

Sorosi turned towards her, a tired but affectionate smile playing on his lips. 'You always know exactly what to say,' he whispered. Then, he leaned over and kissed her—a lingering kiss, one filled not with passion, but gratitude, as if drawing strength from her presence. The moment stretched, tender and fragile, before reality crept back in.

Susan pulled away slightly, her eyes clear, pragmatic. She stroked his face with the back of her hand and said calmly, 'Joseph ... if the Council is avoiding your calls, it means they've abandoned you. And that voice message from Bob?' She gave a small, sad smile. 'That's not a courtesy message. That's Bob telling you that the relationship is over.'

Sorosi's jaw tightened. He gripped the glass without lifting it. 'You think he orchestrated everything?' he asked, a dangerous edge slipping into his voice. 'You think Bob is behind my failures in India?'

Susan rose gracefully from the diwan, her bare feet silent against the marble floor. She walked to the bar, her satin robe swaying around her, and fixed herself a gin and tonic with the ease of a woman who had seen too many power games unfold. She poured a fresh Jack Daniel's over ice and brought it back to Sorosi. Handing him the drink, she sat opposite him, legs tucked under her body, studying him thoughtfully. 'I can't say yes or no,' she said slowly, 'but he has every reason to be.'

She sipped her drink, her eyes never leaving his face. 'If you trust your team and are sure about their silence, then the leaks could have only come from one place: Bob's side. Especially when you tell me he's always resented you. If he's gunning for your job, Joseph, then sabotage would be the easiest way.'

Sorosi's knuckles whitened around the glass. 'He definitely wants my seat,' he said bitterly.

'Why?' she asked.

'Because my seat isn't just money—it's power. Real power. The power to whisper into the ears of presidents, kings and prime ministers. The power to shape the future of entire continents. Bob has been a glorified errand boy for thirty years; sure, he's made money, enjoyed the perks. But never *this*. Never the seat at the real table.'

Susan nodded, swirling the ice in her glass. 'And your fall,' she said softly, 'is his only way up.'

The room was heavy with the unsaid. Sorosi stared at his drink for a long moment, then looked up. 'Even if I know it,' he said, his voice low, 'I can't convince the Council. They trust him. He's been their dog for three decades. He knows their dirtiest secrets; maybe even filthier than the ones I know. They will protect him before they protect me.'

Susan placed her glass down, leaned forward, and spoke quietly, almost conspiratorially. 'Then he's a threat to your existence.'

Sorosi nodded once, slowly, the truth solidifying inside him like concrete. 'Yes. He is.'

Susan leaned back, running a single finger along the rim of her glass. Her smile was calm, almost serene: the smile of a woman who had seen how the world really worked. 'Then there are only two ways to deal with it, my love,' she said, her voice velvet and deadly. 'Either you disappear somewhere peaceful ... or you disappear *him* somewhere permanent.'

Sorosi's face slowly cracked into a grin—cold, ruthless, dangerous. He raised his glass towards her. Susan lifted hers in reply, her eyes gleaming with dark mischief. 'Six feet under,' she said sweetly, 'is a tranquil place to settle him.'

Sorosi chuckled, a low, predatory sound, as he clinked his glass against hers. 'My darling Susan Sorosi,' he said admiringly.

Susan threw her head back and laughed; a rich, carefree laugh that echoed through the penthouse, swirling into the night like a harbinger of the storm to come. Outside, the city lights blinked unknowingly. Inside, a new game of survival had just begun.

8

4 April 2024, 6.30 a.m.
7/17 Akbar Road, New Delhi

RAJNATH THAKUR SAT ON HIS porch with a cup of tea and the day's newspaper, reading an article about him.

> The PCP made a scathing remark at their press conference yesterday. As per party leaders, with just a fortnight left for the eighteenth Lok Sabha elections, Rajnath Thakur, the defence minister with the additional portfolio of the NSA, seems to be more interested in campaigning for the Bharatiya Lok Party than securing Indian borders. There was a satellite shot of China building two towns in the disputed Ladakh region. 'China has been constructing villages near the Line of Actual Control (LAC) in Ladakh, particularly in the Demchok area. Satellite imagery has revealed the development of these "Xiaokang" or "well-off" villages, which serve both civilian and military purposes,' said the Opposition leader. So far, there has been no response from the defence minister.

Rajnath kept the paper aside, sipped his tea and looked at the blooming garden. He knew that the PCP leader, Rahul, was drumming up panic before the elections. He also knew that citizens did not believe a word he said. What truly bothered him was Shahid Faisal's disappearance after reaching America.

It had been months since Dhariwal's assassination, and still, there was no further information on Shahid Faisal. The RAW was still actively searching for him, not as Dhariwal's assassin, but as a potential threat to India. On DD's instructions, Dhariwal's brutal death had been kept a secret from all government agencies and the SPG was sworn to secrecy anyway.

He pondered the situation for a while, then dialled a number. After three rings, a female voice answered the call. 'Good morning, sir; how can I help you?'

'Good evening, Angel. Is it still cold in Canada?' he asked.

There was a slight pause before she responded. 'Here in Toronto, we are transitioning from winter to spring. The temperature during the daytime is around 10°C, but at night, it hovers between 2°C and 5°C.'

'Do you have any good news for me?'

'Not yet, sir. But I may have something for you in a day or two. Pannu and Shahid have a call scheduled for tomorrow. If I can eavesdrop on that call, I might know where Faisal is hiding in America. But I would prefer you keep the information to yourself. As I said before, someone on your team helped him escape by handling his logistics.'

'I know. I had an internal discussion with them and plan to run a private investigation to expose this mole. But tell me, how are you?' asked Rajnath.

'I am fine. It's better than the days in Jamaat-ud-Dawa (JuD), but Pannu has become very suspicious after repeated failures. He hardly comes out of his office or talks to anybody, so getting information is tough. But I will still try.'

'Look after yourself. If you need anything, you know how to reach me,' said Rajnath. He then disconnected the call. Rajnath sat alone in his study, the lamp beside him casting a dim pool of golden light across the documents on the table. The soft hum of the air conditioner and the faint ticking of an antique wall clock were the only sounds in the room. He stared at the computer before him, but his thoughts lingered elsewhere. His mind drifted to a conversation he had dismissed six months ago—a conversation that now, in hindsight, seemed like prophecy. It was Dhariwal who had introduced him to Angel. At the time, Rajnath had questioned the need. She was off-the-grid, never mentioned in official briefings, not even a known asset in the RAW's inner circle. Her existence was a whisper.

Sitting under the weight of Dhariwal's absence, Rajnath realised the truth. Dhariwal had a premonition. He had felt his end coming, and he had placed Angel in his orbit, not as a formality, but as a final contingency.

Angel, the Ghost inside the Devil's den. Her real name was erased long ago. In the world of terror, she was Angel Singh. In reality, she was Dhariwal's most deeply embedded and most dangerous asset. She was only twenty-five when she decided to change the course of her career and South Asian geopolitics.

Then a bright officer in military intelligence, she was married to a decorated army officer and the mother of a toddler. That was when Dhariwal, then joint assistant director at RAW, spotted her during a counter-infiltration briefing. What he saw wasn't just talent—it was adaptability, fearlessness and the ability to blend in. He immediately recruited her into the RAW and personally oversaw her field training. After her training, he gave her the first assignment: Karachi. The assignment was pure surveillance, nothing lethal. But even on that mission, Angel shone like a phantom. She extracted data on sleeper cells, movement patterns and ISI safehouses, all without once triggering suspicion.

Recognising her potential, Dhariwal increased the stakes. She was asked to infiltrate the JuD, a so-called charity front, which in reality was the funding arm of Lashkar-e-Taiba (LeT). The cover identity Dhariwal gave her was flawless. She was the daughter of a martyred Khalistani rebel killed during Operation Blue Star, fleeing Indian 'oppression' and seeking to support 'Islamic causes' for justice.

The JuD did a thorough reference check and background verification, but she came clean, thanks to the backend history created by Dhariwal. Within a month, the JuD took her in. From that moment on, Angel became the ghost behind the veil. She began as a volunteer, but quickly rose through the ranks, helping senior commanders of the JuD with their event planning, social media campaigns and donation strategies.

She also developed funding pipelines from South Africa, Malaysia and the UK for the organisation. She curated online propaganda, created recruitment scripts and helped build encrypted chat groups where radicalisation material was circulated across borders. Her brilliance didn't go unnoticed. The JuD commanders, happy with her work, passed the message upwards. Soon, LeT's overlord, Hafiz Salahuddin, noticed her and made her the head of the LeT communications. This move helped her get deep access to the LeT strategies. To win over Hafiz, she convinced him to rebrand himself. Over the next six months, she started projecting him as a messianic figure fighting for Muslim minorities across Asia. She arranged his first international interviews, coached him on what to say, and even scripted the famous 2017 address where he threatened retaliation if Pakistan's 'brothers' were targeted. She handled his JuD outreach, increased foreign donations by 40 per cent, and managed recruitment festivals masked as religious events. Every word Salahuddin spoke passed through Angel first.

And through it all, she sent encrypted updates to Dhariwal: maps of terror training camps, fund transfers, internal power struggles and lists of targets.

It was Angel who convinced Salahuddin that he was worthy of Pakistan's prime ministership. And it was she who made him believe the world was listening. In 2018, Angel arranged a landmark interview between Salahuddin and an Indian Muslim journalist, convincing him that it would give him global visibility. It was a plan that she and Dhariwal had hatched even without the Panther's Ghosts knowing it. During that interview, the Ghosts assassinated him. A single shot, from 1,500 yards by Sniper Arvind, sent Hafiz Salahuddin to his grave. His assassination, recorded live on a camera feed, was never aired.

On 14 February 2019, while the world celebrated Valentine's Day, Pulwama in Kashmir was bathed in blood. Adil Ahmad, a suicide bomber and a member of the Pakistan-based terror group Jaish -e-Mohammad (JeM), drove a truck laden with explosives into a CRPF convoy, killing over forty CRPF jawans. The massacre rocked the nation and India burned with rage.

Once again, Dhariwal turned to Angel. 'Give me a befitting response plan,' he said.

Angel got herself transferred to the JeM as their recruiter, and within days, she had penetrated their operational tier. Soon, she traced the mastermind of the Pulwama attack—Muhammad Umar Farooq. She found out that he was the trainer and the handler of all terror recruits in one of the biggest terror camps in Pakistan, which was situated in Balakot. Angel provided Dhariwal with satellite coordinates, layout schematics and a narrow three-hour weather window for a precise airstrike on Balakot.

Based on her information, Dhariwal made an attack plan. On 26 February 2019, the Indian Air Force fighter jets struck Balakot. Over three hundred terrorists, trainers, handlers and some JeM leaders along with the entire camp were wiped off the map.

Following Dhariwal's instructions, she faked her death in the Balakot strike using a planted ID, staged DNA and a corpse with similar features. A funeral was held by the JeM leaders where they mourned for their brothers and for Angel. And just like that Angel died a second time.

Three weeks later, she reappeared; but this time in Canada. Dhariwal had embedded her into KHALI—the fast-rising ultra-nationalist Sikh separatist organisation working hand-in-glove with Pakistan's deep state. There, Angel began again.

This time, as a Khalistani lieutenant with a new name and a new backstory. Her fluent Punjabi, encyclopaedic knowledge of Operation Blue Star and fierce articulation made her a sensation among the Punjabi expatriate youth. She joined the team responsible for KHALI's largest youth recruitment drive in North America, indoctrinating hundreds of confused, angry Sikh boys into radicalism; even as she secretly passed names, numbers and digital footprints to Indian intelligence.

She helped build training camps in British Columbia, assisted with money laundering routes and sat in on strategy meetings involving UK-based financiers and ISI middlemen within the KHALI core team. Most importantly, she became Pannu's executive assistant.

While to the outer world, she was a private investigator at a renowned PI firm, in reality, she was a core member of KHALI. She handled Pannu's internal communications, encrypted fund transfers, and even helped vet 'loyal' lieutenants. She was in every room, every discussion. During one such meeting, she overheard a chilling detail: Shahid Faisal had escaped to America. She immediately relayed it to Rajnath. And now, from deep inside the belly of the beast, Angel was trying to locate Faisal's hideout: one last target for Dhariwal's legacy.

Back in the study, Rajnath exhaled slowly, the weight of her story pressing down on him. He now understood why Dhariwal had brought Angel to him. She wasn't just a spy. She was the invisible dagger he had embedded inside India's darkest enemies. And now, she was the only one who could finish what Dhariwal had started.

After breakfast, Rajnath called AV. He always knew that one day, he would have to tell AV about Angel and today, the time had come. He briefed him about Angel and his conversation with her.

'So, this is the source you discussed during our conversation,' AV asked.

'Yes. The most dedicated field agent I have ever come across. She is passionate about her job and protecting the country and has never failed Dhariwal,' said Rajnath.

'Except the time Shahid Faisal murdered Dhariwal,' reminded AV sarcastically.

'No. She did not fail him even then. She told him Faisal was in Odisha, and he arrived in Bhubaneshwar in the evening. Dhariwal had informed the home minister about Faisal's presence in the state, but he never mentioned that his life was in danger. The local police failed Dhariwal,' Rajnath said curtly.

'I am sorry,' AV apologised.

'Anyway, I called to tell you that Angel will get back to me with Shahid's location in a few days, so please have the Panther's Ghosts ready to move at short notice.'

'I will, sir,' said AV. This time, his voice was sincere.

Rajnath sensed AV was feeling bad about judging Angel without knowing her abilities or the situation. He softened. 'I am sure you will, AV. By the way, I spoke to Raj and Lala last night. They plan to enter Drapchi tomorrow.'

9

5 April 2024, 7.30 p.m.
Zhongnanhai Compound, Beijing, People's Republic of China

INSIDE HER PALATIAL SUITE ABOARD the VVIP airborne command aircraft of the People's Republic of China, Paitoon Luan, First Lady of China, waited for the secure SAT line to connect. She had just landed on the private airstrip in Zhongnanhai Compound after a weekend visit to her relatives.

She stood by the tinted window, her elegant silk cheongsam shimmering faintly under the cabin's recessed lights, the faint rumble of twin engines echoing in the background as it taxied towards the private hangar. Her long fingers curled around the sleek black satellite phone, her face composed, but her eyes betrayed urgency. After the third ring, a crisp, reassuring voice answered on the other end.

'Good evening, Ms Luan. What a pleasant surprise,' said DD, speaking calmly through his encrypted Thuraya SAT phone.

Paitoon's lips curled into a soft smile. 'Namaste, DD,' she replied, her voice gentle, warm and tinged with relief.

For years, she had found in him not just a statesman, but a rare equal; principled, visionary, unafraid.

Their bond had begun at Mahabalipuram in 2019, during the informal summit between India and China. While President Xi Wang showcased political pageantry, DD had chosen diplomacy of a deeper kind. He took Paitoon to the ancient seaport, once a bustling hub of the Pallava dynasty's maritime trade with China; a place where cultural and commercial bridges were built centuries ago. On the final evening of the summit, in a candlelit amphitheatre by the shore temples, DD had arranged a special concert in her honour. Paitoon, an accomplished soprano, performed three traditional Chinese folk ballads. When the final note faded into the sea breeze, DD stood up and bowed.

It wasn't a political strategy; it was sincerity. Paitoon could see it in his eyes, and it touched her profoundly. From that moment, a discreet but unshakable friendship blossomed between DD and the Luan family; a rare corridor of trust between Beijing and New Delhi.

But their growing rapport stood in stark contrast to the rising shadow of Xi Wang—the iron-fisted autocrat ruling China with a grip that crushed dissent and buried compromise. To the world, Xi Wang was a charismatic reformer. But to those within China's corridors of power, he was a calculating, obsessive megalomaniac who dreamed not of a superpower, but of an empire.

As general secretary of the Chinese Communist Party (CCP), president of China and chairman of the Central Military Commission, Xi Wang wielded absolute power over 1.4 billion people. However, it still wasn't enough for him. He wanted more. And to get it, he dismantled China's existing power structures.

In an unprecedented move, he purged all those members of the CCP Central Committee who were against him by putting fake corruption charges against them. He replaced them with personal loyalists, like known army generals, intelligence chiefs, tech tycoons and regional governors who owed their fortunes to him. Centuries-old party structures were gutted overnight.

Men like Peng Luan, father of Paitoon and a stalwart of Chinese statesmanship, found themselves isolated, outnumbered and silenced. Xi Wang's next move was even bolder. He unveiled his 'Greater China Doctrine', an ultra-expansionist plan that sought to absorb half of Asia and Eastern Europe under a neo-Sinic order. It included a full military takeover of the South China Sea, where Chinese warships began harassing Philippine fishing boats, building militarised artificial islands and declaring illegal air defence zones over international waters. The PLA and the Chinese Navy ignited daily skirmishes with Vietnam, Taiwan and even American Navy vessels.

Chinese troops began deploying hypersonic missiles under the pretext of infrastructure development, but with the real intent of aggressive land grabs along the Himalayan border with India and Bhutan. And finally, he initiated the rebirth of the Silk Road, rebranded as OPOR (One Path, One Road), a trillion-dollar initiative to create a strategic land-and-sea network from Beijing to Europe.

The first phase of OPOR was the China–Pakistan Business Corridor (CPBC), running through the disputed territory of Pakistan-occupied Kashmir (PoK) and Baluchistan. Xi Wang poured billions into it, setting up military outposts, rail lines and mega-ports. But his dream soon turned to dust. The Baloch Liberation Force (BLF), fiercely anti-China, began systematically targeting CPBC installations. In one year alone, thirty-four Chinese engineers were blown apart by C4. Every 10 km of road laid was bombed back to zero within weeks. Over time, the CPBC became a blood-soaked trail of loss, sinking China deeper into economic quicksand.

Humiliated, Xi Wang was forced to abandon the corridor, the jewel of OPOR, and reroute through the Balkans. There, he handpicked Tefik Metta, president of Albania, to be his puppet. Under Metta, China began setting up satellite bases in the Balkans, forging quiet alliances with warlords, and moving unmarked cargo through the Adriatic. But Xi Wang had underestimated India's silent response.

With intelligence supplied by Mossad and surgical precision from the Panther's Ghosts, India launched a clandestine strike in Albania, toppling Metta's regime and replacing it with an India-friendly coalition in 2022/23. It was during this strike that the Panther's Ghosts lost their eldest member, Arvind or Sniper.

The loss of Albania was a global humiliation. And Xi Wang, desperate to protect his image, needed someone to blame. He turned inward—towards those who had dared oppose his doctrine behind closed doors.

Peng Luan, Paitoon and her brother Chin Luan, the head of her personal security and a former PLA Special Forces officer, had strongly opposed OPOR's direction in CCP meetings. Xi Wang saw not dissent, but betrayal. He accused the Luans of being 'enemies of China's future'. Since he could not jail his wife or father-in-law, he, using manufactured evidence, arrested Chin Luan in the middle of the night, without warning. The judge, a Xi loyalist, conducted an urgent trial, convicted him and sent him to Drapchi Prison in Tibet; the same prison used for breaking Tibetan monks, Uyghur intellectuals, and now, political enemies.

Xi Wang made sure the message was clear: Oppose me, and you will vanish.

Since then, Paitoon had been walking on a tightrope, one misstep away from the same fate. With no one to trust or help her in China, her only window of trust, her only connection to sanity and hope was DD.

As the line stabilised, Paitoon stepped into a soundproofed alcove, her voice hushed but urgent. 'They've stopped letting me visit my brother in Drapchi. The last I heard, he's been kept in solitary for the last fifty-two days straight.'

Paitoon's words were not soothing to DD's ears. Solitary meant the mission was going to be more difficult. DD's tone turned firm, but gentle. 'I am aware. We'll get him out. But, like I had told you before, not through regular channels or special ops.'

There was a pause. Then Paitoon said softly, 'Do what you have to do, DD, but please get my brother out of that hell ... please.' Her eyes glistened and her lips trembled.

'I promise.'

Paitoon had spoken to DD earlier, and DD had already discussed the plans with Dhariwal to extract Chin Luan from Drapchi. Dhariwal had handed over the mission to Raj and Lala, to execute Strike 5 which was a 'snatch and grab' operation. But now with Chin being put in solitary confinement, the dynamics of the mission would have to change.

Pavak and Safi had organised fake Thai Passports and documents from a monastery in Thailand, stating that Raj and Lala were young Buddhist novice monks coming to Tibet to attend special classes at a monastery in Lhasa.

Raj and Lala had entered the city a few months ago, masquerading as Thai Samaneras, Kovit Aromdee and Sirichai Bunchu. On their arrival in Lhasa, Paitoon's confidante, a woman named Pema Ring, organised Raj's and Lala's stay, transportation and access to weapons. Pema, once a member of the Tibetan regiment of the People's Liberation Army, resigned in protest when her brother Gawa, then only eighteen years old, was arrested and sent to Drapchi prison for speaking against the authoritarian rule of the Xi government during a college debate. The police branded him as anti-China, booked him under sedition charges, and sent him to Drapchi.

After leaving the army, Pema moved to Drapchi to be close to her brother and started a grocery business. Through her army networking, she managed to seal a contract with the prison and soon became their primary grocery vendor. She pleased the prison warden and the chef with discounts, home deliveries and special requests, and got Gawa a better job as a janitor in the solitary confinement cell. From then on, brother and sister met once a week when she came to deliver the weekly groceries.

The move helped Paitoon as she got regular information on Chin Luan through Gawa and Pema. During meetings between Gawa and Chin, they often discussed an escape from the prison, but nothing worked out till Paitoon called Pema and told her of the arrival of the Ghosts.

'Help the Indians rescue Chin, and I will ensure they rescue Gawa along with him,' Paitoon told Pema. Pema agreed.

Paitoon contacted DD, and the Ghosts moved into action. After watching her brother spend twenty-five years in prison, Pema was finally hopeful that she would be able to get Gawa out of its dreadful confines.

'Today is D-Day. Whatever the outcome, I wish your people well, and I hope we meet again but during better circumstances,' said Paitoon.

'I reciprocate the feeling, Ms Luan. I am confident my team will deliver on the promise,' DD assured her. 'Or at least die trying.'

'*Yuan shangdi yu ni tong zai*,' said Paitoon.

'May God be with you, too,' said DD.

10

5 April 2024, 7.30 p.m.
Drapchi prison, Lhasa, Tibet

MONTHS OF PLANNING HAD LED to this moment. Raj and Lala, draped in crisp grey Drapchi prison guard uniforms, their faces stoic, their eyes alert, crouched silently inside an old granary behind the prison's industrial kitchen. The dusty storage shed smelled of grain, oil and metal, and the faintest hint of danger. Their weapons were hidden in vegetable sacks, their comms clipped to their collars, and their escape plan mapped down to the last second. All they needed now was Pema's signal.

The tension was suffocating, but beneath it, there was something else: memory. As Raj adjusted his earpiece, his mind drifted; not to the mission, but to everything that led them here ... to Pema.

Six months ago, they arrived in Gongdelin, Tibet, like whispers in the wind. Raj and Lala flew out of Chiang Mai International Airport, Thailand, under perfectly forged identities. Their passports, visas and even the AI-generated letter of recommendation from a senior Chinese general were so flawless that not a single eyebrow was raised at Lhasa

Gonggar Airport. Pavak and Safi were the masterminds behind those documents.

Waiting for them outside the terminal, in the shadow of the snow-cloaked Himalayas, stood Pema. She was no ordinary asset. She was born and raised in Gongdelin residential district, a modest township just 6 km north of Drapchi prison. For decades, she had lived a quiet, anonymous life as a spinster. But beneath her simple attire and calm exterior beat the heart of a rebel. Once upon a time, she was a captain in the Tibetan regiment of the PLA. She took voluntary retirement after her brother Gawa was arrested and put in Drapchi under the dreaded sedition charges for speaking against Xi's policies.

After her retirement, she moved to Drapchi to be close to Gawa. Using her network and connections, she got a contract to deliver groceries to Drapchi prison. Over time, she became friendly with all the staff, management and guards, and managed to get Gawa shifted from hard labour to janitorial duties in the solitary confinement section. This way, she could also spend thirty minutes with him once a week. When Paitoon, whom she knew from the days of the army, told her that there was a chance to get Gawa out if she assisted in helping the Indian team to extract Chin, she jumped at the idea.

When she met Raj and Lala, she knew their cause was righteous. She didn't ask many questions—she didn't have to—and simply took them home. In the beginning, Pema's relationship with the Ghosts was logistical. She provided cover, groceries, transport, storage, and all their administrative work, like organising ammunition, weapons, prison staff uniforms, etc. Most of her conversations were with Raj. Lala, ever the silent warrior, kept to himself; vigilant, disciplined, distant. But over those long Tibetan evenings, something changed.

At first, it was in the way Lala watched her hands as she chopped vegetables for dinner, in the way she moved through her small kitchen like a quiet flame. Then came the walks. They began as strolls for fresh air—short, brisk, wordless. But they became longer, slower and filled with glances, shared stories and gentle teasing.

Raj, the sharpest observer of all, saw it first. He watched his brother-in-arms—the hardened Ghost who had never let love get in the way—turn softer around her.

A hand brushed against hers. A smile lingered. And then one night, Lala didn't return to the guest room. What followed wasn't passion born of urgency but something more profound. Pema, who had known only grief and solitude since her brother's arrest many years ago, found in Lala a kindred soul—someone broken in ways different, but familiar. Someone who didn't speak much, but listened like no one ever had.

Lala also found solace in her. For someone who had buried his heart beneath layers of missions and memory, he let her in. They made love under heavy quilts, their breaths misting the cold Tibetan air. They whispered dreams of a life beyond bloodshed, a home in Punjab, and children with her eyes and his silence.

One evening, as the wind howled outside, she asked, 'What would you do if this ended tomorrow?'

He replied simply, 'Take you home with me on the next flight.'

From that day, they were no longer just lovers. They were each other's only anchor in a world gone mad. Now, crouched in the granary, the scent of Pema's perfume still clung faintly to Lala's collar.

Pema's assistance was very beneficial to the Ghosts because she knew the Tibetan terrain well and showed them the different routes for escape after the extraction. She also gave them the latest blueprint of Drapchi prison, thanks to Gawa, who stole it from files in the administration office while cleaning the place one day. It was she who had got them in. In her weekly grocery truck, she had hidden them behind crates of cabbages and sacks of rice. Her credentials—built over decades of trust with Drapchi's guards—did the rest. The checkpoint searches were mere formalities. No one suspected a thing. The truck had backed into the delivery bay. The men had slipped out under the cover of sacks, ghostlike. Now they waited.

Raj glanced at Lala. Lala was still focused. But Raj saw it—the fire behind his eyes. The rage that Paitoon's and his woman's brothers were locked somewhere in this hell. The resolve that failure was not an option. And beneath it all—the longing to walk out of here, not just victorious but whole. With her. With Pema.

Then, the radio crackled once. 'Thirty minutes to go.' It was her voice. And the Ghosts moved to get their gear ready.

Raj looked at Lala and whispered, 'If everything goes as planned, then we will leave Drapchi with Chin Luan and

Gawa by midnight. Once we are out, Paitoon's men will take over and make sure we board the flight back to Bangkok.'

'If everything goes well,' Lala repeated. 'Remember what Pema said? There are two hundred men here, including soldiers, cooks and administrative staff. They all live on the prison premises.'

'Except for the warden, who stays in a separate bungalow 10 km south of the prison. I remember everything that Pema said, Lala.'

'Gawa said that Chin Luan is in Cell 8, in solitary confinement in the basement,' said Lala.

'The guards bring him to the ground floor every night at 9.30 p.m., when the other inmates are in their cells, and allow him to walk in the central compound for an hour to get some fresh air. Then, he is taken back to his cell,' said Raj.

'Yes. Pema will call us at 9 p.m. That is when we move, right?'

Raj looked at his watch. 'It is 8.30 p.m. After unloading the groceries, Pema would have met Gawa for their weekly meeting by now and briefed him about our plans. In turn, Gawa will brief Chin about when he is being taken out.'

'We have a very short window. We have to finish everything in thirty minutes and leave Drapchi at 10 p.m. That is when Pema leaves the prison compound daily. If we are late, she will be in trouble,' said Lala.

Raj noticed how protective Lala was towards Pema and smiled. 'A thick fog has settled over Drapchi. While that will hinder the prison guard's view, it will help us as we have our night-vision goggles.' Then he turned to look at Lala and asked, 'I am asking for the last time for my comfort. Do we need to blast our way out? Can't we do this discreetly and slip out? It is so much easier when we do it like that.'

'Our principal job is Chin's snatch and grab. In the process, we are taking Gawa with us. But we agreed with Pema that we would help release all the others who have been languishing for decades without a trial. Did we not?' asked Lala.

'Listen, I understand you are in love with Pema and want to settle down with her after Strike 5, but her emotional demands will be the death of us,' Raj said, ruffling Lala's hair.

'She cares for people, Raj, and that is what I love about her ...'

Their conversation was interrupted by Pema's call. The customised version of the CooMax earpieces Raj, Lala and Pema were wearing was a highly sophisticated device that could transmit speech with high clarity even remotely. It had a built-in microphone with an answer key and was compatible with the iPhones they were carrying.

'Time to move. I'll see you in the truck at 10 p.m. Good luck,' Pema said and disconnected.

'And good luck to you, too,' said Raj.

Lala looked at Raj, hugged him tightly and whispered, 'If I become a liability, shoot me.'

'Shut up, will you? Nothing will happen to us. I have memorised every route and know how to get out of here. You have to stay positive,' said Raj.

Raj and Lala were wearing the prison officer's blue overalls. Just like the prison guards, they had silencer-mounted SIG Sauer M17s with three twenty-one-round magazines each in their hip holsters. Both were carrying razor-sharp stilettos in leather sheaths, and their backpacks contained high-powered laser pointers to blind the CCTV cameras, C4 blocks and pagers to be used later as trigger devices, and detonators that were tucked into their belts.

As they got ready to move, Lala stopped Raj. 'On our way to Drapchi, you told Pema that if Plan A does not work, we will move to Plan B. What is Plan B?'

Raj paused for a second and then answered, 'I don't know. Improvise, shoot maybe; we will have to figure it out then.'

Before Lala could argue, Raj wore his night-vision goggles, switched on his COO mic and left the granary. Lala rolled his eyes and followed suit, staying behind him.

As they slipped through the shadows and moved forward slowly, Raj spoke into his mic. 'One more thing. We have a third party to extract as well.'

'What? Who?' asked Lala, stunned by the last-minute announcement.

'Remember Fanny Li?'

'Yes, the half-French and half-Chinese woman in Hong Kong who helped you in Strike 4,' said Lala as he followed Raj.

'Yes. She's the head of public relations for the Macau government,' said Raj as he turned a corner, held his fist up and stopped. Lala cursed softly as he almost bumped into his back.

Raj pointed at three prison guards struggling to cross the narrow pathway between the buildings due to almost zero visibility. 'They are heading for solitary,' he whispered.

Lala looked at the guards and then at Raj and asked softly, 'So what about Fanny Li?

'Her brother, James Li, is in Cell 17,' whispered Raj.

'When did you decide to do this?' asked Lala.

'Before we left Bangkok, I asked her to send me his details. When I was in Hong Kong, Fanny told me about James being in Drapchi, serving a life sentence for protesting against the PLA's atrocities against the Tibetans. They took him away when he was twenty years old. She hasn't seen him since.'

'Do Pema and Paitoon know about this?' asked Lala, glaring at Raj's back as they crossed the road and followed the guards at a distance.

'No.'

'I know now,' said Pema, who could hear their conversation.

'And Rajnath?' asked Lala.

'No,' Raj answered.

'Shit,' Lala muttered. 'You know what your problem is?'

'What?'

'You are emotional and you commit too easily. The tragedy is that you know this is wrong, so you hide it from others and try to execute it on your own. Remember what Dhariwal told you. Teamwork is important.'

'I know. It's just that the thought losing people close to me while I remain safe bothers me a lot. So I end up doing things on my own, without involving others. This is my area of development, and I will work on it. I promise.'

'Remove this shit from your mind that you are responsible for any team member's death. We are at war and we chose this profession. Someday, we will all die, including you. So stop feeling guilty,' snapped Lala, irritated with Raj's continuing habit of carrying guilt.

'Yeah, this is all shit,' said Pema.

Lala glared at Raj and said, 'You are as unpredictable as Veer. You know where it led him. Learn from his mistakes, Raj.'

'I told you I will. So, don't keep on at it,' Raj shot back.

'Who is Veer?' asked Pema.

'I will tell you about him when we are relaxing in Amritsar,' said Lala. Then he shook his head in frustration and said, 'Let's go get Chin, Gawa, James and ...'

'That's enough,' said Raj with a smile as he started moving again.

11

5 April 2024, 9 p.m.
Drapchi prison, Lhasa, Tibet

ZHAO PEN, CHIN LUAN'S SECOND-IN-COMMAND when he was the head of security for Paitoon, was sitting in the driver's seat of his swanky Chery Omoda 5 SUV with black-tinted glasses when his phone pinged.

It was a message from Pema: *Mission is on*.

Zhao called Paitoon and updated her. 'After the extraction, we will meet Laoban (a name they used to address Chin) at the Shubin Dong Meat Store in Gonggar. It is just 2.5 km from the airport. Laoban will change into fresh clothes and take a private aircraft to Hong Kong and from there to New York. Everything has been arranged. Our people are on standby outside Drapchi and in the airport.'

'What about Pema and Gawa?' asked Paitoon, sounding concerned.

'Pema said she would manage everything,' Zhao told her.

It was a foggy night, and everything was quiet as Raj and Lala waited in the darkened alleys for the guards to come out with Chin. Pema's truck stood silently a few feet to the left of the granary. To the right of the granary building, they saw Pema and the chef having soup and chatting. Then, they saw Pema get a call. She was speaking to someone. She excused herself and stepped out of the kitchen.

'Something is wrong,' said Lala.

A second later, Pema's voice came through the mic. 'Problem. Due to the fog, the guards have decided not to bring Chin out.'

'Shit, shit, shit,' said Lala in frustration.

Raj checked his watch. The glowing green digits blinked: 21.22. Time was slipping through their fingers. He looked up at Pema standing at a distance, her face pale but resolute in the moonlight. She stood by the kitchen entrance, silently watching them, clutching her prayer beads—her quiet act of rebellion.

Raj could see the worry in her face, so he softened his voice. 'Thank you, Pema. You keep the chef and the guards in the kitchen distracted. We'll take it from here.'

He saw Pema nod, her eyes looking at Lala for a moment longer—something unspoken passed between them. Love wrapped in danger. Then Raj turned to Lala, his voice low, clipped.

'Lala, look across the compound.' He pointed to two structures under the moonlit haze—one across from the granary, the other crouched like a shadow behind it.

'That's the substation behind us—the heart of Drapchi's power grid. And that,' he gestured forward, 'is the prison petrol depot. If we kill both, we blind the compound and ground their fleet. You take the substation. I'll handle the petrol pump.'

Lala's jaw tightened. He gave a sharp nod. The air around them turned colder, not from the altitude, but from the weight of what they were about to do.

Lala slipped away into the darkness like a phantom, hugging the walls, darting between trees and buildings. He moved with the lethal grace of a seasoned predator, every sense stretched taut. The substation was a squat, concrete block fortified with rusting iron fencing and razor wires, its windows glowing faintly from the inside. A perimeter gate stood locked. Lala crouched near it, pulled out a tension wrench and pick, and opened it in less than fifteen seconds. No alarms. No sound.

He entered silently, boots whispering across gravel. Inside was a humming chaos of metal and voltage—transformers, relays and high-voltage cabinets. He moved quickly, identifying four strategic points on the ground floor: the main junction panel, the distribution conduit, a reserve diesel generator and the massive diesel tank beside it, pulsing with potential devastation.

He pulled out four pre-wired C4 packs, peeled off the adhesive layers and secured each charge. Each detonator was wired to a cell phone–activated microcontroller—a military-grade circuit that responded only to a specific incoming call. Once the circuit was closed, the relay triggered the blast in under two seconds.

Above him, the faint sound of laughter floated down from the first-floor control room. Five guards were watching

TV. Only the shift engineer glanced at the screens. He was sipping tea. They had no idea death was now ticking beneath their feet.

Across the compound, Raj looked at the fuel depot and moved fast, crouching low behind the walls until he reached the petrol depot—a narrow strip of concrete with four massive underground fuel tanks and three fuel dispensers. Next to it sat three garages, their shutters pulled down, housing eleven prison vehicles, including transport buses, riot vans and an old but functional armoured truck. The depot was eerily quiet.

Raj knelt beside the central pump, reached into his rucksack, and pulled out a larger explosive pack. His plan wasn't just destruction; it was escalation. If the fuel tanks ignited and the fire spread to the garages, Drapchi would be paralysed. He placed charges at two vulnerable pump valves and two around the concrete bases of the fuel tank access shafts. Every movement was precise, practised—a dance of fingers, plastic and death.

Like Lala, he connected each C4 to its own cell-triggered detonator, encrypted the frequency and synchronised the call time. Once they were out of range, they would both dial simultaneously from burner phones. After connecting the charges, he paused and looked up. The night was still—too still. He could almost hear Drapchi breathing—ancient, cold, unsuspecting.

Four minutes later, both men regrouped at the granary—hearts pounding, eyes scanning. Raj gave one last look towards the depot. Lala glanced back at the substation. Then Raj pulled out his phone and whispered, 'On your count.'

Lala looked at his phone. The burner screen glowed. He looked at Raj, and both of them dialled the trigger code. 3 ... 2 ... 1.

BOOM. A thunderclap of fire and steel shattered the silence. Flames erupted into the sky behind them—orange tendrils licking at the clouds as the petrol depot exploded, sending fuel-soaked debris across the garages. A half-second later, there was a loud crack, and the substation ignited, shattering glass and tearing through steel, the diesel tank exploding in a ball of yellow heat. The lights across Drapchi flickered within seconds, and then everything went black. A few seconds later, alarms began to wail, screams rang out, and sirens howled. And in the chaos, the Ghosts vanished into the smoke.

Even as the fuel caught fire, the impact of the explosion generated a massive overpressure that shattered the garage's windows, doors and walls 500 yards away. The intense heat and fire travelled to the underground petrol storage facilities, turning the area into a maddening inferno. As the flames hit the diesel drums kept along the boundary and blew them off the ground, fire engulfed the garage, burning everything in its wake. Flames began to lick the cars, causing the petrol tanks to explode and sending the burning vehicles soaring, while the deafening noise rattled the ground. As Drapchi prison was plunged into darkness, the only light came from the burning substation, the petrol pump and the garage. The fog sucked in the dark fumes of burning rubber and metal, making it impossible to see in the night.

'Go to the ammunition dump and prepare it for the final explosion. I will tell you when to detonate. I am heading for the control room. The uninterruptible power supply there would have kicked in. I need to kill that so the CCTV cameras shut down,' said Raj, as he raced towards the control room.

Lala ran to the ammunition dump at the far end of the prison compound. He scaled over a four-foot wall and headed to a door with a red danger sign painted on it and a jeep parked right in front of it. As he neared the door, he noticed beneath the danger sign, the word 'Ammunition' was written in Chinese. He tried the door, but it was locked. Moving on, he approached one of the windows, pulled out his stiletto and wedged it between the shutters, twisting it sharply. The carbon steel blade cut into the wood, cracking one of the shutters near the hinge. He pulled a thick cloth from his pocket, wrapped it around his palm and punched the shutter. The hinge immediately dislodged where the crack had formed. He opened the shutter, slipped in and began exploring the store. At the far end, he found a door and stepped through. Outside, he saw the prison's compound wall, towering 15 feet high. Two hundred yards away, an open area large enough to hold a truck lay between the ammunition dump building and the prison wall.

Lala spoke into his COO mic, 'Pema, once I blow up the ammunition dump, I will place C4s on the rear wall and bring it down. You get the truck behind the ammunition dump.'

'Understood,' said Pema, who was already running to fetch the truck as the granary and the kitchen had caught fire.

In the meantime, Raj stopped a hundred yards from the control room and studied the CCTV camera placed at the building's entrance. There was panic everywhere. Guards and prison officers were running around with torches. Some were moving towards the substation to help restore the power, while others fanned out across the compound, searching for the perpetrators. As Raj had guessed, the control room went dark only for a few seconds when the substation was blown, but then it had switched to the UPS.

Though the fog and the thick fumes had blinded everything, Raj did not want to take a chance. Dressed in his dark blue prison uniform, Raj moved closer to the prison's control room, slightly higher than the ground level. He crawled carefully under the CCTV camera outside the control room and aimed the high-powered laser pointer directly at the lens. It temporarily blinded the camera, and the moment the screens blacked out, Raj slipped under them and ran to the control room. The guard outside the control room heard the sound of footsteps, but could not see anything in the dark.

'Is it you, Lou?' asked the guard, blinded by the fog.

Raj fired his service pistol. The bullet hit the guard squarely on his chest with a slight '*pop*'. After dumping the dead guard behind a bush, Raj rang the control room's doorbell. After two seconds, one of the operators opened the door and peeped out. The moment his head came out, Raj fired. The bullet hit him in the temple. As his body hit the floor, Raj caught him, dragged him out and left him with the other guard. Without waiting, he entered the control room.

The control room was a poorly lit chamber filled with banks of monitors, control panels and blinking lights. Three guards had their backs to him. Two sat on chairs, watching the monitor screens. The third was standing and tinkering with some knobs.

The visibility inside the room was much better than what it was outside, but it quickly reduced as the fog and fumes entered through the open door. Raj closed it gently behind him and walked towards the guards. He had hardly taken two steps when the guard who was standing whirled around. When he saw Raj, his hands went to his hip holster, but Raj beat him to it. Three rounds. One hit the guard standing below between his eyes, and the other two smashed into the backs of the heads of the two sitting—all there died instantly.

Raj went over to one of the monitors, placed his SIG Sauer M17 on the table and entered James's name in the search section. A second later, the screen showed Cell 17. He played with the toggle and focused on the view inside the cell, hoping to see James. The cell was empty. Disappointed, he was about to leave the control room when his eyes fell on another screen. There was an unexpected development. He saw guards with torches moving prisoners to a central hall lit with emergency lights.

'They are moving the prisoners to a common area,' he whispered. Just then, he heard a sound and turned. A huge Chinese guard stood at the door, studying him curiously. With the fog drifting inside the control room, the only illumination came from the monitors' soft glow, casting a ghostly pallor on the man's face. Raj's heart pounded in his chest as the man approached him.

The guard looked at the dead bodies around and then at Raj.

'Who are you?' he asked. He went for his sidearm at the same time.

Raj realised he had left his gun on the table beside the monitor. But he moved like lightning, diving sideways as he pulled the stiletto from its sheath and threw it at the guard. The man had almost levelled the pistol at Raj when the blade punctured his throat. The gun dropped from his hand, and his legs buckled under him. As he fell face forward, the stiletto was pushed further through his throat, increasing his pain. The body writhed on the floor, and blood started pooling all around his huge frame. Raj picked up his weapon from the table, aimed and fired at his head. A classic double tap to the side of the head silenced the guard forever.

Then he turned towards the control panel and fired a couple of bullets through the computer, eradicating any possibility for the prison guards to operate it when the power came on. Raj pulled out a grenade from his backpack, pulled the pin, threw it inside the control room and slammed the steel door shut from the outside. As he sprinted away, there was an enormous blast, and the control room went up in flames.

Back at the ammunition dump, Lala had placed a large block of C4 near the compound wall. He armed it and proceeded to place more bricks in the very centre of the building. Once again, he armed the detonator and linked it to a specific number on his cell phone. He took out a bottle of spirit from his backpack and sprinkled it all over the room and over the crates of ammunition piled up all near the walls. In minutes, he had prepped the entire ammunition dump to explode.

'I am ready,' said Lala.

'Gawa is with me. We are on our way,' said Pema.

'Lala, now,' came Raj's voice.

It was 10.17 p.m., and Raj was just six feet from the rusted steel gates of the solitary confinement wing when the night sky behind him erupted. The earth trembled beneath his boots as a shockwave ripped through the prison grounds when a hidden ammo depot buried deep under the western wall exploded. The blast shattered windows, tore metal off its hinges, and sent the air shivering with heat and chaos. Within seconds, flames clawed into the night sky, engulfing bunkers packed with grenades, mortars and anti-personnel rounds.

Then came the cook-off. Bullets ignited like firecrackers, slicing through the air in every direction, ricocheting off stone, concrete and flesh. It sounded like a battlefield orchestra—violent, unstoppable, deafening.

Raj didn't flinch. His hand reached instinctively for his Sig Sauer M17. Through the smoke, he saw two prison guards posted at the solitary entrance, blinded by darkness, disoriented by the explosions, and unaware that death was just six feet away.

'Good job, brother,' Raj muttered into his comm, a half-smile forming as he raised the weapon and fired three clean shots. Two heads snapped back. One fell to his knees while the shorter guard was thrown three feet back, where he crashed against the prison wall and fell dead. Raj ran forward, dropped to one knee beside the shorter guard, patted his chest, and pulled a heavy iron key ring from his jacket. Behind him, the wind carried screams, sirens and the haunting whine of war from the outer complex. He sprinted down the narrow corridor which was cold, damp and dimly lit by emergency lights that flickered with each fresh tremor.

Outside Cell 8, a lone silhouette stood guard. The man turned sharply. 'Who are you?' he barked, stepping forward, his rifle rising. Raj didn't break stride. One shot. Right between the eyes. The guard's body slumped like a marionette with cut strings. Raj caught the falling rifle mid-air, kicked the body aside, and slid the key into the rusted lock. *Click*. He pulled the cell door open.

And there he was. Chin Luan.

He stood tall—easily over six feet—despite the months of torture and isolation. His face, fair-skinned but hardened, was marked by faint bruises, but his jaw was square, unbroken. His eyes, dark, intense and piercing, held neither fear nor relief. They burned with defiance. Even in the tattered grey prison uniform, Chin looked like a soldier who'd never stopped fighting. For a second, they just stared at each other—two warriors from different nations but the same side.

Raj lowered his gun slightly and asked softly, 'Chin Luan?'

The man gave the faintest of nods. 'You're late,' he rasped, voice dry but firm—touched with a trace of humour.

Raj smiled. 'Blame the traffic.' Then he extended his hand. Chin took it.

'I'm Raj. Here, wear this. We have to get going,' Raj said as he handed him a pair of night-vision glasses. Holding Chin Luan's hands, Raj escorted him out of the cell and proceeded to open the other cells. 'Tell them to go and release the other prisoners.'

'*Qu jiu ni de Xiong di*. Go save your brothers,' Chin instructed the other prisoners whom Raj had freed.

'Yes, Laoban,' they said, running towards the blocks where the prisoners were held captive.

Within minutes, Raj and Chin left solitary confinement. When they were outside, Raj stopped at the entrance and pointed in the direction of the billowing flames. 'See that fire? That is the ammunition dump burning. Behind that, you will find my colleague, Lala, and a lady in a truck called Pema. Run.'

'What about you?' asked Chin.

'I'll see you in a while,' said Raj, already racing towards the central hall.

'He is going to extract James Li,' muttered Lala as he made his way towards the half-blown prison compound where Pema was to arrive with Gawa in her truck.

As Pema raced the lorry towards the ammunition dump, she saw Chin sprinting towards her. She slowed down as she came closer to him and shouted, 'Jump in, Laoban.'

As Chin Luan reached the door, Gawa opened it and leaned out with his right arm outstretched. Chin jumped and held on to Gawa as he pulled him inside the vehicle.

Once Gawa and Chin were safely in the truck, Pem checked her rearview mirror. She saw the chef running out of the main entrance with his helpers. No one was manning the gates; they had been left wide open. The dense fog, combined with the thick, noxious fumes, made breathing difficult. The staff, including the guards, were streaming out of the premises to save their lives, leaving the prisoners to fend for themselves.

'Be there in a few minutes,' she said into her mic to Lala and Raj as she manoeuvred the truck through the rubble and towards the ammunition dump.

When Raj entered the vast common hall, he noticed it was covered on all four sides by a thick mesh made of steel wires. Four guards with headlamps were still standing at the far end of the room. He saw hundreds of inmates sitting inside, shivering under thin blankets; most were monks. Despite the utter commotion outside, the hall was silent.

Raj walked along the mesh and whispered to one of the monks, 'I am here to release you all'. Then he stood up and shouted thrice, 'James Li, stand up.'

The guards ahead turned and saw a man in uniform shouting out for James Li. Confused, they began converging towards the inmates. James stood up to see who was calling out his name. One of the guards approached James and shouted at him to sit down.

As Raj walked towards James and the guards, they assumed he was one of them. But when he got closer, they realised he was not. 'Hey, who are you?' one of them barked at Raj.

Raj aimed and fired two shots. The two shots downed two men, but the remaining guards dived both sides. Raj lunged at the wire mesh door and opened it.

'Run, now …' he shouted at the prisoners. Then he turned to James and said, 'Fanny sent me to fetch you. Run to the ammunition dump. A rescue team is waiting for you. Go, go, go.'

The two guards were overwhelmed by the sheer number of prisoners rushing through the open gates, so they pivoted and fired at Raj. Raj returned fire while sprinting for cover. After several minutes of exchanging shots, all three realised they had exhausted their ammunition.

One of them—a large, beefy man—stepped out of hiding with a knife and growled at Raj, 'If you are a man, fight.'

Noticing the man's confidence, the second guard—of medium build but tough-looking—drew his knife and bravely joined him.

Raj stepped out from behind a pillar, stiletto in his right hand, and stood facing the two. The larger of the two came charging like a bull. As he reached Raj and swung his knife, Raj sidestepped, held his hand and yanked him forward. The speed with which the man had come running made it difficult to stop, and he crashed into the wall in front of him. The knife slipped from his hands and skidded away.

As the man struggled to rise, the second guard rushed to tackle Raj. He attempted to strike, but Raj ducked and countered with a powerful left hook, landing squarely on his attacker's face. The impact was brutal, shattering the guard's nose. He let out a bloodcurdling scream as he stumbled backwards. Raj followed the punch with a kick to his groin, making him howl in pain.

In a flash, the large guard sprang up and lunged at Raj, his massive fist hurtling through the air. Raj reacted with lightning speed, blocking the blow with his forearm and unleashing a right hook that made contact with his opponent's jaw with a sickening crunch. The forceful punch sent him crashing into the wire mesh with a loud clang.

Behind Raj, the second guard scrambled to his feet and swung his knife down in a wide arc. Raj stepped back just in time, but the blade sliced through the air mere inches from his face, catching his forehead and splitting the skin an inch above his left eye. Blood trickled down his face as he spun around to face the guard. Before the guard could strike again, Raj launched a vicious kick into his midsection.

Unfortunately, the big man was back on his feet, looming behind Raj like a spectre. Before Raj could react, a massive fist slammed into his chest, sending him crashing to the ground near the second guard, who was now standing, his eyes blazing with fury. The guard swung his leg in a vicious arc, kicking Raj in the abdomen with enough force to send him skidding backwards. He crashed into the wire mesh. As he struggled to rise, the two men closed in on him together. In a swift motion, Raj sliced the big guy's ankle with his stiletto. The guard screamed as his tendons were slit and buckled to his knees. The other guard tried to back off, but Raj flipped in the air and aimed a kick at his right temple. The guard's head snapped as he crashed against the wire mesh. Raj walked up to the bigger guard, screaming on the floor and kicked him on his left temple, leaving him bleeding to death.

Bruised and bleeding from the wound above his eye, Raj stumbled out of the entrance door and spoke into his COO mic, 'James is on his way.'

The acrid smell of gunpowder lingered in the air, blending with the metallic tang of blood. Lala's eyes locked on Pema's truck as she roared into the prison compound, a few feet away from the ammunition dump, waving frantically from the driver's seat. Hope surged through him, and he ran to be with her. He was just fifteen feet away when Lala's world shifted. A battering ram slammed into his back. An acute and endless pain made his body convulse, driving him to his knees. His vision blurred as he heard Pema scream his name.

Inside the truck, Pema's world shattered. As Lala collapsed, she saw the silhouette of an officer standing behind him, the barrel of his pistol gleaming under the pale moonlight. Her instincts screamed at her to act, and she wrenched the truck's wheel hard, swerving it wildly to avoid the line of fire. But the officer didn't aim at her. Instead, his gun turned back at Lala, now crumpled and bleeding on the ground.

The officer moved closer, the sound of heavy boots echoing ominously. He stopped a few feet from Lala and shined his torch into Lala's bloodied face.

'*Nǐ shì shéi*' (Who are you)?'

Lala's lips curled into a faint smile. His voice, barely a whisper, said, 'Zhèngyì (Justice).'

In an instant, Lala's hand flashed towards the gun in his holster. The officer barely had time to react before the first shot rang out. The bullet slammed into his stomach, doubling him over. A second shot followed, tearing through his skull, and sending a spray of blood and brain matter into the air. The lifeless, headless body staggered backwards before collapsing.

Pema leapt out of the driver's seat, her heart pounding in terror. She reached Lala, who lay in a growing pool of his blood. His face was pale, his breathing ragged.

'No, no, no,' she whispered, her hands trembling as she cradled his head. 'Stay with me, Lala. Please.'

Lala's eyelids fluttered open. He looked at her; his familiar smile, although weak, was back on his face. His voice was faint but steady.

'Prop me up … against that tree,' he gasped.

Pema's heart screamed at her to defy him, but his pleading eyes left her no choice. She gently lifted him and leaned him against the gnarled trunk of an old tree.

Lala held her hand and mumbled, his breathing laboured. 'Don't wait for me. Go.'

'No,' Pema shook her head vehemently, tears running down her cheeks. 'Not without you.'

Lala's gaze softened, the pain in his eyes mingling with quiet resolve. 'My time is up, Pema,' he said. 'Go, save Chin and Gawa. My journey ends here.'

Pema sobbed uncontrollably, clutching his hand.

'If you love me, leave,' he whispered, the words cutting through her heart like a blade.

'No!' she screamed, her voice cracking. 'I will not leave you here to die.'

Summoning all her strength, Pema lifted Lala into her arms, blood soaking through her clothes. She staggered back to the truck, tears streaming down her face. As she neared the vehicle, she saw Raj running towards them. His face was grave.

'We have to get him to a hospital,' she pleaded, her voice choking with tears. 'Now!'

Raj grabbed her shoulders. He didn't say a word, just shook his head slowly.

Pema froze. Her gaze dropped to Lala's limp body in her arms. His chest no longer rose and fell. His eyes were closed; his face serene.

He was gone.

A sound escaped her lips—a low, guttural moan that grew into a scream so raw and brimming with despair that it seemed to split the very fabric of the night. She fell to the ground, clutching Lala's lifeless body, rocking him in her arms like a child. Pema's agonising shrieks echoed into the darkness, the mournful wail of a woman who had lost everything. The world seemed to stand still, a silent witness to her unending grief.

12

5 April 2024, 10.30 p.m.
Drapchi prison, Lhasa, Tibet

THE NIGHT SKY WAS ABLAZE. The heat from the burning buildings grew unbearable, and the air was thick with poisonous fumes. The compound had spiralled into mayhem. The fire consumed everything in its path, setting off more and more explosions in Drapchi's premises. A few of the staff had opened all the cell doors, so prisoners and guards spilled out of the main gates, running to save their lives.

The battery-operated alarms were blaring non-stop, waking up the entire village. Pema had manoeuvred the truck out of the compound from behind the ammunition dump where Lala had blown the wall and reached the main road, but a sea of people was blocking her path even then as they were jostling to get away from the prison.

Beside her, Raj clutched his SIG Sauer M17 in his right hand. In the back, Chin Luan and Gawa sat with Lala's dead body.

Pema, her face deadpan and eyes bloodshot, inched the lorry for a few minutes. Losing her patience, she honked, the blare momentarily cutting through the ruckus of escaped prisoners, guards and villagers. People turned, some scowling, others fearful. But no one moved aside. Pema shifted the gears and gradually moved the truck forward. The vehicle lumbered through the crowd, its bulk forcing people to squeeze to the sides. Progress was painfully slow. She had to stop every few feet and find a new route away from the path of people running. The engine growled in protest as the truck squeezed itself through narrow streets. Sweat trickled down Pema's forehead as she leaned out the window, shouting at the people to move, her voice barely audible over the din. Behind her, Zhao's men followed her in a grey van.

Pema navigated the truck carefully towards an alley to her right that offered a potential shortcut, carefully turning the wheel to avoid crushing people on all sides. The alley was tight, and the walls of the buildings seemed to close in around the truck. She drove cautiously, mirrors almost scraping the sides. Soon, the truck emerged onto a less busy street and picked up speed. She pressed the accelerator, confidently driving past a few remaining obstacles which presented themselves—a bicyclist weaving unpredictably and a stray dog darting across the road—but managed to avoid them all.

Then, as Pema turned a bend, she saw the main road where traffic flowed freely. She also saw a green and white board that said Lhasa Gonggar Airport. She wiped the sweat from her brow, but tears flowed uncontrollably from her eyes as she raced towards the airport with Zhao's men following her at a safe distance.

Police sirens, fire engines and ambulances could still be heard in the distance as she raced. After 2 km, Pema stopped, looked at Raj and said softly, 'I want to spend some time with Lala.'

Raj nodded. Pema and Gawa exchanged places. While Pema sat with Lala in the back, Gawa took over the wheel. She told him he had to stop at the Shubin Dong Meat Store in Gonggar County to drop off Chin Luan. Forty-five minutes later, they were at the store. After everyone had changed into fresh clothes, Pema approached Chin Luan and said softly, 'Lala loved Tibet. We were planning to marry and settle in Amritsar.' After a pause, she added, 'I want a favour from you.'

'Tell me what you want, and I will get it done,' said Chin.

'I want Lala to be cremated with all the honours of a soldier and his last rites conducted in the Hindu custom,' she said, sobbing uncontrollably.

Chin Luan looked at Zhao, who stepped forward and said, 'I will make sure this is done. I will also make sure his ashes reach you.'

'I will send you my new address. Send me the ashes there,' Pema instructed Zhao.

'Yes, ma'am,' said Zhao as he escorted her and Raj into a black SUV. Then he, Chin Luan and James Li got into another one.

The black SUVs stopped in different corners of Lhasa Gonggar Airport, their engines purring softly before the passengers stepped out into the cold night. The atmosphere around them was heavy with the tension of escape. As promised, Paitoon's men, dressed inconspicuously, escorted Chin and James to a private jet waiting. The plane, parked in the tarmac's VIP section, sat cloaked in darkness, invisible to prying eyes. Within minutes, the two disappeared into the jet, leaving no trace of their presence behind.

In the main terminal, Raj and Pema blended into the crowd of regular passengers. Both wore regular, weathered clothes and carried light luggage. Zhao had given Pema a new identity. She was now a Buddhist intern attending a seminar in Thailand. Raj already had a false identity with him.

At immigration and security, Paitoon's men worked silently, their efficiency ensuring Pema and Raj had a seamless passage. No questions were asked, and no documents were scrutinised. The tension lifted as they reached the boarding gate for their flight to Thailand.

Outside the boarding gate, Raj and Pema sat next to each other, their silence speaking more than any speech. The hum of conversations filled the air, but Raj knew neither of them was completely aware of their surroundings. Raj took out his phone and sent a message to Rajnath. *Strike 5 completed. Packages delivered.*

His reply came instantly. *Congratulations. Come home.*

Raj read the message repeatedly. He would be going home, back to Veer's Bungalow, where he and Lala spent so many years together. The weight of his despair pressed against his chest. He blinked rapidly, trying to hold back the tears welling in his eyes. Turning slightly to his right, he looked away from Pema, pretending to focus on something distant, but she noticed.

Her gaze softened as she reached over and embraced him tightly, and whispered, in Tibetan, '*Kong gi tse thung yang ga chö dang dön drub yin. Tse ring dang rab drang mepa las tse thung yang chö dam dang ga chö chewa yin.*'

Raj turned to her, his voice cracking. 'Yes,' he said. 'His life was short, but it was meaningful. A virtuous and fulfilling life outweighs mere longevity.'

Pema's eyebrows arched in surprise. She tilted her head slightly and curiosity flickered in her wet eyes. 'Who taught you Tibetan?' she asked.

Raj's lips trembled slightly as he whispered, 'Lala.'

His name hung in the air between them. After a moment, Raj reached into his backpack and pulled out a small, worn-out envelope. He handed it to Pema with both hands as if it carried the weight of the world. 'He asked me to give this to you if he didn't make it,' Raj said, his voice now barely audible.

Pema's hands shook as she took the envelope from him. She slowly unfolded the documents inside, unprepared to face the enormity of their contents. Her eyes scanned the paper, her breath hitching with each word. It was Lala's will. The neatly typed text declared that everything Ram Madhav Lala owned—his house, his land in Amritsar and his savings—was now hers. Pema traced his signature at the bottom of the page with his finger.

'Why would he do this?' she whispered, clutching the paper. 'Why?'

Raj's voice was hoarse. 'Because he loved you.'

Pema clutched the will tightly, her body wracked with silent sobs. Around them, the world moved forward, oblivious to their unspoken grief. Passengers lined up, announcements blared and boarding commenced. But for Pema and Raj, time seemed to stand still.

Finally, Raj placed a hand on her shoulder, his touch grounding her.

'We have to go,' he said gently. 'For him.'

Pema nodded slowly. She wiped her tears and folded the will carefully, placing it back in the envelope. As she stood up, her body felt heavy, weighed down by their unforgettable loss. Together, hand in hand, they walked towards the boarding gate, carrying not just their luggage but the memory of a man who had lived—and died—with purpose. Lala's sacrifice would not be forgotten.

13

6 April 2024, 10.30 p.m.
7/17 Akbar Road, New Delhi

RAJNATH HELD A FILE IN his hand and looked at the sorrowful faces of the Ghosts as they sat around the dining table. Rajnath had summoned AV, Geeta, Shiva, Raj and Pavak Dahia. Safi Doha had joined from Istanbul via a video call.

'Nothing I say will ease the immense grief that you all are going through, so I won't attempt to console anyone here. All I will say is Lala's martyrdom will not be in vain.'

'Other than us, who will even know Lala existed?' Raj asked. 'We are like mayflies. Born at the crack of dawn and dead by the night. Unheard of, unspoken, unremembered. This is a reality we have chosen, and this is what we have to live with. Lala is history. So will we be, sooner than later. Let us forget the past and move on.'

Shiva cast a sharp glance at Raj. He had never seen him so bitter and insensitive. He was about to react sharply when Geeta held him back and whispered. 'He was closer to Lala than any of us. Let him be. He will have to deal with it on his own.'

Rajnath looked at Raj, then at the others. 'I have information on Shahid Faisal. But I don't want to discuss it if we are not in the right frame of mind. So, you decide.'

Raj glared at him and said, 'If it were Dhariwal, he would have told me what he had to say on my face.'

Something snapped inside Rajnath. He threw the file on the table. Locking eyes with Raj, he said in a voice that was at once commanding and unforgiving, 'If you are guilty that the people close to you often drop dead, then that is your problem, and you need to learn to live with it. Don't try to project your issues and throw your temper around. You might be an ace at the job, but you have no emotional control or a sense of what it takes to be a part of a team. So, I am grounding you for the next strike. You can leave.'

While the others were stunned by Rajnath's ability to read Raj so well, Raj glowered at Rajnath and stormed out of the room.

Rajnath waited for the door to close behind him and said, 'I have information on Shahid Faisal. Angel eavesdropped on a conversation between Pannu and Shahid Faisal.'

Rajnath pressed the remote, and the TV came alive. On the screen was an aerial shot of Queens. 'Angel does not know the exact address, but she said he is now in Queens, New York. I asked my team to dig out everything on Sahid Faisal, and guess what I found?'

The Ghosts looked at him eagerly to answer his question.

'Shahid Faisal has a sister named Shaheen. She lives with his cousin, a truck driver in America, who I am guessing is also in Queens. If he is there, then Shahid is with him. But I am sure they are using their original names. The question is under what names are they living?' Rajnath walked across the room and began fixing some coffee, leaving the team to ponder the situation.

When he returned to the table, Pavak asked, 'What is the cousin's name?'

Geeta, who was going through the file, said, 'Usman Faisal. Why?'

Pavak looked at his cousin. 'Safi, you know how most Pakistanis shorten their names or Anglicise them when they come to America to make it sound more American. Can you find out from your friends what are the most common modifications are for a name like Usman Faisal?'

Safi nodded and called a friend in New Orleans. Everyone waited for his conversation to end.

'The anglicised version of Usman is most commonly Oz or Manny,' Safi informed them.

'And Faisal?' asked Pavak.

'My friend says it will either be Fay or Sal.'

'You'll have to come up with various combinations of Oz, Manny, Fay and Sal and use that to check in the database for truckers,' Pavak told the Ghosts.

'That will be like searching for a needle in a haystack,' said Shiva.

'Probably not,' said AV, who had been silent all along. 'You prepare the various combinations. I will check something out.'

The Ghosts and the cousins started work, while AV took out his iPad and logged into a search engine called Erebus Finder. Lurking in the depths of the dark web, Erebus specialised in tracking personal information, including addresses and financial records. He typed 'Truckers based in Queens, New York'. Within seconds, a long list of fifty-six names popped up on his screen. He sorted the list alphabetically and began searching for Usman Faisal. However, as Rajnath had mentioned, the name wasn't there. He then searched for 'Usman Faisal' and 'Queens'. Still, nothing appeared. Frustrated, AV gave up and decided to wait for their team to come up with a possible name.

After fifteen minutes, Pavak collated all the possible combinations while AV fed them into the search engine. After several tries, one name popped up. *Manny Sal.* AV fed the name into Erebus Finder for the trucker's location, address and financial details. A thirty-second wait yielded Manny Sal's social ID page.

AV read it aloud. 'Manny Sal. Born in Lahore, Karachi. Thirty-six. Unmarried. Working as a trucker with RS Trucking, Queens, NY, since 2008. Offers reliable trucking solutions to ensure efficient freight movement across the US. He lives in …'

AV copied the phone number and email address mentioned under the 'Contact Us' section and entered the information into an Obsidian Mirror application.

After a few seconds, more pages came on the screen. The first was Manny Sal's Facebook page, followed by his Instagram, Snapchat and Tinder profiles. He went through each of them meticulously but found nothing connecting him to Usman Faisal. Just when he was about to give up, Safi pointed at a picture of him with a teenage girl. Someone had left a comment saying 'Nice chick', and Manny Sal had replied, 'Bastard, that's my sister.'

'Trace that girl,' said Safi.

AV cropped the girl's face, pasted it into the app and hit search. Within seconds, her Snapchat opened. Her handle was *FlyShaheenFay*.

'An anglicised version of Faisal is Fay,' Safi said softly.

A rush of adrenaline surged through the room as AV searched for Shaheen Fay. In seconds, he located her graduation certificate issued by Islamabad University. From there, it became easy for AV. Within a few minutes, Shaheen Faisal's address in Queens was on the screen. It was the same as Manny Sal's.

There were smiles of relief. 'Sir, we've got their address,' Geeta informed Rajnath. 'Now, we need to verify whether Shahid is staying with them.'

Rajnath sent the address to Angel, saying, 'Please confirm if Shahid is here.'

'Give me a few days,' came her instant reply.

'Come, let us have dinner,' Rajnath asked the team. 'We can end today's meeting here.'

While everyone else agreed to stay behind, Geeta politely declined. 'My dad is in town and must be waiting for me for dinner. Let me know when Angel reverts.'

14

11 April 2024, 9.30 p.m.
Lahore, Pakistan

KIRAN SINGH PANJWAR FOLLOWED A rigorous diet and ensured he exercised regularly. His daily routine started with an hour-long run on the treadmill, two hours of weightlifting and cardio and a fifteen-minute jog around the housing complex to destress. To the outside world, Kiran Singh Panjwar was a businessman. In reality, he was one of Sorosi's top five hitmen.

Born in Panjwar, he was a bank employee before he was inducted by the ISI and moved to Pakistan in 1986. Under their guidance, Kiran Singh became involved in smuggling drugs and weapons through drones into Punjab. He later joined a global terror outfit, Jamaat E Muslimin, and scaled the ranks by executing several small-scale terror attacks in Srinagar. To date, there have been seven FIRs against him for murder and two under India's Terrorist and Disruptive Activities (Prevention) Act. Nonetheless, he remained protected in Pakistan.

As one of the core commanders of Jamaat E Muslimin, Kiran Singh operated from Lahore. He arranged arms training for radicalised Sikh youths, supplied ammunition, supported subsequent infiltration into India to target VIPs and economic installations, and functioned as a primary conduit between drug smugglers and terrorists. A week ago, Pannu had called Sorosi with a plan to assassinate Ashok Kumar Jakhar, the newly appointed president of BLP Punjab. Pannu was worried that Jakhar's growing popularity and likely victory in the upcoming state elections would sabotage their operations, as his win would lead to the sealing of Punjab's porous border. This would severely impact their drug trade and the movement of weapons and money. Initially uninterested, Sorosi became more receptive when Pannu said that removing Jakhar would create a power vacuum within the party. Sorosi also realised that BLP's loss would benefit the PCP, thereby securing his pharmaceutical contract in Punjab. After some thought, Sorosi agreed to the plan. He asked Pannu, who was capable of executing such a tricky task. Without a moment's hesitation, Pannu said, 'Kiran Singh Panjwar.'

Being meticulous at his work, Kiran knew he had to be in top shape all the time, hence he focused on his physique, and today was no different. He had finished his exercises and was nearly done with his run. Though towering at 6'3" and heavily muscular, Kiran Singh was light on his feet. After finishing the lap, he headed to his favourite tea stall outside his society's front gate for a glass of warm milk.

While talking to a friend on his cell phone, Kiran noticed a motorcycle approaching him from the opposite direction. Seeing the speed at which the biker was driving, Panjwar waited on the side of the road to let the vehicle pass. As the bike came closer, the rider, dressed in black leather pants, a jacket and a black helmet, pulled out a silencer-tipped GLOCK 19, aimed at Kiran and fired two quick shots.

The first bullet hit the centre of Kiran's forehead, throwing his head back. As his body arched backwards, the second bullet went straight through his heart and sent him crashing on the sidewalk. The biker got off the bike, walked up to Kiran's lifeless body, clicked two pictures of it and rode off at breakneck speed. The entire incident would not have taken more than thirty seconds.

Since it was late and the road outside was poorly lit, the owner of the tea stall took a few minutes to register what had happened before he called the police. The police arrived with an ambulance thirty minutes later and took Kiran Singh to a nearby private hospital, where he was pronounced dead on arrival.

In the meantime, the biker arrived at Allama Iqbal International Airport in Lahore, parked the bike in the basement parking and peeled off the bike's black plastic coating to reveal its original blue colour. The number plates were swapped, and the helmet, along with the old plates, discarded in a garbage bin. The biker walked into the women's restroom carrying a leather tote and once inside, changed into brown pants and a white cotton shirt, and stuffed the leather pants and jacket into the bag. Finally, the biker entered the airport and walked to the Malaysian Airlines check-in counter.

The airline's employee looked up at the tall, pretty blonde-haired woman and smiled. 'Passport and tickets, please,' he said politely.

She handed him her passport and the printout of her ticket. The man checked the system and pulled out her boarding pass.

'Miss Selena Draevan, you are flying business class to Kuala Lumpur. Your seat number is 3F, and your departure gate is 14B. Walk straight down; take the elevator to the first floor; it is the sixth gate to your left, please. Have a safe flight, and thank you for using Malaysian Airlines.'

Selena thanked the man and walked towards the elevator. Fifteen minutes later, sitting outside Gate 14B, she dialled a number. After two rings, Rajnath answered her call.

'All okay?' Rajnath asked.

'Yes, dad,' Selena replied.

'What time is your flight?' asked Rajnath.

'Boarding in fifteen minutes and taking off in another thirty. I will land at 7.20 a.m. Malaysia Time tomorrow. The flight to New York is in two days, so I will go home.'

'I will see you at home for dinner the day after,' said Rajnath.

'Really?' a smile spread on her lips.

'Yes. Keep dinner for three. We have a guest coming over.'

'Cool. I love you, dad,' said Selena.

'I love you more,' said Rajnath.

Selena smiled at the thought of finally meeting her father after six long months. The last time she had seen him was when he had come for a meeting of the United Nations Security Council in New York. She put the phone into her pocket and looked at the television in the business lounge airing late-night news from all over Pakistan. The newsreader, an elegant middle-aged woman with a husky, commanding voice, reported: 'In a chilling incident earlier this evening, Kiran Singh Panjwar, a prominent resident of Sunflower Society in Lahore, was gunned down by an unidentified assailant on a motorbike. Police confirm that the precision of the shots, one to the head and one to the heart, points to a highly trained, professional hitman. This marks the fifth such targeted assassination on Pakistani soil in recent months. Like the previous four, the gunman escaped without leaving a trace. No eyewitnesses. No CCTV leads. No suspects.

'While local law enforcement remains clueless about the motive, sources inside the ISI are already blaming India's external intelligence agency, RAW, for orchestrating the hit. What's alarming is the growing pattern—businessmen, politicians and influential individuals with controversial backgrounds are being eliminated one by one by these faceless, silent assassins. The question now haunting Islamabad is: who are these mystery gunmen, and who's sending them?'

An announcement asking business-class passengers to come forward for Malaysian Airlines OD 132 from Lahore to Kuala Lumpur interrupted the news. Selena got up, scanned her boarding pass at the gate and entered the air bridge.

Sitting in his residence in New Delhi, Rajnath called Raj. 'I am sending you a ticket to KL and an address. I will see you there at 7.30 p.m. the day after. We will have dinner together.'

15

13 April 2024, 7.30 p.m.
27, Jalan Mutiara Heights, Bukit Damansara, Kuala Lumpur

RAJ COULDN'T HELP BUT FEEL an overwhelming sense of intrigue as he stood before the bungalow at the far end of Jalan Mutiara Heights. Its structure was illuminated by the soft glow of amber lights along the driveway. The nameplate—etched in sleek, brushed steel—read 'Moonlit Haven', a name befitting the almost ethereal charm of the property. He climbed the two steps leading to the porch and rang the doorbell.

A minute later, a blonde-haired lady opened the door. The first thing that caught Raj's eye was a string of luminous pearls sitting elegantly around her neck. The stunning necklace was perfectly complemented by matching earrings, dangling delicately from her ears. Her tall frame was accentuated by a sleek black dress that fit her athletic build. Her golden hair cascaded in soft waves, framing a kind face. Her lips were slightly curved upward as though she were on the verge of sharing a secret smile. But it was her eyes that held the most intrigue. Beneath the apparent warmth of her demeanour lay a depth that could not be overlooked. Her resolute gaze, a striking shade of sapphire blue, reflected unwavering strength and an unspoken sense of purpose.

'Good evening, Mr Rana. I am Selena. Dad is waiting inside,' she said, as she shook his hand. Her sculpted arms and firm grip hinted unmistakably at a life of discipline.

'Good evening, Selena,' replied Raj.

As he followed her inside, he noticed an air of assuredness in her movements; every step was deliberate, every glance meaningful.

As he entered the living room, Rajnath, seated on a sofa, greeted him. 'Welcome to my humble home, Raj. I see that you've already met my daughter, Selena. Come, please sit down,' he said, pointing to a sofa beside him.

Raj took a few seconds to absorb the information and then asked politely, 'You said this is your home. Do you live here?'

'Sometimes. This is my wife's house. Before I joined politics, I was a professor at a university here.'

'That is where he met Mom. She was a lecturer there, too,' said Selena as she walked in with some hors d'oeuvres and placed them before Raj.

'What would you like to drink?' asked Rajnath, getting up and walking over to a well-stocked bar on the left.

'I will have fresh lime water, please,' said Raj.

'Nothing strong?' Rajnath asked as he poured himself a stiff whisky and added ice.

'Not today,' said Raj.

'I'll get it. Sweet or salted?' Selena asked Raj.

'Salted,' he answered.

As she moved under the bright lights, he noticed the striking resemblance between father and daughter. Except for the upturned lips, blonde hair and complexion she may have inherited from her mother, the rest of her features were like Rajnath's.

'I just noticed; she looks a lot like you,' said Raj.

'She is the better version of me in every way possible,' Rajnath said as he sipped his drink.

'I knew you were married to a Russian before you returned to India and joined politics, but there is not much on you or your family on the internet or in the database lately,' said Raj.

'Like all of you, many parts of my past have been digitally scrubbed clean for confidentiality purposes,' said Rajnath.

'Why?'

'Because I was being groomed to be a part of the Ghosts.' Seeing a scowl cross Raj's face, Rajnath said, 'I was a part of the BCP that DD, Dhariwal and I prepared six months ago.'

'What is BCP?' asked Raj.

'Business continuity plan. A plan in which we assign three names to every key government asset. First, in case of the sudden death of the key member; second, the person who is being groomed to take over from the key member when they retire; and finally, the third name is the person we may have to recruit from the outside in case the one we are grooming doesn't meet our expectations. I was the first replacement for Dhariwal in case of his sudden death.'

'And who is being groomed to take over his role?'

'Angel,' said Rajnath.

'Who is Angel?'

'You will know in time,' replied Rajnath.

'Is there a BCP for us, too?' asked Raj hesitantly.

'Yes. We are working on it. Selena is part of our BCP.'

'What do you mean?' asked Raj, visibly shocked that Rajnath had been training his daughter for such a role.

'She has undergone rigorous training under the best trainers in guerrilla warfare, weapon systems, navigation and the art of disguise. She is an ace hacker and has a commercial pilot's licence. Not to mention her excellent proficiency in evidence-based learning techniques like spaced repetition systems.'

'Languages?' asked Raj.

'Five, but not Arabic and Pashtun,' said Selena as she walked in holding Raj's fresh lime water. She handed it to him, opened a bottle of chilled Corona beer, and sat next to her father.

'How long have you been training?'

'Five years,' she answered.

Raj looked at Rajnath and asked, 'Was your taking over of the Ghosts planned?'

'Like I said, I was Dhariwal's replacement in case of his sudden death.'

'So, you knew everything about all of us for five years,' said Raj.

'Yes.'

'Yet you pretended you knew nothing when you met AV.'

'Yes. I wanted his view on each one of you. I felt that would be more authentic than what I was told or whatever was in the file. A third-party narration or a file can only say so much about a person. It's facts and figures,' said Rajnath.

'And what did AV have to say about me that was not in the file?' asked Raj.

'That you are the most committed to our nation and the Ghosts, and that you would willingly die for any of us,' said Selena.

'And how would you know that?' asked Raj.

'Because I am your BCP,' she confessed.

Raj gasped inaudibly, processing the shock—he was sitting face-to-face with the person who would one day replace him. He shook his head. 'Damn, just when I think I know everything, a new rabbit jumps out of the box.'

'You can expect that as long as DD is the showrunner,' said Rajnath.

'So, do we have BCPs for Sniper and Lala?' asked Raj.

'Unfortunately, their first replacements died in the 2018 Sunjuwan terror attack by Jaish-e-Mohammed when we lost five army personnel and two civilians. The civilians were Sniper's and Lala's replacements. They were undergoing training at the camp. Their second replacements, as well as the replacements for the rest of the team, are being groomed as we speak,' said Rajnath.

'Any reason why my BCP is ready much before the others?' asked Raj.

When Rajnath hesitated to answer, Selena stepped in. 'Seeing your cowboy-esque personality, Dhariwal feared you would be the first to die.'

Rajnath winced at Selena's frank response, but Raj looked at her with admiration. 'Unfortunately, I seem to be surviving everything while those close to me die.' He shook his head in disgust and then looked at Selena. 'I am beginning to like you. You are direct and to the point. There are no shades of grey.'

'I have been trained to be you, minus your areas of weakness.'

'Like?'

'Like constantly whining and blaming yourself for every bad thing in this world. For being an emotional fool. The only area that others say is your weakness, but I see it as a strength, is your one-man army attitude. I like that. Just like how you enjoy a Corona when you are stressed,' said Selena, raising the beer bottle casually yet deliberately, indirectly indicating that she was also under some stress.

Raj and Selena bonded over dinner. Rajnath observed the two as they discussed various topics. Watching them joke and laugh filled him with emotion and brought a lump in his throat. After dinner, they headed out to the beautiful porch with cups of coffee.

'When will you be given an assignment?' Raj asked Selena.

'She has just returned after one,' said Rajnath. Sitting on a rocking chair, he looked over at Selena and nodded.

'Which one?' asked Raj.

Rajnath handed Raj the day's newspaper. 'It is on the second page,' he said.

Raj flipped the sheet. A bold headline announced, 'Businessman Kiran Singh Panjwar killed in Lahore.' He read the article and put it aside. 'Looks like a clean job. Where did you get the intel?' he asked.

'Angel,' said Selena. 'Pannu was planning to take out Jakhar in Punjab. Angel, being part of the core team, knew of Pannu's plans and informed me, and I gave Selena the job.'

Selena entered the living room with a file and a brown envelope. First, she handed Raj the file.

'During Pannu's absence, Angel went through his desk and found two names mentioned in his diary. One was Katerina. You are holding her file,' said Rajnath. 'We don't know much about her except that she is a Czechoslovakian and lives in Prague. But what is more important is the note that is written below her name.'

'What did it say?' Raj asked.

'Katerina and Andy—AD location,' answered Selena. 'And in another place, a second note said: Andy—AD—Odisha. I think AD stands for Ajit Dhariwal, and that message suggests Katerina and Andy were aware of Dhariwal's location in Odisha.'

'So, Andy and Katerina will know who the mole is in our system. And Katerina is somehow connected to Pannu.'

'Exactly,' said Rajnath.

'What about the other name?' asked Raj.

'The other name was the "Dealer". The note in Pannu's diary, next to a date, said, "The Dealer's approval for Panjwar". Angel went through the diary and spotted similar notes next to several other dates. When she cross-checked them, each date coincided with a major worrisome event that happened in India.'

'So, Angel feels the Dealer is at the centre of all these nefarious activities happening in India?'

'Yes. Angel is convinced that the Dealer is the mastermind, and Pannu reports to him.'

'But who is this person?' asked Raj.

'That is what I want you to find out.'

This time, Selena handed Raj the brown packet. 'This contains your new identity, travel documents, credit cards, driving licence and cash.'

'Where am I going?' asked Raj.

'To Prague. To find Katerina. The address is in the packet. Begin from there.'

'What about Shahid Faisal?' asked Raj.

'The other Ghosts will deal with it,' said Rajnath.

'When am I leaving?' asked Raj.

'The flight with Emirates is at 1.25 a.m. There will be a layover in Dubai, and you will arrive in Prague at 10 a.m.'

Raj nodded and got up from the porch steps.

Rajnath looked at his watch and said, 'It is 10.30 p.m. Your bag is packed and in the car. Selena will drop you to the airport.'

'You move fast,' said Raj.

'Time is our greatest weapon; wield it wisely, and success will always follow.'

'Who said that?' asked Raj, standing at the door.

'I did … just now,' said Rajnath with a mischievous wink. 'Good luck, Mr Rana.'

After Raj and Selena left, Rajnath called Angel. 'Anything for me?' he asked.

'Shahid is with Shaheen and Usman in Queens. I am sending everything you need.'

En route to the Kuala Lumpur airport, Raj asked Selena, 'What is your new assignment?

'Have you heard of Amrinder Singh Khanda?'

'No,' replied Raj.

'He is the son of Kushwant Singh, the deceased leader of the Khalistani Separatist Tiger Force (KSTF). He was Pannu's sharpshooter in Toronto but had to leave Canada six years ago because he shot a police officer during a drug bust. Now, he lives in London and handles Pannu's drug trade in the UK.'

'You have to take him out?' asked Raj

'Hmm,' said Selena.

'Why? What has he done?' asked Raj.

'Nothing so far. But it must be done before he does something.'

'Like what?'

'Like assassinating my father,' said Selena as she took a sharp curve and got onto the highway.

'I presume Angel shared the news?' Raj asked.

'Yes. She also gave me Khanda's location.'

'Where is he?'

'Birmingham. I'll leave tomorrow after dad returns to New Delhi. I'll take some time to study Khanda and then go for the kill, so you won't be hearing from me anytime soon.'

Selena parked outside the airport's Departures gate and got out. She went around the car, opened the trunk and pulled out a suitcase. 'It has everything you need.'

Raj smiled and asked his final question. 'Solo assignment?'

'My close friend died when we were on a project a long time ago. I am better at solos.'

Raj hugged her tightly and whispered, 'You truly are me.'

And that is all I want to be, Selena thought to herself as she saw Raj disappear into the crowd.

16

14 April 2024, 2.15 p.m.
119 King Street W, Toronto, Canada

ANGEL SIPPED HER COFFEE AND looked out the cafe window at the cold sidewalks. The temperature hovered around 7°C, and it was windy, too. She saw the school bus drop Mrs Wilkinson's daughter from school; the hot dog vendor was smoking a cigarette and a drifter was sifting through the garbage can in the far-right corner next to the street. She finished her coffee, peeled a $5 bill and placed it on the table.

As she exited the cafe, her eyes instinctively scanned the bustling street. The crisp afternoon air carried the pleasant hum of everyday life and the aroma of freshly brewed coffee, but something was amiss. Her instincts prickled—a subtle unease that she couldn't shake off. Across the street, on a worn pavement bench, a man sat with a newspaper shielding his face. His legs were crossed and his posture was relaxed, a little too casual, and his movements seemed rehearsed. He lowered the paper slightly, revealing the sharp eyes of a seasoned observer watching Angel from behind the pages.

She lingered by the door, pretending to adjust her scarf. The man was pretending to read, his hand turning pages at uneven intervals, but his focus wasn't on the print. His gaze was fixed on the top edge of the newspaper, scanning the street with the precision of a hawk. His demeanour gave it away—the polished boots, the neatly pressed trench coat and the faint bulge beneath his jacket where a holster rested.

Her chest tightened. 'It's the bloody Royal Canadian Mounted Police,' Angel muttered under her breath.

She moved slowly and deliberately, her flat heels clicking against the cobblestones as she made her way down the street. She resisted the urge to look back, though she felt his eyes follow her every move. Instead, she ducked under the awning of a shop and caught a glimpse of him lowering the newspaper, his attention now completely locked on her.

Her pulse quickened. The man on the bench wasn't there for the morning news. He was there for her. She took a deep breath and continued walking down the street towards the building where she lived.

A few minutes later, her phone rang. It was Pannu.

'Meet Jaggi at the office right away. He has some urgent work for you,' he said and disconnected. Joginder Pal was Pannu's right-hand man.

Before putting the phone back into her pocket, she opened the camera and acted like she was taking a selfie. The cop tried to move away from the camera's field of sight but was a little late. Angel clicked his photo and immediately sent it to a contact named Cassy Clark with a message. *Find out who he is. Urgent.* Then she put the phone back into her bag and went ahead.

As she approached the traffic light she increased her pace and, before the RCMP cop could react, jumped into a streetcar. The man tried to race towards the trolley but missed it by a few yards. Angel did not turn back and look lest the cop discover that his identity had been compromised. She wanted him to believe that she was unaware of his presence. She knew that if he were smart, he would return to her apartment building and wait for her there.

Angel exited the streetcar a few stops later, entered a restaurant and called Cassy. 'Did you find out?' she asked as she ordered a cappuccino.

'Yes, I did. He is David Chapman, a senior detective with the RCMP. He was a major in the military, took voluntary retirement ten years ago and worked as a gun-for-hire with a private contractor before joining the force. He has been with the RCMP for the last three years,' said Cassy.

'Anything on his personal life?' asked Angel as she kept an eye on the street outside.

'Not much, but there is an ongoing investigation onto him by the Law Enforcement Complaints Agency.'

'And he is still in the force?'

'Innocent till proven guilty? But why are you interested in him? Are you dating him?'

'No. But he is stalking me.'

'Why?' asked Cassy.

'That is what I want you to find out, Cassy,' said Angel.

The Toronto night crackled with hidden currents, the city's heartbeat pulsing through the concrete walls of the apartment building where Angel and Cassy lived.

Angel had slipped into the neighbourhood a few years ago like a ghost, her arrival marked only by the faint click of her door and the guarded flick of her eyes.

Cassy, though, was a live wire—forty years old but with the glow of a twenty-something, blending into crowds with ease. By day, she was the RCMP's telecommunications operator, her voice a lifeline in chaos, her mind slicing through panic to pinpoint the truth. But by night, she was something else entirely: an ethical hacker, her fingers weaving through digital labyrinths for private clients. It took her less than two minutes to breach the RCMP's administrative database, her custom scripts tearing through firewalls to pull up any file she wanted. She had the skill to even weave through the dark web and get data she could not find on government databases.

Cassy and Angel's first encounter sparked in the dim corridor of the building as they waited for the elevator. Angel lived in the B wing while Cassy resided in C. Angel's quiet intensity drew Cassy to her like a bee to nectar. Something about her—how she moved with coiled purpose, the mystery in her gaze—lit a fire in Cassy's gut.

Back in her apartment that evening, her laptop hummed to life, and within minutes, she'd hacked into a government server hosting public and restricted records. Angel's file flickered on the screen: 'Hmm ... a private investigator for a legal firm, orphaned and no family,' she murmured. Her lips curled into a sharp smile. 'You may be a PI, but I can see parallels in our lives burning bright, sweetie,' she murmured again. 'We are both orphans, tethered only to chosen friends, and we hide behind our carefully crafted lives.' Deep down, Cassy didn't buy Angel's cover. There was something more, something dangerous.

Over the next few years, their bond grew fast and fierce, a sisterhood forged in shared silences and late-night confessions—one true, the other manufactured by Angel, as her role did not allow her to be transparent.

Cassy pulled Angel into her world—cooking her dinners, hauling her to Montreal for rowdy Thanksgivings with her orphanage friends, their laughter cutting through the winter chill. But suspicion coiled beneath it all. Angel's requests for intel were too sharp. She often asked for names from the criminal underworld and details on terror organisations like the JeM, LeT, KHALI, all framed as 'casework'.

Cassy, committed to their bond, obliged, hacking social media accounts on platforms like X to track aliases, scraping dark-web forums for whispers of operatives, even breaching encrypted government databases for social security numbers and travel records tied to Angel's targets.

Each request deepened Cassy's unease. 'A PI doesn't dig like this, and they surely don't ask for dirt that smells like blood,' she thought. Yet Cassy couldn't pull away. Angel was her sister, her mirror, her obsession.

What Cassy didn't know—what she *couldn't* know—was the truth. Angel wasn't a PI. She was Rajnath's weapon, a deep-cover agent for KHALI, and her every step was a calculated move in a deadly game. Her 'cases' were covers for tracking targets, her questions feeding a mission soaked in betrayal. And Cassy, with her relentless curiosity and hacker's skill, was skating closer to a truth that could shatter them both.

About thirty minutes later, Cassy received another urgent call from Angel. 'Any luck with the details about Chapman, Cassy?' asked Angel.

Cassy sensed the urgency in Angel's voice. She had been noticing some strange patterns in her behaviour lately. She was coming late, leaving early and not responding to her messages that often. She wanted to ask Angel if everything was okay, but she decided to do it later when they met.

'Don't get all worked up. I will get you the details, but I can't look into David's file while I'm at the desk. I'll do it tonight at home from my personal computer and update you when we meet for dinner,' she said.

'I may or may not be home in time for dinner,' Angel replied. 'I've got a client meeting and I don't know when it will end.'

Cassy's lips curved into a slight grin. 'Fine. I'll message you the details instead. Call me when you come home. I'm working late anyway.' Something wasn't adding up, and Cassy didn't like loose ends.

She already had a plan forming in her mind. *Tonight, I will dig deeper—not just into David Chapman, but into you as well. If something is bothering you, my sister, then I need to know.* She looked at the clock above her desk and muttered, 'Two more hours, and I'm home to solve a mystery.'

The steam from Angel's coffee curled upward in lazy spirals, dissipating into the dim light of the Toronto cafe. Her eyes traced the vapour, but her mind was elsewhere, clawing at fragments of a puzzle that refused to align. Names, faces, dates, coded messages, everything was a tangle of threads. 'I am missing something,' she thought as her fingers tightened around the mug, the heat grounding her as her thoughts spun.

She remembered Rajnath's words, 'You are a deep-cover agent woven into the fabric of a terror organisation. Even a small incident should warn you that you can be compromised. Never ignore the slightest of doubts that come to your mind, as that doubt will save you.'

Her phone buzzed, a sharp jolt snapped her back to the present. The screen lit up: Pannu. Again. Her pulse quickened as she answered, keeping her voice steady despite the prickle of unease. 'Hello?'

'Where are you? Jaggi's waiting,' Pannu's voice crackled, clipped with impatience that felt too pointed, too deliberate.

Angel's throat tightened. She forced a casual tone, her mind already racing. 'Sorry, I was out running errands. On my way now.' She disconnected before he could press further, her heart thudding against her ribs. She stared at the phone, the screen now dark but screaming with questions. *Jaggi's my colleague. If he's waiting, why isn't he calling? Why is Pannu, our boss, playing messenger?*

A chill slithered down her spine, cold and unyielding. The cafe's hum—clinking cups, murmured conversations, faded as her instincts screamed. *Something's wrong.* Her thoughts spiralled, each one darker than the last. 'Pannu's tone wasn't just impatient. It was probing. Testing.' She replayed their last meeting: his lingering glance, the way he'd asked about her 'cases' with a smile that didn't reach his eyes. And Jaggi—always too quiet, too watchful. Had she missed a sign? A slip in her cover?

And then the realisation hit like a blade: *I'm exposed.* Her breath caught, a wave of nausea churning in her gut—*Pannu's on to me*. The thought wasn't a guess; it was certainty, heavy and suffocating.

She gripped the table's edge, her knuckles whitening as the room tilted. 'Yes ... no ... maybe ...' Her mind raced, sifting through every interaction, every glance. She closed her eyes and the entire last week ran past her like a movie. She went through her entire week hour by hour, and then it hit her. She remembered seeing David Chapman at a grocery store a few days back. Then the familiar car tailing her yesterday, the unmarked car idling outside her building. She'd dismissed it then, but now it clicked. 'He's not just following me. He's looking for the right spot to snuff me.'

Panic clawed at her, but Angel was trained for this. She pushed past the dizziness, her training kicking in like a switch. *Pannu asking me to meet Jaggi must be plan B. He can kill me in the quiet of the office and dispose of my body if Chapman fails.* Scenarios flashed through her mind: Jaggi confronting her in the office, Chapman ambushing her. Then it all became suddenly clear.

'They know I am smart enough to suspect exposure. And if I do, the first place I will rush to will be my apartment to pick up my things. With Pannu pressurising me by constantly calling, I will drop my guard, rush home, and there, Chapman will ambush me.'

Angel realised she had to act fast. She scanned the cafe—families, students, and a barista wiping down the counter. No one was watching—not yet—but the clock was ticking. Her fingers trembled as she dialled Rajnath, her voice a hushed rasp when he answered. 'I've been compromised. Pannu knows. An RCMP cop, David Chapman, is following me. I gave him the slip earlier today, but he'll be waiting when I get back to the building.'

Rajnath's voice was calm, a steady anchor. 'Do you have to return?'

'Yes,' she whispered, her throat dry. 'The passport, the gun, all the KHALI documents are in my safe. I can't leave them.'

He paused, calculating. 'Wait until sundown. Go home, deal with Chapman, pack your bags, destroy every physical document—shred them, burn them, whatever it takes. Then head to the airport. Be at the VIP departure gate by 8 p.m. sharp. Someone will be waiting.'

'Who?' Angel's voice was sharp, her nerves fraying.

'Don't worry. He'll find you,' Rajnath said, his tone final, unyielding.

She checked her watch: 3.30 p.m., four and a half hours until sundown. Four and a half hours to stay invisible, to outmanoeuvre Chapman and whoever else Pannu had watching. She hung up, her pulse still hammering as she paid the bill, her movements deliberate to avoid drawing eyes. Slipping out of the cafe, she pulled her hood up, the Toronto streets swallowing her as she vanished into the crowd.

Every step echoed with suspicion, every glance from a passerby a potential threat. *Pannu knows.* The words looped in her mind, a drumbeat of dread. She was supposed to be a ghost in KHALI, but now the ghost was being hunted—and the hunters were closing in.

Angel weaved through the mall's bustling crowds, her pulse a relentless drumbeat as she darted between racks of clothes and flickering storefronts. For three hours, she played the ghost, blending into the chaos of shoppers, her eyes scanning for tails while Rajnath's orders burned in her mind: *Sundown. Home. Destroy everything. Airport by 8 p.m.*

She bought nothing, her hands empty but her nerves electric. By 6.45 p.m., the sky bruised purple, and she hailed a cab, her hood pulled low as she slid into the backseat.

The cab screeched to a stop outside her building, and Angel's gaze snapped to the cafe across the street. There he was—David Chapman, RCMP cop and Pannu's attack dog, lounging with a coffee, his tinted glasses glinting like a predator's eyes. Her breath hitched, relief warring with dread. *He's not inside my apartment. No ambush. Yet.*

His stare bored into her as she stepped out, but she kept her pace steady, her face a mask of calm. Every nerve screamed as she crossed the lobby, his gaze a blade against her back. Inside her apartment, she bolted the door, her hands trembling as she dialled Cassy. 'Did you get Chapman's details?' Her voice was a taut wire.

'Some,' Cassy said, her tone clipped. 'The Canadian anti-corruption team, LECA's been sniffing around him for money laundering. There's a report linking him to a Khalistani account in the Caymans.'

'Anything else?' Angel pressed, her pulse spiking.

A heavy pause. Cassy's voice dropped, a whisper laced with dread. 'Yeah. I hacked his phone before I left the office. I sent a phishing link from the dispatcher's desk.'

'And?' Angel's grip tightened on the phone.

'There is a message to Chapman. Your photo is attached.'

Angel's breath caught, her chest constricting. 'What does it say?'

'Ice her.'

The words slammed into her like a bullet, cold and final. Her suspicions were no longer shadows—they were truth, etched in blood. 'He's been contracted to kill me,' she whispered, her voice barely audible.

'Where are you?' Cassy's tone sharpened, urgent.

'My apartment.'

'Stay there. I'm coming over.' The line went dead before Angel could protest.

Angel moved like a storm, ripping open her safe and stuffing her GLOCK, passport and a wad of cash into her backpack. She dumped every KHALI document—codes, maps, names—into the fireplace, the flames devouring them in a hungry roar. Her heart pounded as she paced, the clock ticking like gunshots. *Cassy's coming. And so would Chapman. Move.* The doorbell buzzed, sharp and jarring.

'Cassy?' Angel called, inching towards the peephole, her hand on the GLOCK. Cassy's flushed face filled the fisheye lens, her chest heaving. Angel cracked the door, but before Cassy could step inside, a gunshot tore through the hall, a deafening crack that shattered the air.

Cassy's body jerked, her eyes wide with shock as she crumpled, a red stain blooming across her chest as the bullet pierced through her body and embedded itself in Angel's wall. Within seconds, blood stained the marble tiles crimson.

Angel froze, her mind blank for a split second as Cassy's lifeless form hit the floor. Then her eyes snapped up. Chapman stood three feet away, his gun still raised, smoke curling from the barrel, his cold gaze locking onto hers. Time snapped back. Chapman's finger was about to squeeze the trigger when Angel slammed the door. The bolt clicked just as a bullet splintered the peephole, spraying wood shards inside the apartment. A loud bang followed; Chapman was kicking the door.

'Think, Angel!' she hissed, slinging the backpack over her shoulder. Another shot slammed into the door, the frame groaning. No time.

She sprinted to the window, yanking it open. A narrow parapet jutted outside, a precarious ledge snaking towards the fire escape ladder. Another bullet cracked the door, and she moved, stepping onto the parapet, the wind biting as she pressed herself against the wall. Her boots scraped the concrete, inching along the ledge, her pulse roaring.

Just as she stepped off the parapet and onto the iron fire escape ladder, a shot rang out—Chapman was at the window, his gun trained on her. The bullet grazed her ear, hot blood trickling down her neck. She didn't flinch, swinging onto the fire escape ladder, the metal cold under her hands.

The ladder's wall shielded her as Chapman fired again, the bullet pinging off brick. She climbed down, fast, her training a lifeline.

Above, Chapman's curse echoed as he vanished. 'He's taking the elevator,' she said as she reached the eighth floor. She was about to continue down when she had an idea. She kicked open the eighth-floor window and slipped back inside the building. Then she sprinted down the corridor to the C wing. The C wing service stairs were her only shot. She flew down them, her boots pounding, the backpack bouncing against her spine.

Chapman, meanwhile, barrelled towards the elevator, cursing as the display showed it crawling from the thirtieth floor. He pivoted, slamming into the B Wing service stairs. As the predator and prey ran down the two stairs, Chapman's heavy frame slowed him down, sweat beading on his brow. Angel, older but honed for survival, was a blur, her legs pumping as she hit the ground floor and burst through the rear exit, the cool night air hitting her like a slap. She looked left and took a right when she saw a taxi waiting ahead near the main road.

Chapman stumbled out seven minutes later, gasping, his gun sweeping the empty alley. Angel was gone, disappeared into the Toronto night, racing towards the airport with Cassy's blood and Chapman's bullets burned into her mind.

The clock was ticking, and the VIP gate was her only way out—if she could make it.

As the taxi zipped to the airport, her phone rang. It was Rajnath.

'Where are you?' he asked. He could hear Angel panting.

'In a taxi enroute to the airport,' she said.

'Will you make it to the airport?' Rajnath asked.

She looked at Google Maps and saw she was still twenty minutes away. 'If the gods are with me, I will. If not, tell my Angel I love her,' she said.

'In a hurry?' the driver asked looking at her in his rearview mirror.

'Yes, sir. In a terrible hurry.'

The cab driver nodded and pressed his foot on the accelerator. As the speedometer hit 120 kmph, Angel's body began to relax. She may make it after all.

Frustrated by his loss, Chapman dialled Pannu, 'She gave me the slip again.'

'Did she see you?' asked Pannu.

'Yes. I know she will head to the airport as the first thing she would want to do is get out of here,' said Chapman, trying to get his breathing back to normal.

'Then why aren't you headed for the airport, you idiot?' Pannu shouted. 'Get her somehow. You have your badge and your gun. Kill her even if she is at the airport, tell the people she is a terrorist,' Pannu shouted.

Chapman disconnected the call, cursed Pannu loudly, got into his car and sped off, racing towards the airport. Luck was in his favour because the traffic had eased for some weird reason. He floored the accelerator of his Ford and shot off like a bullet.

Five kilometres ahead of the airport, Angel's luck ran out. There was a big traffic jam ahead. She and the driver stepped out of the car and looked at the long serpentine queue of vehicles. 'Is there any other way to reach? I don't want to miss my flight, sir,' she said to the driver.

'Five hundred yards ahead, there is an exit. It is narrow, so cars are generally not allowed, but it is mostly empty. Once this traffic moves, we will take that route,' the driver said.

Angel was about to get into the car when she noticed him. Five yards behind her vehicle, Chapman was inching to the left. Their eyes made contact. 'The bastard is smart. He knows we are taking the old route,' she muttered as she got into the car, called Rajnath and told him what had happened.

'Give me your coordinates and stay calm. He is a cop. He cannot kill you in full public view. He will wait for a secluded spot and then make his move. Do you have your GLOCK?' asked Rajnath.

'I do.'

Let me see what I can do,' said Rajnath, and disconnected.

It took twenty minutes for Angel's taxi to slip into the exit. She knew it would take Chapman another ten. The driver hit the accelerator as soon as the cab eased off the highway. It was a quiet road, with hardly any traffic at night, but it was narrow. Being a taxi driver, he knew his way around the city lanes, so he manoeuvred the taxi skilfully.

They had barely travelled ten minutes down the inner road when the headlights of Chapman's Ford hit them from the back. The man knew the roads, and being a cop, he knew how to chase.

As they raced through the night, dust flew around them as the sides of the by-lanes were not tarred. Chapman was right on her tail in hot pursuit, and just as Angel's taxi whizzed past a side street and re-entered the highway, a black BMW suddenly emerged from nowhere and smashed into Chapman's Ford.

The impact caused Chapman's car to jerk, veer off the road, crash into the highway fender, and roll eleven feet below on a grassy patch. A tall man in a black suit, white tie and a black hat stepped out of the BMW, lit a cigarette, looked at the traffic whizzing past, then walked down towards the Ford.

Inside his overturned Ford, Chapman lay hanging from his seat belt. He heard the sound of feet coming closer and said hoarsely, 'Help. Help me.'

Two legs appeared near his window. After a second, a head appeared at the window. 'Good evening, Mr Chapman,' the man said.

Chapman recognised the accent and realised the man was Indian. 'Help me, I am a cop, help me please,' he pleaded as the smell of the leaking gasoline entered his nose.

The man smiled and said, 'I know you are a cop, Mr Chapman. Unfortunately, a rogue cop.' Then he aimed a silencer tipped gun and fired two shots into Chapman's face. One blew his face and the other, the rest of his head.

The man in the black suit looked at the gasoline pool near the car. Then he straightened up, dusted his suit, and walked towards his BMW. Six feet from the Ford, he stopped and turned, threw the cigarette into the gasoline pool and got into his BMW.

As the BMW hit the highway, there was a loud bang from behind and a split second later, the Ford burst into flames. Within minutes, he caught up with Angel's taxi and followed her till it entered the airport. He parked at a distance and watched Angel step out of the car. Then he called Rajnath and said, 'She's ready to come home.'

In the library of 7, Lok Kalyan Marg, thousands of miles away, Rajnath responded, 'Thank you, Surya.' Then he turned to DD, who was signing some papers Shiva was handing him, and said, 'Angel is safe. Pavak will bring her home.'

'Who did the job?' asked DD as he continued signing some papers.

'Suraj Suryavanshi,' replied Rajnath.

DD stopped signing, looked at Rajnath, then at Shiva, and asked, 'Your BCP?'

'Yes, sir. Surya is doing his primary flight training from the Seneca Aviation School at the Peterborough Airport, so I only recommended that he be sent to assist Angel,' said Shiva softly.

'Is he ready for such missions?' asked DD.

'I had my doubts, but after this job, I am convinced he is ready,' Rajnath replied.

'Ready to retire?' DD asked Shiva jokingly.

'After we complete Strike 6, sir,' replied Shiva. He collected all the papers and walked out of the library.

When Angel stepped out of the cab at Toronto Pearson International Airport, it was 8.15 p.m. She paid the driver his fare, gave him a generous tip, and walked to the VIP's departure area as per Rajnath's instructions.

No one was inside the terminal except a solo attendant who checked her ticket, took her through immigration and handed her the boarding pass. 'Please proceed for a security check,' said the man, pointing to a door on the left.

Walking through security, Angel remembered the GLOCK 19 in her backpack. She thought of disposing of the gun in a bin, but when she looked around and saw the many CCTV cameras, she decided against it. Suddenly, a man in white pants and a beige jacket appeared behind her and held her hand.

'Good evening, Angel,' he said softly.

Angel looked at him. The man was slim, about 5'8" tall and slightly bald. He had a very warm face and a mischievous smile playing on his lips. He patted her backpack and said, 'I will handle that.' Before she could ask anything, he removed her backpack and handed it to the security guard who walked around the scanning area and waited for them near the departure door.

As the man and Angel approached the screening area, an elderly security guard stepped forward and said, 'Good evening, Mr Dahia. It's nice to see you again,'

'Good to see you, too, Benjamin. How are Lara and the kids?' asked Pavak Dahia.

'No change. My daughter and grand kids have decided to live off me,' he laughed. 'Flying yourself this time, sir?' he asked as he and a female guard finished frisking them.

'Yes. My pilot is on leave, and this was an emergency,' Pavak said as the guard with the backpack handed it over to Angel and escorted them out of the gates and onto the tarmac, where a seven-seater Cessna Citation CJ4 was ready and waiting. Just before they entered the plane, Pavak shook the guard's hand and handed him an envelope. 'It will cover everyone,' Pavak said and entered the plane.

The guard thanked Pavak and then helped shut the plane door.

Inside the aircraft, Angel noticed another man sitting at the co-pilot's seat. When he turned and smiled, she noticed that he looked somewhat like Pavak, but was fairer and slightly plump. He was wearing a white Pathan kurta and pyjama. The man greeted Angel respectfully, told her to fasten her seatbelt and waited for Pavak to join him in the cockpit.

After strapping themselves in, they put on the aviation headsets. Pavak punched some buttons, turned on a few switches and spoke into his mic. 'Toronto Tower, November-One-Two-Three-Alpha-Bravo, holding short of Runway 23, ready for departure.'

The ATC tower responded. 'November-One-Two-Three-Alpha-Bravo, line up and wait on Runway 23.'

'Line up and wait on Runway 23. November-One-Two-Three-Alpha-Bravo,' repeated Pavak as he lined up the jet on the runway and waited for clearance to take off.

'November-One-Two-Three-Alpha-Bravo, Runway 23 cleared for take-off. Fly heading 180, contact Departure on 119.3,' said the ATC tower.

'Runway 23 cleared for take-off, heading 180, Departure on 119.3. November-One-Two-Three-Alpha-Bravo.'

The aircraft began taxiing down the runway. Angel looked out the window as the Cessna took off, the twinkling lights of the city becoming a gradual blur as the aircraft started gaining height. She closed her eyes and rested in her seat, her heavy breathing slowly easing.

'Toronto departure, November-One-Two-Three-Alpha-Bravo passing 2,000 for 5,000, heading 180,' said the man in the Pathan suit.

'November-One-Two-Three-Alpha-Bravo, radar contact. Climb and maintain flight level 240.'

'Climb and maintain flight level 240, direct BUF. November-One-Two-Three-Alpha-Bravo,' repeated the man in the Pathan suit.

After a few minutes, when the Cessna was smoothly cruising through the clouds, Pavak handed the charge to the man in the Pathani attire, came out of the cockpit and sat in front of Angel.

'The flight is only an hour long, and we will land at JFK, LaGuardia, at 9.30 p.m. Once we reach the hotel, we can have dinner. If you are thirsty, the minibar beside you has soft drinks.'

Taken aback by the swiftness with which everything happened in the last thirty minutes, Angel took a few seconds to recover and then asked Pavak, 'Who are you?'

'I am Pavak Dahia and that is my cousin, Safi Doha. We are part of Mr Thakur's team. We were in Peterborough for a meeting when Mr Thakur called and told us about you.'

'Pavak and Safi? Right!' muttered Angel, recollecting an old conversation she had once had with Rajnath.

'Yes, ma'am,' Pavak replied softly.

'A Canadian RCMP rogue cop was chasing me and ...'

Pavak cut her off and said, 'We are aware of everything. He has been taken care of by our team member. You can relax now.'

'Team member, as in, one of the Ghosts?' asked Angel.

'The Panther's Ghosts,' corrected Pavak gently. Inside the cockpit, Safi smiled at his cousin's response.

17

24 April 2024, 6.30 a.m.
Josefov, Mikulov, Prague

RAJ'S BREATH CLOUDED THE WINDSHIELD, a fleeting veil in the pre-dawn chill. His sedan crouched in the shadows near Prague's Spanish Synagogue, its Moorish Revival spires piercing the sky like a prayer frozen in stone. Josefov, Prague's ancient Jewish Quarter, was a paradox—compact yet vast with history, its six synagogues and weathered cobblestones whispered tales of centuries. Below, cradled by vineyards that stretched like green waves, four cottages stood vivid against the vines, their red-and-white facades glowing faintly. But Raj's gaze was a laser, fixed on Cottage 5D, home to Katerina Hunt, the woman he was shadowing.

The cottage was a deception, its rustic charm a mask. Stone and wood wove its walls, a red-tiled roof sloped gently, and a chimney breathed faint smoke. Its front garden blazed with defiant blooms—crimson, violet, gold—while ivy smothered the wire-mesh walls guarding its backyard, where fruit trees stood sentinel. Wooden shutters framed the windows, and the oak door, studded with wrought iron, dared intruders to try. It was a haven, serene and timeless, a world apart from Prague's pulsing heart. Yet Raj felt it—a darkness coiled beneath, carried by Katerina Hunt.

Ten days of surveillance had carved her routine into his mind, sharp as a blade, amplified by his Highly Superior Autobiographical Memory (HSAM). Every moment, every detail, locked in perfect clarity. Katerina was a metronome: out at 6.35 a.m., back by 4 p.m., her life a solitary waltz; no friends, no parties, no dives into Prague's neon heart. Every third day, she'd weave through a grocery store, emerging with supplies after two meticulous hours. Then, she'd drift to The Vine Whisper, a vineyard restaurant, where she'd cradle a glass of red wine, her phone a lifeline to some unseen confidant. Raj knew her every move, her every pause. But today, the tenth day, was no mere observation. Today, he would step out of the shadows.

At 6.35 a.m., the dashboard clock pulsed in time with his heart. The door of 5D swung open, and Katerina stepped into the dawn. Her red hair caught the light like fire, starkly contrasting her white dress and tan coat. Tall, mid-fifties, her beauty was a quiet storm, her movements deliberate, regal. She paused, breathing the crisp air, then strode to her yellow Volkswagen Beetle. As she slid inside, Raj glimpsed her face—sharp, unreadable, a mask of secrets. The Beetle roared to life, snaking up the hairpin road past the synagogue. Raj counted two minutes, his knuckles white, then followed.

The hunt had begun.

The morning was a high-wire act. Katerina's Beetle threaded through Josefov's labyrinth, then joined the city's waking arteries. Raj tailed her, a shadow in the traffic, his sedan anonymous. She parked at a grey office building in Vinohrady at 7.10 a.m., vanishing inside.

Raj knew her day: eight hours translating manuscripts with no disruptions. But he didn't wait. His HSAM craved input, a canvas for memory. He drove, weaving through Prague's veins, covering every lane, every alley, every cobbled turn.

Karlova's tourist-thronged curves, Malá Strana's shadowed bends, Žižkov's gritty alleys; each etched into his mind with photographic precision. A left at the butcher's on Dlouhá, a right past the chipped statue on Vítězná, the flicker of a neon sign on a nameless corner. He memorised them all as he drove, a mental map as vivid as a painting, his gift ensuring nothing faded. The entire day went into memorising every street and alley out of the city and onto the freeway. He also discovered some inner lanes by asking local traders and farmers. Satisfied that he was now in command of the layout, he returned and parked a few blocks away from her office at 3.30 p.m.

At 3.55 p.m., Katerina emerged, her coat a shield against the wind. Raj saw her enter the Beetle and reverse, so he looped back, engine humming. She drove to a grocery in Žižkov and parked outside, its neon signs flickering like a dying star. Raj left his car a block away, slipping inside after her, a spectre in a cap and scarf. He watched her glide through the aisles, her basket filling with bread, apples, cheese, a bottle of merlot. She lingered by the herbs, her fingers tracing rosemary, her eyes distant, haunted.

Two hours later, she paid and left, unaware of the eyes tracking her. Dusk painted the sky in bruises as Katerina turned towards the vineyards. Raj followed, the city's clamour fading into the hush of rolling hills and barren vines. A few minutes later, the Vine Whisper emerged, its warm lights a beacon. Katerina parked, her red hair glowing as she stepped out. A few hundred yards behind her, Raj eased into a darkened corner of the lot, killing his engine and waiting for her to settle down.

Two couples occupied tables inside, talking in hushed tones, but she preferred the solitude of the terrace. Climbing the winding stairs that led to the open terrace, she made her way to a table near the edge, her usual spot. From a distance, Raj watched her claim a corner table on the open terrace. She was alone on the large balcony, covered on one side by deep red bougainvillea.

The owner's wife appeared with a glass of her favourite red wine, placing it before her with a warm smile. Katerina thanked her, took the glass, and walked to the railing, holding the glass with one hand and dialling a number on her phone with the other.

Raj slumped in his sedan, the day's tension coiling in his chest like a lead weight. His notebook lay open on the passenger seat, its pages crammed with timestamps, routes and slivers of Katerina's life—each entry seared into his mind with the clarity of his HSAM. Prague's maze of lanes and alleys was his now, a mental blueprint he could navigate blind. But Katerina remained the enigma, her secrets bolted behind the ironbound door of Cottage 5D.

Tonight, he'd confront her. For now, he watched from the shadowed edge of the Vine Whisper's parking lot, a predator cloaked in darkness, his eyes fixed on her as she spoke to someone on speaker mode.

A sleek parabolic microphone hummed softly in his hand, its matte-black surface absorbing the faint moonlight. The device, a cutting-edge marvel, could pinpoint a whisper from fifty metres, filtering out the clink of glasses and murmur of diners to capture Katerina's voice with crystalline precision. Raj adjusted the earpiece, her words trickling through—low, measured but tinged with urgency. She stood at the edge of the terrace, talking on the speaker phone and taking occasional sips from her glass of red wine.

Oblivious to the invisible thread now tethering her secrets to the man in the car, she spoke, and Raj listened, the net tightening with every syllable.

'Hello, Andy. How are you?' Katerina's voice was soft and full of affection.

'I'm okay, love. Did you get the money?'

'I spoke to Henry. He promised to wire it tomorrow. How's the house deal coming along?'

'Everything is finalised. I can close the deal once I have the money. I miss you.'

'I miss you, too. Get everything ready, and I'll join you soon. We'll be in Greece together, forever.'

As she spoke those words, a warm feeling washed over her. Her lips curled into a contented smile, unaware that a man had joined her table. When she turned and saw Raj sitting there, her smile disappeared.

'Excuse me,' she said politely. 'This table is taken.'

'Yes, I know that now,' Raj replied, his voice smooth and calm as he casually lit the candle that had been blown out in the breeze. 'Occupied by possibly the most beautiful woman I've ever met.'

The soft light from the candle illuminated Katerina's striking features, and for a moment, Raj couldn't deny her allure. Her red hair seemed to glow like fire under the fading sun.

'Thank you,' she said, her tone cautious. 'But do I know you?'

'No,' he said, meeting her eyes. 'But I know you, Katerina Hunt.'

Her body stiffened, and before she could respond, the waitress returned to take his order.

'I'll have the same,' Raj said, pointing to the wine. Then with a disarming smile, he added, 'And dinner is on me.'

He gestured for Katerina to join him at the table. As she moved towards the chair, Raj switched on a Dictaphone inside his coat to record everything.

'Who are you?' she asked, lowering herself into the chair, her composed exterior struggling to mask the anxiety that had appeared across her face.

'That is not important. I'm interested in your connection with Andy,' Raj said. He leaned slightly forward, letting his jacket fall open to reveal the grip of a gun in his shoulder holster.

The glass almost slipped from her hand, but Raj moved like lightning and held it for her. Her gaze darted between the weapon and Raj's unflinching expression as he placed the wine glass on the table.

'Did Mr Henry Hunt send you?' she asked, her voice trembling.

'Now why would you think your husband sent me?' Raj asked, catching onto the surname.

'That bastard is not my husband. He is my wretched handler in New York.'

Raj kept quiet. He knew silence created anxiety in your prey. And it did.

'What happens now?' Katerina asked, her voice almost inaudible. 'Are you going to kill me?'

'Not if you come clean,' Raj said calmly. 'I am asking you one last time. Who is Andy?'

'Andy is my partner. We are in love.'

'What are you planning in Greece?'

'We're planning to move to Greece.'

'Why?'

'To get away from Henry.'

'That is understandable. Even I, hate Henry,' Raj acted as though he really knew Henry. And that had its effect. She relaxed a little bit. Raj handed her the wine and asked softly. 'What is your connection to Pannu?'

She paused, her lips trembling.

Raj leaned forward and said, 'Truth will save time for both of us, Katerina.'

'I have nothing to do with Pannu,' she said. 'But Henry does.'

'How?'

'Henry gives him information about important people in India.'

'Like Ajit Dhariwal?'

Her face turned ashen, and she nodded silently.

'And who gave Henry information about Dhariwal?' Raj pressed.

'Andy did. I passed it on to Henry.'

'How does Andy know Dhariwal?'

'Andy and Dhariwal were close. They worked together before he changed jobs.'

'So, Andy is your lover, and he gave you Dhariwal's details, which you gave to Henry. Who did Henry give it to?'

'I don't know. I was just told to get the information from Andy.'

'Have you heard of the Dealer?' asked Raj, his mind racing to process everything Katerina was revealing.

'No, never heard of that name,' she replied.

Raj nodded. 'How did you meet Andy?'

'Long ago, at a party in Delhi. Henry introduced us. I was working for Henry then ... as an escort.'

Raj's expression remained stoic as she continued.

'Andy was a single parent and the father of a girl. He worked in military intelligence and had just got over his wife's death at the time. Henry told me it was the right moment to get close to Andy. He paid me a lot of money and changed my name to Katerina Hunt. Masquerading as the physically abused wife of Henry, I got very close to Andy. Henry wanted me to get classified military and government information from him. Over time, I seduced him and he fell hook, line and sinker for me. But unknown to Henry, I, too, fell in love with Andy. I told him what Henry was up to and we decided to outwit him. We started giving him dumb data and got paid for it. We thought we were smart, but in reality, he was playing Andy.

He recorded every transaction and then used those recordings to blackmail Andy into feeding him real secrets.

'What happened next?'

'Once, Henry demanded information about one of Andy's closest friends. When he refused, Henry threatened to kill his daughter. Andy is very close to his daughter, so he relented. Henry passed that information to his superiors, who passed it on to an Indian politician, a chief minister. Days later, Andy's friend was killed. The death of his friend affected him. A broken man, Andy left MI, lying to Henry that he had been sacked under suspicion. Henry was furious, but there was nothing he could do as Andy had already resigned. For a long time, Henry disappeared from our lives. Andy's daughter grew up and left home, and we dreamt of a new life together. Worried that Henry would re-enter our lives someday, Andy and I decided to disappear to Greece. But we needed a lot of money to start afresh. Nowhere to go, without Andy's knowledge, I met Henry one last time, for the money. Henry told me he would give me the money if I did one last job for him. I agreed.'

'What was the job?'

'To get him details of Ajit Dhariwal's location.' She paused, sniffled and continued. 'Unable to hide anything from Andy, I told him about the deal with Henry. Initially, he was upset, but soon, he, too, realised that the only way out was the money from Henry. We convinced ourselves that even if we gave Henry Dhariwal's location details, no one could harm him as he was the NSA of India. Unfortunately, he lost his father, and in grief, he died a day later. We were worried that Henry wouldn't pay us because Dhariwal had died a natural death, but to our surprise, he paid half the amount immediately. The other half is on its way. It will reach me early tomorrow morning. Once I have the money, Andy and I will disappear from everyone's life. This is the entire truth. Please don't harm me.'

Raj's face was calm, but his voice trembled as he leaned closer, even as his eyes reflected the rage brewing inside him. The Vine Whisper's amber glow spilt across the terrace, and the vineyards stretched into the Czech night like a silent jury.

'Where is Andy now?' he demanded, his words sharp enough to cut.

Katerina's eyes, wide and haunted, flickered with fear. 'In Mumbai,' she whispered, her voice barely a thread. 'Please don't hurt him. We'll vanish, I swear. Forever.' Her plea hung in the air, fragile and desperate.

'Show me his face,' Raj said, his tone icy, unrelenting. 'Do you have a picture?'

She nodded, hands shaking as she fumbled with her phone. When the screen lit up with Andy's photograph, Raj's world tilted. His breath seized, a jagged pain ripping through his chest. Staring back was a face he'd known since childhood—Indrajit Rathode, his father's closest friend, a man woven into the tapestry of his earliest memories. The betrayal sank into him like a blade.

Tears burned Raj's eyes, spilling over as his voice broke. 'This isn't Andy,' he choked, the words raw with grief. 'This is Indrajit Rathode. He was my father's brother in all but blood. And he betrayed him. Because of him, my father was murdered.' His gaze locked onto Katerina, hatred warring with anguish. 'Your Andy is a traitor.'

Katerina's face drained of colour, her lips parting silently. 'Who ... who are you?' she stammered, her voice trembling with dread.

'Raj Pratap Rana,' he growled, each syllable a wound. 'Veer's son.'

Her hands flew to her mouth, muffling a cry. 'Veer's son?' she whispered, her eyes glistening with tears. 'No ... it can't be ...'

Raj leaned closer, his bloodshot eyes blazing with a pain that had festered for years. 'Oh, it is. And let me shatter your illusions. Dhariwal didn't die peacefully in his sleep. Thanks to your precious Andy, Henry orchestrated his death—a terrorist's bullet, paid for and planned. You and Indrajit have blood on your hands. The blood of two of India's greatest men. My father and Dhariwal. How do you sleep, dreaming of a life built on their graves?'

Katerina swayed, her body buckling as sobs tore from her throat. 'I didn't know,' she gasped, her voice breaking. 'I swear, I didn't know it was Veer ... and Andy doesn't know Dhariwal was murdered.'

'Oh yes, he knows. He was one of us, and he knows everything that happens with us. If he has told you that he doesn't know how Dhariwal died, then he is a murderer and a liar,' Raj hissed.

'I thought ... I thought we were ...' Her hands clawed at her chest, as if to rip out the guilt. 'I love him, Raj. Please forgive us.'

Her words pierced him, and Raj's resolve faltered for a moment. He saw her pain, a mirror to his own—a woman caught in a web of lies and hope, her heart as shattered as his. But the memory of Dhariwal's face and his father's lifeless body, the years of grief, roared back. 'Your love or your repentance doesn't absolve you two from your crimes,' he spat, though his voice cracked, betraying the ache within. 'You chose to betray. You chose their deaths.'

Katerina sank to her knees, tears streaming down her face. 'I'm sorry,' she whispered, her voice raw with guilt. She reached out, her trembling hand hovering, pleading. 'Forgive us, Raj. Forgive us.'

Before he could answer, a sharp crack split the night, and a gunshot echoed through the vineyards. A gasp escaped Katerina's lips as her body jerked sideways, a crimson bloom erupting across her chest. Before Raj could hold her, she crumpled to the terrace floor, blood pooling on the stone, staining the night red. Raj dropped to his knees beside her, his hands hovering over her, torn between rage and despair. 'No,' he whispered, his voice breaking. 'Where can I find Henry?'

Her eyes, fading but fierce, found his. 'Forgive ... me,' she breathed, each word a struggle. Her hand grazed his, a fleeting touch of remorse, before her eyes fluttered shut and her body went still.

Raj knelt there, trembling, her blood warm on his hands. The weight of the knowledge that his father and Dhariwal had been betrayed by their own, and his unrelenting pain pressed down, a storm of regret and loss. In the silence, he shed a tear, for Dhariwal, for his father and for the fate he had to live. Then he grabbed her phone and crawled towards the exit.

A bullet shattered the terrace door, wood splintering inches from Raj's head. His heart thundered, a primal drumbeat driving him forward. He dove into The Vine Whisper and rolled across the gleaming floor as glass exploded behind him. A sniper, concealed in the vineyard's black heart, was firing without mercy.

Raj surged to his feet, sprinting for the stairs, his breath ragged and his pulse deafening. As he burst through the main entrance and weaved through the gravel lot, bullets hissed past, grazing the air. Reaching his car, he threw himself into his BMW rental and hit the start button. The engine roared to life with a feral growl. He hit the accelerator and the tyres screamed, kicking up dust, as he tore out of the lot, gunfire fading into the Czech night.

Raj's knuckles bleached white, gripping the steering wheel as the BMW devoured Mikulov's twisting roads. His eyes darted—road ahead, rearview mirror, road again—scanning for threats. The first four hairpin bends were empty, but on the fifth, a dark SUV materialised in the mirror, its headlights predatory, closing fast.

'Henry's men,' Raj snarled, slamming the accelerator. The BMW surged, a sleek beast, weaving through narrow streets. Mikulov's late-night pulse—couples strolling, tourists lingering—erupted into chaos. Raj swerved at a circle, and a fruit cart exploded in a cascade of apples and oranges, splashing into a fountain. Lovers scattered, their screams blending with the chase's cacophony.

The SUV was relentless, a hulking shadow gaining ground. But Raj's memory was his weapon, and Mikulov's labyrinth was vivid in his mind. Every turn, every alley—Svatoplukova's sharp left, Kozí's cobbled dip, the tavern's flickering neon ... everything unfolded like a blueprint.

He jerked the wheel right, the BMW fishtailing on a slick curve, tyres screeching before clawing back traction. The SUV lumbered behind, its bulk struggling against the BMW's agility. As the cars screamed through the night, Mikulov's castle loomed, its Romanesque towers mute spectators to the drama.

A few yards ahead, Raj spotted a narrow alley, barely wide enough for his car. He gunned into it, the BMW scraping stone walls, sparks flaring like a meteor's trail. To Raj's surprise, the SUV forced its way through, metal shrieking as it ground against ancient stone.

After two minutes of metal scraping against the walls, they burst onto a wider road, and Raj saw his opening: a construction site, barricades and machinery sprawling ahead. Before him, a makeshift ramp beckoned. He floored the pedal, the BMW screaming towards it with Henry's men right on its tail.

The BMW raced up the ramp at 200 kmph, then launched itself, airborne for a heart-stopping second. Clearing the roadworks' gap in a giant leap, it landed hard, shocks groaning and tyres biting asphalt. Behind Raj, the SUV skidded to a halt, brakes wailing, trapped by the barrier.

A bald, bearded man—Henry's leader—leapt out, slamming his fist on the hood, his furious roar swallowed by distance as he watched Raj and the BMW disappear into the night.

Raj didn't look back. His memory guided him, every memorised turn a lifeline. He veered onto a rutted path, the BMW jolting through vineyards and fields until the freeway stretched open. A motel's neon sign flickered ahead, a much-needed sanctuary. Raj slid the car into the shadows, killed the engine, and checked into the motel, adrenaline still searing his veins. After a good shower and a change of clothes, he called for room service.

Over a sparse dinner, Raj dialled Rajnath, his voice taut, urgent. 'Katerina's dead. A sniper hit her. I barely got out, but an SUV full of men chased me.'

'Are you safe?' asked Rajnath.

'For the moment, yes.'

'Who were the attackers?' asked Rajnath.

'I am sure they were Henry Hunt's men.'

Rajnath sensed that Raj was holding back something, so he changed his tone and asked gently, 'What is it, son?'

'The Andy we were searching for ... It's Indrajit Rathode,' Raj said.

'What?' asked Rajnath, shocked.

'Indrajit's the mole. He betrayed my father and Dhariwal, too. He has been leaking information. I want to kill him with my bare hands,' said Raj.

Rajnath's silence was a chasm. Then, he said sternly, 'Leave Indrajit to me. Get back home safe and focus on the larger goal. Find Henry Hunt; he'll lead us to the Dealer.' His tone softened, rare and raw. 'I'm sorry about Veer, son. Don't let grief cloud you. We have a bigger war.'

'Yes, sir,' Raj said, his throat tight as he controlled his emotions. 'Understood.'

In the motel's dim room, Raj lay on the bed, GLOCK 19 heavy in his hand, its cold steel grounding him. His mind swirled as he closed his eyes. He could see his mother, Shanti, vividly—her warm smile and soothing voice. He ached to call her, to anchor himself, but Rajnath's words held him back: *We have a bigger war*.

As he lay in bed with his eyes closed, he saw Geeta smiling, telling him how much her father sacrificed to bring her up. Her voice echoed in his ears: 'There is no one better than my dad.' He opened his eyes, lay still for a few seconds, then dialled Geeta, his fingers trembling—two rings, then her sharp, familiar voice came on the line. 'So, you finally remembered me, and that too in the dead of the night,' she teased, glancing at her clock—8.00 p.m. in New York, 2.00 a.m. in Prague.

'Didn't I?' Raj said, a faint smile betrayed by his racing heart.

'Calling this late? No sleep in Prague?' Geeta's tone was light, but worry crept in.

'You knew I was here,' Raj said, steadying.

'Rajnath told us. Said he had sent you hunting moles. Did you find them?'

Raj faltered, the truth too raw. 'No,' he lied, voice tight. 'Katerina was taken out before I got answers. Wasted trip.' After a pause, he asked, 'What about you? Where are you?'

'Queens, New York,' she said. 'We found Shahid Faisal.'

Silence gripped him, the name igniting his fury. 'Geeta,' he said, low and lethal, 'don't let him die easily.'

'I won't. I will make him scream and plead for death,' she replied coldly.

'That's my girl. All the best,' said Raj and hung up.

The next morning, Raj had a quick breakfast and left the motel at 7 a.m. He knew Henry's people would be on the lookout for him at the airport, so he decided to drive to Vienna and then take a flight to Delhi. It was a four-hour drive from Prague. He checked the map on his iPhone—the weather was pleasant, but since it was a working day, there would be heavy traffic within the city limits. But the moment he entered the D1 motorway, the traffic eased. After a three-hour drive, Raj connected to the A5 motorway in Austria, which led directly to the capital. En route, he called Rajnath, who had organised an Air India flight ticket to Mumbai.

A few kilometres before the airport, he took an exit and went over the Danube riverfront, where he dumped the GLOCK 19. As he reached the parking lot of Vienna International Airport, he looked at his watch. It was 10.05 a.m.

Raj pulled his BMW to a halt in the short-term parking lot and glanced in the rearview mirror. His face was calm, but his eyes zipped amongst cars, scanning for any sign of Henry's men. Finally, he stepped out, fetched his black duffel bag from the trunk, adjusted his baseball cap to obscure his face and blended into the swarm of travellers.

Just before entering the airport, his phone pinged. It was a message from Rajnath. He had sent another ticket for Delhi, but it was on a Lufthansa flight leaving thirty minutes later. *Check into the Mumbai flight but board the Delhi flight*, the message read.

As Raj headed towards the terminal, a black SUV pulled into the lot behind him. Raj strode through the glass doors into the busy airport. He moved briskly, keeping his head down, darting through the throngs of passengers heading towards the check-in counters and security gates. As he neared the Air India counter, he heard the boarding announcement for AI154. Standing impatiently in the queue for the check-in, a reflection on a glass panel caught Raj's eye.

Two men in dark suits had entered the terminal. One was speaking into his phone, while the other observed the crowd with sharp, hawk-like eyes. Raj recognised them instantly—Henry's men. Through the glass panes, Raj saw another car screech to a halt, and four more men in uniform got out. One of them saw Raj standing at the Air India counter. Their eyes locked, and the man spoke into his earpiece. Raj knew he had been found.

Raj checked in for the Mumbai flight, then left the line and quickly walked into a souvenir shop, positioning himself behind a rotating rack of postcards and using the shop's glass display to monitor the four men. While two of them had started sweeping the terminal, their colleagues headed towards the Air India counter. They showed the staff a photograph of Raj.

Raj saw the woman nodding and pointing towards the gates for the Mumbai flight. He pulled a pair of sunglasses from a shelf and slapped them on. He grabbed an 'I Love Vienna' hoodie and paid for it in cash. The cashier eyed his rushed behaviour but said nothing. Raj pulled the hoodie over his head, hiding his face even more, walked towards the Lufthansa counter and checked in. With a business-class ticket, he went through security in a matter of minutes and then sat outside Gate 32, carefully watching Henry's men frantically looking for him.

Behind him, two uniformed men continued to wait around the Air India counter, while the others rushed towards the Mumbai flight gate.

After a while, another announcement informed passengers that boarding for the AI154 to Mumbai was complete and Gate 17 had been closed. Two men rushed to the gate, spoke to the attendant there and attempted to board the aircraft. However, the airline staff denied them entry. The guards made some calls, and soon, the airport police arrived. After a brief discussion, they were allowed to board AI154. Not long after, a second announcement over the PA system said the flight had been delayed by two hours due to technical issues.

Raj was sure that Hunt's men were checking every passenger on board A1154, and that the airline was masking the delay as a technical issue. Soon, the boarding process for the Lufthansa flight to Delhi began with an announcement: 'Passengers travelling to Delhi by Lufthansa flight LH762, please move to gate number 32 for boarding.'

Raj went up to the counter, his disguise slightly dishevelled but still holding. He handed over his boarding pass, and the attendant smiled.

'Enjoy your flight, sir,' he said.

As Raj walked down the jet bridge, on the opposite wing of the terminal, the uniformed men stepped out of AI154, disgruntled.

'He is not there,' one of them said to the leader.

The leader thought for a while and then said, 'Check if there is another flight to India now.'

One of the men ran to the house phone and made a call. Two minutes later, he came running back. 'There is a Lufthansa flight to Delhi.'

'When?' asked the leader.

'Now. Boarding for it is from Gate 32.'

The men ran towards the gate, but the plane was already taxiing on the runway.

'Stop the flight!' the leader yelled at the staff, but it was too late. The aircraft was already lined up for take-off. As the leader tried to reach the airport manager on a call, his team watched the Lufthansa flight accelerate and take off from Vienna International Airport.

18

23 April 2024, 8.30 p.m.
Empress Towers, Fifth Avenue, Manhattan, New York City

'I HAVE DECIDED TO MEET face-to-face with Bob,' said Sorosi, peering into the depths of his half-empty whisky glass.

'Why?' asked Henry, who was sitting with him and having a drink in his office.

'The council wants to end their relationship with me, but they don't dare to talk to me directly. So, they asked Bob to communicate the news. I had ignored his calls, but then I called him back yesterday.'

'What did you say?'

'I told him that it was unfair to end this long and fruitful association over a call, and that it would be nice to meet and carry out the final formalities,' said Sorosi.

'He agreed?'

'Not initially, but then I got a little emotional and he fell for it. We are having dinner at my favourite restaurant in Geneva. We will reminisce about old times, have dinner, shake hands and part ways,' Sorosi said with a wicked grin.

'That's it? You will let go of all that power, the money and the connections just like that?' asked Henry with a look of surprise.

'That's it. Why is it hard to accept?' asked Sorosi.

'Because the look on your face tells me you have some evil plan worked out, which you don't want to share with me. No problem. When is this meeting anyway?' asked Henry.

'Tomorrow,' said Sorosi. Then he looked at Henry and asked, 'Did you get Katerina?'

'Yes, I did, but I fear we lost the Indian who was with her.'

'I told you often that she is a liability, but you kept using her.'

'She was in her teens when she helped us with Veer Pratap Rana's details, and she was in her fifties when she helped us with Dhariwal's. So, you can't say she was a liability. I did not take her out sooner because I felt she did her part whenever a job was given to her. But yes, we had doubts that she was trying to escape, hence we kept a watch on her. Yesterday, our suspicions were proven right. So, I decided not to leave loose ends and got her bumped off.'

'What about the stranger she was talking to? Is he the one she plans to elope with?' asked Sorosi.

'No. She was planning to escape to Greece with Andy.'

'Damn. This means you will have to handle Andy too.'

'I plan to. He is in Greece and should be back in India soon. I will take him out there,' replied Henry.

'Again, what do we do with this stranger?'

'The way he slipped out of our hands twice shows he is a professional. I doubt that he is a RAW agent. I don't know what Katerina spoke to him, but we need to trace him. He could be back in India, for all I know.'

'I don't care where he is. Find that man and kill him,' said Sorosi definitively.

Henry nodded. 'Well, all the best for Geneva.'

The Gulfstream G650 pierced the April twilight, landing at Geneva International Airport at 6.30 p.m. with lethal precision. The tarmac shimmered gold, a cruel illusion of warmth as the jet eased into the VIP bay. Sorosi sat in the cabin, his eyes cold as winter, every gesture a study in control. When the air hostess signalled clearance, he descended, inhaling Switzerland's crisp air like a wolf scenting prey, his tailored suit a second skin for the predator within.

A black Mercedes-Benz gleamed on the tarmac, and its driver, a young woman, her smile a fragile mask, waited nervously. 'Welcome to Geneva, Mr Sorosi,' she said, opening the door, her voice steady despite the chill of his presence. He slid into the leather seat, the car a coffin for lesser men.

'I'm Nora, your assistant and chauffeur,' she said, eyes forward. 'Ms Nikolov briefed me. Your table at La Serene Table is reserved. It is 7 km and fifteen minutes away. I'll wait to drive you back; your late-night departure's cleared with the airport already.'

Sorosi's smile was a blade, sharp and fleeting. 'You are very efficient. Thank you, Nora.' He reclined, his mind a chessboard, each move plotted to perfection.

Fifteen minutes later, the Mercedes halted outside La Serene Table, a sanctuary of elegance in Geneva's quiet heart.

Its stone facade glowed under amber lights, the murmur of voices and clink of glasses a siren's call. Sorosi stepped out, his gaze sweeping the scene with a killer's clarity. This was no dinner—it was a guillotine, and he held the rope.

The restaurant's interior was a velvet trap: floor-to-ceiling windows framing Lake Geneva's glittering expanse, a pianist's notes slithering through the air. Couples whispered over wine, blind to the predator among them. A maître d' approached, his warmth tinged with caution. 'Mr Sorosi?'

'Yes,' Sorosi said, his voice smooth, deadly.

'Your terrace table awaits. Mr Azman is already there.' He took Sorosi's coat and hat, gesturing to the open-air stage beyond.

Lake Geneva's waters danced under the twilight sky, but the terrace was a siren's lure. Bob stood as Sorosi neared, his handshake firm but his eyes betraying fear, a rabbit before a wolf. Though they exchanged pleasantries, they could sense the tension crackling like static. A minute later, the whisky arrived, which eased the nerves a bit. They talked about geopolitics and family for a while to maintain the veneer of civility.

Bob loathed Sorosi. Yet, he sat before him, his jaw tight, all set to play the game. He needed Sorosi's signature on the termination letter in his coat pocket to sever ties with the Council's shell company that had hired Sorosi many years ago; a clean cut to avoid future ghosts. Bob was sure that one misstep from their end, and Sorosi would haunt them eternally.

In contrast, Sorosi was a maestro; his words precise, and his smile a stiletto.

Bob squirmed under his piercing gaze, his fingers twitching as he sipped his drink, the liquor doing little to dull his dread. The maître d' returned with lobster thermidor and grilled fish, the lemon butter sauce gleaming like liquid gold. They slowly ate the meal, a cruel counterpoint to the menace simmering beneath. As cafe crème with steamed milk and nutmeg dusting arrived, Sorosi leaned in, his voice a serpent's whisper. 'One last chance, Bob. Reconciliation? Renegotiation?'

Bob's face tightened further, his voice faltering. 'The Council's done with you, Sorosi. India was a disaster—your disaster. Millions were wasted, with no results. So, a relook is out of the question. They don't want your replacement either. I'm taking over.'

Sorosi's eyes flashed, a predator's glint. 'So, you've claimed my throne.' His unspoken thought was venom: *You bastard. You'll choke on it.*

Bob forced a smile, sliding the contract termination letter across the table. 'Sign this. It's finished.'

Sorosi's gaze lingered, his smile razor-edged. He drew a pen, signed with a flourish, and leaned back, exuding triumph. Bob exhaled, pocketing the document, relief warring with unease. Bob pushed back his chair and said, 'Wonderful evening, Sorosi. Let's stay in touch. Thanks for the dinner.'

Sorosi's voice was silk over steel. 'Indeed, a worthy last supper.' Then he stood up and extended his hand. Bob's handshake was clammy. As he shook hands, he felt a tiny prick on his palm. He pulled back his hand and looked at the small prick in his palm.

'Oops, sorry. The edges of my ring are sharp. I need to get it smoothed,' Sorosi said with a smile.

Bob wiped the tiny droplet of blood with a tissue and made a hasty exit.

Sorosi lingered, finishing his coffee, then pocketed the Topaz ring on his right hand, which had a small inner compartment that carried a tiny but potent dose of Thanatide, a synthetic neurotoxin designed to be untraceable and lethal with a precise thirty-minute delay before instantaneous death. The ring had a small needle jutting out to inject it during a handshake. Sorosi signalled for the bill, paid and returned to the Mercedes. A few seconds later, Nora drove him to the airport. En route, he dialled a number and said softly, 'Get the document in his coat pocket and destroy it.'

Unknown to Bob, who was on his way back to his home, the poison had already begun coiling through his veins. Eleven kilometres away, a bellboy helped a sweating and panting Bob to his room. As Bob staggered inside, his suit clinging to his sweat-drenched skin, the bellboy who was helping him put his hand inside his coat pocket, removed the document and quietly walked out. Stepping outside the room, he tore it to bits, dumped in into the trash bin, and walked off.

In his room, as Bob reached for the bed, a fire erupted in his chest. He felt as though a molten blade was twisting deep inside. His breath became shallow and desperate, and sweat cascaded from his brow.

The dull ache in his chest began increasing as the pain clawed at his heart, a beast breaking free. He lurched for the phone, fingers shaking, grazing the speaker button. But his legs collapsed, and he crumpled, gasping, as his vision blurred. His fingers raked the carpet, and his body thrashed as the pain increased. As his breathing became laboured, Sorosi's words, a mocking requiem, echoed in his ears: *A worthy last supper.*

Bob's lips twisted in a silent curse as his body stilled, eyes locked on the clock—1.00 a.m. Robert Azman, the Council's consigliere, was dead.

The late-morning sun streamed through the tall French windows of the stately Chateau Lumiere, casting golden beams across the hardwood floors. Leon Fink, the Council's chairman, sat in his regal home, enjoying a tranquil moment with his tea.

The peace was broken by the sharp trill of his phone. He glanced at the screen before answering, 'Good morning, Brodsky.'

The voice on the other end was grave. 'I just got a call from Bob's assistant.'

Fink's hand paused mid-air, the teacup hovering near his lips. 'What happened?'

'Bob was found dead in his bedroom this morning. His butler discovered the body.'

The teacup clinked against the saucer as Fink set it down. 'How did he die?'

'The preliminary report suggests a massive cardiac arrest. The post-mortem report is underway.' Brodsky paused, then added in a heavier tone, 'His assistant mentioned that Bob had dinner with Sorosi last night.'

Fink sat back, his brows furrowing. 'Sorosi was here? In Geneva?'

'Yes. He flew in for dinner and left immediately afterwards.'

'You're thinking what I'm thinking, aren't you?' Fink asked, an icy urgency filling his voice.

There was a second of silence before Brodsky spoke. 'It has to be him. The document we sent him is also missing. We need to act, Fink. We need to take Sorosi out fast.'

Fink's eyes narrowed. 'Not just Sorosi; Henry and Pannu as well. His entire network has to be demolished. We cannot afford to leave any loose ends.'

'Should I bring the CIA into this?'

Fink's jaw tightened. 'Yes. But keep it discreet. Just between you and your source.'

Fink ended the call and stared out of the French windows at the perfectly manicured garden. The tranquillity of Chateau Lumiere was a stark contrast to the storm brewing inside him. He knew it was time to relook at the Dealer.

19

26 April 2024, 8.30 a.m.
7, Lok Kalyan Marg, New Delhi

DD SAT AT THE HEAD of the table in his grand library, the air scented with old books and polished wood.

'Are you rested, Raj?' he asked, his voice soft with concern.

'Yes, sir,' Raj replied with a nod.

The room was charged with purpose. Rajnath, composed and thoughtful, sat to Raj's right, and Angel, who had just been introduced to Raj, sat to his left.

Raj turned towards Angel, his tone respectful and sincere. 'It is an honour to meet you, ma'am. I can't imagine what you've endured for the nation. It's truly inspiring to see you here, hale and hearty.'

Angel smiled gently. 'Thank you, Raj. Rajnath has briefed me extensively about the Ghosts, especially your missions. Your work has been nothing short of remarkable. I look forward to working with all of you.'

Rajnath, observing the exchange, added with a slight grin, 'I told you she was Dhariwal's BCP. She will be taking over from me. In fact, she will supervise Strike 6.'

Raj nodded and then said softly, 'I didn't expect this transition to happen so soon. We're still deep in Strike 6—Geeta is stalking Shahid Faisal, I'm on Henry Hunt's trail and Selena is targeting Khanda. Even then, we're no closer to identifying Henry, let alone the Dealer. Don't you think it might be better to see how these missions unfold before making the handover?'

Angel glanced at Rajnath for a moment before addressing DD. 'Sir, Raj might have a point. Perhaps Rajnath should finish these missions to ensure a smooth transition. It would help the team adapt better.'

DD leaned back in his chair, carefully considering their arguments. 'The eighteenth Lok Sabha elections have been announced. You're all aware of how many internal and external forces are aligning to ensure the BLP's loss. If we fail, India will face grave consequences. I must lead the charge to secure victory, and I need Rajnath beside me. There's no time for hesitation.'

Rajnath looked at Raj and added, his tone grave, 'The student protests in Bangladesh are spiralling out of control. The ISIS, LeT and the Rohingya Salvation Army are exploiting the anarchy. A CIA-sponsored coup is imminent. Sheikh Nasreen will likely be ousted. If she seeks asylum in India, Yunus will retaliate. There will be border skirmishes, infiltration and the works. I need to focus on that so that DD is free to campaign.' He leaned forward and said to Raj, 'Angel has to take over the Ghosts now. It's your job to help her transition quickly. The rest of the team is already in Queens hunting Faisal.'

The gravity of the situation imposed itself on Raj. Understanding the high stakes involved on every front, he looked at Angel and said confidently, 'Welcome to the Panther's Ghosts, ma'am.'

Angel smiled softly. 'Please call me Angel. It makes me feel younger.'

'Roger that, Angel.'

The trio spent the next hour bringing DD up to speed on the progress of Strike 6. Every detail was laid out, every challenge dissected. DD listened intently, his eyes scanning the faces before him. When the briefing ended, he turned to Angel.

'How do you want to proceed?' he asked her.

Angel, who had been absorbing every little detail, came forward to answer, her decisive tone revealing her innate confidence in her abilities. 'As Raj said earlier, we need a three-pronged approach. Raj will focus on Henry Hunt. Geeta, AV and Shiva will capture Shahid Faisal. Selena will target Pannu through Khanda. The immediate objective of each mission is clear: all three teams will use these targets to uncover the Dealer's identity. After a pause, she added, 'But I don't believe "one man or woman", whoever the Dealer might be, can orchestrate the destabilisation of India alone. I am convinced there's a larger entity funding and protecting the Dealer. Until we identify and neutralise that entity, new Dealers will keep emerging. That should be our ultimate goal.'

'I completely agree with Angel,' Raj said, deeply impressed with her clarity and strategic mind.

Each person absorbed the enormity of the task ahead. The fight wasn't just against individuals but against a network intent on dismantling everything they stood for. It was a web of shadows, and everyone had one question in their minds. Who is the Dealer, and who do they work for?

The white Scorpio carrying Angel and Raj cruised through New Delhi's busy streets, its occupants silent, each lost in their thoughts. Finally, Raj broke the silence. 'Where is your office?'

'I'm using Dhariwal's office,' Angel answered, her gaze fixed outside the window.

Raj was about to respond when Angel cut him off. 'Rajnath told me you found the mole in our system. You never mentioned it to me.'

'Yes, I found the mole, and yes, I mentioned it to Rajnath, and he said he will handle it,' Raj said bitterly.

'Are you convinced Andy is Indrajit Rathode?'

'A hundred per cent. I shared the voice recording when Katerina was speaking, and I saw Rathode's picture. He is Andy. I never imagined in my wildest dreams that this man would be the traitor. He was my father's friend. And to think, I gave that man a job in my company.'

The car came to a halt outside the imposing NSA building. As Raj and Angel stepped out and ascended the two flights of stairs to Dhariwal's office, the tension between them was palpable.

'He was a good man—intelligent, capable and fiercely loyal to his country,' Angel said, her voice quieter than before.

They entered the office, a room that still bore strong traces of Dhariwal's personality despite his absence. Angel walked around the desk and settled into the large chair, while Raj took a seat opposite her. The weight of their unsaid words hung between them.

Her severe gaze met his. 'Katerina's assessment was correct. He lost his way when he lost his wife.'

Raj's curiosity piqued. 'Who was his wife and what happened to her?'

'That's a long story,' Angel replied.

'I have time,' Raj said firmly. He wasn't ready to leave without knowing what had happened to Indrajit and his family.

Angel studied him for a moment, and her gaze softened. 'Many years ago, Indrajit Rathode was in military intelligence and married to a South Indian RAW agent called Sharada Iyer. Within a year of their marriage, they had a daughter. Life was perfect—until duty called. The RAW agent was assigned a long-term mission in Pakistan. It was a choice between her family and her country. She chose the latter.'

'And how did Indrajit take that?'

'She knew he would never let her go. So, with Dhariwal's help, she faked her death and left for Pakistan. Indrajit was devastated. He was left to raise their daughter alone while his wife embedded herself as a permanent mole inside LeT. After losing her, Indrajit was never the same. He abandoned his faith in god, in goodness ... in everything. He had only one goal: to ensure his daughter was well-educated. He succeeded in giving his daughter the best education, but, like her mother, she went against his wishes and joined the army, then the Special Forces. He was assigned to work with Veer but he never had his heart in the job. Then a young Katerina entered his life and you know the rest of the story.'

Raj's eyes hardened. 'I do. He gave them details about my father and Dhariwal, and got them killed. All for money and a life with a Czech escort.'

Angel's expression was sombre. 'Tragedy makes you do things which you can't even imagine. I am not justifying his betrayals but some of Indrajit's actions were done under duress. Of course, that doesn't excuse his crimes. He is responsible for Veer and Dhariwal's deaths, and I am sorry.'

'Why should you be sorry? He'll get what he deserves.'

'And I'll make sure of that,' Angel said, her voice unwavering.

'Why would you do that?' Raj countered, his tone challenging Angel. 'Rajnath has said he'll handle it.'

Angel hesitated for the briefest of moments. 'Because Indrajit is my husband. I am his wife, Sharada Iyer. And Geeta Rathode is our daughter.'

The news hit Raj so hard that it felt like the air had been knocked out of him, the revelation striking him like a punch. A few minutes passed before Raj could conjure the strength to say anything.

'Does Geeta know?' he asked softly.

'No,' Angel replied firmly. 'And I intend to keep it that way.'

Raj shook his head. 'She will find out someday.'

'Not if you and I carry the secret to our graves,' Angel said coldly. After a pause, she added 'And if Indrajit dies.'

Raj's gaze sharpened. 'What are you saying?'

Angel rose from her chair, signalling the end of the conversation. 'I'll be gone for the next two days. Hold fort until I return. I have told the New York team to keep you posted on their progress. If it's urgent, call me. Else you manage the show.' Then, as an afterthought, she added, 'This story of Indrajit dies with us.'

Raj stood, his voice low. 'Does it have to end this way? Can't he be arrested and jailed?'

Angel did not relent. 'If he lives, the pain will linger. If he dies, it ends quickly.'

She turned away and walked over to the window at the end of the room, her posture rigid. It was a silent signal that the meeting was over.

Raj got up, walked to the door, paused momentarily and looked back at her. He could see the storm of emotions she was hiding behind her composed demeanour. As he left, a wave of sorrow washed over him. He couldn't help but feel for Angel. To carry out justice meant killing her husband—a burden no soldier should ever have to bear.

The clock struck 9.00 p.m. as Indrajit Rathode dragged himself into his twenty-seventh-floor apartment in Santacruz, the weight of his sins bowing his shoulders. He longed to leave everything behind and settle down with Katerina in Greece, but deep inside, he knew his sins would haunt him till his last breath.

He flicked on the living room light, and his world fractured. There, in the amber glow of a single lamp, sat his wife, Sharada Iyer; her piercing eyes boring into him, a spectre of a life he'd mourned and cursed. Her calm was a storm's prelude, and Indrajit froze, his breath snagging in his throat. Shock, fear and a desperate flicker of joy warred within him. 'Sharada ...' he whispered, his voice a raw wound. 'Is it you? Truly, you?'

Sharada remained still, her face an unreadable fortress, her gaze unrelenting. 'Yes, Indrajit,' she said, her tone icy, stripped of warmth. 'It's me.'

He stumbled forward, tears brimming, voice quaking with a fragile hope. 'You're alive. After all these years ... you're alive.' Memories flooded him—her laughter, her warmth, the life they'd built before she vanished, leaving him to drown in grief's undertow.

Her eyes narrowed, voice cutting like a blade. 'Alive, yes. But you've erased me, Indrajit. I searched this house—no photographs, no trace of me. Nothing.'

Guilt and sorrow clawed at his chest. 'They told me you were dead,' he said, voice breaking. 'Your car ... the river ... but I saw you everywhere, Sharada. Even months after your death, I saw you everywhere. Your pictures were daggers, tearing me apart. I couldn't move on, couldn't raise Geeta in a tomb. So, I burned them. All of them. And Geeta ... She was so young. She doesn't know your face anymore.'

Sharada's voice turned sharp, a wound of its own. 'That I realised. You erased me from our daughter's memory?'

'I had to!' Indrajit's cry was anguished, tears spilling. You left us! Geeta was a toddler, clinging to me while I shattered. You abandoned us, Sharada, leaving me with lies and a void that never healed. And now, you are here to judge me?'

Her face hardened, eyes blazing with righteous fire. 'I left for a mission, for our country. I had no choice. But you—you chose betrayal. You sold our nation's soul.'

The words struck like a fist. He realised Sharada knew everything about him, and Indrajit recoiled, his voice rising, thick with pain. 'You don't know my torment! When you left, I was broken, Sharada. I gave my life to this country—my youth, my honour—and it spat back loneliness. If you'd stayed, I wouldn't be this … this monster. I made mistakes, yes, for Geeta and her future. But I'm trapped now, drowning in choices I can't unmake.'

Sharada stepped closer, her voice a chilling whisper. 'Choices? You call treason a choice? You let greed and bitterness devour you, and you are blaming me. You spilled blood—Veer's, Dhariwal's, now even Katerina's.'

'Katerina's? What do you mean by that? I spoke to her recently, and she promised me we will be together soon. What are you talking about?' asked Indrajit, panic written all over his face.

'She is no more, Inder. Shot in the head by Henry's men, and now they will gun for you.'

Indrajit let out a wail and dropped to his knees, sobbing. 'Why. Why, why?' he cried.

'Karma's a bitch, Inder. It comes back when you least expect it. What have all these betrayals led you to? You are still the same old broken man you were when you started. And Geeta? Our daughter, who's bled for this country, what will happen to her when she realises she has been raised on blood money? You were so selfish that to gain your peace, you destroyed so many lives. And that, too, of those who loved you more than you loved yourself. Now what, Inder? A confession to Geeta?'

Geeta's name broke him, and Indrajit sank into a chair, face crumpling. 'No. I will not let my shame stain her legacy. I never meant for that to happen,' he choked, tears streaming. 'I thought I could control it, keep it from her. But it grew, Sharada, it consumed me. I'm ashamed. But I can't face Geeta's hatred, can't lose the only light I have.'

Sharada's gaze softened, but her resolve was iron. 'You betrayed us all—your country, our family, Geeta. There's no redemption after all this, Inder.'

He looked up, eyes bloodshot, voice a whisper. 'What do you want? A trial? To destroy Geeta's respect for me? To break her like you broke me?'

'Justice,' she said, placing a vial of arsenic on the table. 'Two paths, Indrajit. You run till Henry's men find you, kill you like a dog and drag your name through the mud. That would surely ruin Geeta. Or you take this, and the world believes it was a heart attack. Geeta keeps her father's legacy. You keep your dignity.'

Indrajit stared at the vial, hands trembling, sins crushing him. 'You're asking me to die?' His voice was a broken plea.

'For Geeta,' Sharada said, her voice cracking, revealing her own grief. 'For our love. For the nation you swore to protect.'

Silence swallowed them, heavy with shared loss. Indrajit's gaze shifted to the vial, then to Sharada, his eyes an ocean of regret. 'I've always loved you, Sharada,' he whispered, voice thick. 'Even when I hated you, I loved you. You know that, don't you?'

Her expression faltered, a tear escaping. 'I know, Inder. I loved you, too.'

'Tell Geeta I love her. That I'm sorry,' he said.

'Tell her yourself,' said Sharda as she handed him his phone.

Indrajit sent Geeta a message: *Missing you a lot, my angel. Take care and do well.* Then he handed the phone back to Sharda and uncapped the vial. With a final, trembling glance, he swallowed the poison, its bitterness a fitting end. For a minute, their eyes met. He reached out to her and held her hand. 'Tell Geeta ...' A smile was beginning to form on his lips when his body seized, and he collapsed, a strangled gasp escaping as he clutched his chest.

Sharada knelt, lifting him gently onto the bed, tucking the sheets around him like a child. Her face was stoic, but her heart was shattered. 'I will,' she whispered, brushing his still face, a promise sealed in sorrow. She sat beside him for a long time holding his hand, remembering the happy days they had spent together, and then with a long sigh, she got up and left.

Back in her hotel room, Sharada's hands shook as she dialled Rajnath. 'It's done,' she said, her voice hollow.

'I'll handle the rest,' Rajnath said, sounding heavy. Then after a pause, he said softly, 'I'm sorry, Angel.'

'Me, too,' she replied, hanging up. Alone, tears flooded her face, a silent wail for the love lost, the broken family, and the pain that would linger forever.

20

27 April 2024, 3.30 a.m.
Willets Point, Queens, New York City

WILLETS POINT BORDERED FLUSHING, CORONA and the Flushing Meadows Corona Park in Queens. It was home to a largely immigrant Hispanic and Asian population. Originally a marshland, it was now a rundown area with auto repair shops, junkyards, homeless camps and isolated houses.

Geeta sat in a parked car away from the main road, her eyes fixed on a shabby cottage 200 yards away. It had a small, dirty quad in the front with some broken tyres lying around. An old yellow Chevrolet, probably Usman's, was parked outside.

A few hundred yards to the left of the house was Cafe Montana, where AV and Shiva sat sipping hot coffee as they kept an eye on Geeta's car and Usman's cottage. There was nothing within a half-a-kilometre radius.

Inside the cottage, Shahid Faisal was still watching TV while his sister Shaheen and his cousin Usman were fast asleep in their rooms.

Geeta shifted in her seat, trying to warm her frozen hands as she sat in her car. The dismal drizzle pattered softly against the windshield, turning the world beyond into a blurred canvas of streetlights and shadows. The temperature had dipped to 10°C, and the cold seemed like it would never go.

'Just because I'm a woman, you've left me freezing in the car while you enjoy the warmth of the cafe,' Geeta complained jokingly into her COO mic.

Shiva's amused voice crackled through her earpiece. 'No, buddy. This is on you. You're leading this mission and you insisted on being closer to Usman's house. Don't blame us.'

Geeta was about to retort when her phone buzzed. It was a message from Rajnath: *Indrajit Rathode passed away in his sleep. Heart attack.*

Geeta drew in a sharp breath. The phone trembled in her hand as the words sank in. The sounds of the rain, the hum of the car and the distant chatter from the cafe seemed to fade into silence.

Her father was gone.

A heavy sensation gripped her chest, constricting her breathing. Tears welled in her eyes, and everything around her became a blur.

She pulled out her personal phone, the one that she used when she was not working and which had only two numbers saved, Raj and her father. She opened the last message and re-read it. '*Missing you a lot, my angel. Take care and do well.*'

Memories flooded her mind: her father teaching her to ride a bike, his rare smile when she brought home her first medal, the way he would scold her but then quietly slip sweets onto her study table, her insisting on joining the army and her father pleading with her not to, at first, but finally relenting, and the look of defeat on his face when she walked out with Dhariwal to become a Ghost. Despite their complicated relationship and their ups and downs, he was still her father. Now he was gone.

The tears fell freely as she looked at pictures of her with her father. She covered her mouth with her hand, trying to stifle the sobs. For a few minutes, she let the grief take over her control, her body trembling as she leaned against the steering wheel.

Her comms buzzed. It was Shiva. 'Geeta, we got the message. We are coming.'

'No,' she said, her voice cracking. She cleared her throat and tried again, firmer this time. 'No. Stay where you are. You're back up. I'm fine.'

Shiva hesitated. 'Geeta—'

'I said I'm fine!' she snapped at Shiva. 'We have a job to do. Stay put.'

She hung up the comms, put her personal phone back into her pocket and took a deep breath, forcing herself to focus. She wiped her tears roughly with the back of her hand, took a sip of water and glanced at the house they'd been watching. The dim lights, the subtle movements inside—it all came back into sharp focus.

Her father was gone, and she couldn't change that. Nothing could. But right now, she had a mission to complete. Her country came first—always.

Geeta straightened in her seat. The grief simmered beneath the surface, but she forced it down, trying her best to replace it with resolve. She checked her watch. It was time to move.

'Guys, eyes on the cottage and the alley behind. I'm going in,' she said.

There was a pause before Shiva responded, his tone laced with concern. 'Copy that.'

Geeta drew in another steadying breath, her focus now unshakeable. She remembered Rajnath's words when she broke down after hearing about Dhariwal's death.

You are a Ghost. And Ghosts don't falter. She kept repeating it in her mind as she moved towards the house.

Geeta moved towards the back of the cottage like a shadow, barely distinguishable from the surrounding night. She gripped a serrated bowie knife in her right hand and had a GLOCK 19 strapped into her side holster.

She approached the kitchen door on padded feet and unlatched it with the knife. Slowly opening the door, she entered a corridor. The house was still, smelling of aged wood and neglect. She moved with the stealth of a predator, her footsteps soundless on the worn wooden floor. The only sounds were the faint ticking of a clock in the hallway and the soft, rhythmic breathing of a person in a room near the back door. She peeped inside and saw Shaheen fast asleep. It was a windowless room. She tiptoed inside, picked up Shaheen's cell phone from the table and walked out.

Once out of the room, she gently closed the door behind her and latched it from the outside. 'The sister's locked in,' she whispered into her COO mic and continued moving through the house.

As she passed the kitchen, littered with empty pizza boxes and unwashed utensils, she paused outside another bedroom whose door was slightly ajar. Inside, Usman lay peacefully in bed. The lights were dimmed; only a sliver of moonlight came through the curtains. Geeta's eyes glinted as she stepped forward, her hand grasping the cold, metallic handle of the knife. She approached the bed and stood over Usman, watching the soft rise and fall of his chest. Then, in a swift motion, she raised the knife and brought it down on the left side of his chest.

As the blade pierced Usman's heart, his eyes flew open with pain. Geeta drove the knife deeper as her left hand cupped his mouth, ensuring no cry for help could escape. She watched as life drained from Usman's eyes. Then, as his body went limp and the final breath escaped in a faint sigh, she withdrew the knife, wiped it clean on the bedsheet and waited for a few seconds to confirm if there was any noise of approaching feet. The house was silent. Only the steady ticking of the hallway clock.

'Usman neutralised, moving towards the target,' Geeta whispered into her mic as she closed the bedroom door and entered the dining room.

She could see flashes in the dark living room, followed by faint voices speaking in Urdu. Initially, Geeta thought the TV had been left on. But quickly, she realised the sound was coming from a phone. Geeta waited for a few seconds. Assuming Shahid was on the phone, she took a deep breath and stepped into the living room. She saw the cell phone on the floor, but there was nobody there. Geeta was about to return to the dining room when suddenly the curtains parted behind her, and Shahid jumped with a knife. Caught off guard, she could not escape the blade. Geeta screamed as Shahid plunged the knife into her right forearm, forcing her to drop her bowie knife.

'We are coming in,' came AV's frantic voice through the earpiece. 'Shiva, you take the rear. I will come in from the front.'

'No. Stand back and cover the perimeter,' Geeta said through clenched teeth as she rolled on the floor and moved away from Shahid before he could stab her again.

As Geeta stood up, she noticed that her right arm was bleeding profusely. In two quick strides, Geeta covered the distance between her and Shahid, and before he could react, dropped to the floor and kicked him on his right knee. The sound of Geeta's heavy boot cracking Shahid's kneecap was quickly followed by his scream as he buckled down. She lashed out with her left foot and planted a second kick to his right cheek. He howled as his left jaw shattered.

AV and Shiva heard Shahid's screams and burst into the living room from both sides with their GLOCKs drawn. They saw Geeta pick her bowie knife from the floor with her left hand, even as blood covered her right arm.

'Which part of "stand back" did you two not understand?' Geeta asked as Shahid somehow managed to get to his feet. AV and Shiva lowered their guns and stepped back. Geeta's grief had turned into rage, and they didn't want to get in her way.

Shahid was holding his broken jaw, still swaying on unstable feet, when Geeta swung her knife and sliced off his left ear. As the ear fell off, blood poured down his left cheek. Shahid screamed and cupped the stub that was once his ear. In a second, he was back on the floor.

As Shiva and AV watched, Geeta pulled out her GLOCK from the side holster with her left hand and calmly sat on a sofa before him. She could hear Shaheen hitting her locked bedroom door and screaming to be let out.

'After I finish with you, I will slice every part of your sister's body while she is still alive,' said Geeta with a calmness that sent shivers down AV's and Shiva's spines.

'Who are you?' Shahid whimpered. He was finding it difficult to speak because of his broken jaw.

'I am your worst nightmare,' said Geeta as she aimed the GLOCK 19 and fired a single shot. The bullet hit Shahid's other kneecap, smashing it into pieces. His agonising shrieks filled the living room.

'Shh ... We don't want to wake up the neighbours, do we?' she asked. 'Did you think Dhariwal's murder would go unpunished?'

'I am a soldier and follow my orders,' Faisal gasped. 'You kill me, but please spare my sister.'

'Beautiful. You feel for your sister but not for the thousands of innocent lives that would have died if your men had succeeded in the Ram Mandir attack.'

'Spare my sister, please,' sobbed Shahid.

'I will, if you tell me who the Dealer is,' she said.

'I have not seen the Dealer, but Hunt knows him. Henry Hunt. He is the CEO of the Open Forum Foundation. I think Henry reports to the Dealer. This is all I know. Kill me, but spare Shaheen, please,' he pleaded.

Geeta turned to AV and Shiva. 'Call Raj and tell him about Hunt. He will inform Rajnath.'

From inside the house, Shaheen banged on her door and bawled, 'Leave my brother alone, please.'

Shahid Faisal looked at Geeta and whispered, 'Please spare my sister.'

Geeta sighed and fired a second shot at Shahid's forehead. His head fell backwards and his brains were splattered across the wall. Then she walked across to Shaheen's bedroom, opened the door, pointed the GLOCK at her and said, 'Usman and Shahid are dead.'

Shaheen folded her hands and fell to her knees. 'Please don't kill me; I have nothing to do with their crimes.'

Geeta kept her GLOCK levelled at Shaheen's face for a full minute, then lowered it. 'Do you drive?' she asked.

'Yes, yes, I drive,' said Shaheen.

'I will give you ten minutes to collect your passport, clothes, money and leave; if you ever talk about us in this life, I will find you and I will kill you.'

Shaheen dashed into her room, put her things in a haversack and ran out of the house. A minute later, Usman's Chevrolet screeched and then raced off down the empty street. Geeta turned to AV and asked, raising her right arm, 'Will you just keep standing there or help me?'

Shiva found a kitchen towel to press against the wound while AV searched the house. He finally found the medicine cabinet in Shaheen's room. He returned to the living room with some cotton and loads of bandages. He wrapped the bandage tightly to stop the blood flow and then, with Shiva, helped her back to the car.

A few thousand kilometres from Queens, in a hotel room in Aerocity in Delhi, Raj sat on the edge of a sagging bed, the GLOCK-19 a cold weight in his palm. The neon glow of the opposite hotel signage seeped through the blinds, casting stripes across his face.

AV's call still echoed in his mind: *Dhariwal avenged. Shahid Faisal is dead. Henry Hunt is the CEO of OFF.* As he tried Angel's number, his heart stayed tethered to Geeta, fighting her own war amidst the mission in New York.

Raj's chest tightened as a tangle of worry and something deeper churned inside him. Something he barely dared to name. Geeta was a tempest, her courage unmatched, but every mission left scars, invisible but heavy. He'd heard the steel in her voice during their call, but beneath it, he sensed a faint tremor of exhaustion, a crack in her armour. He cared for her more than a comrade should, a quiet longing that had taken root in stolen glances and shared silences. The image of her facing Faisal alone, her hands now bloodied, twisted in his gut. He wanted to call her—to hear her voice, to know she was whole—but duty was a chain. Instead, he dialled Angel, his voice steady despite the storm within.

In her hotel room, Angel sat in the darkness. Indrajit's death still clung to her, a wound that bled with every breath. Suddenly, the screen of her phone came alive with Raj's name, stark white against the screen. She answered, her voice taut as a wire. 'Yes, Raj?'

'The NY team called. The mission was successful,' he said, his tone clipped, heavy with unspoken weight. 'Geeta neutralised Faisal. Henry Hunt is the CEO of an NGO called OFF. I am onto him.'

'Have you informed Rajnath and DD?' she asked.

'I messaged Rajnath. I think it's best if he briefs DD directly.'

'Good,' Angel said, her mind racing to the next move. 'I'll take it from here.'

She ended the call, took a long breath and dialled Geeta, her daughter, the child she'd lost to time and secrets. The line connected, and Geeta's weary but sharp voice cut through the silence.

'Angel,' Geeta said, her tone professional.

'Geeta,' Angel began, her voice softening, a mother's heart slipping through the cracks of her resolve. 'Are you okay? I heard about Faisal ... Congratulations, my angel.' She realised the slip-up and quickly covered it by changing the topic. 'I know it wasn't easy given your circumstances, but I admire your professionalism. You stayed focused on the job.' She tried to be crisp and professional, but her words quivered as she realised the Ghost she was speaking to was her only living legacy, wrapped in sheets of secrecy. Her voice sounded raw with the ache of years apart, haunted by the ghost of a toddler's laughter.

And Geeta did not miss it. She also did not miss her boss addressing her as 'Angel'. She hesitated a bit before responding because, somewhere deep inside, she had this weird feeling that she had seen Angel and heard her speak. She jerked herself back to reality and said, 'I'm fine. Then, in a happier tone, she said, 'Like my dad always said, always think of the good part. And the good part is that we now know who Henry Hunt is.'

Sharada's throat tightened. Memories flooded before her eyes: Geeta's tiny hands and giggles as she, Indrajit and Geeta went driving in his open jeep; a life stolen by duty. 'Yes. He was a good man and he loved you more than himself,' she said, fulfilling her promise to Indrajit that she would tell Geeta that her father loved her a lot.

Then the mission loomed before her, a cold reminder, and she caught herself, her tone shifting to steel. She asked Geeta to give the phone to AV. When he came on the line, she said, 'Well done. Raj has already spoken to Pavak and Safi, and they are waiting for you at the VIP section at La Guardia. But before that, take Geeta to Dr Bakshi. I have sent you the location pin. It is en route to the airport. He will fix her up and hand over the boarding passes. Hand over the weapons and the ammunition to him. We will need it again.'

'Sure.'

'Give the phone to Geeta, please.'

'Yes, Angel,' AV replied, and handed the phone back to Geeta.

'I'll wait for you to come home,' Angel said, her voice firm but threaded with a mother's fear, unspoken but palpable.

She hung up, the hotel room's silence crashing around her. Tears welled, unbidden, as she buried the longing for a daughter she could never fully hold, with duty forever standing between them.

21

30 April 2024, 10.30 a.m.
Angel's Office, NSA Headquarters, New Delhi

THE ATMOSPHERE IN DHARIWAL'S FORMER office, now Angel's, was tense, rippling just below the surface of seemingly composed faces.

Angel sat at the head of the table; the weight of command having settled firmly on her shoulders, she looked at the team before her. Her eyes lingered on Geeta, who had just returned from the field.

'I'm very sorry for your loss,' Angel began, her voice steady yet heavy with genuine, sincere empathy. 'Indrajit was a brave patriot. We will all miss him.' Then she looked at the Ghosts and said, 'A two-minute silence for the departed soul, please.'

The Ghosts closed their eyes and whispered a silent prayer for Indrajit. Having paid their respects to the departed soul, the Ghosts and Angel returned to the mission at hand.

Angel rose, crossed to the screen behind her and activated it with the press of a button. A slide appeared, summarising past operations. She turned, looked at AV and Geeta and said, 'In 2014 and 2018, we executed Strikes 1 and 2. Those missions captured the dreaded mafia don, Mohammad Adnan, jailed CM Katyal and neutralised Hafiz Salahuddin. But we lost Veer and Leela.'

She paused, her gaze lingering on Shiva. 'In 2020 to 2022, we carried out Strikes 3 and 4. We thwarted cyber-attacks on BARC and overturned the Chinese-backed government in Albania. But we lost Sniper.'

She turned to Raj. 'In 2024, during Strike 5, we freed Chin Luan, Gawa, James and all monks from Drapchi. But Lala fell.'

Unable to take the highlighting of their failures, AV lost his cool and said, 'Yes, we know we started as six and now we are down to four. You don't have to rub it in. Also—'

Angel interjected before AV could say anything further. 'With one Ghost dying in every mission, can we truly call this unit a success? In my book, success is a mission completed without casualties.' Angel looked at Raj again and returned to her chair. 'Under my command, I will not lose another Ghost. You two,' she gestured at Shiva and AV, 'are nearing the end of your active duty. I want to see you retire with honour, not in body bags.' She looked at everyone and said, 'The BCPs are in place for everyone and I would like to see you hand over to them when you are alive.'

While everyone looked on silently, Raj said, 'Selena Draevan. Rajnath's daughter. She has been recently inducted as a Ghost. She is my BCP and she has already completed her first mission in Pakistan, moving to her second in the UK.'

All eyes turned to Raj, but Geeta was the one to break the stunned silence. 'Where are you going?' she asked tersely.

Raj met her gaze. 'Nowhere. Dhariwal expected me to die before all of you.' Raj's blunt statement lingered in the air. The team sat silently, each person grappling with the brutal truth that had shaped their world. Then Shiva added, 'My BCP, Surya, is the one who saved Angel in Toronto.'

Geeta and AV exchanged glances. After a beat, AV asked, 'Who is replacing us?'

Angel shook her head. 'Not finalised yet. But no one is replacing anyone in Strike 6. However, you will be five instead of four for this mission. Selena will join you in New York.'

'What about Surya?' asked Shiva.

'He has to complete his pilot's training tests,' Angel answered. Then she cleared her throat to draw back their attention. 'I won't proceed with Strike 6 until I have your commitment that you'll all come back alive.'

'That is only possible if we have an airtight plan and we cover each other's backs, no matter what,' AV said.

Angel nodded. 'And the man entrusted to complete this mission and bring back the entire team alive is you,' Angel said in a firm voice, turning to point her index finger at Raj.

'Me? I thought the general impression was that I am emotional and not a team player?' asked Raj, surprised by Angel's decision.

'That you still are—an emotional fool. But I am confident that if anyone can bring this team back alive, it's you. When I say team, it includes *you* as well.'

She looked at the Ghosts and said, 'Raj will lead Strike 6. And this time, he won't work alone. He will ensure the mission is successful, and he *will* bring everyone back alive.'

The Ghosts looked at Raj, waiting for his response.

'That is a lot of trust you are putting in me,' Raj said to Angel. Then he looked at his team and said, 'I promise to bring each one of you back alive and kicking.'

'Good. Take a breather. We will regroup in fifteen minutes,' Angel said, dismissing them, hoping they use the time to think everything through. As they filed out and gathered at the tea stall outside the building, Angel observed them from her window. Their laughter and joking felt oddly out of place, given the tension of what lay ahead.

Her gaze rested on Geeta, who was clinging to Raj as she chatted with everyone. A lump rose in Angel's throat. 'Your love story will also end up like mine, my child. No matter how much you love him, this profession will never allow you to unite,' she whispered.

Sipping their tea outside the NSA headquarters, Geeta asked Raj about Selena. 'What's her background?'

'She's half-Russian, a polyglot, a martial arts expert and an incredible operative,' Raj said.

'Where is she now?' asked Shiva.

'In London,' Raj replied. 'She's preparing to neutralise Amrinder Singh Khanda before he assassinates her father.'

Shiva nodded. 'Will she be useful in Strike 6?'

'If we have to succeed without casualties, then we need her,' said Raj.

'So, we wait for her?' asked Geeta.

'Yes. We will wait for her.'

'How long?' asked AV.

'As long as it takes for her to finish the UK assignment,' replied Raj.

The team exchanged knowing glances. They were warriors, bound by duty and sacrifice. They knew the one rule of success was to follow their leader's command. As they climbed the steps back to Angel's office, each knew the consequences of the mission that awaited them, but, deep inside, for a change, Angel had instilled in them the confidence that they would return alive from this mission. This gave them a new strength and additional courage.

At 7, Lok Kalyan Marg, DD sat across from Rajnath, the library's atmosphere crackling with tension. DD's gaze was sharp as he asked, 'Has Angel taken charge?'

'Yes,' Rajnath replied. 'She's planning Strike 6. Raj is leading it. They're waiting for Selena to return from her assignment in London.'

'And the plan for Bangladesh? How far has the Arakan Army progressed?'

'With our army's clandestine help, the AA is advancing steadily. They're working to seize control of Rakhine state. The Rohingya Salvation Army, along with the LeT and Al-Qaeda fighters stationed there, are either being eliminated or fleeing towards Chittagong. It will progress slowly, and we have to sit tight despite the coup being orchestrated by the CIA. But, in the long run, we will achieve our goal and reinstate Sheikh Nasreen.'

DD nodded, a faint glimmer of satisfaction in his eyes. 'Good. When the coup happens, that's our window. Tell the Arakan Army to secure key regions along the border, including the Maungdaw Township. They must seize the entire 270 km Myanmar–Bangladesh border and work towards getting St. Martin's Island. Once they have control, we'll establish a military base there.'

Rajnath considered this. 'Any message for Sheikh Nasreen?'

'Yes,' DD said. 'If the situation becomes untenable, she should leave for India immediately. She can seek asylum here. We once fought Pakistan to liberate Bangladesh, but if they choose to align with Pakistan again, embrace Sharia and become a hub for terrorists, they leave us no choice. We'll have to dismantle Bangladesh for the greater good, just as we plan to do with Pakistan. You handle this while I fight to secure power here.'

Rajnath hesitated momentarily, then asked, 'What's your assessment of the situation here?'

'Our enemies, both inside and outside the country, have created a powerful narrative,' DD said. He sounded frustrated, a rare occurrence for the usually composed leader. 'They've painted me as anti-minority. They've spread the idea that if the BLP wins, I'll rewrite the Constitution. This is hurting our party's prospects.'

Rajnath interjected, 'And our allies?'

DD's lips pressed into a thin line. 'We need to keep them close. I don't see the BLP achieving a simple majority in the upcoming elections. It's going to be a coalition government.

The political battle will consume me, so you must ensure everything else stays on track.'

Rajnath gave a curt nod. No more words were needed. Both men knew the stakes. The storm wasn't coming—it was already here.

22

1 June 2024, 10 p.m.
11 Dunston Road, Smethwick, Birmingham

AMRINDER SINGH KHANDA STOOD AT the window of his spacious living room, watching the rain lash against the glass. The window was open, so he reached out to lock it and, in the bargain, soaked his shirt sleeves and the front of his trousers. His expression soured.

'It's always raining here,' he muttered, looking at his wet clothes and turning away from the storm outside.

He shuffled into his bedroom, changed into a fresh pair of dry clothes, and returned to the couch. For the past three hours, he'd been engrossed in binge-watching an American series, *I Am a Killer.* On the coffee table lay an empty beer can and a half-eaten bag of chips.

Outside, the streets of Birmingham were cloaked in eerie silence, the usual hum of life drowned by a steady drizzle. Streetlights flickered, casting an uneven, ghostly glow over the asphalt, their reflections shimmering in puddles that mirrored the city's restless sky. A distant clock tower struck ten.

Across the street, Selena Draevan lay flat on the terrace of a house right opposite Khanda's large bungalow. Dressed in black combat gear, she adjusted the scope of her field glass, her focus fixed on the dimly lit living room 200 yards away.

For a month, she had been stalking Khanda, learning his habits, lifestyle and his weaknesses. A week ago, she had hacked his phone with a cleverly disguised phishing video—a pornographic bait he couldn't resist. It had revealed his family's plans to travel to Punjab for a short holiday as the schools were closed. This was her window.

Two nights ago, she'd called Angel, her handler in this mission. 'He's running his drug business from an office at the back of his house,' she said. 'I'll have to take him out at his home. His family is leaving the day after tomorrow. That's when I'll strike.'

Tonight was that night.

Selena's thermal scope painted a clear picture: Khanda sprawled on the couch, a chip halfway to his mouth. His family had flown to India earlier in the day, leaving him to enjoy a rare moment of bachelorhood. Half an hour ago, he had ordered butter chicken and naan from a nearby diner, staying inside to avoid the rain-soaked streets.

She scanned the perimeter. One guard sat at the compound's front entrance, slouched in a wicker chair, his rifle hidden beneath a canvas raincoat. In a bedroom to the left, two more guards were playing cards, their guns propped against the wall. Outside the compound, a third guard sat in a car parked near the main gate, his semiauto pistol resting on the passenger seat beside him. Another patrolled the boundary, his silhouette flickering in and out of the shadows cast by the streetlights.

'Perimeter sweep complete,' Selena muttered. 'One tango in the car, one at the main door, two inside and one on the prowl.' She slightly shifted the scope. 'Cameras on the north and east walls are active. South side's blind. One unmanned entrance. Execution window—fifteen minutes.'

She reached into her tactical pack, retrieved a compact drone and activated it. The tiny device buzzed to life and zipped towards the bungalow. Guided by her tablet, it approached the north wall and dropped a small electromagnetic pulse charge. The device detonated silently, plunging the surveillance cameras into darkness.

With the cameras down, Selena stowed her gear and descended the terrace stairs. Crossing the street on the south side, she silently approached the parked car. The guard inside was smoking, the cigarette's ember intermittently lighting up his face.

Selena pulled a cigarette from her pocket and placed it between her lips. Leaning against the window, she asked, 'Got a light?'

The guard turned to the left, reaching for a lighter on the passenger seat. Selena struck. In a flash, her tactical knife had neatly slashed his throat. The man gasped, a soundless scream escaping as his voice box failed. He convulsed briefly before slumping in his seat. Selena eased his body on the seat, rolled up the car window and pulled on her thermal vision glasses.

Three minutes had passed since the EMP detonation. At the bungalow's southern entrance, she picked the lock and slipped inside the compound. The patrolling guard emerged moments later, his rifle slung carelessly over his shoulder.

Selena held her breath and waited behind a tree. As he passed, she stepped out, grabbed his hair and slit his throat in a single, fluid motion. The guard dropped silently to the ground.

Four minutes.

She rounded the house, her movements fluid and deliberate, her body close to the ground like a prowling hunter. The hazy night and wet grass concealed her presence as she approached the front porch. The guard in the wicker chair was engrossed in his phone, and his rifle lay idly against the armrest, forgotten in his moment of distraction.

Selena reached into her tactical belt and pulled out a nylon garrotte. In one swift motion, she stepped behind him, looped the cord around his neck and tightened it with brutal strength. The guard jolted, his hands clawing instinctively at the cord as he thrashed in a futile bid to free himself from Selena's clutches. He exhaled short, choked gasps before his body went limp, collapsing into the chair.

Selena's movements were mechanical and devoid of hesitation. She propped his lifeless form back into the chair, ensuring his head lolled naturally as though he were asleep. With a glance at the surroundings, she reached up and switched off the porch light, plunging the area into deeper shadow. Satisfied with her progress, she moved towards the living room window.

Inside, Khanda paced the room, his phone pressed tightly to his ear. His voice was subdued through the glass, but his agitation was evident. Selena checked her watch: six minutes since the EMP detonation. She shook off her nerves and prepared herself for the next part of the plan.

The metallic clang of the gate latch startled her. She froze, her body pressing instinctively against the wall. A delivery boy entered, carrying a plastic bag filled with food. He hesitated near the door, his sneakers squeaking faintly against the wet ground and rang the bell. Selena pushed herself against the darkened section of a wall, her breathing controlled and silent.

Moments later, Khanda opened the door. 'What took you so long?' he barked at the boy, snatching the bag from his hands. His face was both impatient and irritated. 'Next time, hurry up!' Khanda slammed the door shut with those words.

The delivery boy lingered momentarily before he turned and walked away, oblivious to the carnage around him.

Selena moved silently like a ghost. Circling to the side of the house, she spotted an open window, wide enough and just high enough. In one smooth motion, she vaulted up, slipped inside, and landed softly on a carpeted floor, her feet barely making a sound. The air was warm, laced with the scent of food and cigarettes. Somewhere deep inside the house, a television murmured lazily in the background. Selena stood silently and listened for a few minutes before moving low and fast. GLOCK drawn, she hugged the walls, eyes scanning every corner, every flicker of light as she progressed towards the bedroom from where she could hear male voices—laughter and the sound of cards being shuffled. She crept towards the half-open bedroom door and peered in. Two guards were seated at a table. They were in the middle of a game of cards. One had his back to her, the other was facing sideways; both too engrossed in banter to notice death approaching.

Two assault rifles leaned against the wall behind them. Too close for comfort. Selena holstered her GLOCK, realising that silence was her best ally now. She drew two throwing knives from her tactical pack, the cold steel pressing into her palms like old friends. She took a breath, squared her stance and struck.

As the first blade flew, it flashed through the air and slammed into the occipital region at the back of the neck. The power of the throw was such that the blade plunged into the suboccipital triangle just where the neck meets the skull, severing the nerves controlling the motions of the head. The guard let out a wet gasp, blood spurting across the table as his head rolled forward first before he toppled sideways.

The second guard jerked up. For a split second, their eyes locked, and then he lunged for the assault rifle, but he was too slow. The second knife was already mid-flight. It sliced the air and buried itself deep into his chest, puncturing his left lung and severing the left anterior descending artery. The guard froze for a beat. No sound came from his mouth as he choked on his blood. Within seconds, the left ventricle stopped functioning, and he collapsed forward, his blood soaking the cards.

As she retrieved her knives and wiped them clean on the guards' uniforms, she saw the red seeping into the kings and queens beneath him, but Selena didn't blink. Two kills. Four seconds passed, and silence returned to the room. Tucking the blades back into their sheaths, she turned her attention back to the hallway.

In the kitchen, Khanda had unwrapped his meal. The rich aroma of butter chicken wafted through the kitchen as he reached for a naan. Then, a faint 'ting' sounded, like a spoon dropping. He barely turned as a flashbang skidded across the tiled floor and detonated with a deafening crack.

A blinding white light flooded the room, and Khanda's reflexes, honed with years of violence, took over. He staggered backwards, his vision swimming with streaks of light and his ears ringing. Cursing loudly, he dove behind the marble kitchen counter, fumbling for the drawer where he kept his compact SMG and a smoke grenade. His hand closed around the weapon as he flung the smoke grenade over the counter. Then, with a growl of fury, he unleashed a spray of bullets into the haze, the rapid bursts ricocheting off metal surfaces, splintering wood and knocking off all the lights in the room.

In the darkness, Selena dived behind a stainless-steel cabinet, her GLOCK 19 steady in her hands. The muffled pops of her suppressed shots contrasted sharply with the thunderous roar of Khanda's SMG. Selena didn't waste her ammunition, calculating every shot to keep him pinned. As soon as the lights went off, her thermal vision glasses flickered to life, painting the room in vivid heat signatures. The swirling smoke was no obstacle to her; she could see Khanda clearly as he crouched behind the counter, the barrel of his gun glowing faintly from the heat of a continuous fire.

Khanda wasn't retreating. He was strategising. His hand darted into the drawer again and pulled out a second smoke grenade. With a vicious grin, he pulled the pin and rolled it across the floor. With two grenades in the kitchen, a thick smoke billowed out, filling every corner of the house and turning it into a claustrophobic labyrinth of shadows.

Selena adjusted her stance. The smoke was irrelevant as she had already pulled on her mask; through her glasses, she could track the subtlest of Khanda's movements. She saw him hold a wet cloth to his face and crouch low before he dashed for the open window. He thought he could escape and that the smoke would be his ally. Unfortunately for him, he was wrong.

Just as he reached the window, Selena's GLOCK barked once, a single precise shot. The bullet found its mark, tearing through Khanda's leg. Khanda screamed and collapsed to the floor in a heap. Blood seeped through his trousers and stained the carpeted floor. His SMG clattered from his grasp, spinning away as he clutched his injured limb, his face contorted in excruciating agony.

Selena moved towards him with measured steps, her GLOCK still trained on him. She stopped just out of his reach, her eyes cold behind the thermal vision glasses.

Despite his pain, Khanda's gaze burned with defiance. 'I don't know who you are, but if you think you can kill me and survive, you are wrong. There are more like me and they will come for you,' he spat, his voice hoarse with fury and desperation.

Selena tilted her head slightly, her lips curving into a faint smile. 'Maybe. But not tonight.' She stepped closer and pressed the barrel to his temple. 'Did you really think you could assassinate India's most powerful minister, Rajnath Thakur?'

Khanda's breath quickened. 'Who are you?' he asked, his bravado faltering and fear creeping into his bloodshot eyes.

Selena ignored the question and said coldly, 'After you, we will go after your boss Pannu.'

'Who are you?' he asked, his tone more of a whimper.

'Rajnath's daughter,' she whispered and pressed the barrel on his chest just where the heart was.

'Let's talk, let's ...' Khanda tried to negotiate with her, but before he could say anything more, she pulled the trigger. The muffled shot echoed briefly in the confined space, even as the bullet blew Khanda's heart. His body arched up and fell lifeless.

Selena didn't linger. She holstered her weapon and searched Khanda's pockets. From his jacket, she fished out a smartphone. Then she searched the living room and his study thoroughly. There was nothing there except a small notebook which had religious verses. She was about to put it back, thinking it was his prayer book, when her eyes fell on a sentence at the bottom of a sheet. It read: 'Rajnath, Katerina and Andy to go. Dealer has approved.' It did not take her long to realise that these three were his targets. But the question was, who were they? And why were their names along with her father's?'

She moved back to Khanda's body and unlocked his phone with a scan of his lifeless face. A cascade of unread messages and notifications came up on the screen. She quickly changed the passcode and tucked the phone and the notebook into her tactical pack.

The smoke was beginning to dissipate, revealing the chaos of the room, the disarray all around them—bullet holes peppered through the walls, broken glass glittering on the floor, and Khanda's lifeless form sprawled in a growing pool of blood. As she walked towards the main door, the faint sound of distant voices and hurried footsteps reached her ears. 'Someone lived long enough to call for reinforcements,' she muttered as she checked around the house. In the bedroom, she found the alarm switch in the hands of the dead guard with the punctured heart. 'Damn, how did I miss that?' she cursed herself.

Her heart rate quickened, but her mind remained razor sharp. There was no room for another error now.

At once, Selena reached into her pack and pulled out another flashbang. She moved to the back door, cracked it open and lobbed the device towards the south gate. A second later, there was a blinding flash and a deafening crack.

An uproar followed as the reinforcements instinctively rushed towards the source of the explosion, their weapons drawn. The distraction bought Selena the precious seconds she needed, and she managed to slip through the front gate.

It was raining quite heavily again, water drumming against the pavement in a steady rhythm. Selena darted into a narrow alley, her figure blending seamlessly with the shadows. She moved quickly but carefully, navigating the streets until she reached a small public restroom near a dimly lit junction. Stripping off her combat gear, she pulled on a pair of jeans, a plain T-shirt and a weathered brown jacket from her pack. She swapped her boots for sneakers and tied her hair into a ponytail. A glance in the cracked mirror confirmed that she now resembled any other traveller caught in the rain. Selena's transformation was complete.

She stepped out into the night, her tactical pack slung casually over her shoulder. The rain was still falling, its cool droplets mingling with the adrenaline coursing through her veins. Ahead, a line of taxis idled outside a nightclub. Selena approached the nearest one, opened the door and slid into the back seat.

'Airport, please,' she said, her voice still calm despite the events of the evening.

The driver, a middle-aged man with a cheery face, glanced at her through the rearview mirror.

'Sure thing, love,' he said with a nod, shifting the car into gear.

The engine purred to life, and they pulled away from the curb, merging into the late-night traffic. Selena rested on the faux-leather seat, her pulse gradually returning to normal. The rain traced intricate patterns on the window, each droplet refracting the glow of streetlights. Her tensed shoulders eased slightly, but Selena's senses remained alert, her mind replaying every detail of the operation.

'Music?' the driver asked.

Selena considered for a moment. 'Jazz, please,' she answered.

The driver's face lit up. 'Ah, my favourite.'

In a second, he tuned into a radio station playing smooth midnight jazz. The soft, soulful notes knit a soothing counterpoint to the relentless rain as the taxi headed to Birmingham Airport.

Selena closed her eyes for a few minutes, letting the music regulate her breathing. Somewhere in the distance, faint sirens wailed, their cries swallowed by the city's sprawling nightscape. She didn't look back. The pandemonium she had unleashed was now behind her, a fading echo. Selena remained motionless. But her mind was working overtime. The mission for the night was complete, but there was more to come. For now, though, she allowed herself a moment of calm, the jazz melodies carrying her away as the city behind her battled the chaos.

23

6 June 2024, 10 p.m.
Empress Towers, Fifth Avenue, Manhattan, New York City

DESPITE ALL THE RESOURCES AT his disposal—money, time and meticulous planning—Sorosi had failed at preventing Damodar Das from securing his position as prime minister of India for the third time. Sorosi's seething frustration seeped through every word he uttered, his eyes glowing red with barely contained fury.

Henry stood at a distance, desperate to find a silver lining. 'But the BLP didn't achieve an absolute majority on its own. They are dependent on their two big allies. Surely, that's a small victory for us?' he ventured gently while still probing.

Sorosi turned to Henry with an expression that bordered on pity. 'Victory, Henry,' he said coldly, 'is absolute. Anything less is a failure.'

He walked to the large bay windows of his plush Manhattan office. Below, the streets of New York bustled with people enjoying the first warmth of summer. Sorosi's gaze was distant, his voice dripping with disdain.

'Look at them,' he said, pointing at the passers-by. 'Happy with their simple lives. No clouds, no snow, just the sun's warmth. They revel when the season changes, but the dampness inside me has only deepened.'

He turned back to the room and downed the last of his bourbon, slamming the glass down on his desk. 'Every attempt we made to remove DD—politically or physically—failed miserably. We tried to weaken him by cutting off both his hands but managed only one: Dhariwal. Before we could act on Rajnath, Khanda was assassinated. Panjwar didn't even last long enough to act on our plans.'

Sorosi's voice grew louder, each failure adding to his mounting anger. 'We failed in Ayodhya. We failed in Gujarat. And Shahid and Usman were found murdered right here in New York, under our very noses. By the time we heard about it, it was already in the papers. The police are so dumb; they think Shaheen did it, but she's sitting in Lahore with her mouth shut.'

Henry, attempting to calm the storm, interjected. 'We did reach out to her. She said an Indian woman and two men killed Shahid and Usman.'

Sorosi's laughter was bitter and hollow. 'Exactly, Henry! That's my point. The Indians are always a step ahead. It's as though they know our every move before we even make it.'

Henry pressed on. 'You thought Bob was the leak and eliminated him. Do you now regret that decision?'

Sorosi's voice turned icy. 'So, you think killing Bob was a mistake?'

Henry shrugged. 'I don't know. What I do know is that even after his death, our operations continue to fail. Our men are dropping like flies. Johan Gunther and his team of four assassins are all we have left.'

Sorosi leaned back in his chair, his frustration finally giving way to exhaustion. 'What do you suggest, Henry? That we admit defeat?'

'My grandfather once told me, "A true leader knows when to retreat, for a battle deferred is not a battle lost, but an opportunity to return stronger than ever." Joseph, I think it's time for you to step back. Take a break, clear your mind and return with a better plan.'

Henry's words attacked Sorosi's pride. His anger flared, but he couldn't deny that the logic was indisputable. He gave a reluctant nod. 'Tell Pannu to stand down. We'll all lie low for now.'

As he got up to fix himself another drink, a thought struck him. 'By the way, did Pannu tell us how he figured out Angel was the mole?'

Henry's response was measured. 'Pannu's erstwhile CIA handler, Cross, tipped him off. After the Ayodhya mission failed, Pannu began digging into everyone connected to Shahid and Pannu but came up blank. Then he tapped Cross to audit everyone in his team. Cross uncovered Angel's link to the LeT and her sudden disappearance after the Balakot strike. It raised too many red flags.'

Sorosi frowned. 'Was she working for the RAW?'

Henry shook his head. 'No proof of that. In fact, Cross found no digital trace of her existence, past or present. Whoever she is, she's connected to someone powerful—someone capable of shielding her from every intelligence agency out there and here.'

Sorosi's head dropped into his hands. The threads were too tangled, the failures too numerous. 'Fine,' he said wearily.

'Tell Pannu to be cautious. I'm stepping away from this for now.'

Six thousand kilometres away, in a meeting room in Geneva, Leon Fink addressed the Council. 'It's confirmed. Sorosi killed Bob, and it's almost as if he wanted us to know. The man's sending us a message.'

Stephen Favier, the oldest among them, muttered, 'We should have dealt with him earlier.'

'It's not too late,' Tim Butler intervened, his tone decisive. 'If Sorosi has gone rogue, we take him out. But first, we deal with Pannu. Without Pannu, Sorosi is a toothless tiger.'

Brodsky's gaze swept across the room. 'This is bigger than Sorosi going rogue. His operations are failing. Whoever is targeting him will eventually trace the connection back to us. And if that happens, everything we've built—Apuni Malo, the Council's legacy, our global control—will collapse. The world will turn against us and against America.'

'Then we take Pannu out first,' Fink said. 'Sorosi will be vulnerable without him, and we'll finish him after.'

Brodsky nodded. 'I'll have Ethan Cross handle it.'

'Who's that again?' Favier strained to remember.

'A CIA agent and Pannu's former handler,' Butler explained.

Favier raised an eyebrow. 'And you think Cross will kill his asset?'

Brodsky smiled grimly. 'The CIA trains you to be heartless. Besides, Pannu is no longer his asset, and Cross has never turned down money. Leave it to me.'

Fink rose from the table. 'Then it's settled. Brodsky, give Cross the orders. Once Pannu is dealt with, we'll plan Sorosi's removal. Let's reconvene after dinner.'

As the Council moved to the private dining area, Brodsky stepped aside and called Cross. He answered at once.

'Good evening, Mr Brodsky. It's been a long time. How can I help you?' asked Cross.

Brodsky did not waste time. 'You need to take out Pannu.'

'No. He was my asset, and I may need him in the future too.'

'$50,000.'

'No.'

'$100,000.'

'No.'

'$120,000.'

'Done.' There wasn't a hint of hesitation in Cross's answer.

'Make sure he is dead as a door nail. No margin for errors here.'

'I never miss my targets. Moreover, Pannu has fulfilled his purpose and now has little to offer,' said Cross.

'So him being an asset and of future use was all bullshit?'

'Not really. Those were negotiation tactics. I learnt it from you, old man,' laughed Cross and hung up.

24

11 June 2024, 10 p.m.
7, Lok Kalyan Marg, New Delhi

DD STOOD AT THE HEAD of the table, his commanding presence filling the room. The Ghosts sat around him, a mix of anticipation and curiosity on their faces.

'So, you finally met your team mates,' he said looking at Selena.

Selena's eyes moved from AV, Shiva, Geeta, Pavak and Safi on the video call, and a soft smile came on her face. She turned to DD. 'Correction, sir,' she said. 'I met the Panther's Ghosts—my family.'

The room, all this while tense with formality, broke into beaming smiles.

'So you're ready for the bigger role with the rest of the team?' asked DD.

'Sir, she's more focused on taking over my role. Look at her, sir, she's even started wearing my clothes,' Raj said, winking at Selena.

Selena's laughter was unrepentant. 'Not true,' she said, looking around with mock innocence. 'My suitcase didn't make it from KL, so when he picked me up from the airport, he offered me his clothes. I agreed out of desperation, sir,' she said to DD. Then she turned to Raj and said with a childish grin, 'It's not my fault if our sizes match.'

Standing beside DD, Rajnath could not hold back. He looked proudly at his daughter, smiled and softly clapped.

After the initial friendly banter, Angel stepped forward and took over the discussion. 'Before we begin, I want to congratulate you, DD, on your third term.' Then she turned to the Ghosts and said, 'Let's give a round of applause to the Panther for winning the prime ministership for the third time in a row.'

The Ghosts clapped excitedly. His victory meant a lot to them as well, as he was their supreme mentor. DD sat down on a chair at the head of the table, his smile gracious yet restrained. 'Thank you,' he said. 'But let's not forget, the BLP fell short of the majority by thirty-one votes. The foreign and domestic interference worked to some extent. Fortunately, our allies stood firm, and we'll continue striving for the greater development of the nation.'

His gaze shifted to Rajnath, who was sitting to his left. 'But the real winner in this room is you, Rajnath. Congratulations on unearthing all the critical intel about the Bangladesh coup and helping us prepare well in advance.' He turned to the rest and said, 'Ghosts, in all likelihood, Sheikh Nasreen will be overthrown by early August. A mass uprising, predominantly led by students, will begin in July. As expected, ISIS, Al-Qaeda, the Rohingya Salvation Army and the LeT will join the protests. The CIA will plan to get Sheikh Nasreen arrested immediately after the coup, which would be by August at the latest.'

Geeta's brow furrowed. 'Where will she go?'

DD's answer was calm. 'Here. I've assured her that she'll be protected if things go south. Rajnath has worked out a confidential deal with one of the generals there who is a Nasreen loyalist. The moment the coup happens, she will be airborne and dropped here in a military chopper.'

Pavak, who had been quiet until now, spoke up. 'Yunus will protest. America will pressure us to return her to Bangladesh.'

DD's resolve didn't waver. 'We've faced pressure before. Remember the Dalai Lama? The world pressurised us. We survived then, and we'll survive now. As for Yunus, if we play our cards well, he won't last long and Nasreen will be back on the saddle in a few years.'

Safi's voice came through the secure video connection from Turkey. 'How can you be so sure? Out here, my source tells me that Turkey, China, Bangladesh and Pakistan are planning to form a bloc and hit us from all sides in the near future. Apparently, this has the US's blessings as well.'

DD's eyes met Rajnath's, and a silent understanding passed between them. Rajnath turned to Safi. 'We are aware of this plan, and we expect a short war between India and Pakistan in early 2025. The most probable scenario is that China and America will join hands in this game, but use Pakistan as their proxy to make the first move. We will be forced to retaliate.'

'Why would the Americans and the Chinese join forces against us?' asked Shiva.

'We are moving towards becoming the third-largest economy in the world. This means we will compete with China and America, which they don't want. Hence, this unholy alliance to retard our growth. They believe an Indo-Pak war, where Pakistan is funded by America through its proxy, the IMF, and armed by the Chinese and the Turks, will turn out like the Russia–Ukraine war and bleed us back to the stone age.'

'Also, the Americans and the Chinese are no friends of Yunus. This is pure economics. They won't allow anyone to come close to them. Once the competition is erased, they will fight to gain world dominance,' Angel added.

'I believe even Azerbaijan will join the anti-India bloc,' said Pavak. 'Who do we have?'

'Israel, Russia, the Arab countries and the entire African Union. Don't worry, we will beat the bloc and come out victorious,' replied DD calmly.

Selena's gaze narrowed. 'How can you be so confident?'

DD's smile was faint but knowing. Rajnath answered for him. 'We have created our own bloc.' Then he turned to Angel and said, 'Sorry for the interruption. Please continue.'

Angel gave a slight nod and switched on the television screen in the library. A slide appeared, dense with information.

'Based on the intelligence we've gathered during Strike 5, we have come to a few essential conclusions. Pannu orchestrated the attacks on DD, Dhariwal and planned assassinations for Ashok Kumar Jakhar and Rajnath. Initially, I believed the CIA was behind it, given that Pannu's handler is Ethan Cross, a CIA agent. But our deeper investigation revealed something else.'

The room was still, heavy with revelations. Angel stood at the head of the table, eyes sharp, her voice steady but charged with urgency. 'The intelligence we gathered so far points to the fact that though Pannu orchestrated the assassination attempts, he wasn't acting alone. He was acting on behalf of this fellow.'

Angel clicked, and the picture of Henry Hunt appeared on the screen. 'Geeta's interrogation of Shahid Faisal before he was killed and the data from Khanda's phone and notebook, which Selena brought us, confirms that this man is the force behind Pannu.'

'Who is he?' asked AV.

Angel exhaled slowly, as if peeling back the skin of a monster. 'His name is Henry Hunt, and he is the CEO of the Open Forum Foundation—OFF, an NGO run by the multi-billionaire Joseph Sorosi.'

Everyone froze as two new names popped up, and then Rajnath's voice cut through the tension. 'What do we have on Henry Hunt?'

'A lot,' Angel began. 'Henry Hunt was not born to privilege. He was born to pain. Raised by a single mother in rural Virginia, Henry never knew his real father. His mother worked two jobs—diner waitress by day, cleaning staff by night—to scrape enough together to send him to a local community college. But inside the house, darkness festered. His stepfather, a drunk ex-Marine with a vicious temper, molested Henry for years behind locked doors. His mother suspected, but fear made her blind.'

Angel paused and continued, 'Silence became Henry's only companion. He survived college, but just barely. Bruised, bitter and emotionally scarred, he emerged a hollow shell, desperate to escape his past. He drifted through menial jobs before landing a low-paying administrative position at an obscure humanitarian NGO in Nigeria. The salary was poor and the work thankless. But it was far from home, and his stepfather—and that was enough until Sorosi walked into his life. When Sorosi acquired the NGO and merged it into OFF, Henry came as part of the package.'

What Angel or the Ghosts were not aware of was that Sorosi had noticed something special in Henry. It was not talent, but rage. Henry came across as controlled, contained and dangerous. And Sorosi weaponised it. He groomed Henry, played him like a violin, slowly manipulating his mind, turning his pain into a tool. One night, after a drunken confession about his stepfather, Sorosi offered him a gift. 'You want to be free from your stepfather and your past?' he asked.

Henry, who now looked up to Sorosi as his mentor, answered, 'Yes.'

'Then kill him,' said Sorosi, and Henry did. He flew back to Virginia, slit his stepfather's throat with a butcher knife he picked from the kitchen while he was asleep, and returned to Lagos like nothing had happened. Sorosi covered it up completely.

From that moment, Henry was his. Mentor became god, and the murderer his disciple. Henry Hunt rose quickly. First as Sorosi's executive assistant, then his personal enforcer, and eventually, with the Council's silent approval, CEO of OFF. Today, Henry doesn't just run the world's most powerful 'philanthropic' institution, he runs Sorosi's darkest operations, which include assassinations, funding of terror cells, false flag campaigns, media blackouts—everything.

'Henry is Sorosi's shadow, sword and shield, but he is only good at executing. He is not a strategist. So, I assume that Sorosi or someone else strategises and Henry executes that person's strategy,' said Angel.

The room went dead quiet. Angel's voice was barely a whisper now. 'That's who we're up against. Not just a man with power, but a man with a purpose. A man built by trauma ... and owned by an evil strategist.'

Raj's jaw tightened. 'So, it is not just enough to break the sword before it cuts deeper. We must also find his evil wielder and god behind him,' he said.

'I agree. Also, apart from the names in Khanda's notebook, another person was mentioned,' Angel said as she clicked again, and a new screen popped up with a sentence. It read, 'Rajnath, Katerina & Andy to go. Dealer has approved.'

'I think someone called the Dealer is approving these hits. And he is the strategist,' said Geeta.

'We find the Dealer's name popping up several times in correspondence. We are convinced that Pannu reports to Henry, who takes approvals for each hit from the Dealer. Now we know Henry is the CEO of OFF, which belongs to Sorosi.'

Selena looked at Angel and asked, 'Who is Sorosi?'

'His full name is Joseph Sorosi. He is a Hungarian-born Jewish financier and philanthropist, as per public records. Still, when we dug deeper, we found that he is a polarising figure often at the centre of major conspiracy theories. The theory he is most famous for is the Black Monday conspiracy, where he allegedly manipulated the Bank of England to amass wealth, but this hasn't been proven yet.

'In the 1990s, the UK joined the European Exchange Rate Mechanism (ERM), pegging the pound sterling to the German mark within a fixed band. By the mid-'90s, economic pressures, such as post-reunification German interest rates and UK inflation, made the pound's peg unsustainable.

'Sorosi, a known figure in England then, went extremely vocal against the pound's ability to stay in the ERM, influencing the market's mood. Having done that, Sorosi's Forum Fund shorted the pound, borrowing billions and selling them for other currencies like German marks or dollars. This increased pressure on the pound's value. The Bank of England raised interest rates and spent billions buying pounds to defend the peg, but it was unsustainable. The UK finally exited the ERM, and the pound devalued. In the bargain, while the market bled, Sorosi's Forum Fund made an estimated $1 billion profit. He recently did the same with an Indian conglomerate and made millions.'

'So, he is a cunning mastermind who orchestrates financial crises, deceives the market and amasses wealth,' Geeta said.

'Our investigations reveal he is a ruthless, shadowy manipulator controlling global economies,' Angel responded.

'I understand that he is a financial manipulator, but could he be the Dealer?' asked AV.

'I don't know but one thing I know is that Sorosi is not what he projects to be.' Angel clicked again, and Joseph Sorosi's face and DD's face came up on the screen.

'What's this?' asked Shiva.

DD's expression darkened. 'This man hates me, and he says it openly. He says his hatred stems primarily from ideological and philosophical differences rather than personal animosity. But I feel that is a front he uses to hide the truth.'

'What truth?'

'The truth is that he wants to destroy India.'

'Why would an American investor, even if he hates you, want to destroy India?'

'We are moving towards becoming the third-largest economy in the world, and America does not want it to happen. I have intel that there is a deep state within America that wants to see India fail. And for this, they are even willing to join hands with China clandestinely. Destroying India economically, morally, culturally and militarily is part of this grand plan. I'm convinced that Sorosi is part of this deep state. Only time and investigation will reveal whether he is the Dealer or not.'

'And as per the RAW, he's funding the protests in Bangladesh,' Rajnath added.

'Sorosi's profile, views about India, his NGO and its CEO Henry's involvement in assassinations and anti-India operations—it all connects beautifully, but this is circumstantial. Where is the definitive proof that Sorosi is the Dealer?' Shiva asked Angel.

The energy became tense, but DD's face was impassive. He was processing the information. After a moment, he spoke in a controlled voice.

'For that, we need Henry Hunt. Strike 6 will begin with him and end with Joseph Sorosi. By then, we will know who the Dealer is.' Then he looked at Angel and said, 'You have my approval for Strike 6.'

Angel turned to the Ghosts. 'In my office in fifteen minutes.' Then, addressing Pavak and Safi, she added, 'Stay back to help finalise the logistics and escape plans.'

As Angel and the Ghosts left for her office, DD turned to Rajnath and said approvingly, 'I think Angel is a good choice to head the Ghosts.'

'Thank you. Now that she's taken over, please declare her as your new national security adviser. That way, she will have access to all the government resources and agencies.'

'I have given it some thought. The time is right. I will make the announcement tomorrow.'

25

18 June 2024, 11 p.m.
Chestnut Haven Residences, Boston, Massachusetts

THE NIGHT WAS COOL IN Boston, the wind whispering through the towering buildings. Gurwinder Singh Pannu stood by the imposing windows of his lavish twenty-fifth-floor apartment at Chestnut Haven Residences, a glass of whisky in one hand and a phone pressed to his ear. His voice was urgent and paranoid as he spoke to one of his shooters.

'No. We have been asked to lie low, which is what we will do. The BLP has won, and DD has taken charge as India's new PM. We need to wait for the right opportunity, so please be patient. And if you want money, I will wire it to you in the morning. Now, don't call me. When there is a need, I will contact you.' After disconnecting, he called Sorosi and told him that his shooters were restless and needed money. Though Sorosi explained the situation and tried to pacify him, Pannu could sense he was evading the topic.

Far above him, hidden in the shadows of a nearby rooftop, Cross peered through the scope of his M24 sniper rifle. The chill didn't bother him. His gloved fingers perfectly adjusted the scope, locking the cross hairs onto Pannu's head. Then, he pulled the trigger.

The bullet tore through the air, shattering the silence of the night, but it missed Pannu's skull by mere millimetres, embedding itself in the ornate mirror on the far wall. The sound of shattering glass startled Pannu. His phone and the whisky glass slipped from his hands, spilling amber liquid onto the carpet. He dove to the ground, his heart pounding in his chest. He was alive only because he had turned towards the TV.

On the rooftop, Cross cursed under his breath. A wind shift had thrown a spanner into his plans, but he was already reloading his rifle.

Pannu called his security guard. 'Get in here now!' he shouted.

Moments later, the guard entered the apartment. He didn't even have time to speak before another shot rang out. This time, the bullet found its mark, lodging itself in the guard's forehead. His body hit the floor with a sickening thud.

Fear paralysed Pannu momentarily as he stared at the guard's body. Then, adrenaline took over. He crawled to the door, his hands trembling as he punched his driver's number into his phone.

'Bring the car to the porch. Now!'

Pannu crawled out of the apartment and into the corridor. He pressed the elevator button and waited nervously. When its doors opened, he jumped in and pressed the button for the lobby. The doors slid shut just as Pannu slumped against the wall. He tried Sorosi's number again. No answer. Desperation clawed at him.

'The bastard,' he cursed.

Within seconds, Pannu bolted out into the lobby, ignoring the curious stares of the concierge and staff. Outside, his car screeched to a halt at the entrance. The driver threw open the door, and Pannu clambered inside.

'Drive!' he screamed at the man.

The driver hit the gas, the car lurching forward. As they sped out of the building's gates, another bullet whizzed by, denting the roof. Cross adjusted his aim. He wouldn't let this one get away.

Cross watched through his scope as Pannu's car disappeared into the steady flow of vehicles. He adjusted his position, moving to the opposite edge of the rooftop and setting up his rifle again. Pannu's panicked voice came through the phone.

'I'm being hunted! Someone's trying to kill me,' he said to Cross.

Cross suppressed a smirk. 'Who wants to kill you?' he asked, feigning concern.

'I don't know, dammit,' Pannu snapped. 'What do I do?'

Cross calmly gave him instructions. 'Tell your driver to head to the McDonald's sign in the next block. Park and go to the bus stand beside it; the killer knows your car. I'm nearby. I'll get you out.'

From his new vantage point, Cross settled behind the rifle and watched the designated spot. He saw Pannu's car stop under the golden arches. His target stepped out, his head darting nervously as he strutted towards the bus stand.

Standing under the dim glow of the bus stand's light, Pannu's mind raced. He suddenly froze, the pieces of the puzzle falling into place.

'Wait, how did Cross know I had a driver with me? It's him!' Pannu yelled, turning to run back to the car.

Cross's finger tightened on the trigger. The cross hairs settled on Pannu's moving figure. He fired with the assurance of a man who knew his job as the back of his hand. The bullet struck with surgical precision. Pannu's head exploded in a spray of red, his body crumpling to the ground. The stunned driver reached for the car door, but a second shot ended his life before he could open it.

Cross watched the scene through his scope for a moment longer, ensuring both targets were neutralised. Then he dismantled his rifle, packed it into a guitar case and left the rooftop whistling a jaunty tune. He blended into the Boston nightlife, just another musician in a city that gave the world the eponymous Boston and Aerosmith.

By the morning, the news had spread like wildfire. Every major outlet ran the story: 'Khalistani Sympathiser Gurwinder Singh Pannu Assassinated in Boston.' Theories swirled, each more explosive than the last. A section of the American media pointed fingers at the RAW, claiming the hit was a politically motivated strike to silence a vocal critic of the Indian government. Others whispered of a different motive, one rooted in Boston's underbelly. Sources close to law enforcement suggested Pannu's suspected ties to a Pakistani gang involved in drug trafficking had sparked a deadly feud with a rival local gang, the South End Vipers, over control of lucrative heroin routes. Insiders claimed a deal gone sour had led to a violent retaliation, with Pannu caught in the crossfire of a turf war.

At the White House press briefing, the spokesperson addressed the mounting allegations. 'There is no evidence to suggest India's involvement in this incident,' they stated firmly. 'Nor do we have confirmed reports linking this to organised crime at this stage. The FBI and Boston Police are conducting a thorough investigation, and we urge the public to avoid speculation.'

Back in India, Opposition parties seized the moment. They accused DD, the victorious prime minister, of killing democracy and escalating global tensions. 'This is not Gandhi's India!' they cried on every news channel. 'This is an India of aggression and violence!' Meanwhile, in Boston's immigrant communities, fear and distrust grew as rumours of gang violence clashed with geopolitical conspiracies, leaving authorities scrambling to uncover the truth behind Pannu's death.

In the library at 7, Lok Layan Marg, DD, Rajnath and Angel watched the situation unfold on television. The prime minister chuckled, his expression that of amused disdain.

Rajnath turned to him. 'You look pleased.'

A sly smile played on DD's lips. 'One less terrorist in the world to worry about.'

Angel sighed, swirling her glass of wine. 'I wish I'd pulled the trigger myself.'

Rajnath frowned, his curiosity piqued. 'If it wasn't us, then who?'

DD's expression darkened. 'Like I mentioned earlier. Either the Dealer ordered the hit or the deep state is cleaning the house. The good news is, if it is the Dealer, then they're scared we are coming for them.' Then, after a pause, he said, 'The bad news is, if it is the deep state trying to clean up loose ends, their next target will be the Dealer. We should assume the latter and get to the Dealer before they do. Move faster, Angel.'

Angel's eyes gleamed with determination. 'Consider it done.'

26

8 July 2024, 8 p.m.
Westchester County, New York

THE EVENING SUN HUNG LOW over Goldstein Mansion's sprawling estate, casting long shadows across the manicured lawns and glinting off the still surface of Schwartz Lake. The mansion itself, a colossal 12,500 square foot masterpiece of Georgian architecture, sat nestled in the quiet embrace of a 10 acre plot in northern Westchester. Its opulence was matched only by the aura of foreboding that seemed to hang over it.

Inside the mansion's west wing, Joseph Sorosi stood by the window of his study. His grey eyes scanned the tranquil lake, a creation he had commissioned in memory of his great-grandfather, Gregory Schwartz. But tonight, the stillness of its water mocked him, reflecting none of the storms that raged within.

He swirled a glass of Kentucky bourbon and replayed the chilling conversation he'd had about Pannu's killing with Henry two days earlier.

'We suspected everyone but the Council. I think they're taking our team down because we failed, and they see us as liabilities,' Henry had cautioned him.

The words echoed in his mind like the toll of a funeral bell. Shahid, Panjwar, Khanda and now Pannu—some of his most valuable operatives—all gone in rapid succession. The evidence was sparse, the motives unclear, but the crippling sense of fear that had eluded Sorosi for decades had taken hold of him. He had always prided himself on seeing the chessboard clearly, but for the first time, the pieces were shrouded in mystery.

His favourite leather recliner in the corner of the room beckoned him. It was positioned to face the lake and served as his sanctuary, his thinking chair. With a deep sigh, Sorosi crossed the large study and sank into the plush chair. The massage rollers got activated automatically, kneading away the tension in his back while its gentle hum soothed his frayed nerves.

Just as his mind had started to unwind, the shrill ringtone of the landline shattered the silence. Sorosi's eyes snapped open, narrowing at the phone's display. It was Henry.

He hit the speaker button. 'Hello, Henry,' he said, his voice tight.

'You sound tired. Are you alright?'

'I'm fine,' Sorosi said curtly, reaching for the bottle of bourbon to pour himself a second drink.

'I'm afraid I have some bad news,' Henry said, his voice dropping a notch.

Sorosi snorted. 'Receiving bad news is now a habit, Henry. Go on.'

'The latest polls are out,' Henry began. 'It's almost certain now. We'll have a Republican president next year, and the Council is already leaning towards aligning with him.'

Sorosi paused mid-sip, his jaw tightening. 'And?'

'You've been very vocal against the Republican nominee. With the Council backing the new sheriff in the offing, you're in a precarious position.'

Sorosi set his glass down with care. He wasn't a stranger to danger and risk-taking, but this was different. Any Republican president would be disastrous for him.

'Why don't you just say it outright, Henry?' Sorosi snapped. 'Now, I'm a marked man, either by the Council or by the new Sheriff. So, what do you want me to do? Disappear?'

'You're too high-profile to simply disappear. But I do suggest you stay out of the public eye. Lay low. Go somewhere quiet, till I figure a way out.'

'Susan has been saying the same thing,' he admitted softly. 'She wants us to leave all this behind and live a quiet life. Maybe it's time.'

'That's a smart move,' Henry said. 'Where will you go?'

'I don't know, Henry. They hate me in Europe and the UK. The Arab countries won't take the risk of allowing me into their country. The only place I can retire is some Asian country but then, even if the Council lets me go, DD will find me sooner or later. Susan and I need to think this through. For now, we will stay at the Bush Wolf Lodge,' Sorosi decided. 'It's remote and secure, and Susan loves it there. Contact Johan Gunther. I'll need him and his team for security.'

'Good call,' Henry said approvingly. 'I'll handle things on this end and keep you updated.'

'Before I go, is there any other bad news I should know?' Sorosi asked sarcastically.

'There's growing unrest in PoK, Gilgit Baltistan, Khyber Pakhtunkhwa and Balochistan. The Baluch Liberation Army has started attacking the Pakistani Army, and so have the Tehrik-e Taliban Pakistan from the Khyber area. Everyone is asking for liberation and the people of PoK are demanding reunification with India. If this continues, DD will annex PoK without firing a shot, and Pakistan will break into four. And that means DD will be back in power in 2029 too.'

Sorosi's grip tightened on the phone. 'It's him,' he spat. 'The attacks by the Baloch Liberation Force, the TTP, the civil unrest and now this uprising in PoK—it's all orchestrated by the RAW. DD has always dreamed of dismantling Pakistan and breaking it into regions he can dominate. If he succeeds, America's leverage in the region is gone. And even the deep state will lose its grip on India. I can leverage this and tell the Council that I am their best bet now.'

Henry's silence was telling. Finally, he said, 'Right now, you need to focus on staying alive, Joseph. There will be enough time to worry about American dominance and a conversation with the Council.'

A bitter laugh escaped Sorosi's lips. 'Stay alive? Easier said than done.'

He disconnected the call, drained his bourbon in one long gulp and dialled Susan. She answered in a second, her voice laced with panic and concern.

'Joseph, why aren't you calling me? It's been a while—'

'Pannu's death changes everything,' he admitted. 'Henry believes I'm next.'

Her voice dropped to a whisper. 'Who's after you?'

'I don't know,' Sorosi said, running a hand through his hair. 'Henry thinks it's the Council. My gut tells me it's DD.'

Susan was quiet for a moment. 'I've been telling you to walk away from all this for years. Come home. Let's go somewhere far away and start over.'

He sighed. 'You were right all along, Susan. Let's go to Bush Wolf for now. We'll plan our next steps from there.'

'What about Rebecca and the kids?' Susan asked.

'They're the least of my concerns,' Sorosi said flatly. 'Tell the chef to make Chinese tonight. I'll be home soon.'

Susan hesitated, then said with a chuckle. 'Alright. But come quickly.'

As the call ended, Sorosi stood by the window once more, staring at the lake. Its surface was still, but he knew still waters run deep. Somewhere in the depth of the shadows, enemies lurked, their blades sharp, waiting to stab him when he was least expecting it.

'Why can't you just die, DD?' he muttered, his voice heavy with venom.

Turning away, Sorosi grabbed his coat and headed for his car. Tonight, he would sit down with Susan, enjoy his dinner and plan his retreat. Deep within, he knew this was just the beginning. The hunt was far from over, and the shadows that had swallowed his allies would soon come for him.

In Imane Keram's office, the small, inconspicuous gadget beeped twice. His sharp eyes darted to the drawer where the device was kept. He slid it open, retrieved the gadget and pressed play. The recording crackled to life, and the familiar voices of Joseph Sorosi and Susan Nikolov filled the room. As he listened to their conversation, his expression darkened.

Let's go to Bush Wolf for a few days and plan our future.

Imane clenched his fingers into a fist. 'The bastard is planning to run,' he muttered with disgust. His hand hovered over the phone, indecision flickering briefly before he dialled Rebecca.

Rebecca picked up the phone on the first ring.

'Imane, what's the matter?' she asked, her voice sharp with concern.

Imane paused, knowing the turmoil his words would provoke. 'Rebeca, they're planning to escape.'

Imane didn't have to take any names. There was silence, and then Rebecca's voice came through, a single-worded response dripping with venom. 'Where?'

'I'm not sure yet,' Imane admitted. 'He mentioned going to a place called Bush Wolf for the time being. They will make their long term plans sitting there.'

Rebecca gasped, her voice shaking with fury. 'Bush Wolf is my father's hunting lodge. It's in Steuben County, deep in the woods. He built it years ago when I was a child. It's been years since the boys and I went there.'

She fell silent again, and Imane could hear her steeling herself. 'This is it. I've had enough. I have been tolerant of his betrayals for long. But now? If he is trying to abandon and run away with that whore, then I know what to do.'

'What do you have in mind, Rebecca?'

'If there is one man on earth he fears now, it is DD, and he thinks DD is after him. If that be the case, then let us make it a reality. We must let DD know precisely where to find Joseph and how to take him down.'

Imane frowned. 'Do you know who's in charge of Dhariwal's operations now?'

'Angel Singh. She took over after Dhariwal. But I have never met or spoken to her.'

Imane's mind was a whirlwind. He knew reaching Angel wouldn't be easy, but the stakes were too high to ignore and Rebecca's resolve to trap Sorosi had hardened beyond belief. 'I'll have to go through official channels, but I think I can get to her. And if I do manage to get her, I will brief her on everything before putting her on to you.'

Rebecca's tone softened, but only slightly. 'Then do it. Quickly. Every minute we delay gives Joseph a headstart.'

It was 11.30 a.m., and Angel Singh, India's new NSA, was sipping her mid-morning tea. The fragrant steam curled upward as she reviewed classified reports on her tablet. All of a sudden, her secretary's voice crackled through the intercom.

'Ms Singh, there's a man on the line—Imane Keram. He claims to be the legal counsel for Rebecca Goldstein, Joseph Sorosi's wife, and says he needs to speak with you. Do you know him?'

Angel paused, her mind flipping through hundreds of past conversations. The name definitely rang a bell. Dhariwal had mentioned Imane once, years ago, in connection with Sorosi's son's health issues. She had never met him or spoken to him. She walked across, pulled out the file on Sorosi, and flipped through the pages. When she reached the section on his family, he saw the names of Rebecca, the boys, and then ... there it was, Imane Keram. He spoke to Dhariwal about Sorosi's son's treatment.

Angel walked back to her table, sat down and said, 'Put him through.'

Moments later, a heavy voice came on the line. 'Good morning, Ms Singh. I apologise for this sudden intrusion, but I didn't know how else to reach you. This is a matter of utmost urgency. Can we speak on a secure line?'

Angel's instincts flared. 'Give me a number to call you back,' she said.

Imane provided a secure line, and Angel dialled it from her encrypted phone.

'Yes, Mr Keram, this line is secure,' she said when the line connected. 'What's so urgent?'

'Please, call me Imane,' he replied.

'Only if you call me Angel,' she countered.

'Fair enough,' Imane said. He then took a deep breath and told her everything: the intercepted conversation, Sorosi's plans to flee to Bush Wolf with Susan, and Rebecca's rage. He painted a picture of a man desperate to escape the disastrous consequences of his twisted schemes, willing to abandon his wife and children in his pursuit of self-preservation.

'She's ready to expose him,' Imane concluded. 'She wants him stopped before he ruins her and her sons' future by transferring everything to that whore ... sorry, I mean, to Susan. She's willing to speak with you directly.'

Angel listened intently, all the while calculating the implications of this deal.

When Imane finished, she said, 'I'm available to speak with Rebecca whenever she's ready.'

Imane's relief was palpable. 'Thank you, Angel. I'll arrange the conversation as soon as possible.'

By the time the call ended, Angel was already planning her next steps. She picked up her phone and dialled DD. 'We have a breakthrough.' She relayed the conversation with Imane in detail. When she finished, DD laughed gently. 'Rebecca Sorosi,' he said, almost to himself. 'She's a remarkable woman. It's a wonder she ever got entangled with that snake.'

'She's willing to help us,' Angel said. 'She wants Sorosi stopped.'

'Good,' DD said. 'Talk to her. Assure her of our support and let her know she has my regards.'

Angel smiled faintly. 'I will. This might be the leverage we've been waiting for.'

'Move quickly, Angel,' DD said, his voice serious. 'If Sorosi gets the faintest whiff of suspicion, he'll vanish.'

After the call, Angel sat quietly for a moment, staring out her office window. The pieces were finally coming together. Sorosi's carefully crafted empire of manipulation was beginning to crumble, and now, thanks to Rebecca's courage, Angel had found a way to bring him down.

She reached for her tea, now cold, and smiled grimly. The hunter had become the hunted, and this time, there would be no escape.

27

12 July 2024, 8 a.m.
Lexington Hotel, Manhattan

THE LEXINGTON HOTEL WAS AN enduring witness to Manhattan's colourful history and elegance. Situated at 511, Lexington Avenue, between the forty-seventh and forty-eighth streets, it was renowned for its blend of art deco architecture and a touch of modern sophistication.

On the eighteenth floor, Suite 1806 exuded an air of nostalgia. The walls were adorned with photographs of Marilyn Monroe and Joe DiMaggio, who had briefly resided there after their wedding. It was here that the Ghosts, minus Selena, gathered around the imposing round table to prepare for their final mission.

Angel surveyed the room, her mind already deep in the intricate details of Strike 6.

'Are we ready?' Angel uttered the words calmly. But they carried the undeniable weight of expectation.

'Absolutely,' Raj answered, poised and confident.

'Let's run through the plan one last time,' Angel instructed.

Raj nodded and spread a large, detailed map of Steuben County on the table.

'This is Steuben County,' he said, his finger tracing the vast area outlined on the map. 'Located in the Southern Tier region of New York State, it's one of the largest counties, spanning roughly 1,400 square miles. The region has rolling hills, valleys, lakes and rivers that dominate the landscape and is frequented by those who love outdoor activities.

'Now, see this secluded spot? This is Bush Wolf, a private colony and members-only hunting reserve built exclusively for billionaires and approved guests. The colony has a single entrance and exit through this gate.

'Access to Bush Wolf is tightly controlled. Each owner has a pass, as do their resident servants or caretakers. Guests require a special pass that must be arranged in advance. The shacks here are far apart, surrounded by dense woods to ensure privacy.

'Here is Shack 66. Susan and Sorosi will be staying here. The distance from the main gate to their lodge is about half a kilometre. It's a luxurious property, with a wide veranda, huge lawns and dense forests acting as a natural barrier. Now, let's study their shack.'

The Ghosts came closer to the centre of the table, their focus intensifying as Raj unfolded another map detailing the layout of Shack 66.

'The compound's gate to the main porch is about 300 yards. From the porch, you enter a large living room. To the right, two bedrooms. Further down the corridor is the master bedroom on the left. At the back, there's a dining hall leading to the kitchen. Next to the kitchen is a smaller bedroom for the housekeeper. There's an entry and exit through the kitchen as well. Behind the house, there's an open area for processing game from hunts and an outhouse with storage and a garage.'

'How did you get these maps?'

'The Steuben County map was public. Shack 66's layout came from Rebecca. She also helped Angel with coordinates and arranged for our vehicle's forty-eight-hour pass.'

'What's our cover?' Geeta asked.

'Horticulturists,' Raj replied. 'We'll pose as landscapers. Imane's men will drive us in. They've been hired for three hours. Once we're inside, they'll leave. We'll set up in the outhouse of a neighbouring shack.'

'When does Gunther's team arrive?' AV asked.

'They're already there and are staying in Shack 66's outhouse to provide security to Sorosi and Susan.' Raj paused briefly before adding another key piece of information. 'Selena confirmed it.'

The revelation caused a ripple of surprise. Geeta's brows knit. 'She's already inside?'

Raj nodded. 'She's working as Martina Diaz, the housekeeper. When Imane overheard Susan talking to an agency for a temporary housekeeper for their period of stay, he informed Rebecca, who then informed Angel. Angel registered Selena with the agency, targeting houses around Bush Wolf specifically. The agency matched both requirements and suggested Selena to Susan. Susan approved her without a second thought because her rates were so low.'

Angel's gaze shifted to Pavak and Safi, who had been silent all along. 'You two handled her credentials, right?'

'Yes. We created the background, forged the documents, hacked the verification company and responded to every inquiry from the agency and Susan.' Safi looked at Geeta and winked.

'Selena's been there for four days. She gathered intel on the house and gained the trust of Gunther's men. She's also befriended the gardener, the cook and the security staff placed at the main gate.'

'After the strike, head to the Pizza House near the Bush Wolf's entrance,' Angel took over. 'Safi will take you to Elmira Corning Regional Airport. Pavak will be waiting there. From there, a private jet will fly you to Syracuse. Commercial flights will handle the rest. I will be here until you finish the mission and return to New Delhi. Raj, when do you move?'

'This evening.'

A heavy stillness fell over the room, the complexity and enormity of the mission pressing down on each person.

Angel exhaled deeply. 'Ghosts, let's make it count.'

28

12 July 2024, 5.30 p.m.
Bush Wolf, Steuben County, New York State

THE SKY OVER BUSH WOLF was a canvas of ominous grey. Thick black clouds spread across the horizon and promised rain. They cast an eerie twilight over the area, blurring the line between day and night. Apart from the security post, there was nothing but dense woods all around. A broad dirt path ran beyond the gate and turned right into the forest. A grey van with 'Floraverde Botanicals' stencilled in fading yellow on both sides rolled up to the colony's main gate.

A security guard stepped out from the check post, smiling as she approached the van. The driver, a middle-aged Mexican man, rolled down his window.

'Gate pass, please?' she asked politely, her tone friendly but professional.

'*Aquí tiene, señora,*' the driver replied, handing her a piece of folded paper. The guard examined it carefully, her eyes darting between the document and the van. She peered inside and noticed the passengers—four workers dressed in green overalls, their faces blank and postures rigid. The company's name was embroidered on their uniforms in bright yellow.

Satisfied, she stepped back and said, 'No vehicles allowed inside the colony. You'll need to park in the shared lot and use a buggy to move your materials. Turn right after you enter, go past the community centre and you will find the parking lot.'

The driver tipped his head. 'Gracias,' he said with a faint smile, shifting gears and steering into the colony.

The van crept along the dirt path, its tyres squelching softly against the wet ground. It passed the community centre, where lights were on, and couples sat around tables, drinking and chatting as waiters ran in and out of the back kitchen. The driver turned right and continued for another 500 yards before pulling into a secluded corner of the shared parking lot. He switched off the engine and waited.

The area was quiet. Too quiet. After scanning the vicinity, he whispered under his breath, '*No hay nadie, puedes salir.*'

The van's back doors opened silently, and the Ghosts stepped out. The overalls hung loosely over their bodies, hiding the bulk of their gear. Without a word, they began unloading large green bags marked with the word 'fertilizante' in bold letters. Each bag was hefted onto a buggy parked nearby. The driver, now their accomplice, climbed into the buggy and took the wheel, guiding it towards a narrow trail leading into the woods.

The buggy's electric motor hummed softly as it trundled down the path, tyres brushing against the forest floor strewn with damp leaves. It took them fifteen minutes to find their way through the dense forest. The shadows of the trees seemed to stretch and merge into a single mass of darkness. A drizzle began, pattering gently against the canopy above.

When they reached Shack 66, the team disembarked. The shack was large, but its wooden structure was weathered and falling apart in places, giving the impression that it was not used much. Nonetheless, it was the perfect hideout—isolated and discreet. The solar-powered porch lights cast a faint glow, a poor match for the encroaching night.

Geeta moved quickly, pulling a compact drone from her bag. She unfolded its wings and instantly powered it on. Using her tablet and a pre-loaded GPS map, she navigates the drone to the shack's side, where the surveillance equipment was stored. The drone hovered briefly, its tiny camera capturing every detail of the wall before she activated the payload. With a silent burst, the EMP charge disabled the lights, plunging the shack into darkness.

The team moved as one and reached the outhouse behind the shack, where AV pulled out his lock-picking tools. The padlock posed no challenge; within moments, the heavy doors creaked open. The driver drove the buggy inside, and the team quickly unloaded the three green bags, placing them in the centre of the room. They stripped off their overalls, revealing tactical gear beneath: body armour, ghillie suits and lightweight helmets fitted with mounts for night-vision goggles. The driver gathered the discarded uniforms and folded them neatly.

Raj handed him a brown envelope. 'Put the overalls on the mannequins in the van when driving out of the colony. Drive the buggy around for an hour and then leave the premises. Make it look like you finished the job.'

The driver pocketed the cash. '*Gracias, señor*,' he said quietly and disappeared into the rain.

As soon as he was gone, Raj closed the outhouse doors. The team unzipped the bags, revealing their contents. The first bag held weapons: silencer-topped AK-74Us, pistols and extra magazines loaded with speciality rounds. The second bag contained advanced gear: night-vision goggles, thermal imaging devices, communication mics and a signal jammer to cut off Gunther and his team from outside help. The third bag had medical supplies, GPS devices, compasses and detailed topographic maps.

Raj checked his watch. 'Six o'clock. Gear up.'

The Ghosts donned their equipment and stowed extra batteries in their side pockets. The rain had begun to intensify and a light mist had lowered around them, masking their movements in a symphony of drops against leaves and soil.

At 8 p.m., a battery-operated buggy dropped Susan outside Shack 66. Sorosi had got off at the community centre to meet his friends. Susan knew he would take an hour to come home, so she was all set to have a luxurious bath before he arrived.

The cottage's warm porch lights were on, and she could see the muted glow of the lamps inside the house as the heavy curtains had been drawn out. Only delicate lace curtains covered the windows. Shack 66 had a rustic charm. Its rough-hewn log exterior featured a steep roof to let rain and snow slide off easily. The entrance had a magnificent wooden door with ornate carvings, a mounted antelope head and a glistening brass lion's head knocker. The veranda had expensive log furniture, rocking chairs in corners and a giant porch swing in the front.

Susan walked up the driveway and the driver followed with her bags. She stepped on the porch and rang the bell.

'How I wish all this beauty were mine,' she sighed as she waited for the temporary housekeeper to open the door.

Five seconds later, the doors opened without a squeak, and a young girl stepped out with a beaming smile.

'Good evening, Ms Nikolov,' she said with a strong accent as she picked up the luggage from the driver and moved aside to let Susan enter. Susan tipped the buggy driver and walked past the housekeeper into the living room.

'Isn't Mr Sorosi coming, madam?' she asked Susan, following her into the living room.

'He is at the community hall meeting his friend, Selena. He will come only after he has had a few drinks.'

Susan removed her shoes and sank into the white sofa with a sigh.

Panoramic windows lined the spacious living area. The centre of attention was a regal fireplace. It was Sorosi's favourite spot, complete with an oversized leather chair where he liked to sit and read while nursing a stiff drink. Hunting trophies, vintage firearms antlers and taxidermy mounts adorned the stone walls.

'Have Louis and Jonas left?' Susan asked, her bare feet sinking into the plush carpet.

'Chef Louis prepared dinner and left earlier this evening. Jonas worked on the spice garden in the morning and has gone as well,' Selena reported. Then, after a pause, she said,

'Gunther and his team are in the kitchen waiting to meet Mr Sorosi.'

'Tell them he will be here by 9 p.m., so they remain in the outhouse until then. Selena, get the bath ready for me and add some herbal salts. They help my nerves. I want a warm soak and be ready before Mr Sorosi arrives.'

'Would you like a drink by the bathtub, ma'am?' asked Selena.

'What do you recommend?' asked Susan.

'For this weather, an Isabella on the rocks would be a perfect fit,' said Selena

Selena's recommendation impressed Susan. That a housekeeper would recommend the world's most expensive single malt Scotch whisky showed Susan that Selena understood her worth. The exquisite decanter itself was made of white gold and came with diamond lettering.

Once Susan had settled into her bath with a glass of Isabella by her side, Selena returned to the kitchen and asked Gunther and his team to wait in the outhouse. Once they had left, she went to the housekeeper's room and called Raj.

'She is in the bathtub; he is in the bar in the community centre, and Gunther with his team is in the outhouse. Sorosi will come by 9 p.m. I expect dinner to end by eleven. Lights out would be at midnight, I think. What will the Ghosts do now?' she asked Raj.

There was a quiet second. Then came his reply. 'Wait.'

29

12 July 2024, 9.30 p.m.
Bush Wolf, Steuben County

THE NIGHT HAD GROWN HEAVIER, the silence in the woods broken only by the rustling of leaves. Inside the outhouse, Raj's phone buzzed softly against the tense quiet. He answered it swiftly, his voice low. 'Yes?'

Selena's voice came through the line, composed but with an edge of urgency. 'Gunther and his team are back. He's in a small room near the kitchen, right opposite mine. The rest of his team is scattered throughout the house.'

'What about Sorosi?' Raj asked.

'Sorosi just walked in. He had a word with Gunther and his men. Now, he's with Susan. Both of them are quite drunk,' Selena updated Raj.

Geeta, restless and eager, leaned closer to the phone. 'What do we do now?'

Raj shot her an irritated glance. 'Like I said before, we wait.'

Geeta rolled her eyes but rejoined the others, her simmering frustration barely concealed.

Time dragged on. At 11.30 p.m., Selena called again.

'The living room is empty. Sorosi and Susan have moved to the bedroom. I can hear loud music and slurred voices,' she said.

Raj slid his phone into his pocket and turned to his team. Geeta's eyes met his for the briefest of seconds.

'Gear up,' he ordered.

The Ghosts moved swiftly, pulling on their black ski masks and checking their weapons. They loaded the necessary gear, synchronised their watches and stepped out of their cottage. They moved in a single file, night-vision goggles illuminating their path as they advanced through the dense woods, slipping from tree to tree like phantoms in the dark as the smell of damp earth filled their noses.

Raj's phone buzzed again. Selena's voice was a whisper. 'Two of Gunther's men just finished dinner. They're patrolling the left and right verandas. The third guy is stationed on the front porch. Gunther is still in his room, but he'll be heading to the kitchen soon for his meal.'

'Open the latches for the glass doors on all sides and the rear,' Raj instructed.

'Roger that,' Selena confirmed.

Raj turned to his team. 'Shiva, take the one on the left. AV, handle the right. Geeta, you're on the porch. I'll deal with Gunther.' He paused, drawing a deep breath. 'Let's get them, Ghosts.'

Selena moved quickly and efficiently. She knocked lightly on Gunther's door. His voice came through, gruff and distracted. 'Come in.'

She entered, finding him seated on the bed, his laptop open, papers spread out around him. Gunther, a towering 6'4" mercenary with a linebacker's build, was a force of nature—muscle honed by years in conflict zones from Aleppo to Bogotá. His shaved head and scarred knuckles spoke of a life spent fighting, his skills in close-quarters combat and surveillance unmatched.

Like Henry, Sorosi met Gunther a decade ago during a hostile takeover of a financial company owned by a warlord in Istanbul. The agency he had hired for his protection had sent Gunther and four of his mates. After the takeover, which was handled with brutal efficiency and professionalism, Sorosi offered him a job; a gun for hire like Pannu. Gunther agreed.

Sorosi trusted Gunther implicitly; his loyalty secured by a debt of honour and a hefty retainer to protect Sorosi's interests. Now, guarding Sorosi and Nikolov in this safe house, his brute strength and razor-sharp instincts were their shield against their hunters.

'Would you like dinner? I need to close the kitchen,' Selena said.

'I'll eat after Sorosi,' Gunther replied without looking up.

'Mr Sorosi and Ms Nikolov have gone to bed,' Selena answered casually.

Gunther's gaze snapped to her. He hesitated, then nodded. 'Fine. I'll eat now.'

A few minutes later, he was at the kitchen table as Selena served him steak, mashed potatoes and bread. She poured herself a glass of wine and sat across from him, watching him silently eat. When he finished, he thanked her curtly and returned to his room. The moment his door closed, Selena moved again. She opened the latches on the glass doors and the rear exit. Then she returned to the kitchen and started doing the dishes. As she worked, she began humming softly, her face serene despite the tension thick in the air.

Gunther, ever cautious, sat back at his laptop, his mind heavy with Sorosi's earlier warning: 'The council and DD are closing in, their agents relentless. This remote house is a temporary haven for Susan and me to lie low till we plan our escape from this tightening net.'

Gunther's role was clear: keep them safe until they could slip away. Every shadow, every sound set his nerves on edge; he couldn't afford a single lapse.

A flicker outside his window broke his focus. His instincts flared. GLOCK in hand, he moved silently into the kitchen, where Selena stood at the sink. She didn't look up as he approached, her tune continuing uninterrupted. He peered out the window and spotted a figure slipping through the trees. His gaze snapped back to Selena, then to the rear exit. It was ajar. Betrayal flashed immediately in his mind.

He turned, aiming the gun at her, but she was gone. Cursing under his breath, he moved towards her room. As his hand reached for the doorknob, it swung inward. Caught off balance, Gunther stumbled backwards. Selena moved like lightning. A blade flashed in her hand, driving deep into his left palm. He roared in pain, instinctively trying to pull the knife free. Selena kicked his GLOCK away as it slipped from his grasp.

Gunther ripped the blade from his hand. Trained to overcome his pain, he swirled around with a swift kick, sending Selena flying into the kitchen wall. Her head struck the wood with a thud, disorienting her.

He wrapped his uninjured hand around her throat, lifting her off the ground. 'Who are you?' he growled.

Selena gasped loudly, feigning weakness. His grip slackened briefly, and she drove her head into his nose. Gunther staggered back, blood now pouring from his face. Selena dropped to the floor and grabbed another knife. Gunther lunged, but she ducked, slashing the tendons in his ankles. He crumpled to the ground, writhing in excruciating pain. Selena went behind him, drove her knee into his spine and yanked his head back. The blade flashed again, slicing through his throat. Gunther's gurgling screams faded as his body folded.

Breathing hard, Selena straightened, blood spattered across her face. A sudden sound made her whirl. Raj stood in the doorway.

'You're brutal,' he said with a faint smile.

She wiped her face with her sleeve. 'You took your time.'

'I was right here,' he said. 'But you didn't need help.' He glanced at Gunther's body and shook his head. 'Get a buggy and be ready for us at the outhouse. Before anything, wash the blood off your face.'

Selena nodded and washed the blood off her hands and face in the sink, ready to disappear.

30

13 July 2024, 12.15 a.m.
Bush Wolf, Steuben County

PAVAROTTI'S SOARING ARIA ECHOED THROUGH the double-walled sound and bullet proof bedroom, drowning out the sounds of the bloody madness unfolding outside.

Susan and Sorosi were entangled in the silk sheets, oblivious to the screams and the gunfire cutting through the night. The deafening music masked everything, cocooning them in their drunken revelry.

Outside Shack 66, a soldier on the right veranda heard Gunther's distant final scream. The sound penetrated the faint noises from the forest. Instinctively, he tightened his grip on the AK-47 slung over his shoulder and moved swiftly towards the rear entrance to investigate.

As he approached the doorway, Raj emerged, a silencer-tipped pistol steady in his hand. The soldier froze for a second before raising his rifle. But Raj was faster. There was a sound of a pop as the bullet slammed into the soldier's chest and sent him sprawling onto the ground.

Sadly, the soldier's Kevlar vest had absorbed the impact. Gritting his teeth, he pushed himself up, his movements sluggish but determined. Before Raj could close the distance, the soldier fired a shot. The bullet struck Raj's pistol, ripping it from his grasp. Pain seared through his hand, and he stumbled back.

The soldier raised his rifle again, his finger tightening on the trigger, but a second pop rang out. The soldier's head snapped back. Raj turned sharply, his heart pounding, and saw AV emerging from the darkness; his rifle still trained on the fallen man.

'I followed him,' AV said. His eyes flicked to Raj's hand. 'Are you hurt?'

Raj flexed his fingers. 'I'm fine,' he replied tersely. 'Thankfully, the bullet hit the pistol, not my hand.' Without another word, he proceeded towards the bedroom.

Both predators and prey were using silencer-tipped weapons to avoid attention in the county.

AV nodded and peeled away, circling the cottage to find Geeta. She was already advancing on her target. The soldier on the front porch stood with his AK-47 slung lazily over one shoulder, a glowing cigarette between his fingers. He was absentminded, unaware of the danger lurking around him.

Geeta moved with laser-sharp focus, the blade of her bowie knife glinting in the moonlight. When she was close enough to feel his presence, she struck. The blade plunged into his back, slicing through muscle and tissue to puncture his left kidney. The soldier gasped, his body stiffened, and before he could react, Geeta shifted her grip, switching the knife to her left hand and driving it into his right kidney.

The soldier collapsed, his hands instinctively clutching at his sides. Geeta wasted no time. Grabbing his head, she yanked it back and slashed his throat. Blood spurted from the wound, soaking the front of his uniform as he fell onto the porch. She stood over him for a moment, before slipping into the living room.

The soldier on the left veranda had witnessed Geeta's attack and quickly hid behind a thick pillar, his rifle ready. Shiva, observing from a distance, saw the movement. He began circling the shack to outflank the soldier.

But the soldier was no amateur. As Shiva crept closer, the man stepped out from his cover and opened fire. Bullets popped through the night, forcing Shiva to dive to the left. He hit the ground and rolled, coming up with his rifle raised. He fired two shots in quick succession. Both struck the soldier's chest, making him stagger back, but the Kevlar held firm.

Realising the futility of aiming for the torso, Shiva adjusted his sights. He pulled the trigger twice more. The first bullet tore through the soldier's left eye, and the second punched into his right temple. The man's body jerked violently before crumpling off the porch.

'Target down,' Shiva murmured into his COO mic.

One by one, the team shared their progress. The confirmations came swiftly, each voice steady despite the violence that had unfolded. But Raj's voice remained absent.

'Raj, where are you? Answer us,' Geeta's voice cut through the static, full of pleading urgency.

There was a pause before Raj's voice came through. 'Hide the bodies. Move to the outhouse. Selena's bringing the buggy.'

'And you?' Geeta pressed.

'I have business to finish.'

31

13 July 2024, 1 a.m.
Bush Wolf, Steuben County

RAJ STOOD NEAR THE MUSIC console, his shadow long against the subdued bedroom lights. Sorosi sat naked on the bed, his face betraying a flash of fear behind the arrogance he had worn for decades. Beside him, Susan had a bedsheet tightly around her shaking frame, her wild eyes darting between the masked figure and her lover. The couple had no clue about his entrance till he switched off the music.

Sorosi's voice cracked as he spoke. 'Who are you?'

Raj's voice was calm but cold. 'You don't know me, but I know you. You are a monster who built his fortune on people's miseries. You have meddled with the world, created riots here, arson there, civil wars in some peaceful countries, and executed assassinations in others with democratically elected leaders. All for money and power. We couldn't intervene then because it wasn't our fight. But this time, you crossed a line. You came for us. That was your biggest mistake.'

Sorosi's face twisted into a defiant sneer, his hand subtly moving near his pillow. Raj noticed but didn't flinch. Tonight, he was feeling immortal, undefeatable.

In an instant, Sorosi whipped out two pistols hidden beneath the pillow and fired. The first bullet tore into Raj's right arm above the elbow, forcing him to drop his GLOCK. The second whizzed past his ear, close enough for him to feel its heat. Sorosi raised the pistol again, ready to fire, but Raj rushed forward, his bowie knife flashing in a deadly arc.

The blade sliced Sorosi's face, and a sickening gash appeared from his forehead to his chin. Flesh split, his lips dividing into grotesque quarters. Blood poured down his chest as Sorosi howled in excruciating pain, the pistols slipping from his grasp as his hands flew to his ruined face. As he fell out of the bed, writhing on the floor in agony, Susan screamed in fear.

Even in this pathetic state, his cries garbled and wet, Sorosi's hand flailed around until he found the edge of a floorboard. With a desperate shove, he opened the secret door embedded in the bedroom wall and disappeared into the living room.

Raj glanced at Susan, naked and trembling violently. 'If you don't want to see what's coming, lock yourself in the bathroom,' he said coldly before following Sorosi.

In the living room, Sorosi stumbled towards the front door, a trail of blood dripping in his wake. He reached for the handle, but Geeta stepped into his path, blocking his escape, her frightening presence looming as Sorosi's bloodied eyes shifted between her and Raj, who calmly followed him into the living room.

'Please,' Sorosi stammered, his voice hoarse. 'Who are you? Are you DD's men? Has the Council sent you? What do you want from me?'

Raj carefully placed the bowie knife on a side table. 'You've spent your life giving orders, letting others fight your dirty battles. Now you get the chance to fight your own. Come on,' he challenged Sorosi, stepping forward. 'Let's do this the old-fashioned way.'

For a moment, Sorosi hesitated, his monstrous face contorting in rage. Then, with a guttural roar, he came at Raj. Sidestepping at the last moment, Raj drove his bleeding elbow into Sorosi's spine as he passed him. The blow sent Sorosi crashing into the wall, where a display of vintage rifles hung. His hand shot out, grabbing one with a fixed bayonet.

He charged at Raj, the bayonet shining under the lights. But Raj didn't wince. Instead, he rushed forward, delivering a powerful roundhouse kick to Sorosi's chest. The impact sent him crashing into the concrete wall, and he crumpled to the floor, gasping for air.

'Are you the Dealer?' Raj asked, his voice low and menacing.

Using the rifle for support, Sorosi struggled to his feet. His breath came in shallow, laboured gasps. 'I am,' he rasped.

'Who do you work for?' Raj demanded.

'I worked for the Council,' Sorosi wheezed, clutching his chest. 'But not anymore.'

Raj pulled a nylon garrotte from his belt and looped it around Sorosi's neck, yanking him close. 'You used to work for them?' he pressed.

Sorosi gasped for air, his weak hands struggling to loosen the garrotte. 'Yes,' he sputtered. 'Yes, I used to. Please … let me go.'

Raj released the garrotte just enough for Sorosi to breathe. The man slumped against the wall. 'I don't know who sent you,' he said hoarsely, 'but if you let me go, I'll tell you everything. I'll tell you who the Council is.'

Raj nodded slightly, motioning to Geeta. She pulled out her phone and began recording.

'Talk,' Raj commanded.

Sorosi spilled everything. He spoke of the Council, their names, companies, ambitions and operations, the Apuni Malo and its insidious meddling in India. His words crafted a vivid image of corruption and bedlam, the strings of every villainous act pulled by unseen hands. When he was finished, his bloody face turned to Raj.

'Now, please,' Sorosi pleaded, 'let me go. Susan and I will disappear forever. You'll never hear from us again.'

'No,' Raj said simply, raising his GLOCK.

'But you promised!' Sorosi sputtered, blood now trickling out of his mouth.

Raj's voice was devoid of emotion. 'I lied.'

The gunshot echoed through the room as the bullet struck Sorosi in the heart. His body jerked once before slumping to the floor, his head falling forward onto his chest.

Geeta stared at Raj; her breath caught in her throat. She had never seen this side of him. Blood dripped from his ski mask and his injured hand. His eyes, cold and fierce, met hers. A shiver ran down her spine.

Raj's voice broke the silence. 'Did you get everything?'

Geeta nodded slowly. 'Yes.'

Raj gestured towards the bedroom. 'Bring Susan here.'

Geeta obeyed, returning moments later with Susan. Raj pointed at Sorosi's lifeless body. 'Wait an hour. Then call the cops. Tell them it was a drug turf fight gone bad. If you say anything else, I will find you. Wherever you go, I will find you.'

Susan nodded frantically, tears streaming down her face. She was too shocked to speak and simply stared at her lover's disfigured state with the deadpan eyes of a person who had lost her senses. Just then, the COO mics crackled to life. AV's voice came through. 'The buggy is here.'

Raj stepped out into the pouring rain, his gait heavy but resolute. Geeta followed him silently, her mind occupied with a maze of thoughts as the darkness consumed them both.

The buggy's engine barely made a sound, creeping along the winding path until it reached Bush Wolf's shared parking lot. From there, the team disembarked. They halted 50 feet away from the check post. The lone security guard sat in his chair that faced the main entrance, his focus entirely on the glowing screen of his cell phone. Earphones plugged in, he appeared oblivious to his surroundings, nodding occasionally to a rhythm only he could hear.

Raj signalled Selena with a subtle nod. She acknowledged and broke away from the pack, her steps as light and graceful as a panther's. Approaching the check post from the rear, she opened the door and coiled her right arm around the guard's neck. The man's body thrashed about as he struggled to free himself, his hands flailing in vain. Within moments, the guard's resistance ceased. His body went limp, slipping into unconsciousness.

Selena glanced back at the group, her fingers forming a silent signal. The Ghosts emerged and advanced, sticking to the periphery to avoid the CCTV camera mounted atop the check post. Soon, they had bypassed the security zone and were on their way to Pizza House.

When they were within sight of their meeting point, AV pulled out his phone and made a quick call to Safi. 'We are here,' he said softly.

In the distance, a pair of headlights flickered twice before going dark. Moments later, a black SUV emerged from the trees lining the roadside, its tyres crunching softly against the gravel. The vehicle rolled to a stop, and the Ghosts quickly climbed inside.

'Are you all in shape?' Safi asked, his hands steady on the wheel.

'Yes,' Shiva replied with a curt nod.

Raj, seated in the back, made a quick call to Angel. 'Strike 6 successful. Departing for Elmira Corning.'

'All okay?' Angel's voice came through.

'All okay,' Raj assured her.

'See you all back home,' Angel said, and Raj thought he caught a slight tremble in her voice before the line went silent.

Safi guided the SUV through the dark woods. Selena sat beside him, her thermal imaging device scanning the area ahead, ensuring no surprises waited to pounce on them. The headlights remained turned off as they navigated the backroads, relying entirely on their night-vision glasses. It wasn't until they had covered a significant distance that he dared to turn them on.

The Ghosts reached Elmira Corning Regional Airport at 3.00 a.m. Pavak was already waiting in the cockpit of the private jet. He had filed the flight plans and secured all necessary clearances from the FAA and Air Traffic Control well in advance. The Ghosts boarded the aircraft without delay. Fifteen minutes later, the engines roared to life, and the jet ascended into the night sky.

Once airborne, the Ghosts cleaned up, discarded their gear and changed into civilian clothes. The tension that had held them tightly wound began to fall away, replaced by a quiet camaraderie. Geeta patched up Raj using the first aid kit on board, while Safi handed each of them their passports and travel documents, ensuring everything for the final leg of their journey.

The jet touched down at Syracuse Hancock International Airport just as the first hint of dawn crept over the horizon. Safi led them to the commercial terminal, where the Ghosts would merge into the crowds of ordinary travellers. At the gate, Safi embraced each of them.

'Have a safe flight,' he said, his voice heavy with emotion. 'Talk to you soon.'

Raj gripped his hand firmly. 'Take care, brother.'

The Ghosts boarded American Airlines Flight AA1218, which was scheduled to depart at 4.55 a.m. They settled into their seats as the plane prepared for take-off. At precisely 5.21 a.m., the captain's voice was heard over the intercom.

'Good morning, ladies and gentlemen. This is your captain speaking. I welcome you aboard American Airlines flight AA1218 with service from Syracuse Hancock International Airport to New Delhi, India, via Chicago O'Hare. The weather en route looks favourable, with mostly smooth skies. Our first leg to Chicago will take approximately an hour and forty minutes, cruising at an altitude of 33,000 feet. Once in Chicago, you'll have a brief layover before boarding the connecting flight to New Delhi. On behalf of myself, the crew, and everyone at American Airlines, thank you for choosing to fly with us today. Sit back, relax and enjoy the flight.'

As the plane took off, Geeta glanced at Raj, who was seated beside her. His head had already tilted back, his eyes closed and breathing steady. Exhaustion had finally claimed him, and she couldn't help but smile faintly. From that bloodthirsty killer, he had transformed back into the innocent, childlike Raj that she loved. She held his hand, leaned on his shoulder and closed her eyes.

32

15 July 2024, 9 a.m.
NSA's Office, New Delhi

ANGEL LOOKED AT THE GHOSTS with pride lighting up her face, but it was only when her gaze met Geeta's, that a sense of relief washed over her.

'Raj, you stood by your promise, and the entire team is back home safe. And thanks to Sorosi's confession that Geeta recorded, we found the precise locations of all the Council members. A private message has already reached them. They want to have a meeting with me in Geneva.'

'Are you going?' asked Shiva.

'No. I told them they should come to New Delhi if they wanted to discuss anything with me,' said Angel.

'And, did they agree?' asked Selena.

'They didn't have a choice. They arrive on 20 July. I have a meeting with them at the Ashoka Hotel. I will brief you after I meet with them.'

'What is the situation in the US?' asked Geeta.

Angel pulled out a newspaper and spread it on the table. It was the *Washington Daily*, and the headlines read,

'Joseph Sorosi, billionaire and philanthropist, found brutally murdered in Bush Wolf.'

> The billionaire's mistress who was with him at Bush Wolf said she was drunk and had slept through the entire tragic incident. She said it could be a drug deal gone wrong as Sorosi had recently started having arguments with his drug dealing partners in Colombia. Strangely, the CCTV cameras were down. Hence, no footage was available. But Sorosi's wife, Rebecca Goldstein, gave a new twist to the murder. She said Sorosi had been receiving many threats from the Khalistani organisation, KHALI, and its head, Gurwinder Singh Pannu who was recently assassinated by an unknown gunman a few days ago. The Boston PD feels there is a connection between the two murders and is assuming that it could be a rivalry between Pannu and Sorosi that could have led to this brutal gangster-style murder. Either way, till something comes out about the murders, Pannu and Sorosi's deaths remain shrouded in mystery. But what is disappointing is that the man considered a philanthropist was having dealings with druglords and Khalistani terrorists. The reputation he had built over several decades lies in tatters and he will be remembered in history as a petty criminal.

Angel looked at the team and said, 'Pavak and Safi prepared the communication for Rebecca and her counsel, Imane.'

'What happened to Susan?' asked Selena.

'Safi got her on a private jet to Greece. She now stays in Loutro,' said Angel.

'Where the hell is that?' asked AV.

'It is a remote coastal village in Crete. Not easy to find and only accessible by boat or hiking. Unknown to Sorosi, she had bought a home for herself there. She wanted to retire there.'

'Looks like she knew deep inside that her lover would die a dog's death so she made her own arrangements.'

'Have the cousins made it back safely?' asked Shiva.

'Yes. Safi is back in Karachi, and Pavak is in Delhi,' Angel replied

'What next?' asked Raj.

'We meet DD tonight at his library. So, enjoy the day and spend time together. Dismissed,' said Angel, standing up from her desk.

As the team left the room, Angel whispered proudly, 'My Panther's Ghosts.'

In Sorosi's opulent Manhattan office, Imane worked quickly but methodically. He opened the safe embedded in the wall and retrieved its contents with an unruffled efficiency that belied the tension in the room.

Sorosi's prized mahogany table soon had an assortment of papers, cash and recording devices. Rebecca's sharp eyes were scanning the items. She picked up a document—the will—and read it carefully. Without a word, she handed it to Imane.

Imane studied it in silence. Then, with a decisive motion, he placed it in a metal wastepaper basket, struck a match and set the paper ablaze. Flames licked the edges of the document, curling it into blackened ash as the room filled with the faint smell of burning ink and paper.

Meanwhile, Rebecca sifted through the recordings that Sorosi had meticulously maintained. Her lips pressed into a thin line as she reviewed their contents. Finally, she handed the most incriminating of them to Imane.

'Make sure these reach Angel,' she said firmly. 'She needs them more than we do.'

Rebecca turned her attention to the rest of the items—the bundles of cash and the piles of documents. She gave a short sigh. 'Do what is necessary with them, Imane.'

As she moved towards the door, Rebecca paused in the doorway. 'Thanks for everything, Imane,' her voice softer now, almost tender.

Imane looked up, his eyes meeting Rebecca's. 'You're most welcome, Rebecca,' he replied with a warmth that momentarily broke through his professional demeanour.

Rebecca lingered for a second longer before breaking into a smile and said, 'Let's have dinner with the boys tonight. Just you, me and the boys.'

Imane returned her smile, this time brighter and warmer. 'That is an excellent idea,' he said.

It was 9 p.m., and the library at 7, Lok Kalyan Marg hummed with subdued energy.

The Panther's Ghosts sat in quiet anticipation as DD poured over the thick dossier Angel had handed him. The only sounds in the room were the rustle of paper as he turned over to the final page and the occasional murmur from the team.

Finally, the Panther closed the dossier and handed it back to Angel. His expression remained neutral, but the weight of the dossier's secrets was palpable around them.

'I've gone through it,' DD said, his voice measured. 'This has everything necessary to expose the Council. The PCP, some key Opposition figures—every sordid detail.'

Angel's fingers tightened on the dossier as she looked at DD. 'If this comes out, many heads will roll,' she said. 'A lot of people will end up in prison and the economies of some developed nations will crash.'

DD nodded slowly. 'We're talking about a global crisis here, Angel. Nations won't trust each other anymore. Alliances will crumble. This isn't just politics—if this comes out, the foundation of international peace and security will be destroyed.'

Closing the dossier with a quiet snap, Angel met DD's gaze. 'What do you want me to do? I'm meeting the Council in five days.'

'We'll talk about this later,' DD said in a tone that left no room for debate. Turning to the Ghosts, DD's expression softened for the first time that evening. 'I'm extremely proud of all of you. This is the first mission where everyone has returned home safely.' He looked at Raj. 'I'm grateful to you for that.'

Raj nodded with subtle humility. 'It was a team effort, sir,' he said, his voice tinged with unconcealed pride. His gaze shifted to Selena. 'And let's not forget our youngest Ghost. She fought with great courage and tact.'

Selena flushed under the attention as a ripple of applause erupted from the team. For a moment, the atmosphere in the room lightened, as laughter and camaraderie replaced the tension.

DD clapped his hands once, signalling the end of the formal meeting. 'Now, let's celebrate this victory.'

The Ghosts had wide grins on their faces as they moved towards the dining room. For the first time in weeks, they allowed themselves to relax. It was a rare evening of triumph—a mission accomplished with the entire team intact.

As the group entered the dining room, Angel walked over to DD and whispered. 'I've informed AV and Shiva that this was their last assignment,' she said softly.

DD's eyebrows rose slightly. 'And how did they take it?'

'AV was happy,' Angel replied. 'He wants to spend time with Ameeta and his sons in Pune.'

DD nodded approvingly. 'And Shiva?'

'He looked lost,' she admitted. 'I'm thinking of asking Raj if Shiva can take over as the head of security in place of Indrajit.'

DD considered this for a moment. 'That's a good idea. A change of place might do him good. Who do you have for future strikes?'

'Raj, Geeta, Selena and Surya, for now,' Angel said.

'So you want to stick to four?' DD asked.

Angel shook her head. 'No. But for now, they will do. I will find the other two soon.'

'And the new leader of the pack?'

'Raj Pratap Rana,' Angel said with conviction.

DD's smile widened. 'The Ghosts have come full circle. It started with Veer Pratap Rana as our first Ghost; now his son will lead the team. It's only fitting.'

He placed a hand on Angel's shoulder. 'Take a break, Angel. Though you cannot reveal the truth, spend time with Geeta. You two have a lot to catch up on.'

Angel nodded but was quick to notice something unsaid in DD's eyes. 'Is there something you want to say?' she asked him.

'Meet me after you see the Council,' he said. 'We may have to get ready for another strike.'

Angel held his gaze, her expression unperturbed and resolute. 'Yes, sir,' she said.

Together, they entered the dining room, joining the Ghosts in their celebration. Laughter and warmth filled the space, but Angel's mind was already on DD's parting words. Somewhere out there, the next threat loomed—a storm waiting to break. And the Panther's Ghosts would be ready.

EPILOGUE

20 July 2024, 7 p.m.
Veer's Bungalow, Pune, India

VEER'S BUNGALOW, FRESHLY RENOVATED, STOOD like a fortress at the end of a kilometre-long driveway slicing through a vibrant field of mowed grass and wildflowers ablaze with colour. A dense tree line encircled the property, cloaking it in secrecy, while a gleaming lake mirrored the starless summer sky. The entrance—a heavy teakwood door framed by tall glass windows—exuded understated grandeur. A stone-columned porch, furnished with chairs and a table, offered a commanding view of the driveway and field, a perfect perch for vigilance. Inside, the lower floor's open layout flowed from a fireplace-centric living room to a stark dining area, its marble floor glinting under a grand chandelier. Two en-suite bedrooms with patio access flanked the space, every window positioned for surveillance. A wooden staircase led to four upper bedrooms, each with a private balcony overlooking the lake and field—a sanctuary designed for comfort and defence.

Tonight, this haven was a trap. The Council—four shadowy titans of global manipulation—had been lured by Angel, blindfolded and flown from Mumbai to Pune on Pavak's private jet, then driven to Veer's Bungalow. Unbeknownst to them, they were encircled by the Panther's Ghosts, positioned silently throughout the house.

In the dining room, seventy-two-year-old Leon Fink glared at Angel, his voice sharp. 'The partial evidence you shared with us is damning and we know when the chips are down. That is why we are here to make a deal. We do not know who you are, but we know that currently you hold the strings. We are businessmen and we value time and money. That is why we survived the Holocaust, two World Wars, and innumerable other global crises.'

Angel smiled and said, 'You survived the Holocaust, two World Wars and innumerable other global crises because you created them. And that too for your dominance over the world. And yes, *we* hold the strings, and your chips are down.'

'Tell us what you want. We will make a deal right here, right now, and part as friends. Otherwise, you will face the wrath of the Council, and trust me, no matter what you have, we can make you and your evidence disappear,' Butler said aggressively.

Angel, poised at the head of the mahogany table, exuded lethal calm in her tailored black suit. 'Mr Fink, this is a sanctuary—away from prying eyes and ears. Just us. And you are inches from your death.' Her smile was a blade's edge.

Suddenly, the mood in the room changed. The Council—Fink, Stephen Favier, Jim Brodsky and Tim Butler—sat like condemned men, their faces carved with decades of deceit. They had orchestrated wars, toppled governments and amassed empires through the Apuni Malo, but their power teetered on a guillotine's edge tonight.

Angel placed a dossier on the table with a deliberate thud, its contents a death sentence in paper form. 'Gentlemen,' she began, her voice slicing the silence, 'you, the Council, have played god for too long—igniting conflicts, assassinating leaders and destabilising nations for your so-called balance. A balance that lined your pockets not just with money but with uncontrolled power. Tonight, that game ends.'

Favier scoffed, his arrogance a fragile mask. 'You're out of your depth. You can't touch us.'

Angel's eyes glinted. She produced a USB drive, its metallic surface catching the chandelier's light. 'This is a gift from you to us. It contains everything about you—every clandestine operation, every dirty deal, every coup, every life you've ruined. Your names, your sins, all exposed.'

Fink's composure cracked. 'You are lying. Everything we did was through secure lines and encrypted communication. Robert ensured—'

'Robert,' Angel interrupted, 'was your Achilles' heel. You trusted him to scrub your tracks, but he recorded every meeting, every transaction, every word, syllable that came out of your mouths—those audios and videos were his insurance against you. He never trusted the Council, and you never suspected him.' Angle tapped another black box on the table. 'This contains the Dealer's confessions, his tapes, Pannu's diary, Khanda's phone messages, notebook and many other pieces of evidence that link you to every global crisis, every civil war, coup and assassination that has happened around the globe. We have enough to bury you for centuries.'

Butler leaned forward, defiant. 'Okay, we thought we had insulated ourselves for decades, but we never knew we had a snake in our backyard. We agree you outsmarted us. What do you want?'

Angel ignored him, her voice rising. 'You've meddled in elections, funded insurgencies and sown chaos across continents, all for your Apuni Malo fantasy—a world under your thumb. But you made a fatal error targeting India. You backed the PCP, Opposition traitors and terrorists to fracture our country because you knew we were going to become a self-reliant superpower, and with our rise begins your fall. What you forgot was that this is not the India of the Mahatma. This is the new India. Bold, fearless, aggressive. We have endured worse than your schemes—and we are still standing.'

Pale but defiant, Brodsky countered, 'India's rise will threaten global stability. We sought order—'

'Order? Global stability? When were you worried about global stability? All you have been bothered about for decades is your stability, growth and control.' Angel's voice cracked like thunder. 'You're vultures, not visionaries, treating the world as your private fiefdom. India's not your playground. This time you failed.'

Favier slammed the table. 'Enough! You can't hold us. Our allies will—'

Angel pressed her tablet. The walls flickered to life with screens displaying damning evidence—videos, bank transfers, encrypted communications. The Council's machinations played out in merciless detail, the room growing colder as their empire crumbled in pixels. Butler's defiance wavered. 'What's your endgame?'

Angel's smile was predatory. 'To be the Dealer—not your kind, but a new one. The Council will answer to India's will, or it will cease to exist.' She turned to the double doors. They swung open, revealing Raj Pratap Rana, his presence a quiet storm. The son of the first Ghost, Raj blended his father's steel with his mother's cunning, a vigilante forged in India's shadows.

'Meet Kaalnemi,' Angel said, 'or Kaal, if that's easier. In our legends, Kaalnemi is deceit and menace, but today, he's justice—a Dealer who wields espionage to protect India. You'll operate under his terms. Your global games are over and now the Council will work for India. Cross us, and you'll meet kaal—death.'

Raj stepped forward, his voice iron. 'You've ruled without consequence for too long. That ends now. DD has placed me as your Dealer, with India's interests at heart. From today, you'll serve her ascent, channelling your networks to strengthen her, not tear her down. Defy me, and you're finished.'

Fink laughed bitterly. 'You think we'll bow to a cheap Indian thug? We have resources, contingencies—'

Raj's hand flashed. A GLOCK materialised, and a single shot rang out, splitting Fink's skull. His body slumped, blood pooling on the marble. The room froze, the Council's bravado shattered.

'Anyone else?' Raj's voice was a low growl. Silence answered, broken only by the trio's ragged breaths.

Raj resumed, his tone unrelenting. 'You're not free. You're leashed. DD sees your networks as tools for India's rise—a superpower unshackled. You'll comply because exposure or death are your only alternatives. Sorosi, Pannu, Henry and Indrajit, the Dealer's mole in India, are all gone. Your secrets are ours. Your assets are ours, and your fate is in our hands. Test us, and the world sees your sins.'

'And yet you will let us leave? Why?' a shaken Favier stammered.

'Because,' Raj said, 'you're more useful alive, serving India's will. But step out of line, and we will find you.'

Butler nodded slowly, his fight drained. 'We ... understand.'

Angel's gaze softened, turning to Raj. 'The Council is yours, Dealer.'

Raj scanned the broken men. Then he walked over to Favier, patted him on his back and asked softly, 'Chairman Favier, dinner?'

Favier, now the chairman of a puppet council, shook his head. 'We'll skip it. I have to be in Mumbai tonight and then Geneva tomorrow.'

'Of course,' Raj said. 'We'll be in touch.'

The Council was blindfolded and escorted to cars, doors locking with a finality that echoed their new reality. Pavak's jet awaited at Pune's airport.

In the bungalow, Angel faced Raj. 'The world's watching, Kaal. Play it right.'

Raj's faint smile held a predator's edge. 'I learnt from the best.'

The lake's ripples whispered in the night, a prelude to the storm awaiting anyone who dared challenge the Panther's Ghosts.

A few hundred miles away, in 7, Lok Kalyan Marg, the Panther received a message from Angel. 'A new Dealer has risen, and India's path to superpower status is unstoppable.'

THE DEALER'S WORLD

The Council: A deep state that owns 80 per cent of the world's wealth. Believes in one totalitarian government ruling the world. Controls nations through a shadow government.

- Council Chairman: Leon Fink, founder and owner, Blue Rock
- Member 1: Stephen Favier, founder and owner, Redstone Group
- Member 2: Robert Brodsky, founder and owner, World News Network
- Member 3: Tim Butler, founder and owner, Bioguard Group

Apuni Malo: The shadow government created by the Council to control puppet presidents and prime ministers of nations.

Puppet Nations: The countries whose governments are controlled by the Council through the Apuni Malo.

The Dealer: The mysterious identity that forces nations to have puppet governments of the Council, either by cutting 'deals' with their president and prime ministers or by toppling democratically elected governments through orchestrated coups, executing assassinations, funding civil disobedience through 'OFF' to Opposition parties and NGOs that would create instability in nations.

The OFF: The Open Forum Foundation, the world's largest NGO, owned by the Dealer, and the front that funds instability in nations, coups and assassinations.